A VOW OF RUIN

ISBN: 978-0-473-60090-7

Series Playlist

- WITCHES' SONG – Marianne Faithfull
- CHURCH – Fall Out Boy
- BLEED IT OUT – Linkin Park
- WHICH WITCH – Florence + The Machine
- YOUNG AND BEAUTIFUL – Lana Del Rey
- I WANNA BE YOUR SLAVE - Måneskin
- I BET YOU LOOK GOOD ON THE DANCEFLOOR – Arctic Monkeys
- SEASON OF THE WITCH – Joan Jett & The Blackhearts
- BLACK OUT DAYS – Phantogram
- CHANGE – Deftones
- THE NIGHT WE MET – Lord Huron
- SOMEWHERE ONLY WE KNOW – Keane
- SAVE A PRAYER (2009 Remaster) – Duran Duran
- YELLOW LEDBETTER - Pearl Jam
- THE PASSENGER - Iggy Pop
- IF I COULD FLY - One Direction
- READY OR NOT - Fugees
- I WANT TO - Rosenfeld

Prologue

Draven

I scented the night air. Cottage fires, roasting meats and freshly baked bread traveled on the breeze from the nearby village. Still no sign of Selene.

Her mother had been accused of witchcraft and would most certainly be found guilty at dawn. Selene was risking much coming to me now, but plans must be made, and time was not on our side.

One of my warriors howled from the shadows.

She approached.

Relief filled me, when finally, her light tread reached me as she made her way through the woods. My wolf chuffed with pleasure. No, I hadn't yet felt the mating call for the beautiful witch, but it was only a matter of time. I would never want another the way I yearned for the sweet and delicate female.

She broke through the tree line, candle in hand, her chestnut hair shining in the moonlight, her blue eyes bright—and as always,

1

her familiar, a sleek white cat, slinked along at her feet among the folds of her gray linen gown.

I strode to meet her. "I was afraid you wouldn't come."

"I almost did not. The magistrate posted a guard at our door, but a sleeping draft in his ale easily remedied that."

My female was sweet but also cunning.

I grinned and cupped her cheek, the intricate markings that had appeared a week ago, stark against her pale skin. I didn't know what it meant, something to do with her coven, but it was just another reason for the humans in her village to turn against her family. "Your family will be safe with my pack. I promise I won't allow anyone to harm you."

She pressed her soft curves against me, and I pulled her closer when I felt her tremble.

Selene looked up at me. "Thank you, Draven. Without you, we would all surely hang."

My stomach turned over at the thought of losing her, which was why my pack mates, six of my finest warriors, hid among the shadows, keeping watch.

The sound of another approaching, making their way through the woods, put me on alert. I pulled her behind me.

"You have nothing to fear, 'tis only Charity," she said.

I watched as Selene's sister approached. The female's beauty was otherworldly. A raven sat perched on her shoulder, her familiar, its silky black feathers the same color as Charity's hair, and when she smiled at me, my hackles lifted. My wolf didn't trust this female, but I had ignored the feeling, afraid if I refused to help Charity as well, I might lose my Selene.

"Leave now," Charity said to her sister.

"Why must I leave?" Selene asked, a frown upon her face.

Charity's eyes sharpened. "I told you why."

"She will stay." I tightened my hold on Selene's hand. "We must make haste." Once they were safe with my pack, I would free their mother and leave this place.

"Go, Selene. Now," Charity said, her voice harder. "The longer you tarry, the more danger our mother is in."

Selene looked up at me. "I must strengthen our wards. Charity will hear your plans."

I studied her beautiful, pleading blue eyes. "And only you can do this?"

"Yes," she said, placing her hand on my chest.

My heart thumped below her palm. I nodded, unable to deny her anything. She smiled, scooped up her familiar, and walked away into the darkness of the woods.

"I have something for you, wolf," Charity said, drawing my gaze back to her. She strode forward, swaying her hips and pursing her full red lips.

"You have nothing that I want." Unease pulsed through me.

Charity pulled a dagger from the folds of her gown.

My hand shot out, and I grabbed her wrist with a snarl.

"I have no desire to harm you, wolf. Instead, I ask that you safeguard it. It is called *voltafaccia*, and it is ancient and powerful and too dangerous to keep in our cottage." Her raven squawked, and several more now circled above us. Selene and Charity both had an affinity with animals, but Charity could control them. I had once seen her instruct her birds to remove a male's eyes after he'd spurned her.

She held out the blade. The dagger was iron, the handle carved wood with leather wrapped around the base, plain, but the magic it held radiated from it. "You wish me to hold this for you?"

"Yes." She smiled again. "Do you agree?"

"It is that important?"

"You feel the magic it holds, yes?"

I dipped my chin.

"The magistrate, he is not human, we wouldn't be in danger if he were," Charity said. "I am not sure what he is, but he is powerful, immortal, and vengeful. He cannot be killed, and this blade in his hands would be dangerous to us all."

Fear for Selene sliced up my spine. "He is other?"

"Yes."

I had not sensed it. "I need to get Selene away from this place." Moving the entire pack would be difficult and not something I wanted to do, but if I had to, I would. To keep Selene safe, I would do anything.

"Yes," she said. "Unless..."

"Unless?"

"If you use this on the magistrate..." She held the blade out to me. "If you drive it into his heart, he will leave here. He will leave us be. None of us will have to go."

"It won't kill him?"

"No. The blade, if used on one such as him, causes a change. Dark tempers become light."

"Selene would be safe?"

"Yes," Charity said, her blue gaze holding mine fast.

I would fight an entire army to keep Selene safe. "Where is he?"

I stumbled through the woods, blood smearing my arms and chest. My warriors in the same condition. Several were injured. The male we had fought had been incredibly strong, and he was not alone.

But it was done. Whatever the male was, he was no more.

Not dead, but changed.

No longer dark, but light.

Selene was safe. My pack was safe.

I broke into the small clearing where Selene and Charity waited.

"'Tis done," I said, rushing to my sweet female.

"Draven," Selene cried, eyes wide as she took in my bare chest covered in blood. Horror transformed her features. "Are you injured?"

"No, I am well."

"It is done?"

"The male still lives but is changed as Charity said he would be."

"We need you to keep the dagger, Draven," Charity said. "For now, it is safer in your hands."

I looked at Selene, and she smiled tentatively and nodded. "We would be most grateful."

"I'll hold it." I would do anything she asked of me.

"You vow this night that you and the warriors with you will safeguard it? That only those who hold proof from my coven may retrieve it?" Charity said.

"What proof?"

"A map that will reveal its truth when held to the moonlight."

I looked at Selene again. She watched me, waiting, that sweet smile still on her lips. "You have my vow."

Charity moved to a large boulder beside me, then made a slice in her hand, a small *X*, with the delicate blade she wore tied around her waist. She pressed her hand to the stone as she muttered words under her breath. A great *cracking* sound echoed through the night, startling sleeping birds from the trees before a large slice slid from the side of the bolder. Charity took the magical dagger back from me and placed it against the hard rock, then muttered similar words, and the stone slid back into place, somehow locking the dagger inside.

I frowned. "But I thought I was to safeguard it?"

"That is exactly what you will do." Then she spun and pressed her sliced hand to my chest.

I tried to step back, but I was held fast by her magic.

"Return to our mother," Charity said to Selene. "You must gather your things. It is almost time for us to leave."

What was she talking about? "Selene! Wait..."

Selene turned to me and cupped my cheek. "Without you, the magistrate would have killed us. You saved us, Draven. Your bravery saved our entire coven, and I will always be grateful to you for what you did this night."

Why did she say that as if she were leaving—leaving me? "Come with me...stay with me."

Regret filled her smile. "I am not your mate, Draven, and you know that as well as I. There are things I must do, for my coven, for my family. I must leave."

Then she turned to walk away.

"Selene, don't go..."

"Goodbye, Draven."

I struggled against Charity's magic. I would not let her go. Whatever this was, I could not let her go.

"She is Keeper of our coven, wolf. We need her far more than you do," Charity said, drawing my attention back to her.

"I don't understand," I snarled.

"You don't need to."

I tried to follow Selene, but I still couldn't move. My joints locked, my muscles seized.

"I name thee guardian of the dagger, and bind you and your warriors to this place until coven Thornheart releases you."

Charity stepped back, and I dropped to the damp forest floor. My pack mates growled from the shadows, snarling and fighting against Charity's spell that had rendered them as helpless as me.

She looked down at me, and her smile returned. "I knew you would eventually prove useful." Then she turned and walked away.

By the time I could move, both Charity and Selene had left the forest, and the thrall I'd been under, the feeling I had believed was love had left with her.

Selene had fooled me, betrayed me in the most heinous of ways. I'd believed myself in love with her, but I did not, had not, *ever* truly loved her.

I shook my head, the fog clearing.

A love potion. I'd heard Charity speak of them before after using one to control a male in the village.

Selene had bewitched me.

With a vicious growl, I tilted my head back and howled into the night.

A warning.

A vow.

She would live to regret her actions this day.

I would not rest until she had paid for her deceit.

Chapter One

Iris

Present day

Draven Moreau was back.

And he was watching me.

I did my best to ignore the male as I worked my way across the bar, carrying a tray of drinks, but as usual, it was impossible when he looked at me with such deep and unsettling intensity. The alpha of the Silver Claw Pack was still fairly new to Roxburgh, or Wolf Hill Woods, to be precise—and he hated me with a fiery passion.

He also wanted me.

At least that's what it looked like from where I was standing. Honestly, I wasn't sure if he wanted me and hated himself for it or hated and lusted after me in equal measure and couldn't decide which would win out.

As far as I knew, in the almost twelve months he'd been here, I hadn't done anything to earn either emotion, besides breathing.

Or why he'd zeroed in on me. He hadn't deigned to inform me of that as yet. But he was often here at Hell Fire, the hellhound-owned bar I now worked at several nights a week, and every time he showed up, he sat in a corner, surrounded by his pack mates, and watched me with what could only be described as murderous hunger.

It was too bad the alpha was completely insane because he was the most gorgeous male I had ever laid eyes on, even when his face was all twisted with lustful self-loathing. Or maybe I was way off base and it was just plain old loathing?

Perhaps the hunger I saw was literal and he wanted to take a bite out of me? Did wolf shifters eat people? I didn't think so, but what did I know?

Not a very comforting thought.

I glanced his way again, unable to stop myself.

His hair was black and wavy, in need of a trim, and every now and then, he shoved his fingers through it impatiently. My gaze dipped. The male was tall, muscular, a body built for sin and violent brutality, and as expected, his vibrant green gaze was locked on me.

His lips curled in a sneer when he caught me looking.

Awesome.

I quickly looked away. Yep, he was a perfect combination of chiseled features, raw, rugged masculinity, and full-on unhinged lunacy.

Maybe the mark on my face offended him? Or maybe he watched me out of morbid fascination? Then again, he might have some kind of fetish?

I should be used to people staring at me by now, and I thought I was until Silver Claw's alpha showed up. I could do without the constant reminder of the ugly mark on my face or how I got it.

How I'd almost gotten my family killed, and how the guilt and shame I felt was a living, breathing thing that had festered inside me for the last year.

I shoved those thoughts out of my mind before they sent me on a downward spiral, delivered my drinks, and headed back to the bar. After my sister mated Warrick, alpha of the hellhounds, we'd all had to make some adjustments. The first was getting used to how protective my new bro-in-law was. Which was why I was now working here at Hell Fire and not the place I'd previously been waitressing at in the city.

But I was fine with it. This place had been in desperate need of extra management. Knox had been doing a pretty good job, but the hounds weren't much into crunching numbers. We worked well together, even though the male was gruff and blunt as hell, but most of the hounds had that in common. I was used to it now.

Maybe I should tell Warrick about Draven's weird obsession with me? I'd held off saying anything because so far, he'd kept his distance, and I didn't want to mess with the agreement the wolves and hounds had come to over territory. They got on, and if I went tattling to Warrick, that might end, and that wouldn't be good for anyone.

It was near closing, and the bar had been packed most of the night. Usually, I'd be exhausted, but tonight I was wired.

Rose was on my mind. She was always on my mind. My sister's sickness had taken a stronger hold on her the last few months. I honestly didn't know how she was still with us but thanked the goddess every morning that she was.

And, of course, there was the mother and when she would finally call on me, and the fear that I wasn't strong enough to pass my coming task, let alone the magical combat trial that would follow. After all Willow had gone through to ensure our coven kept the gifts we were given, it was a constant worry. I couldn't even contemplate failing and letting them all down.

I strode to the back of the bar and down the short hall to the office. We were running low on a few things, and I wanted to write them down before I forgot. The lights were off, and I leaned over the desk to switch on the lamp—

Something moved in the shadows, and the door clicked shut

behind me. I flicked on the light and spun around, but somehow I already knew who it would be.

Him.

My audience of one.

The Silver Claw pack's alpha stood with his long legs braced apart, his arms crossed over his wide chest, and those eerie green eyes locked on me.

This was it, he was going to make his move, whatever that was.

"What are you doing in here?" I said, trying to keep my voice even when my heart was trying to pound right out of my chest.

One moment he was on the other side of the room, and the next, he was in front of me. He took hold of my arm, his grip tight, fingers pressing deep into my flesh. His icy gaze clashed with mine.

All animal. All predator.

"You need to leave," I said and tried to yank my arm free.

He said nothing, and he didn't let go. Instead, he stared deeper into my eyes, like he was trying to see something, pull something from me.

"I don't know what the hell your deal is—"

"Yes," he growled, "you do, and this act of yours has worn thin."

"Act? Seriously? You're the one watching me like a freaking serial killer sizing up his next victim." I tried to pull free again. "If anyone's acting, it's you. The sane routine you've been trying to pull off needs some work. I'm sure as hell not buying it."

"Sane?" he growled. "My sanity was lost a very long time ago." His gaze searched mine, and again it was like he was waiting for me to say something more.

His penetrating stare had my stomach twisting in a way that wasn't good, but not totally bad either. It was messed up, but my body went haywire whenever he was close. It was confusing and addicting in equal measure. "I don't know what you want from me, alpha, but I'm pretty sure whatever it is, you're looking at the wrong woman."

The sneer was back. "Oh, I have the right female...beautiful and fucking treacherous."

I blinked up at him, dumbfounded. "You think I'm treacherous...and beautiful?"

"Am I wrong?"

"Yes, on both counts."

I didn't understand what was going on here. I was confused and aroused, and even though my instincts told me to get the hell out of there, I didn't want him to stop talking to me either.

"Those sweet lips can convince a male to make all kinds of bad decisions, I know that much. And that beautiful face, so fucking innocent, it fools them into believing the lies you spill."

I laughed, and it wasn't a very nice sound. This guy was seriously delusional. As for my *beauty*, half my cheek was black, a star shape of cold, lifeless flesh. The guy was full of it. Even more messed up, I didn't care what he thought or why he was looking at me with all kinds of lustful hatred in his eyes. All I knew was, for some insane reason, I liked it. Needed it.

A year and a half ago, I'd thought dating the sweet boy next door had been playing it safe. Only Brody had turned out to be a monster. I wasn't interested in love or relationships anymore. But right then, I needed what I saw in those cold green eyes looking down at me.

Truth.

He wasn't hiding what he was; it was all right there to see.

Still, I pointed to my face. "You don't find this ugly?"

He said nothing.

"You're not going to ask?"

His gaze slid to my cheek and back. "What am I asking?"

"Oh, aren't you sweet." I smiled, giving him a good look at my lopsided smile. "You're not bothered by it? My face? How I got it? You're not the tiniest bit curious?"

He cupped my cheek right over the damaged flesh, surprising

me. He sucked in a sharp breath, frowning. He wasn't expecting it to be cold. No one did.

"Someone tried to kill me," I said.

A muscle in his cheek jumped.

"I'm not scared of you, Draven." *Not at this moment, anyway.* He gritted his teeth when I said his name, and heat, raw and wild, blazed in his eyes—a look that said if I offered myself, he'd take me like an animal on the dirty ground in a heartbeat. I pushed on and pushed him when it was the last thing I should do. "I'm as cold as the dead flesh on my face," I lied. I'd tried to shut off my emotions, to harden my heart, and had failed miserably. He didn't need to know that, though.

"Oh, I know that, little witch," he said and swiped his thumb over my cheek, the rough skin making me shiver when it hit a spot by my ear that wasn't dead but still very much alive.

I looked up at him. "And yet, you want to kiss me right now, don't you?"

He dipped his head closer. "Yes," he said, voice raw and laced with fury.

He hated that, there was no missing it in his voice. Again, he concealed nothing. After Brody's deception, the way he'd used me, hurt me, tried to break me, I wanted more of this. I craved it. I wanted this male to reveal the twisted truth, the darkness inside him, the thing I saw in his eyes when he looked at me. I wanted him to admit it. "You want to punish me too," I said.

"Yes."

"And you want to fuck me while you do it." *What the hell are you doing?*

His nostrils flared and he bared his teeth.

My heart thundered in my chest. This whole exchange was strange and dangerous. I didn't understand what this was, but I also didn't care. I was chasing an escape, something I realized I desperately needed, and that was all that mattered.

"If you stick around until closing, I'll let you take me back to your place and maybe we can help each other out?" He was close enough that I could feel the heat of his body against mine. Like most shifters, he ran hot.

"Is that right?" he growled, and I felt it low in my stomach.

"Sure, why not."

He leaned closer still, and my lips parted in anticipation.

But his mouth bypassed mine, skimmed along my jaw, and touched my ear. "I would rather douse my dick with gasoline and set it on fire than stick it inside you." I froze as he lifted his head and stared down at me, his expression cold. "You're right, you are ugly. Inside you are so rotten, so hideous, it can't be concealed by your beautiful face, not from me." He tucked my hair behind my ear. "I know you for what you really are, little witch."

Then he released me, turned, and walked away.

I stood there as a million thoughts and feelings pounded through me.

How was I still standing? I should be nothing but a bloody stump after the way Draven Moreau had just verbally eviscerated me.

Instead, I walked back out and started collecting the empties scattered around the bar, because I was terrified—that he might be right.

Chapter Two

Iris

Nia whined and nudged my hand with her wet nose. When I didn't wake fast enough, she jumped on the bed and licked my face.

"Okay, all right, I'm getting up."

She graced me with her gorgeous doggy smile, licked my face again, and jumped off the bed, dancing around with excitement.

Happy. Nia happy.

I laughed and shoved back the covers. I didn't need my magic to interpret how she was feeling, I could see that for myself. Still, I heard her loud and clear, her voice filtering through my mind.

No, animals didn't speak like you and me, or even think like us, but my power worked as a kind of translator. Whatever an animal was putting out, or trying to communicate, my magic delivered it to me in a way that I would understand. Nia was my familiar, our connection was incredibly deep, and communicating with her was as natural as breathing.

Other animals, well, I was getting there. My magic had grown a lot stronger over the last several months. Animals had always been drawn to me, though, they trusted me, wanted to please me. I often had stray cats follow me home—I was now very good friends with the lady who ran the local cat sanctuary and rehabilitation center. Birds liked to flutter around me, and squirrels were often sitting in the tree outside my bedroom window, much to Nia's excitement.

"Come on then, sweet girl, let's go get breakfast." I pulled on my robe and walked into the hall. Rose's door was ajar, and I eased it open as quietly as I could, not wanting to wake her if she was still asleep.

"I'm awake," my sister said, her voice so incredibly weak.

I gripped the handle, took a steadying breath, plastered a smile on my face, and pushed the door open. "Hey, Roe." Nia followed me in, rushing to my sister, then carefully jumping up to lick her hand, sensing the need to be careful. Rose was twenty-two, two years younger than me, and had been sick her entire life. No one knew what was wrong with her, and every year, she'd grown more and more unwell. She lay in a sea of pillows and blankets, so tiny and fragile. She felt the cold now. God, her skin was like ice most of the time.

I sat on the edge of the bed and took her hand, biting back my tears at how frail she had become. There was nothing to her, and her skin was paper-thin. I barely recognized my sister anymore.

Her pale blond hair was spread out on her pillow, her blue eyes faded and huge on her drawn face. They blinked up at me. "Can you help me dress? I'd like to go downstairs."

"Of course." I could carry her, she was so small now, but Rose hated that. "You need the bathroom?"

She shook her head. "Mom helped me earlier."

"I'll just grab a washcloth." I rushed to get what she needed.

When I pulled back her covers, I kept my expression neutral, not letting the heartbreak I felt show on my face. I helped her sit up, keeping her that way by propping pillows around her, and quickly undressed her. Rose hated this as well. She didn't like anyone seeing her body now, so we did this part as fast as possible. I handed her the cloth, and she slowly, painfully, washed under her arms and between her legs while I grabbed her clothes from the drawers on the other side of the bed.

I picked out a shirt and tights and glanced over at her. Her back was to me, and I almost let a sob escape. She was like a skeleton covered in pale skin, but what upset Rose the most was the hump that had appeared on her back. We didn't know what it was or what it meant, but it was big enough to be noticeable even when she was dressed. Else, our aunt and a great healer, didn't know why it had appeared and neither did any of the other healers she'd spoken to.

So we didn't mention it, all studiously pretending it wasn't there.

I helped her dress, slid her slippers on her feet, then wrapped my arm around her narrow waist, taking all of her insubstantial weight, and we slowly made our way downstairs.

Voices reached us before I walked into the kitchen. The whole family was up by the sounds. Mags, our baby sister, jumped up from the table as soon as she saw us and cleared off the chaise in the kitchen by the window for Rose.

Magnolia was nineteen and had recently graduated from high school. She was working full time with our aunt Else now, making tonics and potions for my sister Willow's store, The Cauldron. The money from Else and Mags' hard work was our family's main income, and I helped out with what I earned at the bar. But the shop did more than all right. Else's tonics were highly sought after, and she had trouble keeping up with demand. Thankfully, she now had Mags to help.

Bram, Magnolia's familiar, a crow shifter, leaned against the wall. He was dressed all in black, as usual, his dark eyes watching her every move from under his tussled, glossy black hair. Bram had just started a new job. I didn't know much about it, but he seemed to mainly work nights, and Mags wasn't overly happy about it.

Elswyth, our seventy-two-year-old great aunt, limped over—her prosthetic leg gave her more trouble in the mornings—and tucked pillows around Rose, then covered her with a blanket. "I've got a new tonic for you this morning, sweetness," Else said to Roe. "I'm hoping it'll help with your appetite."

Rose smiled at our aunt indulgently. My sister thought our efforts to find a cure for her were a waste of time. But she'd never argue with Else. None of us would.

"Don't give me that look," Else said.

"What look?" she said innocently.

"You know what look." Else shuffled to the kitchen, grabbed her tonic, and shuffled back. "Now take your medicine, no arguments."

Rose smiled wider. "I wouldn't dream of it."

"Good," Else said, fed her a spoon of tonic, then planted a kiss on her forehead. "Now I'm gonna make you some eggs, because I'm expecting to hear your belly start growling any minute."

Rose chuckled weakly and rested back against the chaise.

I sat at the table and stole a sip of Magnolia's coffee. "Where's Mom and Art?"

She threw a balled-up napkin at my head and took her mug back as Else put another one in front of me. "They went out for a breakfast date; it's their anniversary."

My mug paused halfway to my mouth. "It's already been a year?"

"Yup."

Arthur was Mom's familiar. He was an owl shifter, fierce and loyal to all of us, and he'd been in love with Mom for as long as they'd been together. That sometimes happened, familiars falling for their witches. Mom had been clueless up until a year ago—or in denial—now she was the happiest I'd ever seen her.

I glanced at Bram. Sadly, those feelings were not always reciprocated. And when that happened, you had a familiar tied to his or her witch, suffering when they were forced to stay, their unbreakable connection keeping them there. But it was even worse when they had to stand by and watch the person they loved find and fall in love with someone else.

Bram sat by Mags, and she smiled and slid her toast in his direction to share. She loved him, as her best friend, as family; I just didn't know if there were any romantic feelings on her end or not. Mags had closed herself off after what happened a year ago. After Brody and his aunt Cora finally showed who they really were and tried to kill my entire family. Mags had been used as a pawn in the worst way to get to us and she was still struggling. She leaned on Bram, almost clung to him, but other guys and dating weren't something she would even contemplate—and especially not with her best friend. Not that Bram had ever broached the subject with her.

All eyes had drifted in my direction. I knew what they were thinking because I was as well. "I'm fine."

"How can you be?" Mags said. "The mother could call you at any time, aren't you scared?"

"Willow's prepared me," I said instead of what screamed through my mind. I was utterly terrified, but saying it out loud would only make that fear worse and worry my family even more. I could fight—nowhere near as good as Willow, but I could handle myself if push came to shove. Unfortunately, I didn't have a magic blade like my sister, but I did have my own special magic and my affinity with animals. Hopefully, all the practice I'd been doing would pay off.

"Wonder where she'll bite you?" Else said unhelpfully.

"As long as it's not the other side of my face, I don't care," I muttered and grabbed a piece of toast that Else had just put in the middle of the table.

There was this whole ritual that included a demon-infested forest, followed by face time with a giant serpent possessed by

19

Mother Nature. After she bit you, you ended up with permanent tattoo-like markings made by her magical venom. They started off black, and *if* you passed the task she gave you, they became colorful. Just what every girl wanted on the side of her face. And no, that wasn't out of the realms of possibility. We'd all seen the painting in our library of Selene Thornheart. She'd been a Keeper in our family a very long time ago, and the mother had marked her face. Why the hell would she do that? Seemed kind of bitchy to me.

And, of course, then there was the magical combat trial that came after that. I tried not to think about it.

Willow, our oldest sister, was the Keeper of our coven now, but the mother had decreed, after Willow had passed her tasks and trial, that since the position of Keeper had moved to a new branch of the family—again thanks to Brody and Cora's treacherousness —each of us, me, Rose, and Mags, had to pass a task and trial of our own to prove our line was worthy of keeping the magical gifts she'd bestowed on our coven over the centuries. To lose those gifts would be devastating to not only our family but to our entire coven.

This all happened a year ago. The mother had given us time to prepare, and a year was more than we'd hoped for. But time was running out. I felt it; we all did.

"Surely, she's not that evil," Mags said. "Though, going by what Willow told us, maybe she is."

The rumble of bikes came from outside the house.

"Speaking of your sister," Else said.

I'd just topped off my coffee when Willow and her mate, Warrick, walked in. Relic, one of the younger hounds, and by younger, I mean only several hundred years old instead of a thousand like my sister's mate, followed. Warrick greeted us with that low, rough voice, then sat and pulled the plate of toast toward him. Relic leaned against the counter, the handsome hound grinning and somehow managing to flirt with all of us at once.

Willow perched on the edge of the chaise and took Rose's hand, kissing her pale skin and smiling down at her before her eyes came to me, that familiar anxiety there. "How's everything going?"

As my turn drew closer and Rose got sicker, the tension in the house grew. My family tried to hide it, but I knew them too well.

"She just realized it's been a year," Mags added.

"It's fine, I'm fine," I said, repeating myself. "Nia and I totally have this." My familiar sensed my stress and pressed against my thigh. I gave her side a rub to calm her down.

Willow leaned forward, resting her elbows on her knees. "You're going to need help when the mother calls, more than Nia." She tilted her head toward Relic.

I looked at the hound, and he smiled, or more bared his teeth. "Whatever you need, Iris. Just say the word."

Okay, no. Willow had been throwing Relic at me every chance she got for the last twelve months. She'd been trying to fix us up and was more than obvious about it. Her obsession with getting me mated bordered on obsessive. She didn't seem to care that Relic and I weren't *actually* mates. Theoretically, they could mate with someone of their choosing, not the one "destined" for them, but what happened when Relic's real mate eventually showed up? He'd drop me like a flaming turd, and I wouldn't blame him.

"Thanks for the offer, Relic, but I'm fine," I said. That word again, and the complete opposite of how I felt.

"Why would you turn down his offer?" Willow said and shot to her feet. "You don't know what'll be thrown at you, you need help."

"Forcing me to spend time with Relic isn't going to change anything. We're not into each other." I glanced at Relic. "No offense."

He smirked. "None taken."

Willow planted her hands on her hips. "Iris..."

"I don't know why you have this obsession with finding me a mate, but you need to cut it out. I'm not you, and Relic isn't

Warrick. I promise you, Relic isn't going to see me across a bloody battlefield and suddenly realize that I was there all along, and that he can't live without me."

Relic threw his head back and laughed.

"I knew Willow was my mate as soon as I met her," Warrick said, slathering butter on his piece of toast.

"See," I said to Willow. "Thank you, Warrick."

Warrick shrugged. "You still need someone to take your back. You don't want Relic, we'll find someone else."

I hated owing people, and I didn't want my brother-in-law to force one of his brothers to follow me everywhere against their will. "It's not that I don't want Relic..." Relic winked, and I shook my head at his brazenness. "But I want to find someone myself—"

"You're running out of time," Willow said.

She wasn't trying to freak me out, she was worried, but this wasn't helping.

Relic's flirty grin slid away. "I've got no ulterior motives, Iris. Happy to take your back, babe, if you need me."

"Thank you, I appreciate that, and I may take you up on the offer, but it feels important to work this out myself. The mother wants all of us to prove ourselves, not get our big sister, the Keeper, to fix it all for us. Besides, help from family or coven is forbidden, and Willow finding backup for me could be construed as help. That seems too close to crossing the line, and I won't risk it."

Willow cursed, "I guess you're right. Shit."

"What about the wolves?" Else said. "We've been without a pack here so long, we've overlooked 'em. The local pack and the witches here in Roxburgh have always worked together."

The look in Draven's eyes from the night before filled my mind, and my belly clenched. "I don't know about that..."

"Silver Claw is a solid pack, good, honorable people," Warrick said. "Draven is a strong alpha, trustworthy, and I know he's looking to increase their power. I think they'd be open to some kind of exchange."

Witches had exchanged magic with the packs for protection in the past—incantations, healing, or wards to protect their territory. But I doubted Draven would want to do that with me, not after the things he'd said at the bar.

"I'll think about," I said, lying through my teeth.

Mags cursed suddenly, and we all turned to her.

She looked up from her phone. "Amy Sartori and Imogen Lewis have gone missing."

We all froze around the table. "What do you mean, missing?"

"It's all over Nightscape," she said, face pale. "They never came home last night. They found Amy's car not far from Oldwood Forest, but no sign of either of them. Someone said they saw Amy walk into the woods. They thought she was alone and called out to her, but she ignored them."

Nightscape was a social media app used mainly by witches and shifters and was magically hidden from humans. It was also our main source of news and information.

Unease filled me. Both girls were Rose's age, and both had fathers on the witch's council. Cesare Sartori was fairly powerful and a major asshole. I didn't know much about Imogen's family; I'd never spoken to councilor Lewis.

"That forest is swarming with demons, do you think they could have..." Mags trailed off, the thought too horrible to say out loud.

"Both of their fathers are on the council," Willow said, saying out loud what I'd been thinking.

Mags leaned forward. "Do you think that means something?"

Willow shook her head. "I'm not sure. I just hope they're found...and quickly."

Chapter Three

Iris

The bar was busy again tonight, and *he* was back.

The alpha sat in his usual spot, his green gaze looking almost black as he watched me from his favorite shadowy corner. I did my best to ignore him and delivered my drinks. Thankfully, he wasn't at one of my tables, something I had to guess he did on purpose.

But yeah, close enough, I wouldn't miss his death glare.

Warrick was also here tonight. There were always hounds here keeping an eye on things, but Warrick didn't come that often anymore. But I knew exactly why he was here when he finished talking to Jagger, his lieutenant, and headed across the room—straight for Draven.

Goddammit, Willow. I bet she made him come here tonight to talk to the other alpha, and there was no way of stopping the train wreck that was about to happen.

Warrick and Draven shook hands in greeting. I kept my eyes on

A VOW OF RUIN

the two alphas while trying to look like I was working. Warrick sat and started talking while Draven listened intently, their mutual respect obvious. Draven nodded, and then his head jerked back. It was slight, but I didn't miss it. His gaze sliced to me, darker than before, and his nostrils flared.

Nope, he sure as hell wasn't interested in helping me out, and after our little conversation the last time he was here, I had no intention of asking for it.

Warrick said something else and Draven dipped his chin. They shook hands again, and Draven stood and walked away. My knees actually weakened as he left, the brutal tension he brought with him draining from my body as he vacated the room.

Get it together. I gave myself a mental shake and headed back to the bar. I unloaded my empties, and when I turned back, Warrick was striding my way.

"What's up?" I said, playing dumb when he stopped in front of me. If I told Warrick what the wolf had said to me, things would go south fast. My protective, hulking, brother-in-law would start a fight, and no one wanted that.

"Draven agreed to speak with you. He's in the office," he said, shocking the shit out of me.

"He agreed to talk to me?"

"Yeah."

Okay, *that* I was not expecting.

"You're right, you are ugly. Inside you are so rotten, so hideous, it can't be concealed by your beautiful face, not from me."

His hateful words filled my head. They'd been on repeat since he'd said them. My face heated, mortified all over again. Why the hell would he agree to that? "Are you sure?"

"Yeah, I'm fucking sure. Now go talk to him. The sooner you get some backup, the sooner my mate stops worrying." His gaze grew intense, but his eyes had grown soft-*ish*. "We all want you to get through this in one piece, yeah?"

That was as mushy as Warrick got with anyone who wasn't my

25

sister. "If Willow had anything to do with this, I can't accept his help, anyway."

"She didn't, this is all me, and I didn't ask him. You'll do that."

Shit. I didn't want to talk to Draven again, I'd promised myself I wouldn't. I sure as hell didn't want to be alone in the same room with that prick, but I would endure it for my family. I'd hurt them enough when I'd brought Brody deeper into our lives, when I fell for his lies, then almost got us all killed. I'd do anything to protect them, no matter the cost to me. And it wasn't like Warrick would take no for an answer, either. "Right. Fine. I'll go talk to him." Though I was sure it was a complete waste of time.

"Good," Warrick said and gave me a gentle shove toward the office.

I straightened my spine and strode across the bar, then stopped outside the door. My heart was racing, and my palms felt clammy. I reached for the handle, then stopped. This seriously sucked.

Come on. Open the freaking door.

Dragging in another breath to steady my nerves, I rubbed my sweaty palms down my apron and reached for the door—

It opened before I could touch the handle. Draven filled the space in front of me, his expression blank.

Embarrassingly, I shrieked a little. "I was just...I..."

His lips flattened, and he stepped back, telling me without words I was wasting his precious time.

Shit. "Right, sorry," I said stupidly and rushed in. This male seriously threw me off my game. *Who are you kidding? You don't have game.* I ignored the snarky bitch in my head and turned to face him. "Thanks for agreeing to meet with me."

He shut the door and leaned against it, crossing his arms over his wide chest. All the bravado I'd had the last time I spoke to him was gone, shattered by his cruel words. I don't know why I cared. He didn't know me. Whatever he thought he saw when he looked at me wasn't something I could control. He didn't know one thing about me.

And as much as I hated this, Willow was right, I was running out of time. A deal with the wolves would mean there was no chance the mother could accuse me of getting help from my family or coven. Witches and wolves had made these kinds of deals for centuries, and Draven didn't have to personally help me, he could assign someone else in his pack, right?

I stayed on the other side of the office. "Okay, so...I don't know what Warrick told you. You're a wolf shifter, so I have to assume you have some knowledge of witches, covens, what a Keeper is?"

He said nothing, just continued to study me.

I struggled on. "I guess that depends how old you are?" I said, musing out loud. "Well, I have this task and a trial—"

"I'm three hundred and sixty-two years old, I know a lot of things," he said.

Well, shit. Wolf shifters weren't immortal, but they were long-lived. How long, I wasn't sure, but Draven looked like a male in his late twenties or early thirties. "That makes it a little easier," I said and tried not to fidget. Then I mentally kicked my own ass because I was not going to let this guy make me feel like crap. Brody had done a good job of destroying my self-confidence, my sense of self, but I was not some meek female. I was strong. I'd always been strong. This would be a business arrangement, right? I wasn't going to grovel. Our working together would benefit us both.

I straightened my spine, and he watched me, eyes narrowing.

"Look, I know you dislike me. I mean, you don't exactly try to hide it, so I'm probably wasting my breath here..." I let that hang between us, desperate to know what his deal was. I waited for him to try to deny it or tell me what his problem was. He said nothing. I took him in, that granite jaw still tight as hell. "Wow. You really do hate me, huh?"

The muscles in his forearms flexed, his gaze still locked on mine. "You repulse me."

I blinked, stunned that he'd just said that out loud, then I threw my head back and laughed, startling us both. I laughed so hard tears ran down my face. I guess I should be hurt or offended? I couldn't work up the energy this time.

He didn't move, just watched me, his expression growing darker by the minute. *Awesome.* I was pissing him off even more. It was hard, but I managed to pull myself together. "Please, don't hold back on my account."

Again, he said nothing, the fucking weirdo.

Why did that make me want to push him into reacting? His self-control seemed tenuous at best, I doubted it would be that hard. Aggression and lust now saturated the room, so thick it was impossible to ignore. Except this time, I wasn't dumb enough to bring it up. I could pretend it wasn't there if he could. I could pretend my body wasn't humming for the unstable male across the room, which only told me I was as unstable as he was. And considering I'd just laughed in his face, I'd say that was an accurate assessment.

The male had me behaving in all kinds of fucked-up ways, and apparently, I was just going to go with it.

"Fine, let's just get to the point, then. So every two hundred years, the Keeper of each coven has to complete a task set by the mother, then win against another witch in a magical combat trial or lose the powers she gifted them. Willow did this, she won, but for *reasons*, the mother wants my sisters and I to complete a task and trail as well. I'll need help with my task when the mother calls me. Things often get dangerous and the rules say no members of my family or coven can assist me. I'm fairly powerful, but there are places I might need to go that I shouldn't go alone. I'm not helpless, but I'm not a fighter either. Warrick said you might be willing to trade services? I would get the backup I need, and you would... well, you tell me what you want, and hopefully, I can provide it for you. Wards for your home or land, spells, potions, an IOU for a later date? Whatever you want within my abilities."

"How about giving me the last three hundred and twenty-nine years back?" he gritted out cryptically.

I frowned. "Um...that one's beyond my skill set. So I take it that's a no, then? I guess I expected it, but..."

He moved, quick, and took my jaw in his rough-skinned hand. "Stop," he barked out. "I won't play these games with you anymore, witch. I have waited, bided my time, but I am done with this play acting of yours."

That wasn't the first time he'd said something like this. The first time I met him, six months ago in the clearing behind our house, he'd acted like I'd personally wronged him. "I don't know what you're talking about." The ice in his gaze sent cold dread down my spine. "Who do you think I am?"

He walked me back, pressing me against the wall, trapping me with his body.

"Come now, Selene, you forget me so easily?" he said, fury making his voice shake.

I froze.

He thought I was... "Selene?"

He snarled.

The painting of her in our library flashed through my mind, her face so like mine. God, he'd *known* her. "I think I can explain—"

He snapped his teeth. "No more lies. Admit what you did."

"I-I didn't do anything. You have me mixed up with someone else. Where have you been the last three hundred and twenty-nine years, Draven?"

He leaned in, his nose sliding over my cold, blackened cheek. "Where you left me, witch. Where you left me and my warriors to fucking rot."

Oh goddess. What had Selene done? "I'm not her. My name's Iris. Selene died a long time ago."

"Lies," he growled. "And if you do not break this spell you have over me..." He shook his head as if he was trying to shake something loose. "Making me want you again, making me think about you, dream about you." He snarled. "End this hold you

29

have over me right the fuck now, because it won't save you this time."

"Draven..."

He shoved away from the wall and stormed out of the room, slamming the door behind him.

Draven

I strode out of there before my wolf broke free and I did something I couldn't undo. Her professions of innocence, *her lies*, ran through my head on repeat, and I snarled again as I walked through the bar, through the door, and out into the night.

I fucking hated her. I wanted to end her life for what she did, for the pain she'd caused my pack. But I'd lied. She didn't repulse me, not physically, anyway. Far from it. I was ashamed to admit how much I wanted the deceitful little witch. When I'd first met her, I'd believed myself in love with her. But it had all been a twisted ruse. She'd bewitched me so I'd do her bidding. But even under her witch's spell, I'd never burned for her like this.

I burned for her now.

I'd wanted her then, but nothing like this. Resisting her charms had been hard, but now—

I growled and paced across the parking lot.

I'd only kissed her once—one chaste kiss was all she'd allowed —and that's all it took for me to let her lead me and my warriors to our doom. Now she was doing it again, bewitching me, trying to control me, and if I touched her again, I was afraid of what I might do.

What she had me feeling now? I growled. Her magic was poisoning my mind, and somehow I had to fight it.

I gripped the sides of my head and my wolf whined and clawed to run free, to run to her. Yes, she was doing it again—a spell, a curse, a potion. Another fucked-up attempt to make me want her, crave her. To control me like a puppet on her strings.

I would not let her win. Despite how different it felt this time, stronger, more all-consuming, I would fight it. She'd had over three hundred years to perfect her magic, but I'd had the same amount of time to plan her end.

My wolf whined again, demanding I go back to her, and I wanted to roar my frustration.

The beast wanted to take her, keep her.

I wanted to slit her fucking throat and watch her bleed for what she did. To finally free myself of her and her treachery and never look back.

I couldn't do that, though, not with the hellhound alpha mated to a female claiming to be Selene's sister. They'd fooled him as well, and I had to find a way to make him see the truth for himself before I took my revenge.

"Fuck." I needed to run as far from her as I could get, especially while I was this close to the edge of my control. I strode to my truck, stripped off my clothes, tossed them in the back, shifted, and sprinted into the forest.

As I headed for Wolf Hill Woods, my mind raced, the past twisting with the present. The forest closed in around me, but all I could see was her face, her deceitful fucking face. After more than three hundred years trapped, the seven of us confined to a small piece of woods—our wolves unable to run as far as we needed, never able to fully unleash—our sanity had suffered. Food had been scarce, and two of my warriors had starved to death.

If it hadn't been for one of the Knights of Hell—half demon, half angel, demon hunters—stumbling upon us in his search for the dagger Charity had hidden, along with the map to set us free, we'd still be trapped.

It was my job to protect my people, to keep them safe, and I'd failed. I'd lived. Fuck knew how. I could only assume my hatred and thirst for revenge had kept me going.

Now Selene was finally within my grasp, and I'd hesitated.

I howled in fury and frustration. Kenric, one of our elders, had gladly given up his position as alpha when I'd returned. The old wolf had stepped up to take care of the pack while I was gone, even though he'd never wanted the position. I fucking hated that I was failing him now, that I was failing my entire pack, again. I needed to end this—end her—or I would never get any peace, and my pack wouldn't either.

I let my wolf take the lead, running faster, harder. The wind ruffled my fur, the earth soft beneath my paws. Yes, I needed this. I needed to run, to clear my head.

A familiar scent reached me.

Demons.

More than one, encroaching on my territory. We'd been reclaiming this part of the Roxburgh State Forest the last year, land that had always belonged to the local pack. The previous one had been driven out, depleted by the demons that lived here. The place had been infested with the evil fuckers when we'd arrived, and there were still some reluctant to move on.

Killing these twisted pieces of shit was exactly what I needed to work off the rage still pumping through my veins.

I burst through the trees.

There were four of them.

They all turned to face me. One of them grinned.

Stupid fuck was about to die and didn't even know it.

I howled into the night, then charged my prey.

Chapter Four

Iris

Brody covered me with his body and pushed my legs wide, his gaze intense, like he was trying to draw every one of my thoughts from me, to learn every secret I might have.

"You have everything," he said, and it wasn't the first time he'd said that to me. "You didn't even have to work for it. It all just landed in your lap."

"That's not true."

"You don't even appreciate it. While I watched my mom slowly die, you were living in that big house with your big family. Powerful, safe."

I hated when he got like this, like he was jealous of me. Shouldn't you be happy that the person you loved hadn't had an awful life? I hated that he'd lost his mom, no one should suffer that.

"I'm sorry you lost your mom," I said, like I always did when he spoke this way because there was nothing else this could be about. He missed her, and sometimes he took that out on someone else he loved, someone that was still here.

"You'll never understand what it's like to feel helpless, Iris. To feel like you've been left behind and forgotten. Powerless."

"Your aunt loves you...I love you. I'll never leave you behind."

He leaned in, pressing his lips roughly against mine, the kiss hard, bruising, and when he lifted his head, his expression was strange.

"What are you thinking?" I whispered.

His lips curled up, an expression he sometimes got when he looked at me, a warning. That's how I'd come to think of it. I hated when he got like this, but he needed me. Sometimes, he needed more from me than I knew how to give, and I'd learned to go with it. It was easier than making him angry. His hand slid up my chest between my breasts and wrapped lightly around my throat.

I whispered his name in the shadowy room as the look in his eyes darkened. Yes, he was in pain, and it was my job to get him through it, even if I didn't want this. But when you loved someone, you took the good with the bad, right? My father hadn't; none of my sister's fathers had. They'd left Mom sad, broken, and feeling abandoned. I would never do that to the person I loved.

And the bad wasn't very often. I could take it.

His fingers tightened a little more, and he slammed inside me with a grunt. It hurt, I wasn't ready for him. But I let him work out his frustration on me, his pain, because I was his and he was mine. He needed this from me for some reason, even though sometimes it felt like he was trying to inflict pain rather than soothe his own.

I shoved that thought away.

No.

Brody loved me.

He would never intentionally hurt me.

He looked down at me, teeth gritted, eyes filled with rage, and my stomach gripped tight.

"You're not so powerful now, are you, Iris?"

I woke with a start, sitting bolt upright in bed.

My heart pounded in my chest, vomit churning in my gut. Why had I let him treat me like that? Why had I put blinders on, refusing to see the person he truly was? He'd shown me repeatedly, and I'd been so scared he'd leave me, like most of the men in our lives, that I'd refused to see it.

Another ex once told me I had daddy issues. I'd always been needy, desperate for attention from the guys I'd dated, and the desperate way I'd clung to Brody, the way I'd rationalized the awful things he'd said and done, made me think it might be true. I'd been so desperate for Brody's love, I'd blinded myself to the truth.

I rubbed my eyes, trying to force his hated face from my mind, his voice too. It lingered now. A voice I used to look forward to hearing, like the needy idiot I was.

Tingles goose-bumped their way across my shoulders and down my spine before a cold blast hit me out of nowhere. I blinked into the dark room as a weird *hum* spun around me.

Come to me, child.

I jolted at the voice filling my mind. Definitely not Brody's.

Come to me now, daughter of coven Thornheart. The voice repeated—a female voice.

Oh shit. It was happening.

Mother Nature, the Great Goddess, the Creatress of all life— or Mother, as she was called by the witches who worshipped her, was calling me to her.

I exploded out of bed, and Nia flew off the end where she'd been sleeping, her ears pinned back, on high alert. I quickly rubbed her head to calm her, even though my heart was like a jackrabbit in my chest. "We have to go out now, Nia." Just like I could understand her, Nia could understand me. "And there could be danger."

Nia will kill it. Keep Iris safe.

Her reply didn't surprise me. My hands shook as I quickly dressed. "You must wait for my command. There could be demons, and there will be a monster, a serpent. Do you remember what I told you about the serpent?"

Nia remembers everything Iris says.

"Of course you do. She'll look scary, and she'll bite me, but I'll be okay. She's good, and you mustn't attack her, okay?"

No attack unless Iris says.

"Exactly." I crouched in front of her and cupped her fuzzy face. "I'm going animal while we walk through the woods, so the demons won't sense me, but you can't get too excited, you have to stay calm and alert for me."

Nia quivered *with excitement,* unable to help herself. She loved it when I embodied an animal. I couldn't shift forms—I was a witch, not a shifter—but I'd discovered that talking to animals and drawing them to me wasn't all my magical specialty allowed me to do. I could take on some of an animal's physical abilities, whatever animal it was that I chose. No, I didn't physically change as such, instead it was like the spirit of that animal encompassed me. Nia called it a shadow; it was translucent, surrounding me in the form of the animal I chose.

It was the newest trick in my arsenal. Something I'd been practicing nonstop, and from what we knew, a power that was extremely rare.

It was a weird feeling, and it'd scared me when I first did it, but it might be the thing that would save my bacon during this task, not to mention the combat trial that would follow if I was successful.

We run in the woods?

"Yes, we'll run," I said to Nia.

Nia couldn't contain her yip of happiness. I held my finger to my lips, telling her to stay quiet, and quickly put on my running shoes. I didn't want to wake the rest of the family. They couldn't come with me, and if they knew where I was going, they'd be up all night worrying when there was nothing they could do to help me.

I either made it back or I didn't.

We tiptoed our way downstairs and let ourselves out as sound-lessly as I could. The house next door, Brody and his aunt Cora's house, now stood empty and cast a long shadow across our yard. Brody was dead, never to return, and I had no idea where Cora was. The council had taken her away. But seeing that house, some-times it was like they were still there, plotting and scheming. A shiver slid through me before I could stop it. If I had my way, the place would be torn down.

I rushed to my car and opened the door. Nia jumped into the Toyota's passenger seat, and I slid in behind the wheel. My gaze darted to our house when I started the engine. No lights came on. So far, so good. Putting the car in drive, I rolled out onto the street and headed toward Oldwood Forest.

Planting my foot on the gas, I battled my nerves. I knew what was coming. Willow had prepared me. We'd gone over it so many times that it felt like a memory, not someone else's recollection. I was as ready as I'd ever be.

The dark entrance into the southernmost part of the Roxburgh State Forest loomed ahead as I pulled off the road and parked as deep into the shadows as I could get.

"Stick close," I said to Nia when we got out. "No chasing, okay?"

Nia won't chase. Except squirrels?

"Not even squirrels."

Tomorrow?

"Yes, you can chase squirrels tomorrow."

She bounced up on her back legs and gave me her beautiful grin.

The only thing left to do was summon my animal. I'd already chosen which one would be best for tonight. A wolf. Silver Claw had been taking back territory around Wolf Hill Woods, killing the demons hiding out there. So I had to assume the demons here would want to avoid any wolves they came across. Wolves could also run extremely fast and had an excellent sense of smell, both traits I could use tonight. A pity I couldn't summon their sharp teeth as well.

Closing my eyes, I breathed in the scents around me—pine, earth, moss, animal, and let it sink deep. I envisioned a wolf, strong, proud, fast, and my heartbeat accelerated—

There she was.

Ash gray with arctic blue eyes. Every time I called on an animal, the more in tune we became. I didn't know if they'd always been a part of me or if they were spirits that came to me and I became a part of them. Either way, the connection was like nothing I'd ever experienced before. It was breathtaking, empowering. And so incredibly *right*.

Nia whined beside me, sensing the wolf as it surrounded me.

I opened my eyes—eyes that I instinctively knew were now blue—and Nia ran in a circle around my feet. Despite my riot of nerves, I laughed. It was impossible to ignore the exhilaration of the transformation firing through my synapses, the feeling of the wolf's strength pulsing through my veins and muscles.

I took off, sprinting into the forest, Nia at my side. My running shoes hit the packed earth, and I dug deep. My eyes were clear, sharper than ever before. I could easily scan the woods around me as we ran at full speed, darting around trees, jumping over dead logs, a small creek, running faster with every second. I'd always jogged, stayed fit; it had come naturally to me my whole life, but this was on a whole new level.

The scent of the forest grew heavier, and my skin buzzed and tingled, a sense of rightness filling me, making me smile with a kind of joy I never knew existed until this part of my magic became fully realized.

A part of me that had made me whole when I hadn't even realized something was missing.

The scent of demon reached me, but it wasn't close. My plan was working. They were staying away, avoiding the wolf they sensed nearby.

Oh goddess, this is actually going to work.

Nia stayed close and alert at my side. She growled a little when she scented the demons as well and veered to the right, as I did, moving farther away from them.

The clearing was close; I could feel its vibrations. My nerves grew.

There.

It loomed ahead.

We made it to the edge of the clearing and I crouched by Nia. "You must stay, Nia, yes?"

Nia stay.

"That's my good girl." I rubbed her head. "When the serpent's gone, you can come to me. But if I'm hurt and the demons come, more demons than you can fight...that's more than one." I held up one finger. "Nia, you must run for help. And if I stop breathing, you must run away as fast as you can, run home, don't let any demons come near you, okay?"

Nia will protect Iris.

"No, Nia will go to safety."

She growled low and pawed at the ground, not wanting to do as I said, but good girl that she was, finding it hard to disobey to me. She moved restlessly, struggling to stay in place as I stood, to hold herself back. Nia was sweet, but she was my familiar and could be vicious if I was threatened. Nia could save my life tonight, if it came to that, but she could also lose her own if she was outnumbered. Leaving her at home wasn't an option because I needed backup, but I had to make sure she would obey my command. I couldn't bear for anything to happen to her. My heart wouldn't survive it.

"Stay, Nia," I said, making my voice firm, unyielding.

She growled again but agreed. *Nia stay.*

I crouched back down, kissed the top of her furry head, and, releasing the wolf surrounding me, walked out into the clearing.

The night was starless, with low clouds making the sky look

like a yawning nothingness. The moon had been peeking through on and off all night, and as I reached the middle of the clearing, it made another appearance.

I glanced back. Nia's eyes shone from her spot at the tree line, focused on me. I turned back to the ring of small stones on the ground and held out my hand, muttering the spell to summon fire as was expected. It instantly ignited, and I quickly stripped off my clothes.

Our coven often used blood to spell, and I took the small jewel-handled blade Mom had given me when I turned thirteen and made a slice in my thigh. Blood instantly bubbled to the surface and ran down the side of my leg, soaking into the soil. I pressed my bare toes deeper, tossed the knife aside, closed my eyes, and raised my arms.

"Guide me, old ones. I am your servant, the Keeper's sister chosen to fulfill the rite of Coven Thornheart." Wind came out of nowhere, blowing faster and faster, carrying dried leaves and small twigs, battering against my naked body. "I'm here to accept my task. Whatever you ask, I will undertake."

The wind increased, whipping around me, and I gasped for breath when the power the mother brought reached not only flesh and bone but went soul-deep. My soul *felt* her. The Great Goddess, her power, her greatness, her darkness, and her light.

Then I heard it, a rattling sound that could only be one thing.

I kept my eyes closed. The mother would tell me when I could look at her. Something scraped across my thigh, rough and oily, followed by the tickle of what had to be her forked tongue across my skin, tasting my blood. Making sure I was the witch she'd summoned here.

Look at me, child.

Her voice flowed through me, and as much as I didn't want to, I forced myself to do as she bid and barely managed to hold in my gasp when I finally got a look at her.

Nothing could have prepared me for the sight. The mother

didn't have a corporeal form, she was everywhere, at all times, so when she needed to get up close and personal with someone, she chose to inhabit her pet serpent.

Its massive head hovered in front of me, shining ivory fangs on either side of her wide jaw. I shivered and forced myself to stay still. The mother didn't like weakness.

You are a brave one. I did wonder if you were as stubborn as your sister and... Her forked tongue slid out again and she tasted the air. *I see that you are.*

"Thank you, Mother."

I wouldn't congratulate yourself quite yet, witch. You may be stubborn, but to pass this task, you will need to be cunning and clever, and you will need courage. You will need to prove to me that coven Thornheart should keep my gifts.

"I will, Mother. I will do anything you ask of me."

You must complete the task I give you by the time the vines meet. If you fail, you will be unworthy of trial, and gifts past will be returned to the mother. If you complete your task yet fail to win your trial, again, your coven's gifts will be returned to the mother.

Apparently, the mother referred to herself in the third person. "I understand," I said.

Her enormous head moved to the side, and her huge glossy black eyes slid over the side of my face.

You know betrayal.

"Yes."

Then you know how rare loyalty is.

"I do."

It is a quality I admire.

Her eyes flashed, then her head reared back, and she struck. It was so incredibly fast I didn't see it coming. Her fangs sank into my upper thigh, her venom instantly pumping into my veins. She widened her mouth, sliding her fangs free of my flesh, and even though I knew this was part of the deal, I stared up at her in shock.

Nia barked in the distance but didn't leave her spot at the tree line. Probably because I was still standing, though I didn't think I would be for much longer.

The serpent's head came close again, its head tilting to the side, then she leaned in—and for one horrifying moment, I thought she was going to bite my face as well. Instead, her forked tongue danced over the black, dead skin on my cheek.

I stood frozen, not by choice but because my limbs were paralyzed as she whispered words I couldn't understand.

Somehow, I remained standing as she spun and finally slithered away. My legs gave out a second later. I collapsed onto the ground, my limp body cushioned by the damp grass, leaving me prone and naked on the ground.

Nia exploded from the trees, tearing across the clearing.

Iris get up. Demons. They come.

I couldn't move.

And as the seconds ticked by, darkness began to creep in at the corners of my eyes.

Nia pawed at the ground and jumped around me, nudging me, trying to tell me to stand, but I couldn't hear her anymore, my head only buzzed, static filling my mind.

The shadows moved in the distance, among the trees.

No, not shadows.

Demons.

They were creeping slowly toward us, curiosity drawing them closer, and I was in no condition to call on my animal magic to play wolf in the hopes of scaring them away.

They came faster now, sensing an easy target.

I was dead.

I wouldn't make it out of here alive, and my family, my coven, were going to suffer for it.

"R-Run, Nia. Run h-home as fast as you can," I managed before everything went dark.

Chapter Five

Draven

Nothing but ash remained of the demons who had dared encroach on my territory, something that happened when you removed these fucker's heads.

I snarled, adrenaline throbbing through me. I was covered in their blood, and one of them had pissed himself. I sniffed and scowled and searched for more. I wasn't done, the tension inside me was far from burned out.

The wind swirled, increasing in strength—

I stilled and scented the air again.

Selene.

The witch was close. I scented again. Blood. Hers.

And demons.

I shifted back to my wolf and exploded through the forest. I should let them have her and save myself the trouble. But that wasn't the way it was supposed to end. She didn't get off that easily.

I broke free of the trees and into a large clearing. Magic hummed all around, saturating the place. Demons, five of them, surrounded a small fire.

A dog growled in the center, snarling, teeth bared, standing over Selene's still and naked body. I'd seen the dog with her before, and the outnumbered beast snapped at the laughing demons as they edged closer.

The dog wasn't a shifter, and it was going to get torn apart if I didn't do something. It didn't deserve that, not for being loyal to its master, even if she was a twisted, evil bitch.

A demon swiped at the dog, and I rushed them, taking the closest one down, tearing out its throat. Not dead but incapacitated. I took down another the same way, then shifted, grabbed the small blade lying by a pile of clothes, and, when the next demon came at me, slashed it across the stomach, spun it around, and stabbed it several times in the chest. It dropped, and I faced the next two.

One snarled...then ran away, like a fucking coward.

I waved the last one forward. "This ends one way, you decide if that's now or later. You're in my forest now, demon." The stupid fuck charged, and I had him down and decapitated in minutes.

I worked my way around the others still writhing on the ground, removing heads, turning them into ash, and sending them back to Hell where they belonged. Then I turned and faced the dog. She was still crouched over Selene, her lips pulled back and trembling as she growled fiercely at me.

"I won't hurt you, or your master," I said, trying to keep my voice even. And it wasn't a complete lie. The dog was safe from me. The unconscious witch she stood over, not so much.

I held her gaze and let the dog see my wolf, let her taste my dominance. Showing her that I meant her no harm and that I was strong enough to protect them. It was hard, but I held my aggression back, hiding my hatred for her master. She finally whined and stepped back, nudging Selene with her nose, then sat.

I bit back my curse and scooped up the witch, looking down at her beautiful, traitorous face. She was unconscious and there was no sign of her waking.

I could return her to her home, to her coven. But I had no intention of doing that.

I'd been waiting for my chance, and I'd finally been presented with it. It was obvious no one else was here with her, and—I scented the air—no one was coming. If she vanished off the face of the Earth, no one would ever know what happened to her.

I scooped up her clothes and set them on her, then hitched her higher in my arms and started for Wolf Hill and my keep. No trace of her remained here. I glanced down at the dog. I'd have no trouble finding a new owner for the creature among the young in our pack.

Selene was finally going to pay for her crimes. We'd lost people because of her, and those of us trapped, had lost half of our lives in that hellhole—in my pack, we were all about an eye for an eye.

A life for a life.

I ignored the howl of my wolf, the unwanted hunger for the female in my arms that was already growing in the pit of my gut and making my heart pound. The spell she had over me grew stronger whenever she was near. And when my wolf tried to push forward, tried to take over, and roared for me to claim her, it took everything not to obey, not to get lost in the euphoric feeling pulsing through me.

But it was a lie. A sick, twisted, evil, fucking lie.

I would not let her dark witchcraft destroy my life again.

This she-devil was not my mate, no matter what my wolf was roaring in my head. No, fate could not be so cruel.

It was more of her sick fucking treachery.

I would not let her do this to me again.

～

It took over an hour to carry her to our mountainside keep, and her dog stayed glued to my side the entire way. When I drew near, my warriors on watch, stationed farther down the mountain, followed me, curious. Dirk offered to take her from me, but her witchcraft had sunk too deep, and I couldn't bring myself to let her go. I snarled, my fury rolling higher.

"What do you plan to do with her?" Dirk asked, looking down at her with hatred in his gaze.

As one of the males who'd been trapped with me, he despised her as well. His thirst for revenge ran almost as deep as mine. Still, it took all my will not to snap at the male, to warn him away from her.

I glanced down at her again. She had yet to wake, but she'd made little whimpering noises every now and again that had me gritting my teeth and my wolf's protective instincts roaring forward. "Stop her from hurting anyone else."

As I walked through our settlement, my pack mates watched in silence from in front of their cabins that lined the sheltered valley concealed in the side of the mountain.

Asher strode toward me. She was one of my fiercest warriors and, after me, had the highest demon body count since we came here. She scowled when she saw who was in my arms.

"You're going through with this, then?" she said, her displeasure unmistakable.

"I told you I would." I carried on walking, and Ash kept pace beside me.

"This bitch did us wrong, Drave, but we don't execute indiscriminately, no matter what they are or what they've done. Even the demons we've killed were given the choice to leave first."

I stopped with a growl. "Have you forgotten what it was like trapped in that place so easily? She is the reason Fisher and Amber are dead. And Boone may not have been with us, but she's the reason you lost him. You can just forgive her for that?"

Fury lit her gaze. "Of course not, but this..." She motioned to Selene. "This isn't us."

I let my wolf flash through my eyes. "Last time I looked, I was alpha."

"Seriously? You're gonna pull that with me? You need to—"

"I don't need to do a fucking thing." I strode off, heading for the keep.

The place looked like a medieval castle, and the previous pack hadn't done anything to modernize it. I walked through the great room and up the stairs to the bedrooms, but instead of taking her to one of the guest rooms, I carried on down the hall to the west wing, to my quarters.

I wanted her close. Of course, it was a terrible idea, but I couldn't risk having her out of my sight. I might not get a chance like this again, and I wasn't going to waste it.

Shoving my door open, I carried her into the large room. The bed was to the left, an en suite beside it that we'd added when we moved in. The whole place had gone through some upgrades, despite the way it still looked on the outside, and there was a small living room to the right. Some of the females had added rugs and throw pillows to make it seem less cold.

I looked at the couch in front of the fire, then carried her to the bed instead. I lay her on it, and her dog jumped up beside her, resting her head on Selene's shoulder.

"Down," I said. She whined but did as I said. I was an alpha wolf, it was impossible for her to refuse, but she rested her head on the bed as close to Selene as she could get.

I strode to the door and opened it. "Ebony!"

"Coming!" The young wolf was never far when I was in the keep, and she rushed down the hall. "What do you need, alpha?"

"Take the dog to the kitchen, give her some water, and feed her."

Ebony frowned. "What's the creature's name?"

"No idea."

She peered around my shoulder. "Is that her master? The witch?"

"Yes."

"Is she your mistress now? Am I taking the dog so you can bed her? Or have you already? Is that why she's asleep?"

Jesus. "No. Now do as your alpha asks and take the damned dog down to the kitchen."

Ebony scowled but walked in and, after petting and beckoning her, it finally followed without too much resistance. Which was fucking odd, considering how protective she'd been an hour ago.

I returned to the bed and looked down at Selene. She was on her back, her arms up, hands on either side of her head, her chestnut hair splayed around her face. She was as beautiful now as she had been then.

No. Somehow, she was even more so. Witchcraft, no doubt. How else could she have remained so youthful?

She whimpered suddenly and writhed against my mattress, and only now did I take in the rest of her properly. Her naked curves were lush, rounder, softer than I remembered, but then I'd only ever seen her clothed. Her skin was deeply tanned instead of the ivory it had once been. My gaze drifted over her chest. Her tits were high and full, topped with pinkish-brown nipples, tight and small.

My mouth went dry, and my wolf started fighting, demanding I get closer.

I growled and fought it, even as my gaze continued to traverse her naked body. There were two red marks on her upper right thigh and a black tattoo curled and twined around her leg above her knee. There was an expanse of smooth, unmarred skin, then the design picked up again, its thorny vines snaking around her upper thigh and the side of her hip.

My hand lifted, about to touch, and I curled my fingers tightly and snatched them back. Carrying her the last hour had been torture of the worst kind. Lust, fierce and demanding, had almost choked me, and as soon as I made her break this spell she had over me, I would execute her for it. For what she did to my pack and me back then, and what she was trying to do to me again now.

I fucking hated her, but I couldn't keep my gaze off her. *Fight it.*

She moaned softly, and it was like the sound reached up and took me by the throat, snaking inside me and gripping tight until all I could see was her.

Her beauty was...dazzling, mesmerizing, and even as I internally roared for her to release me, struggling against it, my wolf pushed forward, filling me with a desire to get closer to her. I was unable to resist. Fuck, my head spun. I felt drunk from need, starved of touch.

The animal in me took hold, and I couldn't stop myself from lowering my head and pressing my nose to the skin at the base of her throat, and breathing deep. I gritted my teeth, struggling in vain against the magic she'd wrapped around me like chains, drawing me closer. I greedily dragged her scent into my lungs a second time and fucking groaned.

Her scent was different—not lemons, like it used to be, but something richer, darker, earthier: orchids or some other exotic flower.

I breathed her in again, and her scent sunk deeper. My mind roared for me to back away, but instinct and that feeling of rightness were so intense, so strong, that I found myself climbing onto the bed with her. I kept telling myself it was false, it was a lie, but I couldn't bring myself to back away.

I looked at her more closely and felt my mind fracturing all over again as I tried to come up with ways to explain away her treachery. Memories grew hazy, and I had to struggle to remember why I hated her. Why I wanted her to suffer so badly. I should be protecting her, shouldn't I? The female was delicate, unprotected, and she was mine.

Yes, mine.

We were both naked, and the heat of her skin was fierce, drawing me closer. She writhed restlessly again. Was she sick? Did she have a temperature? I pressed my hand to her forehead. She was burning up.

I slid my hand down the side of her face, over her shoulder, the back of my hand brushing the side of her breast, and down over her small waist. I leaned in again and pressed my nose to the skin beside her belly button, nuzzling the softness.

Another moan escaped her lips, and she squirmed. I looked up at her face, but her eyes were still closed, and when I breathed in again, the scent of her cunt hit me.

Another groan escaped. I wanted to fucking rub against her, cover her in my scent, have hers all over me—

Someone banged on the door. I jolted, snapping out of my haze.

With a growl, I sprang off the bed and backed up several steps. What the fuck was I doing? The twisted enchantress on my bed had crawled into my head, and I was losing more control with every minute that passed.

Fury and hatred roared through me, and I was torn between choking her and climbing back on that bed, shaking her awake, and taking her the way she was tempting me to.

She moved restlessly again. Her face was darker, sweaty. Fevered.

I stalked away, snatched up a pair of jeans, and pulled them on, watching her the whole time. Even unconscious, she was spinning her foul magic around me.

The door opened before I could get to it, and Ebony walked back in with the dog. Her gaze darted between me and the bed.

"Watch the witch while I get Marisol." Our healer. Selene needed to pay for her crimes, and I wasn't letting her die of whatever it was that afflicted her now, not until she admitted who she was and what she'd done to us.

I ushered Ebs back out. "You stay out of the room. Watch

from the door and if she wakes, lock her in, and come find me," I said to Ebony.

"You got it, alpha."

I tried to resist, but I turned back to her before I walked out. My wolf growled and struggled, trying to make me stay. I felt tethered to her, and I fucking hated it.

I'd spent over three hundred years tethered to one small patch of forest and I would kill us both before I allowed myself to suffer that again, especially if it was her I was tied to.

I tore my eyes from her naked, restless body and strode from the room.

Chapter Six

Iris

My body ached everywhere, and my eyes were heavy. I tried to open them, but my lids weren't cooperating.

Something wasn't right—

Then it all came rushing back—the mother, the forest, the demons. Nia. My eyes snapped open, and my gaze shot around the room. Where the hell was I?

I struggled to sit up and couldn't. I was naked and in a massive wooden bed, dwarfed in an equally large room made of stone. Nia whined against my leg, and I sighed with relief and buried my fingers in her fur. Through the windows, I could see it was still dark outside. I scanned the room again, it was washed in golden light from the wall sconces and the fire blazing on the other side of the room, making it feel ominous and warm all at the same time.

"Finally," someone said. "I've been waiting for you to wake up forever."

I spun around.

A girl sat by the bed, staring at me with big brown eyes.

"Where are we?"

"The alpha's keep, in his quarters," the girl said, eyes narrowing.

"The alpha?" But I knew, didn't I? She was a wolf, I could recognize it easily now with my magic. And there was only one pack in the area.

Silver Claw.

"You're in Draven's room, witch," she said, telling me what I already knew. Her face screwed up. "Are you guys, like...doing it?"

I cursed.

I would say the night couldn't get much worse, but I was alive, so that wasn't true. But this wasn't exactly a freaking wonderful development either.

Draven had rescued us. Of course, I was thankful. But now, I was indebted to an insane male who hated my guts. And I owed him big.

"Was it your alpha who brought me here?" I asked, desperately hoping for another answer than the one I knew deep down to be true.

"He carried you for over an hour." She stood and crossed her arms. "He asked me to guard you. I'm one of his warriors, so I wouldn't try anything if I were you."

I fought my smile. I guessed she was no more than twelve years old. "I promise. But I'm not sure why you think I'd try anything? I'm grateful to your alpha for rescuing me."

"You can go, Ebs," a deep, growly voice said from the other side of the room.

My stomach plummeted, and I turned to the now open bedroom door. Draven stood there with his arms crossed over his wide chest, tall and lean and impossibly handsome, even with a scowl on his face.

"Are you sure?" the girl asked. "You might need me again."

Draven scowled harder. "Your mom has supper waiting for

you. And I told you to stay out of this room, to come and get me as soon as she wakes, remember?"

"Fine. Sorry," she grumbled, patted Nia, and walked out.

The pissed-off alpha closed the door behind her, closing us in together. "Still as cunning and manipulative as always, I see."

Still dazed from what happened out in that forest, I'd momentarily forgotten he believed I was Selene. I struggled to sit up again, but I still didn't have the strength. My skin felt clammy and hot and tight. "We need to talk," I said.

"No." He prowled toward me. "You need to listen."

I had no choice but to shut my mouth and wait for him to lay whatever accusations he had on me. I couldn't exactly make my argument and defend myself if I didn't know what my...*Selene's* crimes were.

I pretended to zip my lips and motioned to the chair by the bed.

He watched me, looking momentarily puzzled, then he bared his teeth. He stayed where he was, and I wondered, not for the first time since I'd encountered this male, if he truly meant to do me harm. Right now, he looked like he wanted to wrap his hands around my throat and choke me out. If I wasn't so weak, I would be running like hell.

His arms unfolded, and he fisted his hands at his sides. His black, slightly wavy hair looked like he'd been running his fingers through it, and his jaw, covered in a dark shadow, was clenched. Every muscle in his upper body, a body that was scattered with scars, seemed tight as if he were physically restraining himself. This whole situation did not bode well for me.

His green eyes were sharp and filled with a wildness that made my heart pound and my palms sweat.

He took an abrupt step closer and planted his fists on the mattress near my hip. "Release me."

I waited for more, but nothing came. "I don't understand."

"Release me from the spell you have me under and I might allow you to walk out of here." That deadly stare never faltered from mine.

A lie.

He had no intention of letting me leave—of letting *Selene* leave.

"What spell do you think I have over you?" I asked, trying to remain calm when I realized my life literally depended on me convincing him who I was, and even then, he still might not let me walk out of here.

He rushed me, a blur of movement like he had in the office, and gripped my throat. "A witch's most vile of tricks, a spell to make me want you. Break it now, or I break your neck."

I blinked up at him, my fingers wrapped around his thick wrist. He thought I'd given him a love draft? "There is no such spell," I rasped. "There is a draft, but I have not, would not use it, not on anyone."

His eyes darkened. "At the bar, you would've had plenty of opportunity to put it in my drink."

I shook my head. "Why? Why the hell would I do that?"

"The same reason you did it the first time, Selene. To control me. To entrap me," he said through gritted teeth. "To use me and my pack for your evil machinations."

"I am n-not Selene. I told you at the bar, my name's Iris. Selene's a distant relative of mine. We h-have her portrait in our library at home. I look a lot like her, but you need to look closer, Draven."

He snarled as his eyes slid over my face. "I don't believe you."

"Her eyes were blue, mine are brown."

"More tricks."

"Not tricks. She's buried in our cemetery. Witches are not immortal, they're not long lived, and if there was a spell that granted eternal life, no witch would grow old, and cemeteries would not be one of the main sources of our power. What you are proposing is impossible."

He shook his head in that way he had before, as if he were trying to shake something loose. "No, you're lying."

"If you knew Selene, then you've been around witches. They weren't all young, were they? You were in Salem, you know that, you saw it yourself. I can take you to her resting place if that will help?"

His lips pulled back, and he flashed his teeth, his canines extended. "Your tongue is poison, the lies drip from it so easily."

How the hell was I going to get him to believe me? "Do you think Warrick is so easily fooled? That Willow gave him some love draft?"

"Possibly," he said, fingers tightening around my throat. "I believe he is somehow under her spell. Your family is twisted and evil. You are all capable of darkness."

Okay, right, maybe I could work with that. "Warrick spent most of his life in Hell, did you know that? Do you think he wouldn't sense evil when it was right in front of him? In bed with him?"

Draven stared, gaze still wild, but he seemed to falter.

I rushed on. "Warrick has powers. He wouldn't be fooled by my sister's magic, even if she had used it on him. He'd sense evil in me, in the rest of my family, if it was there. Warrick was void of emotion when he met Willow. Other than anger and lust, he didn't feel anything else. He's a brutal warrior. He executed his brother and sentenced him to eternal limbo. Do you really think my sister could win him over unless she were his mate in truth?"

"Lust, it was lust that blinded him," he said, looking triumphant, as if I'd somehow slipped up and given him the ammunition he needed.

"To Warrick, loyalty comes first. When Lucifer created him and his brothers, it was loyalty that kept them together. It came before anything else. He wouldn't have mated with Willow unless what he felt was real. And he sure as hell wouldn't let me live or be near his mate if I was the dark, twisted witch you're accusing me of."

He searched my eyes for long, painstaking seconds, as if he were trying to see inside me. Finally, he pushed away with a vicious growl and strode to the other side of the room. When he turned and walked back, those fists were still clenched tight. He looked at me once more, then paced to the window and stared out into the night.

He was quiet so long, I thought he was done talking, then finally, "You say she's dead?"

Had I gotten through to him? "Yes," I whispered, afraid to shatter this moment of sanity. Draven was broken and, unbelievably, blamed Selene for causing that damage. "She died when she was sixty-eight years old. She was one of our Keepers. She passed her task, and her magical combat trial, and ensured we retained our magical gifts and succeeded in acquiring more power for our coven. The markings I'm sure you saw on my leg, she had something similar on her face."

His gaze moved over the side of my face to the black mark there caused by Brody. "She wouldn't tell me what it was." His lip curled. "Then she left."

"In 1692, she left Salem after completing her trial and moved here to Roxburgh. She married and had three daughters. Our line came from the youngest of them. Selene died of influenza and was laid to rest in our family burial grounds."

His gaze moved over my face again before catching and holding mine. His nostrils flared, and he dragged in a sharp breath. He cursed so loud I jumped. Then he spun and slammed his fist into the stone wall.

I watched in silence, afraid to move, to speak. His back heaved with his labored breaths.

It took time, but eventually, he had himself back under

control, and though it was probably a terrible idea, I dared to speak. "What did she do to you, Draven?" I had to know.

He snarled, and the sound was filled with loss and anger, with hatred. "She fooled me into believing I cared for her, loved her, then she bound me to a dark and cold place, tethering me to a fucking rock, forcing me and my warriors to guard one of your family relics. For over three hundred years we were stuck there. Two of my warriors died of starvation, and one of them lost their mate. Many others, including my grandparents, my parents, died while I was stuck there." His eyes flashed brighter, his wolf coming to the fore, and I braced for him to shift, but again, he pulled it back, regaining control. "That's what she did," he finished.

Horror rocked through me. Selene had always been a heroine in our family's eyes. What Draven was saying didn't match up with all the good we'd read. "She was revered by her coven, by her family. No...I can't believe she would do that...why would she..."

"Yes," he roared, looking as unhinged as I'd believed him to be when I first met him. "Witches have used my kind for centuries. But instead of making a fucking deal, as is custom, between wolves and witches, she fed me a love draft, lied to me, trapped me, and walked away. She did it for herself, for her *coven*, and spared no thought to me or my pack, or to our families that we'd never see again. My pack was vulnerable, and with its strongest warriors gone, we lost people, good fucking people because you..." He snarled again, chest heaving. "Because *Selene* was a selfish, evil, cunning bitch. She sacrificed us and never looked back. I don't give a fuck what was written about her. I knew her. I know her for what she truly was. She was a fucking monster, *that's* what she was."

Tears stung my eyes. What he said, it cut me to the bone. But I believed him. It was all there in his voice, in his posture, in the pain and fury in his gaze. That she had done that...*Oh goddess*. I felt sick to my stomach. He had suffered so much, and Selene had caused his pain, and the pain of his people. How did you make that up to someone? Somehow Draven and his warriors had been freed, but there was no way to give them back time that was lost or the loved ones they never got the chance to say goodbye to.

"I'm sorry."

"I don't want to fucking hear it. It's meaningless coming from your lips."

I shoved back the covers, about to go to him—I don't know why, what it would achieve, I just needed to get closer to the male. I froze in place when I remembered I was naked. Nakedness didn't bother me, a lot of our spells required it, and shifters were used to it, but we didn't just walk around like that unless it was necessary and neither did they.

His gaze sliced down my body and he hissed.

"Draven..."

"If you have not bewitched me, then why—" He stopped himself and the blood drained from his face.

"What is it?"

His chest heaved. "Just...stay the fuck away from me," he said and walked out the door, slamming it behind him so hard the sound bounced off the stone walls.

Draven

I strode from my room and down the hall, not sure where I was going. My mind spun, and my lungs ached from my desperate fucking breaths.

Asher blocked my path.

"Not now, Ash," I said and tried to walk past.

She planted her ass in front of me and wouldn't move. "I want her dead as well, but killing the witch won't change anything," she said. "Selene broke one of her own covenants. Approach the witch's council, let them deal with her. We've only just claimed this territory. We take out this female, we'll start a war with the hellhounds and the witches. Are you ready for that? For what that will do to your people? We finally have a home, they have you back, don't allow your pride and thirst for vengeance to destroy everything we're trying to build here."

"It's not her," I said, knowing it for the truth as the words left my mouth.

"What?"

"She is not Selene." I was about to walk past but stopped myself, and instead, pulled my fiercest warrior into my arms and hugged her, pressing my mouth to her dark hair. "I'm fucking sorry, Ash, for bringing up Boone, when you were just trying to do right by the pack. I know how much his loss cost you."

She thumped my back. "It's okay."

But it wasn't.

I needed to get my head on straight and fast. My pack, my people were everything, and I shouldn't have to remind myself of that.

I released her and carried on down the stairs and out the door into the night. Iris, her face, the things she'd said, filling my head.

Somewhere inside me, I'd had doubts, hadn't I? There had been small differences, her voice, that slightly lopsided smile, the ice-cold skin below the markings on her cheek. The way she moved, the way she smelled. I'd brushed the truth aside, desperate for someone to take my anger out on.

Stripping, I shifted and ran into the woods. I had to see for myself.

I didn't stop, didn't slow until I reached the clearing where I first saw her...Iris.

Not Selene.

Gray headstones, some glossy in the moonlight, some older and dull, sprouted from the ground on the other side of the field in the distance. I shifted back to human form and strode toward it. The area would be warded like all witch's cemeteries. They were brimming with power. Even after death, witches exuded magic; it flowed from the bones of their ancestors and into the earth. Everything in their burial grounds was useful and held power. Selene had taught me that. The dirt, plants, the grass, all of it. And having a big and old cemetery like this made the Thornhearts very powerful.

I worked my way around the perimeter, searching the dull headstones, the ones that were rough and old, unpolished. There was a group of them on the far side, and my gut gripped tightly as I reached them.

My sight was excellent, and the stylized *S* carved into one of the crumbling stones was easy to see, the rest of what it said readable.

Here lies Selene Thornheart. Wife of Jacob Williams, beloved mother of Jasmine, Cassandra, and Susanna.

I didn't finish reading it, I didn't need to. She was here, in this place. How could I doubt it?

Beyond the cemetery was a path that led to the house. It was dark, everyone was asleep—except for Iris. She was where I'd left her, in my bed, in my keep.

I'd planned to end her life.

I dragged in a deep breath, needing the night air to calm me, but it didn't work.

Selene was dead, but she was still ruining my life.

All my secret hopes and dreams for the future, shattered before my eyes.

Iris, the descendant of my worst enemy—was my mate. And there was nothing I could do to change it.

Chapter Seven

Iris

I hadn't planned on falling back to sleep, but the next time I opened my eyes, it was morning. Sun streamed into the large room, and the smell of coffee and bacon had my stomach rumbling.

I rolled over and startled when I found Ebony sitting by the bed again, Nia at her side this time. The girl was running her hand down my familiar's back, and Nia was lapping up the attention.

"Breakfast," Ebony said and motioned to the plate on the bedside table.

"You made this?"

"Nope, Sally did. Don't worry, she didn't put poison in it, I watched her."

The thought hadn't occurred to me. It did now. I gave the food another once over. "They don't like me here, huh?"

She shook her head, her long wavy hair falling over her shoulder. "You're the bad witch who used your magic on our alpha."

I sat up and pulled the plate onto my lap. My muscles shrieked in protest, but it wasn't as bad as last night, and I wasn't feverish anymore either. I gave the food a sniff and my stomach growled loudly. I hoped it wasn't poisoned because I was starving, and this looked so damn good. "You know that wasn't me, right?" I said and took a sip of coffee then scooped up some of the scrambled egg.

She shrugged. "I still don't trust you."

"Fair enough. That just means you're smart. I wouldn't trust some random stranger either. But again, just for the record, I'm not the one who hurt your alpha or your pack."

"How old's your dog?" she asked, changing the subject as I slipped Nia a piece of bacon.

"She's four and she's not mine. Nia chooses to be with me, she's my familiar. Our connection goes beyond any normal pet–owner relationship." I grinned. "And we can talk to each other."

Ebony screwed up her face. "Do you think I'm an idiot?"

"You want me to prove it?"

Her eyes narrowed with a good dose of disbelief. "Go on, then."

"What did you have for breakfast, Nia?"

Girl gave Nia sausages. Nia loves sausages. Nia likes girl.

I chuckled and looked at Ebony. "Sausages. They're Nia's favorite, and now you are as well."

Ebony's mouth fell open. "There's no way you could know that!"

I cut a piece of bacon and topped it with some egg. "Like I said, we can communicate."

Ebony leaned forward. "How?"

"Some witches have a little something extra. We're given special magic abilities, and mine is the ability to speak to animals." I looked up from my food and stilled.

Draven stood in the open door again, like he had the night before.

63

Ebony spun away from me. "Alpha!"

"You're good at that," I said.

He lifted a brow.

"Sneaking up on people."

He studied me for long, uncomfortable seconds. "Yes, I am."

There was a lot of warning in those words and the tone of his voice.

Okay, so he hadn't woken up this morning and decided to not hate me. The fact I wasn't who he thought I was didn't seem to have made much difference.

Then he ignored me as Ebony stood and ran to him. He didn't bark orders at her like he had last night. Instead, he pulled her in for a hug. Wolves were tactile, a lot of shifters were, but I'd yet to see it from this particular wolf. He pressed his nose to the top of her head and breathed in her scent. "You've been a big help, Ebs. You've pleased your alpha."

She tilted her head back and beamed up at him.

The smile he gave her back was gentle and filled with affection, and my heart almost stopped in my chest at the beauty of it. He loved this child, and I strongly believed after witnessing this exchange that he had looked at every member of this pack like that at one time.

"Your mother will be missing you. You head on home."

"Okay, alpha." She turned and rushed back to Nia, kissed her furry head, then turned and ran from the room.

"You're good with her. She loves you—"

He turned back to me, and the smile was gone, the look on his face stopping me in my tracks. "Don't talk to me about her or anyone else in my pack."

Why did that sting? It shouldn't. I didn't know him, and he didn't know me. "You still hate me then?" I asked. He didn't reply. "I was hoping we could try to mend bridges between my coven and your pack. We owe you, Draven. What Selene did was inexcusable. That's not the way we treat our allies. But now that you know the truth, who I really am...and well, I still need someone to help me with this trial. My coven would give you whatever you wanted—"

"Mend bridges?" he said, voice filled with silent fury. "You think I would help you? I owe you not one fucking thing, little witch."

I couldn't hold his icy stare. God, I just kept putting my stupid foot in my mouth. "I'm sorry, that was insensitive. There's nothing we could do to take back what she did or return what you lost." But for some reason, I didn't like the idea of him hating me, so I pushed on when I knew I shouldn't because some stupid needy part of me wanted him to know that I wasn't like Selene. "But if you'd consider my offer..."

"I don't want anything to do with you, Iris. You are a Thornheart, which means you have the same toxic blood running through your veins as the rest of your twisted family."

Another blow, and again, I didn't blame him for it. There was nothing I could do or say to convince him otherwise, and I understood why.

"When you're finished gorging yourself on our food after your comfortable sleep in my bed, I'd like you to get the fuck out of my territory."

I didn't remind him that he was the one who'd brought me here.

My clothes were folded on the chair by the bed, and I reached out and grabbed them. "I'll leave now." I looked back up at him. "I know you don't want to hear it, but thank you for saving my life."

"I saved your dog. You were just lucky enough to benefit from it."

And there it was, the final blow to make sure I didn't darken his door again. "Understood."

His jaw worked for several seconds like he was battling with himself, his eyes flashing to his wolf and back. "You need to watch yourself," he barked at me suddenly, making me jump, anger still in his voice. "The woods aren't safe. You're clumsy and inexperi-enced, and I sure as fuck won't be there next time to save you."

Was that concern behind the anger in his voice? "Thanks for the warning." No, of course not. He just wanted to make sure I stayed out of his forest, that he wasn't forced to save me again.

His expression darkened further.

I pulled on my shirt, and he didn't look away. He watched me with those cold green eyes, impatience in every flexing muscle. He was going to personally escort me out of here.

I awkwardly shoved my jeans under the covers to pull them on, then stood and swayed to the side when I was hit with a wave of dizziness. I would have collided with the rough stone wall if Draven hadn't moved like lightning and grabbed my arm, stopping me.

"For fuck's sake, I said, watch yourself," he snarled.

I looked up at him, my heart beating faster being this close to him. "I guess I still have a bit of venom pumping around in there."

"Venom?"

"It's this whole thing...but long story short, Mother Nature inhabited a serpent, bit me, which is how I got the new 'ink' on my thigh," I said, adding air quotes. "And thanks to you, I survived, so next up is passing whatever task she has planned for me."

His expression showed his disgust, and when I had my balance, he released me like I was the carrier of an infectious disease. "I thought it was some kind of magic that had knocked you out, not..." He scowled. "That's fucked up."

"Yeah, agreed, the whole thing is just freaking weird. But that's the way it's always been." I shoved my feet in my boots and glanced up at him.

He'd gotten closer, and, again, his nearness made my skin tingle like he'd hit me with an electric charge. Draven was impres-sive at any distance, but this close, he seemed a whole lot bigger. He towered over me, and then he leaned closer still, his gaze suddenly becoming all predator.

I didn't know what was happening, but I didn't dare move. The male was unpredictable and unstable. So we stood there like that for long, tense seconds. Me, staring into the eyes of his beast, while the beast stared right on back. Then his head dipped and he scented me. I'd seen shifters do it before, mainly Warrick to Willow, but I had no clue why Draven was doing it to me now.

"Draven?" I whispered.

His head jerked away, and his gaze flashed back to its usual green.

"What are you..."

"Move. I want you gone."

Was that desperation I heard in his voice?

I quickly did as he said, calling for Nia as I rushed for the door, and thankfully didn't fall on my ass. The dizziness was still there, though. I hadn't fully recovered, and I didn't have one of Else's elixirs to help me. She'd made several while Willow was in the middle of this last year.

God, my family would be worried out of their minds. "Do you have my phone?"

Draven pulled it from his pocket and handed it to me. It was dead. *Shit.*

"You can charge it in my truck," he said and walked ahead.

I followed him downstairs, where several of his pack mates were gathered in a massive dining room—all warriors, without doubt.

And they looked at me as if I were an unwelcome rodent.

Draven led me outside and down a steep path on the side of the mountain, and several birds left their tree branches to fly around my head, chirping and singing, something that happened often. Sadly, I didn't have any birdseed with me. It was in my other jacket.

Draven glanced over and frowned at their antics, and I resisted the urge to explain it. It'd probably only anger him more.

There were several vehicles parked down here, and he opened

the door to one of the trucks. I climbed in and plugged my phone into the charger already there as he started the engine. "My car's on the other side of the forest."

He grunted, put the truck in drive, and we headed down the rough dirt road, heading back to civilization.

Draven

Iris's phone started beeping a few minutes after she'd plugged it in, alerting her to all her messages and texts. Her family.

Christ, I hadn't even thought about her car, so focused on my revenge. It was parked on the other side of Oldwood Forest. Eventually, they would have figured out where she'd been taken. The hounds were the best trackers around. I'd acted recklessly and risked my entire pack. How could I have done that? After everything they'd already been through. After everything we'd already lost.

I glanced at the little witch beside me. I didn't know what she planned to tell her people, but I was prepared to face the consequences of what I'd done. If that included trouble with the hellhounds or her coven, I'd make sure it fell on my shoulders and mine alone. My pack would not be touched by another one of my fuckups. I gripped the wheel tighter. The anger was still there, shit, even more so than before. I felt like I was being torn in two. My wolf, every one of my animal instincts, fought with me to get closer to the female at my side.

Every part of me recognized who she was now—there was no denying it—and I wanted to roar at the injustice. All those years trapped, my warriors and I had been forced to accept that some of us would miss our chance to ever connect with our mates. They'd be out there waiting, and we wouldn't be able to reach them. I assumed I was one of them. I never dreamed she was still out there.

I'd hoped, though, in a deep, needy part of me, I had hoped.

And she was.

She was sitting right next to me, and the idea of claiming her made me sick to my fucking stomach. I'd seen the birds flock to her, the way she communicated with her dog. Witches couldn't be trusted, and I sure as hell would never be able to trust Iris. Not only did she look like Selene, but she had the same power as Charity. No, I could never, would never, accept her.

The lust riding me, the curl of rightness in my gut, the stiffness of my cock disgusted me. My body wanted her, my wolf howled for her, and my mind raged against all of it.

Her scent filled the cab, and I bit back the growl of hunger crawling up my throat, then cracked open the fucking window. I didn't want her scent in my lungs, all it did was drive me closer to insanity.

She still held her phone in those delicate little hands, hands that I'd dreamed of having on me, of touching my bare skin too many times—then I'd wake, hard and drenched in sweat, forced to work out the burning lust with my eyes screwed shut and my dick wrapped in my fist. Fuck. I tore my gaze away as she tapped at the phone and lifted it to her ear.

"Iris!" a voice yelled down the line.

It wasn't on speaker, but with my hearing, I could hear every word.

"I'm okay, Mom."

"Where are you? Magnolia and Bram have been out all morning looking for you. They just found your car outside Oldwood Forest. Wills and Warrick are on their way there."

"I'm heading back now. You can call them off."

"Else, call Willow and Mags. Iris is on her way home...what happened, sweetheart? Were you summoned? Is that what happened?"

"Yes, but I'm fine—"

"Oh my goddess. Is someone driving you?"

"Yes. I'll explain when I get there."

"She's got a ride," her mother called to someone again. "Tell Bram to drive her car home."

"No, don't do that. I'll get my car," Iris said.

"You'll do no such thing. You'll be in no condition to drive. No arguments. And you must be starving. I'll make food."

"Mom..."

"Pancakes and sausages. We'll be waiting."

"Hang on a minute..."

The phone went dead.

"Mom?" Iris sighed and cursed under her breath. She looked my way and winced. "Um...would you...could you. I feel like a total dick asking, but would you mind driving me to my house?"

Christ. "Sure. It's not like I have anything better to do," I said, letting her hear my aggravation because this female frustrated the hell out of me. I didn't want to be nice to her. I didn't want to forgive her, even though she hadn't actually done anything to me personally.

And I didn't fucking *want* to want her.

We drove in silence, the only sound her constant texting to her sisters, I assumed, because from what I knew of her family, she had a lot of them.

Someone named Rose called her next, and I gritted my teeth at the way Iris's voice softened, at the sweet way she spoke to her sister. Like a shifter, not a witch. The other female's voice had been weak, fragile, and I wondered if there was something wrong with her, then got pissed off at myself for giving a fuck.

When we pulled up at the house, Warrick was standing out front by his bike. His mate, Willow, at his side. Another female with black hair stood beside a tall male, a bird shifter of some kind. And both females rushed to Iris when she got out of the truck, pulling her in for a tight hug, fussing over her.

Warrick frowned at me and strode over.

Iris untangled herself from her sisters and I braced. I may despise her family, but Iris had not personally wronged me. I'd threatened her life, though, and there would be consequences, but I alone would face them. Two other females walked out of the house, one who was obviously Iris's mother and an older female.

"What's going on? Why was Iris with you?" Warrick asked.

"I took her to my keep," I said, holding the other male's direct gaze.

His expression darkened.

"He saved me," Iris said, shocking the hell out of me, "Demons surrounded Nia and me and Draven found us. I was unconscious and he carried me for an hour. I'd be dead if it wasn't for him."

Her mother made a distressed sound and ran at me, throwing her arms around my waist. "Thank you," she said, emotion making her voice shake. "Thank you for saving my baby."

I stood there stunned, not knowing what to do, and patted her back awkwardly. Wolves were affectionate, we were huggers, but this female, her coven, had been my enemy, in my mind, at least, for over three hundred years.

"Let the man take a breath, Daisy," the gray-haired woman with her said as she walked up.

Iris's mother finally released me, and the gray-haired female grinned. "Anything you need, alpha, you just say the word. Coven Thornheart is in your debt."

"Yes," Willow said. "We won't ever forget what you did for us, Draven. Anything you need, please ask."

Warrick's approving look lifted my hackles, and I reluctantly took his outstretched hand and let him shake it.

"I need to go." I was desperate to get the hell away, away from these people.

"We have food if you're hungry?" Iris's mother said. "Please, let me at least feed you."

"I need to get back to my pack...but, thank you." *Goddammit.*

71

I didn't want to thank them either. I turned from their smiling faces and strode back to my truck.

I heard Iris follow, and she stopped me from getting in with a hand on my arm. There was no holding in my low growl as fire sparked in my gut, just from that simple touch.

She yanked her hand back, mistaking my reaction for aggression instead of raw, animal lust, and I was glad of it.

"I'm sorry," she said. "For everything."

"I didn't ask you to lie for me, little witch," I said, low, so her family wouldn't hear us. "If you think to use that against me..."

"I would never do that. I just think you've suffered enough at the hands of my family," she said gently.

Her soft tone sent tingles across my scalp and only increased my need for her, and my anger, because being close to her weakened me. *She* weakened me. "This doesn't change anything," I said, my beast coming through loud and clear in my voice. "Stay the fuck out of my way."

She nodded and stepped back, and I got in my truck and drove away, ignoring her smiling, waving family, and didn't look back.

Chapter Eight

Iris

The kitchen table was covered in food. Mom must have started cooking as soon as we ended our call.

"Sit, eat," she said, her hand lingering on my shoulder.

Art handed me a mug of coffee as soon as I sat down. "We've been worried sick."

"I'm sorry," I said to everyone gathered around me. "I would have called, but I was, you know, unconscious."

Warrick sat in the seat across from me. "Why didn't Draven call me?"

"I asked him not to," I said, lying through my teeth. I hadn't had a chance to tell Warrick or anyone that Draven had turned down my request for help, and I didn't plan to. They were already worried enough about me.

"How? You were unconscious," Mags added unhelpfully.

"I came around for a few minutes while he was carrying me back." More lies. "I didn't want anyone to see me like that. I didn't want Mom to worry. I thought I'd recover in a few hours and be back here before you woke."

Else nudged me. "Well, you were wrong, sunshine, and you almost gave me a heart attack." She walked to the kitchen, opened her medicine cupboard, and pulled down several bottles. "You got a fever?" she asked over her shoulder. "Shivers, delirium? Did you throw up or get the trots?"

I inwardly sighed in relief when the conversation turned from Draven. The toughest warrior would struggle against my family when they were in interrogation mode. "Fever, but that's mostly gone, and some dizziness. Other than that, just general aches and pains."

Else scooped up several bottles and a big spoon, and Mags smirked at me behind Else's back when she started feeding me spoonful after spoonful of foul-tasting liquid. Else was a powerful healer, but some of her elixirs were utterly disgusting.

"Right, my girl, you just need some rest and you'll be right as rain by tomorrow morning," she said.

"Yeah, I don't think that will be hard. I'm wiped."

Mom planted a kiss on the top of my head.

"So how was it?" Mags asked. "Did it hurt?"

"It didn't feel great, but it could've been worse." No point freaking Magnolia out. It'd be her time soon enough. Now I understood why Willow had been so worried. I hated the idea of any of my sisters going through this, so much, the very thought had my heart galloping in my chest, and my ordeal had only just started.

"Where did she bite you?"

"My thigh, it's...big." A lot bigger than I'd expected, honestly.

"I like what she did to your face," Else said. "The mother must've taken a shine to you."

My hand lifted to my cold cheek. "What do you mean?" I shot out of my chair, then grabbed onto the table when I almost fell on my ass because my legs were still weak, and stumbled to the mirror in the hall.

I took in my reflection, and a cry escaped before I could stop it. The black star was still there, and it was still cold, but it wasn't solid black and ugly, it was swirly, with small flowers and curls, it was...pretty. Tears filled my eyes as I took it all in.

"You okay?" Mags asked, poking her head around the door.

"Yeah." I blinked faster, fighting back tears. Every time I'd looked in the mirror since the day Brody did this to me, I was taken back to that nightmare, to nearly losing everyone I loved. Of when he'd fired his dark magic at me and left me with this. It would still be a reminder of that awful time, but now it wouldn't be as ugly as the thing that had happened.

I ran my fingers over the design—it kind of looked like hope. Maybe that sounded silly. But it was like the mother had offered me a glimpse of it, of the beauty that was possible if I only looked for it.

"I'm just...I don't know how to explain it."

"I get it," Mags said.

And if anyone did, it was my baby sister. Her entire body was covered in scars. Brody's aunt Cora had attacked her, cutting her body over and over again using her own dark, twisted magic, and even Else's balm couldn't make the scars totally fade away. If anyone knew what it felt like to have a physical reminder of one of the worst moments of your life, it was Magnolia. My baby sister had been through so much.

Mags grabbed my hand, and I gave hers a squeeze when she tugged me back into the kitchen. I was about to sit back down when Wills pulled me in for a hug. "Proud of you," she whispered. "You've got this."

I hoped she was right. I'd do everything I could to succeed. And despite my weak limbs, I felt stronger than I had in a long time. Nia nudged my hand, and I rubbed her ears.

Nia want to play with little wolf.

Ebony. "Maybe another time," I said, not wanting to make her sad by telling her that would never happen again.

"Now you look as badass as Selene," Else said. "The markings on her face were different, but yours are just as cool."

"It's definitely an improvement," I said and sat, not meeting my aunt's eyes. I'd talk to her about what I found out later and not in front of the whole family. And especially not in front of Warrick. I wouldn't throw Draven under the bus like that, and Else was good at keeping secrets.

Mom took the seat between Art and me. There was a big botanical book on the table in front of her.

"You looking to plant something new?"

I wanted to talk about anything besides me and the task ahead, whatever it would be, and my family would understand that. Going through this with Willow, at least they knew talking about it constantly before I worked out what it was would only cause all of us more stress and worry.

"There's a dead patch of grass in the cemetery," Mom said, going with the change of subject straightaway. "I don't know what's caused it. I've taken a sample of dirt and Art's doing some tests." She frowned. "I think for now, I'll dig out the diseased section, reseed it, and see if it germinates."

"Sounds like a plan." I stood. "I'm going to head upstairs." I seriously needed to lie down.

Else threatened to wake me in a couple of hours for more of her elixir as I walked out the door. I checked in on Rose, gave her a quick rundown of what happened, then finally headed to my room and collapsed on my bed with Nia.

I blinked up at the ceiling.

What was Draven doing now?

My belly fluttered just thinking about the male. God, I hated knowing that he thought the worst of me. I wanted the chance to prove to him that I wasn't the bad person he believed I was.

He didn't want that, though; he didn't want to know me.

And I didn't blame him.

～

"I'll need some help harvesting," Mom said to me from the bedroom door. Her eyes softened when they moved to Roe. "Do you need anything before I head out, sweetheart?"

"No, I'm fine, Mom," Rose said.

I was sitting on the side of my sister's bed, brushing her hair. It had thinned out, lost its shine and the wave that she'd always had. I kissed the top of her head. "Mags is making Roe's breakfast now, so I'll be right down."

"Excellent!" Mom said and rushed off.

"Mom looks tired," Rose said, burying her fingers in Nia's fur. "She sleeps in here, in that chair every night. I can't get her to go to her room. She's exhausting herself. Art has to carry her out most mornings after Else comes to take over."

We didn't like to leave Rose alone for long periods of time, especially during the night and early morning. That's when she seemed to have most of her "turns," where she'd lose consciousness or sometimes stop breathing altogether. She didn't seem to be fully aware of it happening. To her, it was like she'd drifted off to sleep, and we let her believe that's all it was, for her sake.

The growl of bikes reached us from outside. "Warrick and Willow must be here." I put down the hairbrush and moved to the window. There were a couple of bikes and Willow's truck. "She must be here to pick up supplies." Mags and Else had been working on restocking the shop the last few days. They had their regulars—witches, some shifters, and a few demons as well, who used my aunt's elixirs and potions.

Yes, there were demons who weren't completely terrible, though they preferred to keep to themselves. The rest were easily identifiable as creeps because they tended to run at you with their teeth bared.

77

My phone chimed, telling me I had a Nightscape notification. I scanned the screen and a cold shiver slid down my spine. It was about the missing witches, how there was still no sign of either of them.

"What is it?" Rose asked.

I glanced up, a weird feeling in my belly. "Nothing yet on Amy or Imogen. It's like they've vanished into thin air."

The sound of someone coming up the stairs had us turning to the door.

Ronan walked in, expression stoic as always and dressed in his usual trousers and button-down shirt. The dhampir—half human, half vampire—spent his time between the hellhound clubhouse, and well, no one knew where he went the rest of the time. He just seemed to vanish for a while, and then he'd show up again. And for some unknown reason, the emotionless male had taken an interest in Rose. The guy may not have emotions, but he seemed to under-stand loyalty and had a strong sense of it when it came to his sister, Luna, and those she associated with, which included us.

Rose blushed when he moved closer, a tray of food in his hands.

"Hey, Ronan," I said and shoved my phone back into my pocket.

"Good morning, Iris." His lavender gaze slid to Rose, and something shifted behind those unusual eyes that were impossible to read. "Rose, how are you feeling this morning?"

I smiled. Because dhampir were void of emotion, they often struggled with social interaction, unable to read emotion and body language from others. The hounds had been teaching him how to be more tactful, which I found hilarious. They weren't exactly the most diplomatic guys around, but they'd managed to teach him the basics, like asking her how she was instead of telling her how ill she looked. That alone was a seriously big improvement.

"Good, thank you," she said huskily.

"I have your breakfast, and some fruit," he said in his deep, mesmerizing voice. There was a container of strawberries next to her plate. We didn't have any downstairs. They were from him. He always brought Roe food and tried to get her to eat more.

Rose blushed harder. She had a crush on the male that was easy to see, something else we never mentioned. Thankfully, Ronan was utterly clueless to the fact. She hated him seeing her like this, but he insisted on visiting with her. "W-where's Magnolia? I thought she was bringing up my breakfast."

"There's some issue with the cemetery," Ronan said, his gaze sliding to me. "Your mother said you were needed."

"I better go see what's happening." Rose was safe with Ronan, I knew that without even the smallest of doubts. "I'll be right back, promise," I said to my sister and headed down the stairs. There was no one else in the house as I walked outside and down the path to the cemetery, Nia bounding along beside me. Relic stood beyond the ward surrounding our burial grounds, unable to pass, and he gave me a chin lift as I strode by.

Then I saw the rest of my family. Mom and Art in the center. Mags and Bram beside them.

Willow was closest. "What's going on..." My words trailed off when I saw for myself. There were dead patches of grass all over the place. Plants drooping, most of our herb patches shriveled and brown. "What the hell is this?"

"I don't know," Willow said. "I've never seen anything like it."

Mom turned in a slow circle, the blood draining from her face. The cemetery was hers to look after. She and Arthur spent hours every day out here making sure everything was healthy and thriving, making sure Else and Mags had everything they needed, so we had a steady income. This place was not only the resting place of our ancestors, our loved ones, our most sacred of places—it was one of the major sources of our power.

"I don't understand," Mom said, tears welling in her eyes. "How could this have happened?"

Art wrapped his arms around her. "We'll figure this out, Daisy."

Mom dropped into a crouch and started breathing heavily, like she was trying to stop herself from being sick. Art rubbed her back. "We'll take soil samples. There has to be an explanation for this. We'll get to the bottom of it, my love."

Mags strode over to me. "What the actual fuck is going on? Everything Else and I planted for our next batch of orders is dead." She shoved her fingers in her hair. "This can't be happening."

Else hadn't moved. She stood by Mom, and her face was a mask of devastation. Nia ran to her and pressed against her leg. Else absently reached down and petted her.

"I don't understand this. How?" I whispered.

Mags paced away and back. "Do you think this could be some kind of sabotage? Retaliation?"

I turned from Mom and back to my youngest sister. "What do you mean?"

"Isaac and Sapphire Eldridge. Maybe they've been biding their time?"

Sapphire was a *very* distant cousin of Gran and Else, and up until Warrick killed her son Elmer, protecting Willow a year ago, she'd treated us as if we were an extension of her coven, or at least she'd tried to. The woman was formidable, powerful, and no one wanted to piss her off. And yes, we were now in her crosshairs. But this?

I took in the devastation again and shook my head. "Sapphire covets this place. She wants it above anything. She couldn't bring herself to destroy it."

Isaac, though, was a different story. He'd said many times that he wanted to destroy everything we loved. He'd actually said the words, "Burn it all down." Poisoning our cemetery was far from a stretch when it came to him.

Mags planted her hands on her hips. "Then it has to be Isaac.

You know that creep's capable of anything," she said, saying exactly what I was thinking.

"If this is sabotage, I can't think of anyone else who would do this." Besides Brody and his aunt Cora. But with Brody dead and Cora locked up somewhere, it could only be Isaac, he was past caring about anything beyond his thirst for revenge, and he'd made no secret of his hatred for us since his brother's death.

It didn't matter to him that his brother had tried to murder Willow or that Warrick took him out to protect her.

All Isaac cared about was that they'd been humiliated in front of everyone. Willow had defeated his brother in their combat trial fair and square and Elmer had lost his shit. Warrick's actions had been justifiable, and the witch's council had agreed. No action had been taken against our family. The Eldridges had lost the mother's gifts as a result, losing a great deal of power, and the guy was desperate for revenge.

Mags was quick to point the finger where the Eldridge's were concerned, but this time, I had to agree with her. I looked around the cemetery. Who else could have done this?

"Nia, stay," I said when she turned toward me. I wouldn't give the asshole ammunition by putting my girl in his sights. He was the kind of male to hurt her just to get to us.

Willow grabbed my arm. "What do you have planned?"

"I'm not sure yet, but I won't let him get away with this."

Willow's green eyes burned into me.

"What?"

She crossed her arms. "You need to approach this carefully. You don't know that it was Isaac. You have no idea what your task is, if this is part of it, or how dangerous it could get. You need to think through every step."

"I know, I do." I had a reputation for being a little brash when it came to my family and people trying to fuck with them. My older sister knew this and was trying to rein me in before I ruined everything. It sucked, but her worries were justified. Look what happened with Brody. "I'll be careful, Wills. I know what's at stake here."

She nodded, but the concern was still there in her eyes.

I turned to Relic, still standing beyond the cemetery boundaries, and started toward him. "You got a minute?"

"What are you doing?" Magnolia asked, following me. "Are you going to see him? I'm coming with you."

That wasn't happening. Mags had become more and more unpredictable lately, losing her temper, lashing out. The situation was volatile enough. "This could have something to do with my task." I didn't know if that was true, but it seemed like a good excuse. "No family help, remember? We can't risk it."

Mags cursed a blue streak.

"What do you need?" Relic asked.

Willow was right, I had to be smart about this. And right then, Relic was my only option. I wasn't stupid enough to meet with Isaac alone. I didn't have a death wish. And this was me asking for help, not my sister, so that should cover my ass if all of this did end up being part of my task. "I need to pay someone a visit and could do with some backup."

Chapter Nine

Draven

Something had called me here to the city, and if I'd learned anything over the centuries, it was to listen to my gut. Ignoring it usually ended with something going wrong, like being trapped in one spot for over three hundred fucking years.

We'd ended up in the main business center of Roxburgh. All skyscrapers and concrete and traffic. I fucking hated it. My wolf was already getting antsy.

"What are we doing here?" Dirk asked.

"No fucking clue."

Dirk went on high alert, scanning the area. He'd known me long enough to trust my gut as well.

I froze as I caught a familiar scent and growled under my breath. "Fuck."

"What is it?"

I dragged my fingers through my hair. "It's her."

"Your witch?"

"Not mine," I bit out, even as my wolf strongly disagreed with my denial.

"There," Dirk said.

I followed his gaze, and a snarl was torn from me before I could bite it back. She was striding toward an office building, her chestnut hair shiny and wavy down her back, her face flushed, her deep brown eyes bright.

She was angry.

She unclenched her fist and reached for the door—someone stopped her. That's when I managed to tear my eyes off her long enough to notice that Relic was with her. My wolf bared his teeth, not liking that the hound was touching her.

"Is she with him?" Dirk asked. "Has he claimed her?"

I scented the air. If another male had claimed her, I'd be able to smell it. Iris's scent seemed to come straight to me, and I ignored the swell of relief when I got nothing but orchids, dark and intoxicating. Yes, the hound's scent was there but not blended with hers. The other male hadn't been inside her, not yet, anyway. "No."

Iris turned to the hound, and he dipped his head, getting closer. My wolf shoved to the surface, wanting to charge, to attack.

"Keep it tight, Drave," Dirk said. "You go after him with all these witnesses, there'll be a price."

I did my best to shake it off, but it wasn't working. "He can fucking have her."

"She wasn't the one who wronged you, brother. Not claiming her as your mate will only do you more harm."

I'd confided in several of my warriors; I'd been forced to when a couple of them had noticed how erratic I'd been behaving.

I watched as they spoke, as Relic held out his fist for her to pound. She did, then he held open the door and they disappeared inside.

Dirk was closer to the truth than I wanted to admit. The more aware of her I became, the more unhinged I felt. My wolf wanted her and didn't understand why I was denying myself the one thing I'd wanted my entire life.

"You think I could ever grow to care for her? To accept her? She has Selene's face. She has her blood in her veins." I turned back to where Iris had just been. "How could I ask our pack to accept her after the harm her kind has caused us? After the losses we suffered?" I mourned them every day, the family we'd lost because of Selene and Charity's treachery. I couldn't ask my pack to just *shove* their pain aside like it was nothing for a mate I would never trust.

Dirk shifted beside me. "If you reject her, you will forever be without a mate."

My wolf howled in pain at the prospect of living without her, but there was no other choice. I'd just have to find a way to live with it. "I would rather that than bring another member of that poisonous coven anywhere near our pack." Still, I couldn't look away from the door she'd just walked through.

"If that's your decision, something needs to be done and soon," Dirk said.

"I know."

"And you're prepared to do that?"

I'd do what was necessary to protect my pack. "You doubt me?"

"If you go this route..."

"You may as well head back, I'll be right behind you," I said to Dirk, not wanting to talk about this anymore.

He cursed, and if I could bring myself to look away from the fucking door Iris had walked through, I knew I'd see a look that said he thought I was full of shit, and he'd be right. Because no matter how hard I tried, I couldn't bring myself to move from that spot.

"Drave...you know I'm here for you, yeah?"

There was worry in his deep voice. He loved me just as I did him, as I loved all my people, so I forced some of the growl from my voice. "I know, brother. You always have been. I promise I have this under control." We both knew that was a lie as well.

But instead of calling me out, Dirk gave my shoulder a nudge and left, and I stayed right where I was.

Just once more.

I just had to see her one more time.

I was growing addicted to the sight of that little witch, and if I didn't find some other way to satisfy this craving, to escape this fixation I had with her, I'd be trapped all over again.

Iris

The Eldridges were in real estate, and they were loaded. There was no missing it as we walked into their offices.

Relic strode beside me like a massive, threatening bodyguard, looking around the wide marble foyer like he expected a hoard of demons to crawl out of nowhere.

Honestly, right then, a hoard of demons would be preferable to Isaac Eldridge. Walking in here felt a little like jumping into a shark tank without a cage and expecting to jump back out with all your limbs intact.

A stunningly beautiful woman dressed in what had to be designer clothes sat behind the reception desk. A nymph, going by her flawless beauty and the amethyst pendant hanging around her neck. The amethyst neutralized their effect on males. Going out without the protection was highly dangerous for them, just being around a nymph threw males, especially, into an uncontrollable lust. I glanced up at Relic. He was checking her out, but there was no sign he wanted to throw her over his shoulder and drag her back to his den, which was a relief because Relic was a big male and there would be no stopping him.

Her gaze slid over my jeans and long-sleeve T-shirt. She pursed her lips. "Can I help you?" she asked, voice cool and professional.

"I'm here to see Mr. Eldridge."

She swiped her finger across the tablet in front of her and read the screen. "Name?"

"I don't have an appointment."

Her gaze lifted. "Then I'm sorry, he can't see you this morning."

"You want me to sniff the fucker out?" Relic asked.

I wanted to say yes, but us barging in without an appointment and accusing him of sabotaging our cemetery would give him ammunition to take to the witch's council. I needed to stay as calm as possible, which was easier said than done. I didn't feel calm; I wanted to wrap my hands around his neck and squeeze.

"I'd like to make an appointment, then," I said to her.

"Name?"

"Iris Thornheart."

Her gaze shot back up, her expression changing to one of shock. "I'm sorry, that won't be possible. He has no available appointments."

"What about next week?"

"None."

She hadn't even looked back down at her tablet. "The week after that?"

She shook her head.

Security appeared out of nowhere, several burly shifters. They barred the way, like they expected us to make a run for Isaac's office. Relic moved forward and bared his teeth. The shifter in front faltered but held his ground.

"You need to leave," the nymph said.

Well, wasn't this an interesting turn of events. "No problem. I'm sure I'll catch up with him eventually."

We walked back out, and Relic looked down at me, brow raised.

"Seeing him wasn't necessary. Letting him know we're onto him was."

Relic nodded and grinned. "Savage little thing, aren't you?"

I laughed, which was a nice change. "I'm working on it."

He'd followed me on his bike into the city, and after he left, I drove to The Cauldron, Willow's shop. My sister wasn't here, I assumed she was still at the house, but I could still stock up on a few things. Whatever my task was, I had to be prepared. And if Isaac was involved in this, even more so. We kept most things at the house, but not everything.

I moved around the shop, loading up my bag, then headed to the back room where we kept our more specialty items, in other words, things that were not for humans.

The shop had an apartment at the back, and I'd thought about moving in now that Willow lived with Warrick, but I didn't like to leave Rose. My family needed me with them, and honestly, I needed them too. Until our trials were over with, we had to stick close to each other.

I wrote a quick note for Willow, listing everything I'd taken, locked up, and headed to my car—

Tingles danced along my spine, and I looked up, stopping in my tracks.

Shit.

Draven stood on the other side of the street.

His hands were at his sides, fingers curled into fists, legs braced apart. He stood there motionless, looking right at me. I was frozen in place by his cold gaze...no, not cold, *frigid*.

He told me in no uncertain terms that he never wanted to see me again, so what was he doing here? I had to assume this was some kind of coincidence.

You don't believe in coincidences.

He had reason to hate Selene, to mistrust my family, and

although I felt sick over what Selene had put him through, she and I were not the same person. All that rage he was directing at me belonged to a ghost. I'd done nothing to deserve his hatred.

It was probably a bad move, but I was feeling seriously overwhelmed and angry about everything that was going on right now. I sure as hell didn't have time to deal with a psychotic wolf shifter, so I lifted my hand and waved, giving him a wide, beaming smile. "Hi, Draven!" Though I doubted he heard me over the traffic.

His eyes narrowed, and I grinned wider, gave him another overly enthusiastic wave, and climbed into my Toyota. He started toward me, moving quickly, darting around cars.

I wasn't sticking around for whatever poison he wanted to fire at me this time and quickly started my car. As I pulled out onto the street, I realized my heart was pounding, my palms were sweaty, and there was this flippy, zip-zappy feeling in the pit of my stomach.

Exhilaration? Excitement?

Maybe Draven wasn't the only one who'd lost their damned mind. This was not a game—playing with that male was a seriously stupid thing to do. But he brought out a side of me I thought was long dead, a side that I should let stay dead.

It wasn't like I'd done anything wrong. I told him I'd stay out of his way, and I'd planned to, but he wasn't staying out of mine.

You're asking for trouble.

Trouble was the last thing I wanted, so why the hell had I done that back there?

I turned up the music and tried not to think about the surly alpha, or my task, or Rose—or what the hell had happened to our cemetery.

I failed, but I did sing at the top of my lungs, the best stress relief there was besides sex, and since I planned on being celibate for the rest of my life, there would be a lot more loud-car-singing in my future.

I left the city and headed for home. The busy streets and

people and cars slowly thinned until I was driving along a forest-lined road, one I knew like the back of my hand. When I took the next bend, the steering grew heavy, then I was bumping along and the wheel jerked in my hands.

Shit. Flat tire.

I quickly pulled off the road so I didn't damage anything. Shoving the door open, I grabbed the spare from the trunk, leaned it against the side of the car, and hauled out the jack. I couldn't remember the last time I'd had a flat, but, thankfully, I still remembered how to change a tire. Arthur had taught us when we got our driver's permits.

I'd taken off the wheel nuts when I heard a car approaching. I kept my head down and hoped whoever it was could see I had things under control.

When the car slowed, I cursed under my breath, then plastered a polite smile on my face and stood.

The car stopped behind me, and both front doors opened. Two males climbed out, big, muscled, and both with black, cold eyes. My internal alarm shrieked. Demon.

Now, not all demons were scum or dumber than bricks, but the way this pair looked at me, I knew I was in trouble because some were just plain evil. I preferred the demons who behaved like wild animals over this kind. I understood acting on instinct. Demons like this were smart and cunning and vindictive as hell.

"Iris, right?" the tallest one said.

He knew my name. *Not good. Not at all.* "Nope, I think you have me mixed up with someone else."

The demon smirked. "I don't think so." He tilted his head at the creep beside him. "He made sure we had the right witch before we fucked with your tire."

The other one nodded.

Someone had sent them after me. I planted my hands on my hips and carefully slid free the knife sheathed against my back. I was no Willow with a blade, but I knew how to use one if I had to.

The one who liked to talk took a step toward me, and the other one grabbed his arm. "She's mine."

Smirky scowled but backed up. "Fine, but I get the next one."

The scary, quiet one aimed his black eyes at me and stomped forward. I backed up, colliding with my car. When he reached for me, I slashed his arm with my blade. The demon cursed, and his friend threw his head back and howled with laughter.

"Stop playing with our food," he said as I swiped at the big demon a second time.

He jerked back, then swung his ham hock of a fist at me, knocking the blade from my hand. I wasn't sure I could outrun these guys, and my blade was now on the other side of the road. I dove for the tire iron, snatching it up. He growled and came at me. I swung the iron, getting him around the side of the head, ringing the fucker's bell good, going by the way he swayed a little before he came at me again.

His friend was still laughing. *So glad I'm amusing you, asshole.* The demon faked left, then right, then grabbed for me, and I cracked him across the head a second time.

He growled and spat out several teeth. As each one pinged off the road, his friend laughed harder still. My fear spiked. Even if I could somehow take out the demon in front of me, there was a second guy to deal with.

If I wasn't fighting for my life and had more experience with my new magic, I could call on my wolf spirit or maybe a lion and freak these fuckers out. But sadly, I couldn't do that without serious focus, and that wasn't something I could spare right then.

I swung again, and this time when he reared back, I spun and sprinted for the forest. Pounding footsteps followed, and the other demon's obnoxious laughter grew louder as he joined the chase.

It cut off suddenly, and a gurgling sound followed.

I didn't dare stop or turn around. I kept running.

A scream came next, and then the pounding of boots started again.

I'd almost made it to the tree line and the cover of the forest when an arm hooked me around the waist, and I was yanked off my feet with a snarl. I struggled, swinging the tire iron wildly. Another hand grabbed my wrist, stopping me.

"Stop," a deep voice growled before planting me back on my feet and spinning me around.

Draven.

He stood there covered in demon blood, so much of it soaking into his clothes and splattering his handsome face.

"What did I tell you?" Draven snarled, his large hands gripping my shoulders. "I told you to fucking watch yourself, and as soon as I turn my fucking back, you're almost eaten by fucking demons."

And going by all the blood, they were no longer a threat. "You're angry," I said stupidly. Not that it wasn't hard to figure out with all the F-bombs he'd just dropped.

"And you're a reckless fucking idiot."

I tried to yank out of his hold, but he held me fast.

"Reckless? I got a flat tire. How the hell could I know that was going to happen?"

"Well, if you'd waited for me and hadn't taken off in the city, I could have told you I'd seen one of those assholes tamper with your car."

Anger pulsed through me now, thick and fast. "Why would I do that? You told me to stay away from you. I was only doing what you asked."

He bared his teeth, his canines sharp and extended. "You're a pain in my ass."

"And you're a major asshole," I fired back.

He leaned in. "An asshole who just saved your life."

Goddammit. That's exactly what he'd just done. "Well...*thank you*, I *appreciate* it," I said, still yelling.

He opened his mouth to fire something back, then shut it again when my words registered. He blinked down at me; the wind momentarily knocked from his sails.

He didn't let me go, though. If anything, he held me tighter. His green gaze flickered, then changed, going wolf, and he made a low, rumbly sound. Shifters, especially wolves, loved touch, affection, and the way he pulled me closer, as if controlled by his wolf, then drew in a breath, scenting me, I knew that part of him was still drawn to me.

I held his animal gaze. "Still want to kiss me, huh?"

What the hell is wrong with you?

I mentally kicked my own ass. The male scared the shit out of me. He was unstable, dangerous, and he hated me. Yet when I was around him, the urge to goad him, to push him, was damn near irresistible.

"You'd love that, wouldn't you?"

"I'd sooner kiss that demon's half-severed head."

His snarling lips curled into a vicious smile. "If I kissed your devious mouth, you'd drop to your hands and knees and offer up your cunt like I know you're desperate to. You'd beg for it."

I wanted to slap him hard, and my face heated because right then, I was turned on, which was twisted and humiliating. What did that say about me? Nothing good, that's what.

When I didn't reply, he laughed darkly.

I pulled away, yanking from his hold, and this time he let me. I strode to my car and Draven followed. The demons were torn up but still alive on the side of the road. I stepped over one, and got back to changing my tire while Draven walked to the writhing, bleeding demons and finished removing their heads, turning them to ash.

I hauled the flat into the trunk, ignoring him when he moved to stand beside me. Instead, I walked past and opened my door, but he grabbed my arm, stopping me from getting in.

"I want to leave."

He said nothing, just stared down at me for long seconds, those eerie green eyes searching mine before sliding over my cheek. Finally, he said, "It's different." His hand lifted like he was going to touch the new and improved black star on my face, but stopped himself.

"The mother took pity on me."

His gaze slid back to mine and locked on. "You're not like her, are you, Iris?"

It was the first time I'd heard him say my name, and tingles moved over my skin and my heart beat faster. He was talking about Selene. "I wouldn't know."

"You'd be better off if you were like her, little witch. You're not nearly as cunning."

"I'll take that as a compliment."

He dipped his head, his nose almost grazing my neck he was so close. He breathed me in again, and when he lifted his head, his eyes had darkened. "I wouldn't. She apparently lived a long life. You carry on the way you are, you won't be so lucky."

"I'm capable of more than you realize."

"If you say so," he said, then breathed deep again. "I can smell him on you, the hound. Are you going to fuck him?"

The change of subject gave me whiplash. "No."

"He wants you."

"That has nothing to do with me."

"So he's your backup?"

"He was happy to help since the local pack refused to do as the previous one had and form a mutually beneficial alliance with the local witches."

"And where is your hound now, Iris?"

I pulled free of him and shoved my car door open. "He's not my hound, not that it's any of your business. And thanks for helping me out, even though it's obvious that saving my life is the last thing you wanted to do. Next time, save yourself the regret and drive on past."

His nostrils flared and he took a step toward me. "Iris."

I ignored him, got in my car, started it up, and got the hell out of there.

Chapter Ten

Iris

The wind howled through the trees outside, making Else's chimes under the porch an eerie, chaotic soundtrack. I stared at the ceiling, another night without sleep, thinking about so many things—including Draven, whose face filled my head, his presence a visceral sensation that wouldn't leave me.

Our conversation two nights ago had been on replay in my head. How could I be so drawn to him? I knew I had bad taste in guys, but this, god, this twisted crush I had on the alpha bordered on masochistic.

A loud crack came from outside. Followed by the thud of something heavy hitting the ground.

I shot up.

Nia lifted her head.

"Stay, girl."

Nia come.

"I'll be right back. Nia stay."

She remained alert but did as I said. I climbed out of bed, yanked on my robe, and padded downstairs. The rest of the house was silent. I crept past Else's room, past the kitchen to the back door, and pulled the curtain aside. I couldn't see anything, no heavy branches broken off laying in the yard, and I was sure that's what I heard.

Shit. I spotted the new seedlings Mom and Art had planted earlier. They'd left them out on a table in the afternoon sun. They were covered, but this wind might blow the seed trays onto the ground.

I unlocked the door, tugged my robe around myself tighter, and slipped out. One of the trays had already tipped over. I slid them off the table and put them underneath, out of the wind that whipped my hair around my face, the rain stinging my skin.

I rushed for the door.

Another crack echoed through the night, making me jump. It was coming from the cemetery. Then another, louder this time, followed by a crash so loud I was surprised the ground didn't shake. *What the hell was that?*

A tingling sensation danced across my thigh, right over the markings the mother had made under my skin with her venom.

My heart exploded in my chest. Whatever had caused that noise had something to do with my task.

I raced around the side of the house and down the tree-lined path that stretched from our yard to the cemetery behind it. I didn't get far, though, because a massive tree, an ancient oak just outside the ward surrounding the cemetery, had blown over. Pulled from the ground like a giant had yanked it from the earth and tossed it on its side. It lay right across the path, its huge, twisted roots sticking up, exposing a massive hole where the tree had once been anchored.

Lightning cracked, forking across the sky, lighting up the shadowed path beyond it. I looked into the large hole.

Something was down there.

I stood at the edge as thunder rolled above me. I couldn't get a good look. Gripping one of the massive roots, I wriggled through the twisted mass and eased my way down. My feet sank into the soft soil, and when I took another step, something hard pressed against my bare foot. I dropped to my knees and brushed away as much dirt as I could.

A box.

I kept digging. The top was polished metal of some kind, but it was too dark to see what it was clearly. I found the rim with my fingers, and with a groan, shoved it open. Another flash of lightning lit up the sky—

I froze.

Oh goddess.

Bones.

No, not just bones, an entire skeleton. This wasn't a traditional coffin, it was too short for that, and whoever this was had been curled up inside, forced to fit.

I scrambled back out, stumbling.

Who the hell was that, and what were they doing here? I searched the shadows frantically, as if whoever had put this body here could be watching me now, when I knew that had to be impossible. These bones were old. Seriously old. This was my task? What the hell was I supposed to do with this?

I was going to hyperventilate.

Pull it together. I didn't have time to freak out, I needed to move the box before anyone in my family saw it. If they did, they'd have theories, questions, their first instinct would be to help, and they couldn't do that. I ran back to the house, grabbed a shovel and one of Mom's garden trollies that she used to cart plants around, and rushed back to the hole.

The wind had grown more intense; the rain was icy now and coming down heavier. My robe was drenched and plastered to me, my hair stuck to my neck and the sides of my face.

My teeth chattered as I climbed back into the hole, slipping in the dirt that had now turned to mud. I started digging, dragging the muddy soil away from the edges of the box to try to lift it out. When I finally cleared the dirt from around it, I started to pull.

My fingers were numb, and the rain was like icy needles against my skin. I heaved, but the box was too heavy for me to get out alone.

I grunted and pulled harder. It slid a little farther, but there was no way I was lifting it out of this hole and onto the cart.

There was movement beside me, and I spun around.

A large orange fox sat several feet away.

A fox I would know anywhere.

"Ren!" Tears immediately sprang to my eyes. I hadn't seen him for a whole year. None of us had. During Willow's task, he'd been possessed by an evil spirit and forced to do things that would make even the toughest warrior shudder in horror. Now Ren lived in the woods, preferring his animal form. The fact he was still breathing after what happened to him twelve months ago was a miracle.

He was Willow's familiar, and she missed him so badly she couldn't even bring herself to talk about it. He would occasionally text her, but when he did, he kept the conversation short. It hurt her badly. Ren was family, and Willow didn't know what to do to bring him back.

He shifted to his human form, and I stared at him, stunned.

Ren had changed in every way possible. He was bigger, lean and tall, but more muscled. His hair was longer, and his beard was thick. Dirt streaked his skin, and there were scars, old and new, wounds healed and some fresh all over his body.

"I've missed you," I said. "We've all missed you."

His amber gaze hit mine, then darted away. Without a word, he jumped into the hole and, gritting his teeth, lifted the large box out, sliding it onto the path. He climbed out and motioned to the trolley.

"Yes, thank you."

He lifted it again and placed it onto the trolley with a grunt.

"Why don't you come back to the house?" I said. "Everyone's asleep. It can be just us. Come and have something to eat."

He shook his head. "Thanks, though," he said, finally speaking.

Even his voice had changed, now deeper and a lot rougher, like he'd spent hours yelling or roaring. "Please let me give you something."

"I'm okay, Iris."

He wasn't okay; he was far from okay. But he was engaging with someone who wasn't Willow, and in person, so that was a win, even if it was only for a short time.

"Can I tell Willow I saw you?"

"If you want," he said, and his gaze turned hollow, the pain in his eyes grew more acute. He looked behind him, already wanting to leave, to get away.

"It's you, collecting the food she leaves at your place?"

He nodded.

"But you don't sleep there?"

He shook his head. "I need to go."

"Ren..."

He shifted back to his fox, blinked up at me, then turned and ran back into the trees lining the path. How often did he come here? Was he watching over us? It wouldn't surprise me. I watched him disappear into the woods, until lightning cracked above, making me jump.

I rushed to the trolley and towed it off the path and around the massive hole, so I could get to the other side of the tree, and down the path to the cemetery. There was a small unused garden shed back there that was rickety and close to falling down. Art had been meaning to dismantle it after they got their new one, but he hadn't gotten around to it yet.

I dragged the trolley past headstones, noting the dead patches of grass had grown larger, and pulled the shed door open, towing the trolley inside and shutting the door behind me. It smelled stale, but there was still an underlying scent of potting mix. Rain tapped against the rusted tin roof, and the wind whistled through the boarded walls. Matches and an old lantern were still sitting on the potting table like they had been the last time I came in here, and it lit without any trouble.

I carried the lantern over to the box and brushed away the mud from the top with an old rag. There were symbols on it, engravings I didn't recognize. I had no idea what any of them meant, but it was witchcraft, a spell or ward of some kind. Leaving this here without binding it in some way would be irresponsible, possibly dangerous. I had to assume whatever it translated to wasn't good. I needed to protect my family from whatever this was.

My blade was back at the house, and I was going to need blood for this. Thankfully, the new shed had all sorts of sharp tools I could use. Yanking the door open, I ran back out into the rain, grabbed what I needed, and rushed back. I pulled open the old shed door, then froze when one of the shadows at the edge of the cemetery moved.

Not a shadow.

A wolf, huge and black, with eyes that were as cold as the wind battering me.

Seriously? Anger, and something else I didn't want to name, fired through me, and I changed direction, marching over to Draven. "What the hell are you doing here? It's the middle of the night. You're a goddamn stalker."

He shifted suddenly, towering over me—all naked and muscled and wet. "I could ask you the same question. Do you have no fucking sense of self-preservation?"

I waved the pruning shears in my hand and glanced down at his seriously impressive junk. "I don't know why you're here, but if you don't leave, I'll use these, and I won't feel bad about it."

He sniffed, scenting me.

"Stop that."

"You're up to something, female." His gaze slid to the shed. "What did you take in there?"

"You're unbelievable. It's none of your damned business. Why are you here?" I yelled over the wind. "And why do you even care?"

"I assure you, I don't." His lips curled.

"Keep telling yourself that, but you're the one stalking me, not the other way around." I turned and headed back toward the shed. The sound of Draven hitting the ward surrounding our cemetery when he tried to follow had me grinning, and for some reason—blame it on the fact I'd just towed an unknown dead body into our garden shed and wasn't exactly myself—I momentarily dropped the ward, letting him through. If he caused me any trouble, I could expel him from the cemetery easily enough.

I heard his feet stomping through the mud behind me, following me back into the old shed. He crowded in after me and shut the door, closing us in together.

"So, are you going to tell me why you're here?" I said as I moved around the box. I slid my phone free and took pictures of the symbols painted on the sides.

"I like to keep a close eye on my enemies," he said, but there wasn't the same anger in his voice as there had been when I first met him or the times after.

I glanced up. He was frowning down at the box, watching as I crouched to get a closer look. I studied the markings more closely. "Is that..."

"Blood," he finished, and scented the air.

Some of the symbols were painted in blood.

That wasn't good.

He moved closer. "What's inside?"

I should probably keep it to myself, but it wasn't like he'd go and rat me out to my family. He hated all of us. "A body...well, bones."

His gaze sliced to me. "What evil have you been up to, witch?"

"You think I did this? That I killed someone, buried them,

then dug the body back up and brought it into this shed to...what? Reminisce?"

He didn't answer, just stared at me, which was answer enough. "If you must know, the bones are old. A tree fell over in the storm and this box was under it." I snapped another photo to study later. "I'm sure you won't believe me, but I've never killed anyone. Can you say the same?"

"If I killed anyone, they deserved it," he said in his low, gritty voice.

I scoffed.

"What?"

"Nothing."

"Tell me," he demanded.

I shrugged. "Only, you're not exactly the best judge of character. I wouldn't be so sure they did deserve it."

He crossed his arms over his scarred chest, the muscles in his forearms flexing. "I am."

"If you say so."

He moved, it was subtle, but it brought him closer to me. "You're the one with poor judgment, little witch."

"You would say that, you hate me."

"I say that because I'm in here with you alone, in the middle of the night." His voice had dipped lower still, and it set off tingles in my belly. "No one even knows you left the house."

He was trying to scare me. It wasn't going to work. "I'm not worried. If you wanted to hurt me, you would've done it already."

"Maybe I like to play with my prey," he said, eyes growing brighter.

"Maybe, but I'm still not worried."

I grabbed the pruning shears and held one of the blades to the palm of my hand.

"What are you doing?" His voice held a note of alarm.

I looked up at him and sliced.

He flinched.

"I told you why I needed backup, that I'd be called by the mother, well it happened, and this"—I motioned to the box—"has something to do with it."

His brows lowered.

"Now stand back." I fisted my hand and blood dripped through my fingers and to the floor as I walked in a slow circle around the box. "Bound with blood, in this circle you will stay," I said, starting the simple yet highly effective binding spell.

I didn't know what these symbols were or what spells had been used on this box, which meant treading with care. Simple was the best way to go with things like this. If powerful magic had been used here, and I had to assume it was, using a spell equally as strong could set off a safeguard, if the witch who did this had spelled one, and again, I had to assume they had—which would be really, really bad.

A simple spell like the one I was doing would be less likely to activate any counter spells that might have been built in. The only downside was it wouldn't last indefinitely, and the strength of magic used here would decide just how long mine held.

When I completed my second circle around the box and finished reciting my spell, I looked up. Draven was watching me, and he was doing that lip-curling thing he often did around me. "Let me guess, I disgust you?"

His nostrils flared. "The smell of your blood, it...I don't." He snarled a little. "I don't like it."

"You don't like the smell of my blood?" I forced a laugh. "I guess that's not surprising since you don't like anything about me. Still, that's a new one. I'm trying to decide if I should be insulted or not."

His eyes changed color, brightening to his wolf.

"There he is, the wolf's back, huh? He pops out a lot around me. Do you want to tear my throat out, then? Or does the scent of my blood offend you so much it turns your stomach?"

"Don't..." He held himself impossibly still. "Don't taunt me, little witch."

"I'm not *doing* anything to you. I don't have time for it," I said, even as nerves spiked in my gut. I grabbed his arm, about to usher him to the door.

He moved fast, so incredibly fast, pushing me against the wall. "Don't touch me."

I stared up at him, my heart hammering in my chest. "Don't touch you, don't taunt you, don't bleed in your presence." Yep, he had me pressed against a wall and I was still pushing the male, testing his control like a freaking lunatic. "Everything I do pisses you off. I see the way you struggle to hold yourself back, how close to the edge of your control you are."

"Iris," he growled, putting so much warning in my name that I shivered.

"Why are you here, Draven? Why the hell do you put yourself through this? You told me to stay away from you, yet you follow me around like a stray dog."

His lips peeled back and his incisors elongated.

I lifted my hand slowly, and he watched me, eyes so bright they glowed in the dim light of the lantern. He shook his head, warning me not to touch him.

I ignored him and pressed my palm to his bare chest, petting the beast, pushing him harder. *What are you doing?* This wasn't me.

But as I stared up at him, something like exhilaration filled me, and I realized I was lying to myself. Because I felt more like myself around this male than I had in a long time. Fearless. Strong and, yes, reckless—the Iris that Brody had slowly stripped from me. "What are you going to do about it, alpha?"

He snapped his teeth with a vicious sound and grabbed my wrist, pulling it off him and shoving it over my head. His face was in mine, harsh breaths hissing between his teeth. His chest brushed my nipples and he dipped even lower.

His gaze dropped to my mouth, and I stilled.

He was going to kiss me.

"You want me," he hissed between clenched teeth, the words angry. I wasn't sure if he was angry with me or himself because he wanted me as well.

"No," I lied. "And seeing as I plan on being celibate for the rest of my life, as well as a whole lot of other reasons, nothing between us will ever happen, I suggest you back up."

He dipped his head closer, ignoring me. "You want me to fuck you, don't you, little witch? Right up against this wall."

His chest heaved, and he pressed deeper into me. He was naked, hard, and I was obviously twisted because his hateful lust had me craving exactly what he said.

But I was not doing this. I may be a masochist when it came to this male, okay, no maybe about it, but if I allowed this to happen, if I let my body's reaction to Draven override literally everything else, I'd turn a new corner, right into certifiable.

He growled and took my jaw in his rough fingers, his lips moments from touching mine—

"I rescind your invitation," I said and grabbed the handle, flinging the door open.

Draven's eyes widened a moment before he was pulled away from me, the ward around the cemetery, our magic, extracting him, like he was connected to a bungee cord.

He flew through the air, tossed out of the grounds. I rushed out as he jumped back to his feet and charged forward, hitting the ward again and getting knocked back.

I walked up to the barrier but kept a safe distance away.

His chest heaved. "Let me back in."

I shook my head. "Not happening."

"Let me in, Iris," he said again, not a request, a demand.

The wind was wild and plastered my damp robe to me. I shivered but held my ground. "I won't let you take all that rage you've been holding on to, rage for Selene, out on me. And sure as hell not like that. I don't know what went down between you and her, but we are not the same person. We may have the same face, but that's where the similarities end."

He froze.

"Go home, Draven."

Then I walked away.

Chapter Eleven

Draven

W *hat the fuck was I doing?*
Panting, I watched Iris walk away. I fisted my hair as my wolf fought me harder. I should never have come here.

Every muscle in my body tightened. I could still smell her blood. She thought the smell disgusted me. She couldn't be more wrong; what it did was send my wolf into a frenzy. The beast recognized Iris as mine, it didn't matter if I wanted that to be true or not, and her blood was like a siren going off in my head, firing to life every protective and possessive instinct I had.

What the fuck was I going to do? How did I fight this feeling? My mind was fracturing more with every day that passed. I could feel myself falling backward. Last time I'd felt my sanity slipping, I'd been physically trapped, knowing my people were suffering and not being able to do anything about it.

This time, it was like the little witch had a vice grip on my mind...and my wolf.

I didn't know what the answer was. How to stop this? Everything was spinning out of control. My focus needed to be on establishing our pack here, on clearing and maintaining our territory—instead, I was out all night, compelled to follow that female, to be close to her, to protect her.

I didn't fucking want her.

Liar.

I didn't *want* to want her.

I paced away and back to the edge of the cemetery, my gaze moving to the shed.

Goddammit.

The female was reckless by nature, it was easy to see that. And this task she was doing, having to prove herself, was going to get her killed. I thought Mother Nature was supposed to be good and kind and nurturing? Instead, the goddess was a selfish, twisted bitch, sending unprepared witches to their fucking deaths for her own entertainment.

Her task had something to do with that box of bones. I didn't know what it meant, but I knew she was in danger.

Go home.

That's exactly what I needed to do, but I didn't. Instead, I shifted back to my wolf and drifted through the shadows, back to Iris's house in time to see her slip inside and shut the door behind her.

She was safe, locked inside a warded house.

Still, leaving felt wrong.

If I could cut out the part of me that recognized her as my mate, I would. Since that wasn't an option, I stayed where I was. A light came on upstairs, a silhouette moving behind the sheer curtains, and I knew it was her instantly.

Mine. The beast roared the word inside me.

But I couldn't have her.

And somehow, I had to convince my wolf of that before I sunk deeper into insanity.

Iris

"Whatcha looking for?" Else said behind me.

I turned from the ladder I'd scaled and sneezed for the hundredth time. "Just doing a bit of research." I grabbed the massive, dusty, leather-bound tome that had records of births and deaths in the Thornheart line and made my way down carefully.

Else watched me as Nia pressed into my aunt for pats, her gaze moving between the extremely old book and my blank expression. As always, nothing got past her.

"This has something to do with your task, yes?" she said, scratching Nia's ears.

I plonked the book down with the ancient spells book I'd been reading. "You know I can't answer that."

"So that's a yes. Not asking for you to give me all the deets, pumpkin. But you don't need to be so cagey. We knew what Wills was up to, we just couldn't help her. Share with your old auntie, it might make you feel better, or at least make you feel less like you're swinging your behind in the wind all on your own."

There was nothing that I would like more. Keeping this all to myself was so hard, having the weight of it on my shoulders was straight-up terrifying, but this was way too close to home. Those bones were on our land. They could be one of our family members, or equally as horrific, put there by one of us—because generations of Thornhearts had lived here.

Else would not be able to stand by and not be tempted to look into it, even if she didn't mean to. "I can't do that," I said, holding her gaze and hoping she'd end it at that.

She went still, her face paling. "That bad, huh?"

Not a question.

I said nothing.

She gave me a nod. "Okay, pumpkin, I'll leave you to your research. And FYI, if you want a more in-depth peek at the family tree, the council has better records. Sometimes families choose to omit things in their own for various reasons. The council has never given a shit about appearances. All the ugly that people try to hide is documented there." She leaned more heavily on the cane she used a lot more lately. "I don't like to think we've got that kind of ugly in our past, but you never know." She shrugged and walked away.

I watched her go, and an unhappy feeling curled and twisted in my belly. I'd planned to tell her about Selene, but seeing that look on her face...if Selene was as awful as Draven said, I didn't have the heart to burst Else's bubble.

I prayed to the mother I was wrong, but someone had put those bones just outside the cemetery, burying them deep, and planted a tree over the top, hoping no one would ever unearth them, and I was terrified of what I might find when I looked deeper.

Several hours later, bleary-eyed and exhausted, I headed upstairs, Nia on my heels, to get ready for work. I'd found nothing on the symbols I'd taken pictures of and nothing untoward in our family history records, which meant my best bet was a trip to the council chambers in the morning.

The bar was busy when I got there, the place full of hounds and other shifters, mainly.

The wolves were there, of course, at least a handful of them were there most nights.

I glanced over at their table. Draven wasn't here tonight. I kind of thought he would be, just so he could yell and snarl at me, since that seemed to be his favorite thing to do. One of them glanced up, catching my eye. A female warrior that I'd seen at Draven's keep. She gave me a hard stare.

I quickly looked away.

Of course, she hated me as well.

The female could kick my ass all around this bar if she wanted to, and going by the number of bottles on their table, she'd been drinking a whole lot. She'd also been making out with some huge guy most of the night, a bear shifter. I'd never seen one before, but my magic let me know easily now that it was growing stronger.

Bears didn't travel in packs, they didn't need to. They were incredibly loyal, though, especially to family.

I got back to work.

Half an hour later, standing at the bar, someone bumped my elbow.

The wolf must have gotten bored with scowling at me from across the room, and she'd decided to make sure I hadn't missed the fact she loathed me as well.

"Hey, witch, why do you keep ignoring me?" she said, and for the amount of beer she'd had, sounded surprisingly coherent. I was impressed.

"I assumed that's the way you wanted it," I said, not in the mood to play games with this female, even if she could snap me in half if she wanted to.

"Why would you think that? Oh…" She chuckled. "The resting bitch face? It's not personal. It's just the way I look."

I didn't believe that for a second. "Did you want something?"

"A 'thank you, Asher,' would be cool." She leaned against the bar and motioned to the hound behind it to fill up her glass.

So that was her name. I turned and leaned on the bar as well and looked up at her. Asher was tall. Not as tall as most of the guys, but a hell of a lot taller than me. She was also utterly gorgeous. Rich brown hair and golden eyes. Her brown skin was flawless, and her lips were full and wide. "Okay…what am I thanking you for?"

She tilted her head to the side. "You're still breathing, and you have me to thank for that."

I stilled. "What do you mean?"

She reached out and took a piece of my hair between her fingers. "Draven's been waiting for the right time to strike. He'd planned to take you out. No, you're not her, Selene, but he didn't know that. He would have torn you apart first and asked questions later if I hadn't told him to stand down."

He had planned to kill me. A lump formed in my gut. *Are you truly surprised?* "Then thank you. Being torn apart doesn't sound much fun."

She smiled and it was genuine. "No worries, I'm glad I said something. Despite your shitty family, you seem all right for a witch. You'll remember that, right? How I saved your ass?"

This whole conversation was confusing as hell. "Uh...sure."

"Sweet." The bear bellowed at her to "get her ass back here" from across the bar, and she turned and flipped him off, then winked at me. "Don't want to seem too interested."

"Shoving your tongue down his throat probably wasn't the best way to go, then," I said.

She stared at me for several seconds, then tossed her head back and laughed. When she got herself together, she gave me a friendly punch on the shoulder, which freaking hurt, and turned to leave.

"You can do better than the bear, you know," I said for reasons unknown. But a female like Asher? No one should be bellowing at her across a bar, they should be worshipping her.

"Oh, I know. But Buck fucks like a champ." She chuckled. "I'm not going to mate with the guy, I just want use of his giant dick for the night," she said and winked.

I laughed as well, nervously. Asher was kind of unpredictable, but yeah, surprisingly, I liked her as well. "In that case, I won't hold you up."

She walked away, still laughing, and I got back to work.

The rest of the night passed without drama. Asher left with her bear, and the bar slowly cleared out.

"I'll walk you to your car," Relic said when we were done closing up.

"Thanks." One of the hounds always walked me to my car after work, Warrick's orders. But these guys would have done it without their alpha telling them to.

I unlocked my car and tossed my bag onto the passenger seat.

"How's everything going?" he asked.

"Oh, you know, pretty shitty."

He nodded. "Yeah, you got a lot going on. You need me to kick someone's ass or you just need some backup, remember I'm here, no strings."

"That's really cool of you." Because as much as I hadn't wanted to ask Relic for help, he was the only one offering, and I'd be a fool to say no. "I have a feeling I might need to take you up on that."

"Good," he said in that deep, insanely rough voice. "Now get the fuck home, it's late."

I mock saluted him and got in the car, fired her to life, and headed out.

But as I hit the crossroads to leave Linville, I was hit with a weird sense of urgency that I couldn't explain. It rose up inside me, and when I went to turn for home, my gut screamed at me to go the other way.

My thigh started to tingle.

Shit.

My task. I had no choice but to go with it.

I turned right instead of left and let my instincts guide me. I drove for a while and ended up on the outskirts of the city, an affluent area where a lot of the rich and influential witches lived. I'd only been here once, to a party when I was in high school. Fantasia Cotter had thrown a graduation party and invited nearly everyone at school. It hadn't been my scene, and they hadn't been my people. I'd had a few beers and then called Willow for a ride home.

Nothing much had changed. It still wasn't my scene, and they still weren't my people.

But I pushed on, and when I rounded the next corner, I had to slow right down. There were cars, people all gathered outside someone's house, including several reporters from Nightscape. Was this some kind of press event?

There were more people arriving as I got out of my car and headed over. Lorenzo Leone stood there, face bloodless, eyes filled with fear, hands shaking. Lorenzo had several businesses but had made most of his money from his fast-food chain.

"...send my daughter home, please. If you want money, it's yours. Whatever your demands, you can have it, just...please, send our girls back."

"I can't believe this is happening," a girl said beside me. She looked about Mags' age.

I joined their huddle. "What's going on?"

"Marina was taken last night. You didn't hear?"

I shook my head. I'd been so preoccupied searching for answers about the body I'd found and thinking about a certain alpha-hole who couldn't decide if he wanted to kiss me or kill me, I hadn't been on social media at all. My family had been caught up with the cemetery and what was happening there, and I assumed they hadn't seen it either. "So, this is the third witch to go missing?"

"Yeah, I can't believe it."

"Lorenzo isn't on the council," I said, mainly to myself. The last two girls had been councilors' daughters, and I'd thought that might be a link.

"They're all friends, though," the girl said. "I've seen them at The Bank together. Come to think of it, I saw Marina there with Kristi the night she went missing. Not to talk to, of course, I'm not part of her inner circle, but they stand out, you know?"

I stayed and listened to Lorenzo answer questions while I checked out Nightscape and the two other missing girls' feeds. Both had been to The Bank the night they went missing as well, and people were speculating about it all over the app. I clicked on one of the pictures. It was Amy, Imogen, Marina, and Kristi. The four of them had been friends since they were little. They were all smiling, and they'd put #thespecials below it. I clicked on the hashtag, and hundreds of pictures of them together came up, a lot of them at that club.

The tingling had been steadily growing stronger while I'd been talking, which meant I knew exactly where I needed to go. As I strode back to my car, my heart was going nuts in my chest, my mind spinning with questions. I knew this task was going to be hard, but I never imagined it would involve anything like this.

What did the mother want me to do? Search for the missing witches? Find whoever was responsible? Like I was Sherlock-freaking-Holmes? I was just me. I didn't know how to do any of this.

Wiping my sweaty palms on my jeans, I got in my car, took several calming breaths, that didn't do shit, and headed into the city. Because I had no other choice. Whatever this task involved, I had to do it.

I parked a block away from the club. My clothes weren't exactly suitable, but I had to get in there, and it had to be tonight. That sense of urgency was at an all-time high.

I stripped out of my Hell Fire shirt, so I was just in the black tank top I had on underneath, grabbed my jacket from the back because it was cold as hell, shoved it on, grabbed my phone and wallet, and got out.

I could call Relic, but the streets were busy. All I had to do was scream and I'd have every set of eyes on the street on me.

I was perfectly safe.

The line to get into the club was insane. You would assume having three witches go missing after coming here would be a deterrent, nope. Danger was sexy apparently.

Standing out here all night freezing my nips off, waiting to get in, wasn't my idea of a good time, though. Working in bars, I knew there'd be another way in. I slipped down the alley. Bingo. There were two doors. One would be the fire exit from the club itself, and exit only, and the other would take me into the back of the staff-only area, most likely the kitchen.

I tested the first door, and, as expected, it opened.

I slipped in. The guy loading the industrial-size dishwasher had headphones on and had his back to me, so I rushed past, through the next door, and out to the bar.

Chapter Twelve

Iris

The club was packed. I worked my way through the crowd of sweaty bodies moving to the music, fighting my way to the bar. But the staff was slammed. Talking to them right then was out of the question.

So I made my way around the perimeter of the room. I wasn't sure what I hoped to achieve coming here, only that the urge to do so had been impossible to ignore—

A tingle danced down my spine.

I looked around the room, searching for I didn't know what, and glanced up...

And froze.

A male in a suit stood behind a large glass viewing window that oversaw the club. His expression was stony as he scanned the room.

Oh yeah. He was definitely who I needed to talk to. I mean, I didn't want to. I *really* didn't want to go up there. But a guy like that, this was his place, and he'd know everything that happened in his club.

No one was going to just let me up there, though. He was the big boss, that was obvious, and I was nobody. But after working in bars and clubs for years, I knew exactly how I'd get up there. So I headed back to the bar, the staff was scrambling and rushed off their feet. I waved over one of the guys. He ignored me at first, but I persisted.

"What can I get you?" he asked.

"I'm a new hire. You have an apron back there, and I'll get to work."

"Experienced?" the barman asked.

"I've worked in bars for the last four years."

"Thank fuck." He reached under the bar, grabbed me an apron, and tossed it to me, then slid a tray my way. "You can start by gathering the empties. Kitchen's through that door."

I gave him a thumbs-up, then he was gone. I kind of felt bad for fooling the guy. I'd been in this situation before myself. It sucked. And they did look like they needed help. *Shit*. I'd make a couple quick rounds of the room, then do what I came here to do. It could only help my cover, right?

I rushed around the club, loading up my tray with empties and delivering them to the kitchen, then did another couple of rounds.

The staff here shouldn't suffer because of all the morbid sight-seers hoping to learn something about the missing girls. Why people were drawn to tragedy, I'd never know. I sure as shit didn't want to be here. And what could the missing witches possibly have to do with the box of old remains I'd found? I had no clue, but they were somehow linked. I felt that tingle across my thigh for both.

I dropped off another load of glasses to the guy in the kitchen but was stopped by one of the bar staff before I could make a final run.

"Can you take these up to the VIP?" He pointed to the glass viewing window.

I'd think luck was on my side, but then I didn't believe in luck, like I didn't believe in coincidences. "Sure!" I called back as nerves exploded through my belly.

Mr. Suit had been watching me, and he knew I didn't belong here. But the result was the same, no matter how it came about—I got to talk to him, which I had to assume was at least one of the reasons I was drawn here.

I made my way to the nondescript door that'd been pointed out to me on the far side of the room. Another guy in a suit watched me approach. He opened it when I reached him and stepped aside. His dark eyes locked on me, but he said nothing as I squeezed past. Not a shifter, possibly a demon? I wasn't sure what he was, but he wasn't human.

Classical music drifted down the staircase that led to the upper level, a complete contrast to the music playing in the club. My nerves grew as I reached the top, dread rushing up from deep inside me as I knocked on the open door.

"Enter," a low, rich voice said from inside.

I didn't know what was about to happen, but as wrong as this felt, I also knew this was where I needed to be. Every instinct told me as much.

He didn't turn to face me when I walked in, and I stood there unsure what to do as he continued watching his club below. In the end, I cleared my throat. "I have your drink."

"I didn't hire you, witch," he said mildly, still not looking back. "Why are you here?"

In for a penny, in for a pound. "I have some questions, and I think you might be able to answer them."

He turned to face me then. His skin was deathly pale, and I sucked in a startled breath as his incredibly dark eyes met mine. "And what makes you think I'll answer them? Who are you to come into my club and ask anything of me?" His handsome features remained hard, unreadable.

"I'm nobody, and you probably won't, but I'm going to ask anyway."

He tilted his head to the side, that dark gaze moving over my body slowly, taking me in from head to toe before returning to my face. His gaze lingered on my cheek. "You misunderstand me, witch. Who are *you*? You made the effort to come here, to pretend I hired you, then do actual work for the last hour. I know why you're here, there's only one reason a witch would invade my sanctum under a guise right now, but you are a confounding creature, and I find you have piqued my curiosity."

He knew why I was there.

Dread slithered down my spine. Maybe coming here wasn't such a great idea. I reached out with my magic. Not a shifter either. Like the guy at the bottom of the stairs, I didn't know what he was, and the realization that he could be behind all of this hit me like a brick upside the head.

There was a darkness rolling off him that I'd felt before, but I couldn't place it. I'd met a lot of different kinds of demons in my life, but I'd never met one like him. He was powerful, and I would guess, very old. I didn't feel an evil vibe coming from him, at least I didn't think so, just...void. The male was cold, like a reptile.

No, a dragon.

The kind of creature who could kill you in one breath, then walk away from your bleeding corpse and never think of you again. The last thing I wanted was to pique this monster's curiosity.

But the way he was looking at me now—I knew it was already too late. And with a male like this, lies would only make him angry or murderous. Either didn't bode well for me.

So I decided to go with complete honesty. He'd already said he knew why I was there, the same reason I'd been compelled to drive to Lorenzo Leone's house. "Three witches have gone missing, and all three of them were seen at your club the night they vanished. What do you know about that?"

He didn't move, not one bit. It was disturbing how still he was. "Are you accusing me of something, little female? Brave as well, I see, or perhaps stupid?"

"I'm not either of those things. I'm here, in the...dragon's den, because I have to be."

"You think me a dragon? How delightful."

He didn't look delighted. "So...do you know anything?"

"You have no sense of self-preservation, how interesting," he said mildly.

"Oh, I assure you, despite evidence to the contrary, I'm fond of the whole living and breathing thing, and I would never purposely offend you." Whatever the hell he was. "But I do need to find out what happened to those witches. If I don't, my family suffers. So here I am, putting my neck on the line because I have no other choice, because I'd do anything for them. So, if something or someone here at this club had anything to do with the disappearance of those witches, I need to know."

"I had a family once. I'm sure I loved them as well," he said, that frigid gaze wide and still locked on me. "I can't remember what they looked like anymore."

Okay, not old, ancient. "I'm sorry."

"You can't miss what you can't remember."

"I guess not."

"I don't know what happened to your friends. Witches aren't to my taste these days. My palate is more refined," he said and grinned.

And I couldn't stop my startled step back, then several more. Fangs, and not like Draven or the hounds, these were sharp and long and pointed, made to pierce skin with precision, not tear shit apart.

Vampire.

He was a vampire.

I knew they existed, obviously, but I'd never met a full-blooded one myself. Only Ronan, and he was half-human.

"And if I want a female, I don't have to kidnap her—she comes to me willingly, enthusiastically," he carried on, as if I hadn't just propelled myself across the room to get away from him. "But, perhaps, I could make an exception for you? You do intrigue me so."

I ignored that last part and asked what needed to be asked. I had one foot already out the door, but there would be no getting away if he chose to come after me. If he wanted to drink my blood, he would. "So, you're telling me, you know nothing? That you've seen or heard nothing?"

"I know a lot of things, and I hear and see almost everything, but nothing that would help you in your little quest."

Okay, he was difficult as well as arrogant. "Would you allow me to see your security footage? Something either happened to the females here, or someone followed them when they left. I'm positive of it." The markings the mother had given me still tingled, telling me I was on the right path.

"You will not have access to any part of this club. If you would like to see my bedroom, however, I would be more than happy to accommodate you."

My heart accelerated, and judging by the way his gaze, which I now realized was deep purple, had darkened even more, he'd heard it as well. "Thank you so much for the kind...um offer, but old dudes aren't to *my taste,* and I make no exceptions."

He blinked, saying nothing for several long seconds.

I'd surprised him, apparently, throwing his words back at him.

"You are delightful," he said without even the tiniest hint of a smile.

"Thank you."

"You're sure you won't stay?"

"Positive."

He inclined his head. "Maybe we'll see each other again some-time soon."

"Maybe, but probably not."

His lips actually curled up in a seriously rusty imitation of a smile. "Well, sadly, it seems we've come to the end of our conversa-tion. I would advise you to leave my club as soon as possible, or I may change my mind and decide to keep you after all."

And that predator stare told me he meant it. *Shit.* I turned and got the hell out of there.

The stairs were a blur under my feet as I ran down. The goon in the suit, vampire as well, probably, watched as I rushed past. I pushed my way through the pulsing crowd, getting bumped and smothered by people laughing, dancing, and unaware of who stood above watching them and totally oblivious to the danger they were in.

I didn't know if he was the one who'd taken Amy, Imogen, and Marina, but he was a threat to everyone here.

The club was dark, and the lights flashed, the music so loud I felt disorientated as I struggled through the throng. I spotted an exit sign glowing across the room and only realized it was an exit to the back alleyway when I reached it. There was no way in hell I was risking that.

I turned and took two steps back the way I came—

Someone grabbed my arm and yanked me back so hard I momentarily thought my arm had been pulled from the socket. Hard fingers dug into my skin and shoved me into the darkened corner.

A shadowed face got in mine. "Not so fast," the male said, and this one *was* a demon—one who could pass as human, just.

"Let me go," I said as calmly as I could. "I'm a friend to the knights. You hurt me, they will hunt you down and send you back to Hell."

He flinched, freezing momentarily. No demon wanted to draw the attention of the Knights of Hell. The demon hunting warriors kept Roxburgh city clear of scum like him. But then he seemed to rally. The creep must think he'd get away with whatever he planned. "How will they know, if there's nothing of you left?"

I pulled my small knife from my pocket, and he laughed at it. But I had no intention of trying to cut him—though I was pretty sure I could cause some damage, I was angry enough. So much so, it smothered my fear.

I held up my palm and sliced a wide *X*. He frowned, thrown by what I'd just done. I took advantage of his confusion and slammed my palm to his forehead, pumping *everything* I had into him. His body locked in place. "In this spot you will rot," I hissed into his face.

He dropped to his knees, the tendons and veins in his neck standing out, jaw clamped tight.

I leaned over him. "Weren't expecting that now, were you?"

He growled at me through clenched teeth.

"No matter how hard you try, you won't be able to leave this spot. If someone tries to move you, you'll feel pain like nothing you've ever experienced."

I'd never used the spell before, I hadn't even known if it would work, honestly. It'd just kind of come to me one night, and using it now had felt like second nature. I'd asked Willow if she'd heard of the spell. She hadn't, neither had Else or Mom. So I didn't know for sure if the whole pain thing was true, but he didn't need to know that.

I'd also seriously overshot my power, draining myself almost dry. Fear did that sometimes, especially if you weren't used to using magic in combat. Now I'd messed up and left myself vulnerable.

I needed to get out of there.

A figure in dark jeans and a black hooded sweatshirt appeared out of nowhere. Another vampire. I lifted my blade. "Stay back."

He ignored me and something silver flashed. A moment later, the demon frozen in front of me was ash on the floor. The hooded guy took a step back. "My master apologizes for what just happened. You're free to go."

"Your master?"

He pointed to the viewing window above us on the other side of the large room.

Of course, who else could it be?

The vamp tilted his head back, and I got a flash of his face. Vibrant lilac eyes stared back. He was...beautiful, the most beautiful male I had ever seen, looks so stunning I felt momentarily mesmerized. "What are you? Like his Igor or something?"

"I'm known as Pretender, but please call me Ender. And you're welcome," he said sarcastically, though he kept his body rigid.

"I'm not sure what I'm thanking you for. I had it under control, the demon was already incapacitated."

He was silent a beat. "A word of advice, Iris?"

"I'm all ears." Shit. I needed to tone down the snark, but it tended to come out when I felt threatened, which was a seriously bad personality flaw.

"Leave this place and never come back. The next time, Nero might not be in such a good mood."

"Your master's name is Nero?"

"Yes."

"And how do you know my name?"

He said no more, just turned and walked away, melting into the crowd. I glanced up at the window again, and though the lights were now off, I could still see the outline of that tall, terrible male standing there. I tore my gaze from him and rushed out the nearest exit—

And right into the goddamn alley.

Shit.

A group of males stood there, and they turned. All eyes now on me. I assumed they were shifters of some kind, not wolf, something unpleasant—rodent. My first instinct was to open the door and run back into the club, but I got the feeling if I went back in there, Dracula would make good on his threat. Right now, these guys were the lesser of two evils.

I put my head down and, ignoring the crude things they called to me, tried to rush past. One of them moved in front of me, not letting me get by.

This night just got better and better.

It was late, or should I say early, close to three in the morning, and I'd pumped almost all of my magic into that psycho in the club. I could fight a demon one on one, but shifters were something else. They were strong and even more vicious if they chose to attack in their animal form, which meant I was in serious trouble.

"Let me by," I said. Why the hell hadn't I brought Relic with me or called him to meet me here? Though I hated to think what might have happened if he had come with me. Mr. Vamp and Pretender might not have been so accommodating if I brought an aggressive-always-ready-to-fight hellhound into their club.

"No, I don't think so. You can stay here with me. We're going to have some fun, you and me."

I tried to visualize a dim light, my power, then imagined it growing, trying to ignite the dwindling embers of my magic. It didn't work, I was totally drained. The shifter grabbed my shoulder roughly, and I knocked his arm away and slammed the heel of my hand into his throat. I couldn't win this, but I wasn't going down without a fight.

He cursed and choked but didn't go down. His friends snickered, and he hissed and grabbed for me again before I could run, more roughly this time—

A growl tore through the alley.

I spun as Draven emerged from the shadows and stalked toward us, all sexy and furious and insane.

The rodents turned to him, and the alpha of the Silver Claw pack stared them down with eyes that were terrifying. "Were you about to touch what's mine, rat?" he said, voice so cold and filled with violence, I shivered.

His?

The rat shook his head.

Draven approached, and the male who had just threatened me tried to hold his deadly gaze then just...dropped to his knees.

"Stay down," Draven snarled. "You're lucky I don't disembowel you where you sit, you fucking coward."

The rat kept his head down, and his buddies did the same. The other male was shaking and, judging by the smell, had peed himself.

Draven turned to me and held out his hand.

And I was so damned thankful to see him, I took it.

Chapter Thirteen

Draven

Iris clung to my hand as I strode from the alley. She didn't fight or try to pull away, letting me lead her from the pieces of shit who were about to hurt her.

The idea of anyone causing her pain, of touching her—touching what was *mine*—filled me with fury.

"Where are you taking me?" she said, trying to keep up.

"I don't know." The words came out blended with my beast. "I just know I need to get you away from those fuckers back there or I'll turn around and tear them to pieces one by one."

Wisely, she said nothing and let me pull her around the side of the next building and into the parking lot behind it. It was dark, heavy in shadow, quiet. My wolf was right there at the surface, and there was no holding him back this time. I needed a taste of her, and if I didn't get one, I would literally lose my fucking mind.

I closed in on her, unable to keep my distance another

moment. The fear I'd felt rolling off her had all but gone, but I still wanted to go back and kill every male in that alley. "You okay?"

Her big brown eyes were wide, and she blinked up at me as if she were surprised by the question. Which was fair. So far, she'd only seen the worst of me. But then, when I was with her, my emotions were so fucking conflicted, so raw, there was no holding any of it back.

"I am now," she said.

Christ, she was beautiful. Need clawed at me, thick and hot and urgent. It felt like a molten fire burning through my veins. I needed her. I wanted her. She was mine, and I was going to have her.

I pressed her small body against the brick wall at her back.

She stared up at me, her deep brown eyes searching mine. "You're going to kiss me, aren't you?"

"Yes."

She didn't tell me to back the fuck up or try to run. No, she submitted, licking her lips and waiting for me to claim what was my due. My right.

Maybe if I was in my right mind, I could still walk away. But that wasn't going to happen tonight, there was no walking away. There was only her and me and the burning need between us, the desperate aching thing that buzzed in the back of my head and sparked and fired across my skin whenever she was near.

The thing that told me that on every level she was mine. My mate. And not tasting *my mate* at that moment was impossible.

I drew in a ragged breath, my hands hovering at her sides above the curve of her hips.

"Go on then, do it. You earned it," she said, goading me, something she seemed to enjoy.

Maybe she thought her taunting would snap me out of it, would make me stop, that I'd turn away. Not going to happen. With a snarl, I scooped Iris up in my arms. She gasped, the sound turning into an alarmed cry when I slid a hand up her back, thrust my fingers into her hair, and fisted, holding her still.

Her lips parted to fire more of her attitude at me—

I claimed that smart mouth and kissed her hard.

Yes. This was what I needed, what I'd been missing my whole fucking life.

I forced her mouth open with mine and slid my tongue deep inside, needing more, *taking more*, and still not being able to get enough.

She moaned against my lips, and that sound—*fuck*—had my heart beating so hard I thought it would explode out of my chest. I shouldn't want this. I shouldn't want her. But fate had other ideas.

Christ, nothing had ever felt this good, this right.

She clung to me, letting me take everything I needed from her.

Submitting to her male.

So I took what she offered, and I kept on taking.

Only when we were desperate for breath did I lift my head. She was panting, her gaze heavy, lips full and swollen, glistening from my kiss.

I growled, hovering on the edge of sanity, ruled by need, by the dizzying drive to claim her. "You did this." I pressed my forehead to hers, struggling to catch my breath. "You pushed me to my breaking point. What the fuck were you doing in there? I told you...I told you to be careful, not to put yourself at risk. And you kept on doing stupid shit. You have a fucking death wish. Do you know what could've happened to you in that alley?"

Her throat worked. "I miscalculated, okay? And I didn't ask you to come to my rescue. I mean... I appreciate it, I do. But I didn't ask for it, for any of *this*...whatever it is that's happening right now."

"Why won't you just stay the fuck at home?" I bit out. Every time she put herself in jeopardy, my protective instincts shot higher, and my drive to claim her increased.

Her gaze narrowed, and she studied me harder. "Why are you here, Draven? You're following me again, aren't you?"

I didn't answer, because she was right, and we both knew it. I stalked her day and night. I hadn't been eating, barely sleeping. The only thing in my damned head was her and the urge to be close to her, to have her.

"What's your deal? I don't... I don't know what you want from me." She blew out a shaky breath. "I won't lie, I feel this thing, an electricity between us, but it's just lust. Ignore it and eventually it'll go away. We've kissed, so hopefully you got it out of your system. Now you need to forget I exist because *this*"—she motioned between us—"can't happen. It would be a monumental mistake. You don't want me, not really. You don't even like me. You want Selene. You hate what she did to you, but you cared about her once, and it's messing with you. You see her face"—she pointed at her own—"and you forget everything else. That's what this whole twisted lust-hate situation going on between us is all about."

I shook my head and couldn't stop myself from breathing in her scent again. "I don't want Selene. I despise her. She fucked with my life, my pack, and left me to rot. I never kissed her like I just kissed you, and I never wanted her this way. You're right, though, I don't want it. But I also can't stay away from you. Believe me, I've tried. Every night I tell myself to stay the fuck where I am, but every night I leave the keep and hunt you down..." I drew in a ragged breath. "Because you are mine, little witch, whether you or I want it is irrelevant."

Her eyes widened. "I don't belong to anyone." A tremor moved through her. "The last guy I got involved with did this..." She touched the cold black skin on her cheek. "I've had this kind of twisted. I've had someone who wanted me and hated me all at the same time. I've been there, I've done that, and I sure as fuck won't be doing it again with you." She pressed her hands against my chest and pushed. "Now, back up and let me go."

I didn't want to. Letting her go, letting her walk away from me, felt impossible. I wanted to pick her up, throw her over my shoulder, take her to my keep and never let her leave. Instead, I ignored the clawing, growling desperation of my wolf and stepped back. "We are not done, Iris. It doesn't matter what you say, or what I say, this is happening."

She stared up at me in disbelief and shook her head. "Just...you need to stay the hell away from me."

I bit back my growl of denial. My concern over her safety was overwhelming, and I was talking again before I could think better of it. "You're not a warrior, little witch. This task you are on will get you killed. Despite the blood running through your veins, I know you're different than Selene. And I find that I don't want to see you hurt. If you need me to help you ..."

"Pass. You turned me down and that was the right move. I have someone else who can help in the future, and I'll make sure to use them next time. I don't need you."

"The hound," I growled.

"It's none of your concern."

A mournful *meow* came from beside us.

I looked down at a scrawny alley cat rubbing against Iris's leg. She shoved away from me, fished something from her pocket, and crouched down. "Here you go, pretty girl." She gave the cat a treat and patted its matted fur. "I know." She petted her again. "You won't be lonely anymore." Then she scooped up the cat and walked off.

"What the fuck are you doing?"

Iris didn't answer, she just strode off with the damned cat.

I stared after her, confused and frustrated. A state the female had me in every time I was near her. She'd been communicating with the cat, hadn't she? Just like Charity used to. A knot formed in my gut.

I shook my head, like I could shake that witch loose from my damn mind.

I focused back on Iris, and even after what she'd just said, I was helpless against the urge to follow. Only now, when she got in her car and sped off, I stayed back so she wouldn't see me following in my truck. But every protective, possessive instinct inside me prevented me from walking away from her. Not yet. So I followed her like the crazed stalker she thought I was.

I pulled over a little down the street from her when she stopped at a house on her way home, despite the hour. There was a sign out front in the shape of a cat. The Cat Sanctuary. Iris got out, opened the passenger side, scooped up the cat, and carried it to the front door. An old woman in her dressing gown answered, smiled when she saw Iris, took the cat, as well as the cash that Iris handed her, and after giving the cat one more pat and saying something to the pitiful creature, Iris left.

It was obvious this wasn't the first time she'd done this, rescued a stray. Jesus, I didn't know what to make of her.

She drove off, and I followed her all the way back to her house, unable to return to my keep until I watched her walk through the front door and the light in her bedroom upstairs turned on.

Did she truly think that kiss would be enough for me? She couldn't be more wrong. I'd tasted my mate, I had her scent branded on me, and the feel of her warmth, her soft curves, imprinted against my body.

That one taste had only deepened my craving for her even more.

Iris

I rummaged around in my bag for my ID and flashed it to Gunther, the security guard, ignoring the tingle dancing down my spine. I was still reeling from what happened the night before— learning the missing witches were part of my task, going to the club, and then what happened afterward. Draven had called me his, and he'd kissed me. I'd told him to stay away, but he was out there now. Somehow, I *felt* him. The guy was still stalking me. It should horrify me, or alarm me, something, but it didn't. Instead, it kind of thrilled me.

Stop it!

Gunther handed it back.

"This way."

Gunther Morgans was tall and thin, and I assumed in his late fifties. He'd worked here at the council chambers for as long as I could remember. I'd been here before with Else when I was a kid and with Mom as well for different things over the years, and Gunther was always the one to greet us.

He led Nia and me through the main rooms, her claws tapping on the marble floors, then through a set of wide double doors. I felt the *hum* of magic as we passed. If Gunther wasn't with me, there was no way I'd be able to pass. This place was warded to the gills, and for good reason.

We reached an office, where a small desk sat between two doors, one we were about to go through, the other to the public records room. Gunther's daughter, Penny, sat there, and she smiled wide when she saw me. She was the same age as Willow.

"Hey, Pen."

"Iris." She stood, her familiar, Jasper, a pure white ferret, sat on her shoulder. "It's so good to see you. You look...so great."

I looked like a wreck. I hadn't slept, and my hair wasn't playing the game today. "Thanks, you're too kind," I said and laughed. "But we both know that's a lie."

She blushed. Pen was shy but incredibly sweet. "You always look nice."

"Have I told you lately that I love you?"

She giggled.

"I think you have some work to do?" Gunther said to his daughter.

Penny's cheeks grew pinker and she sat back down.

"Down here," he said to me and opened the door.

A steep staircase descended into shadow, and the cold from the belowground library drifted up, making me shiver. Gunther flicked on a light, and we made our way down, then rounded a corner at the bottom and carried on along another short hall. Finally, he stopped at a huge wooden door. It was intricately carved and the deepest of mahogany.

He motioned to the middle of the door. There was a darker patch, and it was surrounded by a carved ring of ivy. "Your blood, Miss. Thornheart."

"The door, it's gorgeous." I pulled my knife from my bag and pricked the tip of my finger. Nia whined, she didn't like it when I made myself bleed, no matter how many times I did it. When the blood had swelled to the surface, I pressed it to the darker patch of wood. My blood mixing with the blood of many witches before me, generations of them.

"It's more than just a door. It remembers. It knows many things about the witches who have come here, and it can recognize bloodlines. The door knows if you should be granted entry."

That was impressive. The magic was so incredibly old; I felt that now. The hum of it was deeper, richer. Like it'd become one with the ancient wood. There was no separating them, even if there was a witch powerful enough to try.

The click of the heavy iron locking mechanism echoed off the stone walls and marble floor before the door slowly swung open on well-oiled hinges. Gunther walked in, leading me to a wide oak desk.

"Please sit."

I did as he said, Nia doing the same beside me, and we waited while he gathered several large books from around the room and stacked them in front of me.

"Is all of this about coven Thornheart?"

"Yes. And you may look through them here, but please wear

the gloves at all times." He placed a white pair in front of me. "All the shelves in this room are restricted. You are prohibited from looking at another coven's records." He motioned to said shelves. "They are also heavily warded."

In other words, don't even try it, or you'll be sorry. "Thanks, Gunther. Much appreciated. Does it matter how long I'm down here?"

He shook his head. "Take all the time you need." He placed a small bell beside me. "Ring this if you need me. It's enchanted, so I'll hear it no matter where I am in the building."

"Awesome, thanks again."

Gunther left, closing the heavy door behind him, and I took in the stack of books in front of me.

The answer was in here...it had to be.

I shivered, thinking about Amy and Imogen and Marina, and what they must be going through, how scared they must be.

Failure wasn't an option.

Chapter Fourteen

Iris

There were four books, all leather-bound, and Gunther had stacked them in order of age—newest at the bottom.

I stood, slid on the white gloves, and took the first book from the top. The leather was thick and worn, rich brown in color. The hinges were iron, and it was seriously weighty. I lowered it to the table's surface and undid the buckle, holding it closed.

I scanned the first page. *Whoa.* It was dated 1302, and I was no expert, but I was pretty sure some of it was written in Italian, or at least an early version of it? Which made sense since our ancestors originated from Italy. I worked my way through, but this was farther back than I needed.

The next book, again, was still too far back.

I opened the third book. *Bingo.* We were in the right century.

The leather of this book was black and velvety smooth, the pages thick. I carefully turned to the back, where the others had the family trees written, along with lists of births and deaths. I ran my finger down the list of births first. Selene's name was on the second page, alongside her location and date of birth. The date had been entered twice, again right below. The name under Selene's had been crossed out, though, a red line right through the middle. It wasn't thick enough to conceal what was written, but the line through it was definitely blood.

A spell.

I snapped a picture and enlarged it on the screen to get a better look.

Charity.

What the hell? I'd never heard that name before, not once. Had Selene been a twin? That's what this looked like. I turned to the family tree drawn on the inner back cover. Selene and Charity had both been added, but again, Charity's name had been crossed out in blood.

I carefully flipped to the beginning of the book and started reading the scribes' entries: recollections, our histories. Important events, births, deaths, marriages, along with funny little anecdotes, recipes, and, of course, spells, more or less of the latter two, depending on who had inherited the book over the years. Some provided more information than others.

The author had written about Beatrix Thornheart and her wedding to Giles Pickering. Beatrix was our great-great-great-aunt and one of the most powerful witches in the history of our family. She would have used Pickering as her surname, but only because that's what the humans of the time would have expected. To her coven and other witches around her, she would have remained a Thornheart. We didn't take our husband's names, and our children didn't either. That's how it worked in a coven.

I skipped ahead. Beatrix had become pregnant soon after. The story of the birth was harrowing, though some of the thick, sloped writing was hard to decipher. From what I could read, Beatrix had almost died, but in the end, she and Giles were blessed with...twin daughters.

Selene and Charity.

I sat back.

Well, shit.

I read the rest of the book, but there wasn't much mentioned about Selene and Charity again. I slid it aside and pulled the next book closer. The red leather was heavily tooled, the corners tipped with silver. I opened the book to the back like I had the others. It spanned a longer time frame. Being a newer book, the pages were thinner, so there were a lot more. Else and Gran's births were there, Mom, her sisters, me, and my sisters, our cousins, right at the bottom of the list.

I flipped it carefully to the front again and started reading. The first entries were written by Selene. She must have inherited it at some point.

I ran my finger down each page, reading Selene's words. When she married. The births of her daughters.

But no mention of Charity.

I reached almost the end of Selene's section before it was handed to another to take over the task of scribe—then I saw it.

It was her handwriting, but it was also different, unsteady, darker, like she'd been pressing down hard on the pen.

Charity returned.

Her magic more powerful, her skills in the dark arts as great as her desire to cause harm. We were forced to do the unspeakable to protect our loved ones.

My sister is no more.

Both Jacob and I were badly injured. A trip to Shadow Falls is impossible. We have secured and buried her remains beyond the cemetery grounds until we are well enough to journey to the falls.

I stared down at the passage, my heart beating hard in my chest.

Selene and her husband had fought and killed Charity.

It said she'd returned. Charity had obviously been cast out of the coven, and this was why there was no more mention of her in our family history, not passed down verbally or in books.

The bones in our garden shed belonged to Charity. She'd been using dark magic and had returned to cause harm. Selene had killed her sister to protect their family, the coven. Rowena was the head of our coven now and the current scribe. She'd never mentioned it, but then she may not have ever seen the passage, and talking about such things wasn't done even if she had. A dark past like that was never spoken of, covens didn't want that kind of thing getting out.

Which meant Else and Mom wouldn't know either.

They'd planned to move her remains to Shadow Falls, but in the end, they'd never done it. I thought about my sisters. There was nothing they could ever do to stop me from loving them. Nothing. Even the thought of taking their remains to that awful place would break my heart. Is that why Selene had never moved Charity? I guess we'd never know.

I snapped a picture of the passage, closed the book then rang the bell. Gunther walked in a short time later. He inclined his head and put away the books as Nia and I headed up the stairs.

"Did you find what you were looking for?" Penny asked when I surfaced.

"I'm not sure." I'd found something, and as horrific as it was, I still wasn't sure how or if it was linked to my task and the missing witches. "I think so."

Penny glanced at the door. "I saw you at The Bank the other night," she said in a hushed tone.

"You were there?"

She nodded as she offered Jasper a treat and glanced at the door behind me again. Worried her father would hear? I wasn't sure why, she was twenty-seven years old. "I didn't realize you were working there now."

"Oh, I'm not. I was just...you know, helping out a friend." I liked Penny, and I was sure I could trust her, but she didn't need to know what I was doing. I barely knew myself. "The place was so busy." I had to be careful how I worded this. "You must have seen on Nightscape that Amy, Imogen, and Marina were all seen there right before they disappeared?"

She nodded, her eyes wide. "Do you think Kristi could be next? Whoever's behind this seems to be targeting that group."

The thought had occurred to me. It was always the four of them together. But getting to Kristi wouldn't be easy, especially now. "Her family has her locked down from what I've heard. They'll keep her safe." She'd posted a video this morning, crying and shaking, begging whoever had her friends to let them go. They weren't crocodile tears. She'd looked utterly distraught and scared out of her mind. She'd said her father had hired security and she was somewhere safe.

"There's no way she could've...you know, had something to do with it, could she?" Penny asked, looking freaked out.

"I don't think so." I didn't know her that well, but Rose had when she'd been at school. She'd always said how sweet she was, and a little naïve, kind of like Penny. From what I'd been told, the girl didn't have a malicious bone in her body. "Maybe you should avoid that place, Pen. At least until we know what happened to them."

She pouted a little. "I guess you're right. Hey, we should hang out sometime? I mean, if you want to? We could go somewhere else?"

"Love to. I have some family stuff to deal with right now, but after that, absolutely."

Penny bounced in place. "Awesome!"

I headed back the way I'd come, my mind racing with what I'd found out.

Nia bumped into my leg. *Nia hungry.*

I rubbed her ears. "Me too. Let's go get some food."

A door opened ahead of us, one of the offices the councilors used from time to time, and Isaac Eldridge, the asshole himself, walked out. I paused mid-step and he did the same, then his shoulders straightened and he turned to face me fully, standing in my path, waiting for me.

I stopped in front of him, ignoring my nerves, and smiled. "Surprised to see me?"

"It seems they let anyone in these days." He didn't even try to disguise his sneer.

Nia growled, and I ran my hand down her back to calm her.

"No, I mean alive. Some of your demon buddies followed me from your building the other day, after they'd messed with my car." My heart was racing, but I used every bit of courage I had to stare him down. Well, technically up, but I refused to let his height intimidate me. "Kind of cowardly, don't you think? I just wanted to talk, Isaac."

His gaze was dark and filled with rage. "I have no clue what you're talking about. Why the hell would I send demons after you? If I wanted to hurt you, Iris, I'd do it myself."

"Sure you would," I said, probably not wise to goad the male who wanted to see my entire family dead, but I was still pissed off. Willow was right; when people fucked with my family, I had trouble thinking first, but this asshole made it impossible to stay calm.

He leaned in. "Your allegations are baseless. You're making a fool of yourself. I'd stop talking now, if I were you."

"Or what? You'll keep poisoning our cemetery?"

His head jerked back. "What?"

"Don't play dumb with me," I fired at him.

He tilted his head back and laughed, deep and throaty, then finally looked down at me. "Oh, that's perfect. You're losing the only thing that makes your family valuable." He shook his head. "I mean, yeah, it does sound like something I'd do. But sadly, it's not me. I kind of wish I'd thought of it first, though."

Dammit. I thought I might actually believe him. The cemetery part anyway. There was no missing his surprise at my accusation.

"As fun as this was, I find being around you brings out my bad side." His fingers curled into a fist at his side, then he turned on his heel and strode off.

I watched him go, and then it hit me.

It wasn't sabotage. Something else was poisoning our cemetery.

Oh goddess.

Charity's remains—it had to be. Our magic didn't leave us even after we died, and that included dark magic. It poured from our bones into the ground, making our cemeteries a huge source of our power. The damage to the cemetery had only started recently. The box she was in, somehow her dark magic had to be leaking out.

I rushed from the council building and instantly felt Draven when I stepped outside. I couldn't see him, but he was close by. He was always close by. The memory of that kiss washed over me, and I squeezed my eyes closed for a moment. He was all wrong for me. In every single way. He was also obsessed with me. And let's not forget that he wasn't totally sane.

I didn't know what to do about him. But I guess I had backup, whether I wanted it from him or not. This couldn't go on, though. I knew myself, and as messed up as it was, I wanted him as well, and if he kept this up, eventually, I would give in. Like I had with that kiss.

I'd let him kiss me again, and I wouldn't make him stop next time. Because, obviously, I was as insane as he was.

I tapped out a quick text to Knox, letting him know I couldn't make my shift.

I had to make sure the bones were secure.

Mom and Art were at the table in the kitchen poring over books when Nia and I finally got home. Mom looked exhausted, what with Rose and the cemetery, she'd barely slept at all. But right now, she looked scared.

"Mom, what's going on?"

"It's worse," she said, her voice breaking. "The cemetery. If this carries on, if I can't work out what's happening, your task won't matter, we'll lose so much, all on our own."

How could I keep what I knew to myself? My mom was suffering.

I sat beside her and took her hand. "I think I know what's causing it, but if I tell you, you'll want to help, and that can't happen."

She gripped my hand tighter. "You can't tell me? It's your task?"

"I think so, and at the very least you'll want to offer advice, and the mother will see that as you helping, right?"

She bit her lip. "Yes."

"Whatever this is, I don't want you doing it alone," Art said, worry lining his face.

"It's okay. Relic said he'd help if I needed him, and...Draven has been as well." He was with me constantly, I may as well use that to my advantage and put Art and Mom's worries to rest.

Mom lit up a little. And I could almost see the hearts and flowers dancing in her eyes. She was a hopeless romantic.

I shook my head. "Don't get any ideas. I promise you, there is no love lost between the alpha and me." Which wasn't a lie. There was a whole lot of something else though. Something that made my skin tingle and my heart race. Something that made me want to move closer to him and run like hell the other way all at the same time.

Mom patted my hand. "I won't ask any questions. I know you can do this, sweetheart. I believe in you."

God, I hoped her trust wasn't misplaced. I stood, kissing the top of her head, and walked out of the kitchen, my belly in knots, and rushed upstairs to change. The sound of murmured voices drifted down from Rose's room. I assumed Mags and Bram were with her. But I was wrong.

Not Mags.

Ronan.

He sat behind Rose and brushed her hair. "Like this?" he asked in his low, smooth voice.

Roe's cheeks were flaming. "You don't have to... Oh l-look, Iris is here now. She can do it."

Ronan's gaze lifted to me. "Iris."

"Hey, Ronan. You're here again." There was a box of Turkish delight on the bedside table and a little powdered sugar on Roe's chin. He'd been trying to feed her again.

He nodded, highly focused on slowly dragging the brush through my sister's blond hair. "Yes."

Ronan always looked the same, but today he looked tired. There were dark circles under his eyes. "Is there...something you need?" I asked him.

"No."

Rose was looking at me with pleading eyes. "Um...I was just going to help Rose with her bath, so I can take over."

Ronan glanced up at me. "I can bathe Rose."

The guy seriously had no idea. Rose looked utterly horrified. "Thanks for the offer, but Rose would probably feel unconformable with that." Sometimes you just had to speak plainly to the guy or he'd never get it. "Most females try not to get naked with guys they aren't in a relationship with, you know?"

Ronan froze, then blinked those purple eyes at me. "Of course. My apologies, Rose, if I was inappropriate."

"It's okay," she whispered.

Ronan slid out from behind her, handed me the brush, and walked out. We both stared after him.

"What's going on with him?" I asked, turning back to my sister.

Her eyes were wide, huge in her thin face. "I don't know. He... he just keeps coming back. I'm not sure why."

I wasn't either. He didn't feel love or lust or even affection. Yes, he had a bond with his sister, but he never showed Luna affection. The times I'd seen her hug her brother, he'd looked baffled. He was loyal, though, to those that he deemed worthy.

"Do you want me to ask him to stop coming over? I don't want you feeling uncomfortable. The guy's intense. I'd understand if you didn't want him to visit so often."

Her hands fluttered over the covers, and Nia carefully climbed up beside Rose, laying against her side and butting her nose against Roe's hand for a pat. "No...I-I like it. He..." She chewed her lip and gave Nia what she wanted.

"What?" I sat on the edge of her bed. I needed to take care of the remains, but I would always make time for my sister, no matter what. While I still had her, she came first, always.

"He doesn't tiptoe around me. He's blunt, and he doesn't seem to care about my...m-my back, and he makes me laugh, obviously without meaning to, and..." Her cheeks went pink again. "He's...he's seriously hot. I-I deserve some eye candy, right?"

I laughed, and her soft giggle had my heart squeezing painfully tight. Tears stung my eyes, for all the things Rose would miss out on, that she'd already missed out on, and for us. Because I wasn't sure how we were going to go on without her.

I swallowed the tears away and soaked in the joy on her face. "Uh, yeah, girl, you so do. I promise not to kick him out next time he comes by. But when he does something that you don't like, you have to say so. He's blunt, you can be as well."

I stayed with Roe until she fell asleep. I needed to get to the cemetery, but these moments with my sister were too precious to pass up. I kissed her hand when Mom walked in, taking her seat beside the bed.

"Nia, stay with Mom and Rose. I'll be back soon."

Nia did as I asked, and I rushed to my room to change.

It was drizzling outside, so I pulled on some tights and a sweater, grabbed my raincoat, shoved on my boots, and headed back outside. As I walked down the path to the cemetery, I reached out with my magic, my wolf spirit, she was how I sensed Draven, I was sure of it. What else could it be? But I didn't feel him anymore.

He must have assumed I was staying in and gone back to his pack. Good.

I didn't want him here.

Sure you don't.

I ignored my inner twisted glutton for punishment and walked through the wide iron gates to the cemetery and pulled up short.

Mom was right, it was so much worse.

The dead patches had spread, and, shit, there was now an obvious ring around the old shed where I'd stored the bones. The dark magic embedded in Charity's bones was leaching out into the soil. The roots of the tree she'd been underneath must have been poisoned by it, and carried it underground right into the cemetery.

I rushed forward and opened the door to the rickety shed and cursed. My ward hadn't held. Her dark magic was still too power-ful, and the ground around the box was black and smelled of rot. It was cloudy, but light still filtered through the windows, and I could see more clearly as my eyes adjusted. The box had several cracks around the bottom edge, and the seal of the lid had been compromised.

I hadn't seen the damage in here when I brought it in. But we'd battled here at the cemetery a year ago. The ground had been torn up in several places and could have easily caused this damage. And I wouldn't be surprised if the roots of the tree hadn't done some of this as well.

I gripped the edge and opened the box—

A force knocked me back, and I hit the wall, my hands flying to my head as voices filled it, so many voices all talking over one another. I fell to my knees, my eyes rolling back in my head, and everything went black.

I was standing in a cave, witches, so many of them stood around me. Their eyes were black, their hair matted and limp, faces pale, skin and bone. They smiled at me with yellowed teeth. Three of them stepped forward. The elder crones.

"Bring Charity to us. Bring our sister home," the crones said as one terrifying voice.

The room spun, and I was floating down a dark tunnel, moving deeper into the cave. I tried to scream, to fight, but hands covered my mouth, held my arms. It was so dark I couldn't see anything, the blackness closing in, suffocating.

I came to a stop and a single candle was lit.

A row of bottles filled with different colored potions.

"You must pay the price. Skin, blood, potion."

My body was jolted, hard.

I gasped, my eyes flying open.

I blinked several times. It was dark. I looked around. I was still in the shed. I'd been unconscious for hours.

And I knew what that vision meant, what I had to do.

I had to take Charity's bones to Shadow Falls, where all dark witches went to be with the crones.

An image of those bottles was still in my head.

Skin, blood, potion.

I had to offer the crones my blood, and I had to drink whatever potions were in those bottles, I knew it without the crones having to spell it out, and I had to go alone.

When a witch turned to dark magic, their remains had to be placed in Shadow Falls to stop what was happening to us right now. To stop the evil from poisoning their family burial grounds. But there was a price, a test that must be taken by a member of the dark witch's coven.

This was the mother's task for me. It had to be.

I didn't know what it had to do with the missing witches yet. Maybe I'd find out when I got to Shadow Falls? But I needed to do this now, before the cemetery was completely destroyed and before more innocent witches were taken.

I stumbled to my feet and searched for a bag.

And before I had too much time to think about what I was about to do.

Chapter Fifteen

Iris

I carefully took out the canvas duffel filled with Charity's remains from the back seat of the car and grabbed a smaller bag with the things I'd need to lay her to rest. Not the most elegant of transportation for her, but there was no way I could carry the box she'd been buried in. I realized after I removed her bones that it was lead-lined, which was probably why there hadn't been any noticeable magic leakage before the box was damaged.

I rubbed my arms when goose bumps lifted. Shadow Falls had that effect on people.

The woods here were all but barren, the trees unhealthy, some dead, all sparse, a result of having so much dark magic pumping into the earth. But it'd be a whole lot worse if the witches here hadn't been laid to rest in the caves.

I locked my car, placed the bags over my shoulder, and started down the path that led to the falls. I'd left Nia with Rose. Anything could happen here tonight, and I wasn't going to risk

Nia being hurt. This wasn't something she could fight or run from. The crones were spirits, and they were evil.

The flashlight I had with me lit the way, and I had to fight not to run back to my car as the sense of dread slowly built around me until it felt like it was being absorbed through my skin, sinking to my bones. I'd never felt anything like it, and I never wanted to ever again.

And god, it grew stronger the deeper I got.

The dark magic saturated this place and was the reason I didn't have to worry about demons attacking me. Even they stayed away.

I heard the falls before I saw them, moonlight glinting off the torrent of water exploding from the top of a sharp cliff. The stone underfoot was slippery, and I clung to the rocky wall along the path that led behind the falls and into the cave.

It was cold and musty inside, the dread so thick it was an effort not to succumb to a panic attack or run away. I had the strangest urge to curl into a ball and sob.

You can do this. You have to do this.

I shone my flashlight around the cavern. There was a dais to the right of me, and I took a closer look. Willow had come here during her own trial, forced to perform a ritual of a different kind. It was exactly as she'd described it, down to the rusty stains. Blood, my sister's included.

I shivered as I flicked the light across the walls, the dug-out sections made by different covens for the purpose of laying the bodies of their own evil family members to rest. Each set of remains was wrapped in linen, now only bones, and placed on their stone ledges.

I didn't stop here, though. The crones had shown me where I needed to go.

The cave went deeper, and my fear spiked when the flashlight lit up the cave I needed to walk down. The light was swallowed by the incredible darkness, and it took every bit of courage I possessed to make myself step toward it.

The air grew cooler, danker as I walked—

Something brushed my shoulder, and I shrieked and spun, aiming my light at it. Nothing. Then someone whispered close to my ear, and I swallowed down my scream. The crones were playing with me, this was all part of the test. If I ran, I failed, and this was the only place Charity's remains could be left safely.

I had to do this for my family, my coven.

My flashlight went out.

I froze and bit my lip to stifle another scream. The darkness was oppressive. I couldn't see an inch in front of me. I shuffled forward blindly as the whispering continued, growing in intensity, vicious, repulsive words that had my pulse pounding so hard I felt dizzy. I thought I'd experienced fear before.

Not even close.

This was my every nightmare come to life.

Something brushed against me again, then again. Tears slid down my face as I ignored every instinct I had and kept moving.

Every step forward felt like a lifetime, not knowing what I was walking toward. Afraid of what the hand I had out in front of me was going to come into contact with.

A faint light ignited ahead.

I focused on that light like a lifeline and carried on, moving deeper into the cave.

A glow was coming from a small room off the main tunnel, and when I walked inside, there was another dais, this one glossy black obsidian, and on the opposite side was a ledge in the stone. There were small bottles lined up, the same ones I'd seen in the vision.

I knew what I had to do because the crones had given me that knowledge. I'd heard whispers about it, of course, among other covens, but no one had ever admitted to being here or doing this.

The council covered up these things, along with the covens themselves. Yes, it was there in our histories. But there was no way

I'd know who had actually done this or how many witches had lost their lives performing this ritual.

I lifted the duffel onto the dais and unzipped it, carefully removing each bone and placing them approximately where they belonged. The other bag held my knife, linen strips, and a jar of soil from our cemetery.

One by one, I sprinkled the bones with dirt, then wrapped them in raw linen, saying the chant that filled my mind. A chant I'd never seen or heard before in my life but instinctively knew.

"Lay to rest, your sister now, take my offering, and hear my vow." More words filled my head, and my pulse thundered in my ears. "On the taking of my mortal blood, your visions I will receive, and if the sun rises while darkness cloaks..." I swallowed, my body shaking with a fear like I'd never known before, as I said the last line. "...forever more, my soul will be yours, and in this cavern deep...I will remain."

In other words, if I didn't make it back out of here before sunrise, I was dead, and the crones would keep my soul for eternity.

I wanted to throw up. I wanted to run out and never come back. But this wasn't just about me. My entire coven needed me to pass this test. If I failed in this, not only would my coven lose their magic, we could lose our cemetery as well. Until Charity was laid to rest properly, we couldn't stop the damage from spreading, not as long as these bones were unbound. They needed to be bound by the kind of magic this place held or there would be no killing the rot seeping into our most sacred earth and the source of so much of our power.

I had no choice. I had to do this.

First—skin.

I stripped off my clothes and placed them on the floor, shivering as goose bumps covered my body, the frigid air soaking right into my bones. I took my small knife from the bag and drew in a desperate breath, the cold, musty air stinging my throat.

Now—blood.

The crones whispered to me, telling me what I needed to do, and I realized that surviving the vision wasn't going to be my only test. Biting back a scream, I sliced the length of each forearm and blood rushed from the cuts into my cupped hands. Shaking, I smeared it all over my body, my face and chest, stomach and thighs, covering myself with my own blood.

I was growing weak; I had to move quickly. I picked up the needle and thread on the stone shelf and repeated the spell the crones again whispered in my ear as I crudely sewed up the slices down my arms. The spell caused the wounds to tingle and burn, stopping the flow of blood before I fully bled out. I finished sewing, and my head spun as I put down the needle.

Now—potion.

I picked up the first bottle with a trembling hand, then removed the cork and forced myself to sip. I was already so weak, and I gasped as pain shot through my body. I needed to take a sip from each one. Shaking hard, stomach churning, I picked up the next and did the same, then the next.

I was on fire, burning, drowning, beaten.

All the ways the crones had been killed over the centuries. I felt their pain, and fear, and rage with each bottle I drank from.

I screamed and dropped to my knees.

An invisible hand shoved me hard, and I fell to my side. I hit my head on the stone floor and my vision flickered in and out a moment before pain sliced through my skull. I gripped the sides of my head as light and darkness flashed behind my lids, the darkness pressing in until the light was suffocated and there was nothing but blackness around me, so dense and thick I couldn't move.

My world spun, and suddenly, I wasn't on the floor anymore. I was above, looking down at myself, my body below, curled in a ball, naked, and covered in blood.

I watched as the ghostly figure of a crone walked from the shadows toward my still form, singing as she slowly crouched down. She reached into the pocket of her brown and tattered cloak and pulled out another needle and thread.

I tried to move, but it was impossible. I wasn't with my body anymore, and I watched in horror as she pressed my upper and lower lids together and started to sew my eyes closed. I screamed, somehow feeling every bit of it, and unable to look away, unable to move, still watching myself from above. She did the same with the other eye, then moved to my mouth.

"Please, no, don't," I cried.

She turned suddenly, looking up at me, the me watching this all happen, and pressed her grubby finger to her lips. "*Shh*," she said.

Then she turned back to my body and sewed my mouth shut with black cotton in a cross-stitch pattern along my lips.

I don't know what I was expecting, a vision that showed me what was coming or what had been. Not this. My soul forced from my body, forced to watch as I slowly perished, as I died. Because that's what was going to happen.

The crone stood and turned to me. I still couldn't move. "What are you doing?" I whispered.

She smiled.

"Was there ever a chance of me passing your test?" Had anyone ever passed it? Or was this the price? A soul in exchange for bringing the bones of a dark witch to this place.

She didn't answer, just laughed and shoved me out of the room. The sound of a stone scraping echoed around me before it slid over the entrance, locking my body inside with the crone and my soul outside in the dark cave.

I turned, spun around, there was nothing but darkness. Something bumped into me, then again, then more. That's when I realized I was surrounded.

Surrounded by souls.

"Hello? What do I do?"

No one spoke.

Instead, they screamed, the tormented souls screaming so loud it was all I could hear. I realized why as my visions began. Blood. So much blood and horror filled my mind. Every fear, every nightmare, played out in my head, so real I smelled it, felt it, breathed it.

I was going to die.

~

Draven

Why did I even try to sleep? It was a waste of time.

I paced the great room for the hundredth time, trying to stop myself from leaving, from going in search of Iris. I had to conquer this because the pull to her had me balancing on the very edge of sanity, and being close to her and not being able to have her made it so much worse.

Who the fuck was I kidding?

Being apart from her made it ten times worse. My wolf constantly howled for her, clawing and fighting to be free. I couldn't take much more.

"You can't fight this, you know that, right?" Asher said behind me.

I'd told her repeatedly to go to her quarters and get some rest. She refused.

"She's your mate. You'll lose your mind if you keep this bullshit up."

I shook my head and gritted my teeth as my wolf shoved harder against my subconscious. "I won't let that happen."

"You're so damn lucky to have found her, Drave. You have no idea, how lucky. Claim her already. Your only other option is severing the tie between you. You're seriously willing to do that?"

My gaze shot to her.

"Those are your choices. The pack needs you." She straightened her spine. "Maybe if you can't bring yourself to do what needs to be done, then I will."

I didn't want to hear this. I knew Ash was just trying to force my hand, to get me to claim Iris with her threat, but her words struck their mark. "You were the one who stopped me from killing her in the first place."

Asher scowled. "Don't get me wrong, I like her. I'd rather we not unlive her, honestly. But what you're doing to yourself... instead of just claiming her?" She shook her head. "You're making a mistake, a huge one. But, I'll do whatever it takes to protect you and the pack if I'm forced to."

I snarled and got in her face. "You will not touch her."

Asher didn't back down, she never did, which was why she was one of my fiercest warriors. Her lips curled up, triumph in her eyes before they filled with regret. "You want her, Drave. Fucking claim her. Because if it's between you and her, I choose you. We all choose you. We need our alpha, whole and sane. You've been through enough. We all have."

"No," I growled.

"I tried to fight it when I first realized Boone was mine and all I did was waste precious time with him that I'll never get back." Her voice grew hard. "But if your mind is made up about this, if you won't claim her, taking her out is our only option."

"No," I roared, louder this time. "You will not touch her."

I paced away, nausea gripping my stomach and not only from the thought of killing Iris. It wasn't just my mind that was in distress, so was my body. I craved her above anything else, above food and sleep, nothing else mattered.

I strode to the window and looked out. Below was the field where our young played during the day, running and hiding among the long grass. They trusted me to keep them safe.

"Your pack loves you, they only want what's best for you.

Don't deny yourself because you think it's what's best for them... or do you think they won't accept her?"

"You think they would? A witch who looks just like the one who hurt us?"

"If you want her, you have to talk to them. I don't know, hell, bring it to a vote. You might be surprised," Asher said. "But you have to end this, one way or the other. I know this fucking sucks, but you have to put your people first."

I didn't answer, because she was right. This did fucking suck.

And If I didn't do something about Iris, and soon, I would be hurting my pack. I'd be letting them down all over again.

Chapter Sixteen

Iris

R ats. They were everywhere.

I screamed as they ate at Rose's corpse. Her body gray and shriveled in her bed. She was dead. *Oh goddess*. She was dead.

NO!

I tried to scare them away as tears streamed down my face, but they wouldn't leave, ignoring me and nibbling at her lifeless body. They bit into my flesh, and I cried out as they surrounded me. Without thinking about it, I called on my power, it had become second nature. "Stop," I commanded.

All the rats around me suddenly stopped what they were doing, backing away from me, and jumping off Rose's bed.

The room spun now, and I was in the woods—Rose, the house gone.

The rats remained—all of them stared up at me, waiting, as if they were under my spell.

This wasn't real, I reminded myself.

The crones were in my head. They were projecting this into my mind, but the rats, they'd changed visions with me. I'd commanded them to stop, and they had, and now they were with me in the next vision. Were they somehow linked to me by my power?

Maybe they were here, or maybe they were in the room with my body.

A figure cloaked in black appeared in the distance, watching me. I stumbled back a step, my heart pounding. He flickered, there one moment, then vanished. I searched the forest around me wildly—he appeared again, closer this time.

Something snarled, the vicious sound coming from the opposite direction. Demons, a lot of them. *They're all just part of the vison,* I told myself. I did my best to ignore my rising terror and focused all my power on the small army of rats staring up at me.

"Do you know the alpha wolf?"

Their little heads nodded.

"Do you know where he lives?"

More nodding.

"Come here," I said to the one closest.

The rat obeyed.

If they were surrounding my body on the cave floor, like I thought...hoped, they were, then my blood was right there.

"You want to please me, don't you?"

I felt his eagerness to make me happy.

"If you roll in my blood, the alpha will scent it, and then you can lead him here to me. That would please me very much."

Another nod.

The demons were drawing nearer, closing in on me.

"Go now, friends, and bring me the wolf."

Draven

Asher walked back into the great room.

"I'm done talking," I said from my spot by the window.

She held up a bottle of bourbon. "I'm done talking as well. Let's get hammered instead. And if nothing else, it might numb the cravings for your witch, for a little while, anyway."

No, it wouldn't. I'd already tried that, more than once. Still, it was better than pacing around the keep aimlessly. "Fine."

"We can get wasted, then go on a demon killing spree," Asher said and grinned.

Sometimes I thought the warrior had a death wish. She pretended that she was fine, but I knew she wasn't. I was there when she felt Boone slip away, and for a while, I thought we'd lose her as well. "If you ever want to talk..."

Someone screamed.

I ran for the door, Ash right behind me.

Anna, one of our females, stood in the middle of the field screaming as rats, at least fifty of them, swarmed around her, heading straight for the keep.

I ran out, trying to divert them, but they didn't stop. What the fuck was this? Asher cursed, kicking at them as they surrounded us.

They stopped suddenly, beady little eyes all staring up at me.

Asher glanced at me. "So...this is fucking weird."

I stomped and waved my arms, but they didn't budge. No, they sat like a pack of little fucking dogs.

One of them scurried up to me. It stopped at my feet, watching, waiting expectantly.

It was dark, but I could see something matted its fur. Was that...

Blood.

A lot of it. The rat didn't appear injured; it just stayed there, staring up at me.

"Draven, what the hell is it doing?" Asher said.

I crouched down. "I don't think the blood is his...." Iris's scent hit me, and my wolf exploded to the surface. "Iris!"

My heart smashed against the back of my ribs as my wolf spun in frantic circles. I needed to find her. She was hurt. She needed me.

The rat turned and headed back the way it came, then stopped and looked back at me.

"I think it wants you to follow," Asher said.

She was right.

Fuck.

Iris had sent them for me. She was using her magic to control them—the same way Charity used to. I growled, shoving Charity from my head, stripped off, and shifted. Asher did the same, along with Dirk and a couple more of my warriors who had come to see what was going on.

The rats turned and ran.

And we followed.

I just hoped I wasn't too late.

It was nearly dawn by the time we reached our destination, a wood, dank and dead and forgotten. Shadow Falls. We never came here. Everything about this place repelled us. This was a place for witches, a place of dark magic, of evil deeds, and death.

What the fuck was Iris doing here?

The rats didn't slow, didn't change course.

Asher was on my right, Dirk on my left, and I felt their trepidation as we neared the falls themselves, as the thunder of water crashing into the river below roared around us. The rats scurried along a rocky path, disappearing behind the massive curtain of water.

You don't have to follow.

I projected the thought to my pack mates.

We've got your back, alpha.

That was Asher, the rest agreeing.

There was no point arguing, they wouldn't let me go in there alone. So I rushed ahead and into the cavern. It was dark, but I ran on, easily following the sound of fifty rats scurrying and squeaking. They ran deeper and deeper, leading us blindly into the depths of the caves.

Until, finally, they stopped, throwing us into a deafening silence.

I waited, listening.

Was this some kind of trap? Panic started to build inside me. What the fuck had I done—

A scratch came from beside me. One of the rats. Was Iris behind the wall?

I shifted and ran my hands around the cavern wall, searching for some kind of opening.

"There's a lip," Asher said beside me. "An opening. This stone is blocking the way."

Iris was behind it. "I can smell her blood."

My warriors shifted as well, moving up beside me and pressing their hands to the massive stone.

"Now," I said and planted my shoulder against it. We pushed, but it barely moved. Witchcraft. It had to be. Iris wouldn't have been able to move this on her own. "Again," I growled as growing panic rocked through me. Iris was behind this fucking slab of rock. She was being kept from me, and she was bleeding.

She could be dying. I could lose her.

A surge of strength filled me, adrenaline pumping hard and fast through my veins. I snarled and pushed with everything I had.

The stone shifted.

Muted light spilled through the crack, and my shoulder popped, but I ignored it and, with another growl, shoved again, my warriors along with me.

It slid open a little more, enough for me to force my way through sideways.

Then I saw her.

"Fuck." My heart stopped at the sight of her.

She was lying on her side, naked and covered in blood. I dropped to the ground beside her. She was alive, I didn't need to touch her to know that, the bond between us was just as strong as ever. I carefully rolled her to her back, searching for the source of all that blood. She didn't move, didn't speak. Her hair was matted with blood, and I brushed it away from her face and groaned in agony.

Oh fuck. Her eyes and her mouth were sewn shut. "Asher!"

She was at my side a moment later, her cry of alarm echoing around the room.

"I need something to cut these threads." I searched the rest of Iris's blood-covered body. *Jesus.* Her inner forearms had been sliced, then hastily sewed back up. How had she survived this? My wolf cried in agony because she still might not.

"Here." Asher held out a small blade.

It was Iris's. I'd seen her with it before. "My shoulder," I said to Ash.

She grabbed my forearm, gripped my dislocated shoulder, planted her foot against the wall, and jerked it back into the socket. I grunted and took the blade from her. My hands shook as I carefully sliced through the stitches along her lips, but there was no way I was attempting her eyes, not with the way I shook.

I needed light and something smaller than this knife. I scooped Iris up. Asher rushed ahead, back out through the gap in the stone, and I passed Iris through, then reclaimed her once I squeezed out after Ash. I held Iris close, taking comfort from the warmth of her skin, the sound of each one of her shallow breaths.

She was alive. And I had to make sure she stayed that way.

We started back the way we had come through the darkness—

the sound of the falls growing louder as we neared the cave opening.

A scream echoed behind us.

A scream that morphed into a roar of fury, building louder by the second, then joined by more voices.

The crones, their dark souls haunted this cavern, that's what I'd been told by other shifters in the area. They'd done this to Iris, and they wanted her back.

"Run," I barked.

The sound grew behind us, louder, closer. I ran blindly, full speed, toward the sound of the falls.

Finally, the beginnings of dusk flickered across the cave walls ahead of us, turning the falls into the deepest of blue, its glow leading us out of this hellhole.

I exploded from the cavern, cradling Iris in my arms, and ran along the stone path, my warriors right behind me. As we stepped off the path, the echoes of rage from within the cavern were silenced.

I looked down at Iris, and fear filled my heart, taking its place beside the rage and pain I'd been carrying around for so long. I didn't want her to die. She may have Selene's face, but she was not that female.

The first streaks of morning sun rose over the horizon and shone across her blood-covered face.

Iris gasped.

Then she exploded into action, fighting as hard as she could in her weakened state.

"*Shh,*" I said. "I've got you."

She stilled. "D-Draven?"

"You're safe now."

She slumped in my arms, instinctively trusting me, even after everything I'd said and done to her. Then her hands lifted to her face. I gently brushed them away. "Don't try to open your eyes, they're still sewed shut. I need to get you back to the keep to take care of it."

Her lips trembled, and she nodded. Then she hung on to me, seeking comfort from me as tears slid out from between the crude stitches.

A moment later, she went limp again, losing consciousness.

"Run ahead," I said to the others. "Find her car. Bring it to the keep." I could get her there faster on foot, cutting through the forest.

They shifted and did as I said.

I held her tighter and ran for home.

She would not die. I wasn't letting her.

Chapter Seventeen

Iris

I woke with a jolt.

"Easy," a deep voice said above me.

Draven.

I tried to open my eyes and cried out in pain.

"Keep your eyes closed, Iris," he said and cupped the side of my face, his skin warm and rough. "They're still sewed shut, remember?"

Everything came rushing back, and my hand shot up to grab his, hanging on to it. I needed him to ground me so I wasn't still floating, stuck in that place, surrounded by lost souls, screaming in fear and pain.

A door opened and closed, and Draven murmured a thank you to someone, then I heard retreating steps and the sound of the door again.

"Y-you came for me. You got me out before sunrise," I rasped.

"The sun rose just as we ran out."

I gripped his hand tighter. "One more minute and my soul would have been stuck in those caves for eternity." I was trembling, relief mixed with the horror of what could have been. "Their test, it was designed for failure. How many witches have been sacrificed doing the same thing?" I swallowed, my throat dry. "You saved me." There was a long silence. "Draven?"

He made a low, rough sound. "Hold still."

His fingers gently moved over my eyes, and I felt the coldness of something metal against my skin. A snipping sound. Nail scissors probably. A tug, the feeling of the stitches being pulled from my skin.

Something damp and warm was gently wiped over my lids. "Okay, open your eyes."

I blinked. My sight was a little blurry as I looked up at Draven. His expression was stony. I glanced down at myself. I was still naked and covered in blood, but he'd thrown a blanket over me.

"You sent the rats to me, didn't you?" he asked.

I had, hadn't I? For some reason, he'd been the first person I'd thought of. The only person I'd needed. "Yes. I mean, I hoped, but I wasn't sure it worked."

His gaze moved over my face, his expression unreadable. "That was clever."

"I have my moments."

A scowl slid over his face. "Last night wasn't one of them. You should never have gone into those caves alone."

"I had to, that's the way it's always been done," I whispered, because the world seemed to have narrowed to just him and me.

"What had to be done? What was so important that you needed to go to that evil place all alone?"

Did he think I was in there doing some dark and twisted deed? God, I didn't want him to think that. He'd saved my life—again. He deserved the truth, and I wanted to give it to him for both our sakes.

"Selene's sister...Charity."

He stilled, every muscle bunching tight.

"The bones I found that night, I discovered they were hers, and because she'd turned to dark magic, I needed to lay her remains to rest at Shadow Falls to save our cemetery." I studied his guarded expression. "You knew her, didn't you?"

His face twisted. "Yeah, I knew her. Selene didn't do what she did to me alone. She and Charity worked together to tear our pack apart. Selene was just a lot better at hiding what she was. Though that probably had more to do with the love potion she gave me than her acting skills." He made a rough sound. "So it was her remains poisoning your cemetery?"

I licked my dry lips. "The box was lead-lined and managed to contain her magic for a long time, but then it was damaged a year ago during some trouble at the cemetery, the same time this happened." I pointed to the markings on my cheek. "And the dark magic still in her bones leaked out, contaminated the roots of the tree she was under, then carried it into our cemetery, poisoning it. Shadow Falls is the only place I could take her where she couldn't cause more damage. The crones, their spirits, they demand you pass a test first. If you pass, you can leave the remains there and go. If you fail, they keep your soul." My throat worked as memories of what I'd seen while I was in there, what I'd felt came rushing back. "If it wasn't for you...I-I would have failed. I would have died."

"I thought you had; there was so much blood. The rats...if you hadn't sent them..." A muscle in his jaw jumped, and his chest expanded as his gaze locked on to mine. "You have the same power as her, as Charity."

I realized I was still holding his hand, and I gripped it tighter. "I do?"

"She could control animals as well."

I blinked up at him, stunned. "I had no idea. I didn't even know Charity existed until I went to the council and searched our family records. She and Selene, they eventually parted ways. In the end, it was Selene and her husband who killed Charity to protect the coven."

That muscle in his jaw tightened again, but he said nothing.

"Selene hadn't turned to dark magic, that was Charity alone. Are you sure she knew what was happening back then? Are you sure it wasn't just Charity?"

He pulled his hand from under mine. "I'm sure." He reached for a tray sitting beside him and grabbed cotton pads and antiseptic. "Close your eyes."

I did as he said, and he gently cleaned them. When he was done, I looked up at him again. His handsome, scowling face made me feel safe.

"Now your mouth," he said.

He got another cotton pad, more antiseptic, and ran it slowly, carefully around my lips. He was looking down, focused on my mouth, his lashes thick and dark against his cheeks. Goddess, he was brutally handsome. He swiped over my lips a second time.

"So what exactly happened a year ago, at your cemetery?" His gaze slid over my damaged cheek.

I swallowed thickly, my palms immediately growing sweaty. "Some twisted people tried to take what was ours. They unleashed evil spirits and tried to bring a monster back from Hell to do it. My boyfriend...Brody, had been using me to get to my family. I didn't realize until it was too late." I shook out my fingers when I realized I'd fisted them so tight they ached. "We fought at the cemetery. He fired his dark magic at me, but missed his mark, which I'm guessing was my heart, and got my face instead. I was left with this." I brushed my fingers over my cheek and shivered as memories flashed through my mind.

He said nothing, the silence stretching out. I couldn't meet his eyes all of a sudden.

"Iris," Draven finally rasped, his voice full of something I was too scared to name.

The door opened, and an older female carrying a bag walked in

A VOW OF RUIN

—their healer. Draven had called for her the last time I was here, but I'd fallen asleep before she arrived. "Right, let's see what you've done to yourself."

Draven stood, and I wanted to reach for him, to keep him close. I resisted, barely. I was glad for the interruption, I hated talking about that awful time, but I could admit, having him close while I did, made it easier.

The other female sat on the side of the bed and lifted one of my forearms. Her hold was soft and her hands warm. She reminded me a little of my gran when she'd been alive.

"Your arms are a mess. I'm going to have to restitch these, honey." Her kind brown eyes met mine. "Did you do this?"

"Yes. I mean, I had to, for a ritual."

She screwed up her face. "Witches and their rituals, always cutting themselves." She shook her head. "You could have died. I need to get in there and clean the wounds out. Best you're asleep for that." She rummaged around in her bag and pulled out a bottle. "Take this, it'll knock you out while I do it."

"No," the word burst from me.

Her brows lifted.

I took a steadying breath. "No," I said again, more gently. "I don't want to sleep." I couldn't bear it, not yet, not after those awful visions.

She gave me an exasperated look. "It's going to hurt like hell."

"It's fine."

"Is there something else you can give her, Mari?" Draven asked, like he knew I was too scared to close my eyes.

Mari turned to him. "I can use something to help numb it, but she's still gonna feel it. You'll need to hold her still."

He nodded and moved back to the bed. That's when I realized he was only wearing a pair of jeans. The button was undone, and his scarred chest was streaked with blood, my blood.

"I'll be fine," I said. Having him that close again was dangerous because I liked him close. I liked it too much.

171

"No, you won't be," Mari said. "And I can't have you jerking and pulling away and hurting yourself even more."

Without a word, Draven slid in behind me, his thick, solid thighs going to either side of mine, then he wrapped his arms around me from behind, taking one of my forearms in his hot, rough-skinned hands.

Mari gathered what she needed, and I barely noticed. I was far too aware of the way Draven's heart was beating against my back and his slow, even breaths beside my ear. And then there was the heat of his body against mine. So much heat. I'd been cold, so impossibly cold. Now the warmth of his skin soaked into mine, going right into my bones. Whatever strength I had washed from me, and I had no choice but to let him hold me up.

He made a growling sound, so low, I didn't even think Mari heard it, and his arms tightened around me a little more.

"Don't let her pull away," Mari said to him.

"It's okay, Marisol will take care of you," he said against my ear, his voice soft, intimate.

I shivered and nodded, unable to speak all of a sudden.

Mari smeared her numbing cream on my forearms, then carefully snipped the rough stitches I'd hastily done. She made a tutting sound and winced a little. "Yep, these will need a good clean out." She placed a towel under my arm, then, using a syringe, she started flushing out the wound.

"That's not so bad," I said.

She nodded. "That's the numbing cream, but I have to go a little deeper now."

Draven's hand tightened under my arm, his other locking around my waist. Marisol pressed on the wound, opening the slice wider. I jerked and instinctively tried to pull away. Draven held me fast. His face pressed against the side of my mine. "It'll be over soon," he said in that calm, soothing voice. "I've got you. You're nearly done."

It hurt like hell, and with him talking to me like that, in a tone of voice I'd never heard from him before, I felt overstimulated. Pain shot up my arm while tingles from his whiskers and his smooth yet rough voice continued in my ear.

When Mari finished, I slumped, realizing I'd held every one of my muscles stiff as she worked. My head rested against one of Draven's shoulders, and he started running his hand over my thigh, massaging lightly, soothingly.

He wasn't being a creeper, he was being a wolf. Affectionate, nurturing, tactile. It was just their natures. And right then, I was the beneficiary of all of that from Draven. Someone was hurt and he couldn't help himself but try to soothe. I didn't kid myself that it meant anything. He may be kind of insane, at least around me, but his pack loved and trusted him.

And this was why.

The male was brutally fierce, deeply loyal—and as he was proving now, capable of providing comfort, even to someone he'd not long ago seen as an enemy.

Mari did the same with the other arm, and Draven held me tight the entire time. She resewed both cuts, which was less painful since her numbing ointment was still doing its job. Else's healing balm would help as well when I got home.

Draven slid out from behind me as Mari finished up, and I missed his heat instantly.

"Thank you so much for this," I said as Mari packed her things. "I owe you. Whatever you need."

She nodded and grinned. "Excellent. I'm sure I'll think of something you can do for me."

I chuckled. "Good, because I meant it."

She winked and walked out, shutting the door behind her. I turned to Draven, who was by the window across the room.

"Thank you. I know you don't think much of me and my coven, and I don't blame you, but you saved my life again and I owe you as well, even more than I did before."

He studied me a moment. "How are you feeling now?" he asked, ignoring what I'd just said.

"Still a bit out of it." I felt nauseous and dizzy, but I was pretty sure I could drive. I needed to get home. "If you could help me to my car, I'll be heading home. I don't want to impose on you any longer than I have to. You've already done so much."

He slid his hands into the pockets of his jeans, which tugged them enticingly lower, and tilted his head to the side. "Oh no, little witch, you won't be going anywhere."

Chapter Eighteen

Draven

"What do you mean, I won't be going anywhere?" Iris stared at me wide-eyed.

The way she said the last two words of that sentence, deep and growly, was obviously supposed to be an imitation of me, but there was no missing the alarm there as well.

I moved toward her but stopped myself from saying what I wanted to say because her reaction to what I had just said had kicked off her fight-or-flight instincts, despite her mocking tone. I could smell it, her fear. It was like she'd instantly thrown up a protective wall.

I may not know much when it came to relationships, but I knew saying the words flying around my head right then would only freak her the fuck out. They freaked me out, honestly.

"You're not well enough to travel," I said instead. "I'll contact your family and let them know you're safe. I'll take you home later...after you've rested some more."

I thought I could fight it, deny it, what was between us. I was fooling myself.

Iris Thornheart belonged to me.

She was *mine*.

My mate.

Resistance had only caused harm. I hadn't been able to stay away from her no matter how hard I'd tried, not when I knew she was putting herself in danger, and my sanity was at its breaking point because of it. Ash was right, my pack needed an alpha who could take care of business, not one constantly pining for his mate. Ending her life wasn't an option, and if I was honest, never truly had been, not once I knew who she was, or more importantly, wasn't. Which meant there was only one thing I could do.

Claim her.

If she was with me, not only could I satisfy this unstoppable hunger for her, but I would have some control over her, I could keep her safe.

Christ, the things she'd just told me. She'd almost fucking died a year ago. Some piece of shit had hurt her. He'd tried to take her from me. I could have lost her before I ever found her.

The urge to keep her here, to not let her leave, grew stronger.

But I realized now, I'd have to ease her into this. Telling her she was mine and then expecting her to offer herself to me was probably not going to go down well with my feisty little witch.

She watched as I moved closer. "No, I wouldn't want to impose."

"You're not." Now that I'd finally accepted my fate, my wolf calmed. My gaze moved over her. I liked the way she looked in my bed. "I think you know me well enough to know I'd tell you if you weren't wanted here." No, I didn't see Selene when I looked at Iris, not like I had before. They were nothing alike, but that didn't mean I trusted this female yet.

I could look past who her ancestors were, though, if I got to wake up next to her warm body every morning. If I had her there, naked and wanting, in the middle of the night when I woke hard and hungry for my female.

Because stroking myself to thoughts of her hadn't been enough. It was never enough.

"This is true. You certainly don't hold back," she said and winced. "But I need a shower. I can't rest like this."

"No problem." I closed the space between us. She did need a shower. Her scent was fucking with my wolf. I couldn't breathe easy when each inhale was full of the scent of my female's blood. I scooped her up in my arms. She gave a little cry of alarm, and I ignored it and carried her to my bathroom.

"I can walk," she said.

"Sure you can."

"I can."

She was leaning on me, struggling to even hold her damned head up. "You lost a lot of blood. If I set you on your feet, you'll fall on your sweet little ass," I said and grinned when her eyes narrowed.

"It's probably best you don't look at my ass."

I sat her on the edge of the tub. "I've seen a whole lot more than your ass, petal."

"Petal?" Her cheeks turned pink.

I shrugged. It suited her as far as I was concerned. Pretty, color-ful, delicate. I got the temperature right in the shower and shoved my jeans down.

"Whoa, dude! Put it away."

I ignored her protests, and my wolf preened at the way her gaze slid over my body. "You're covered in blood, and you can barely stand. The bath is out, unless you like the idea of soaking in your own filth, and you need someone to hold you up in the shower, so you're stuck with me." I stood in front of her. "Stop being a prude, let's go."

Her cheeks grew even darker, but her eyes spat fire. I liked that, the fire. Seeing her so defeated earlier had twisted something deep inside me.

"I'm not a prude," she said. "Do you have any idea how often witches get naked?"

"Exactly, so let go of the damned blanket and let's get you cleaned up." *Before my wolf loses its shit and lets you know exactly how badly I want you.*

She straightened her shoulders and let the blanket drop. I'd seen her naked before, of course, but now that her life wasn't on the line, I had to will my dick to stand the hell down. Pretending I was unaffected was not fucking easy.

I lifted her again and stepped under the spray, putting her head under it to wash the mud and blood from her hair. Getting her wounds wet wasn't ideal, but it couldn't be helped, which was why Mari had left the bandages off until she was cleaned up.

Iris sputtered. "Are you trying to drown me?" She slapped me on the chest.

A chuckle escaped before I knew it was coming.

"This is funny to you?"

"Sure," I said and lowered her to her feet, keeping my arm around her waist so she didn't fall. My laugh died, though, when my arm slipped higher, and her breasts were suddenly resting on my forearm, all warm and heavy and slippery.

I growled and grabbed for the shampoo, then squirted some on her head and went at her hair.

She squawked. "I'd like some hair left at the end of this, if that's all right."

"Be quiet and suck it up," I said and tried to ease up a bit. I'd never done anything like this before. I'd certainly never washed a female's hair. The ones I fucked took their pleasure and left. There was no lingering or showering.

"*Ouch!* Watch the head."

"Don't be a baby."

"How can you not feel the giant egg there? I hit the floor hard earlier."

I moved my hand over her head carefully. *Shit.* There was an egg.

On an indrawn hiss, Iris's hand shot out, and she groped wildly. "What now?"

"You got shampoo in my eyes."

Fuck.

I quickly grabbed the washcloth I brought in with me, held it under the spray, and carefully pressed it to her eyes. "Hold it there while I rinse your hair." Her eyes were already causing her pain and now I'd made it worse. "Sorry," I muttered, feeling like an idiot.

"It's fine. Let's just get this over with."

I unhooked the shower head, doing it that way instead. At least I had more control and could avoid her face and stitched arms more easily. "Better?"

She nodded.

I pumped out some conditioner, and this time was more careful, running my fingers through her long hair, making sure to avoid the bump on her head, then rinsed it out.

I took the washcloth from her eyes next and tilted her head back, inspecting them. She blinked up at me, and I had to fight not to kiss her. The kiss we'd shared was seared into my brain, onto my fucking lips. I thought about it constantly, and I wanted a taste of her again more than anything.

"How are your eyes now?"

She licked her lips, and there was no stopping the sound of hunger that escaped me.

"They're okay," she said.

I rinsed the washcloth before dragging it one-handed over the soap a few times, then carefully cleaned the remaining blood from her face, then rinsed again. Next up was her body, and I slid the cloth slowly over her shoulder.

"I can do that," she said breathlessly.

I shook my head and ran it down her arm. "It's my job," I said, because that was what my wolf was projecting the loudest, and I couldn't stop myself from saying it.

"Your job?" She looked up at me, all pink-cheeked and sexy and, goddammit, adorable.

My female was irresistible.

"I found you, I take care of you," I said improvising.

"I don't think that's a thing." She licked her lips again.

"It is to me." And then I couldn't hold back anymore. I dipped my head slowly, and when she didn't pull away, I pressed my lips to hers and kissed her softly, so very softly.

She was no doubt sore from what had happened, but I couldn't stop myself from tasting her mouth again. And just that soft, barely-there touch set me on fucking fire. I ignored the driving beat in my chest and the throb of my groin, though, and lifted my head, making myself stop, and looked down at her.

"W-what are you doing?"

"Kissing you."

She blinked once, twice. "Well, yes, I worked that out for myself. I'm just not sure that's a great idea."

I shrugged and carried on with what I was doing, running the cloth down her chest and over one of her full breasts. "Don't read too much into it. I'm a wolf, I'm affectionate."

"So, you kiss Marisol like that as well?"

I shrugged again, my lips twitching.

"Your hand is on my boob."

"It has blood on it." I moved the cloth over it, then did the same to the other side and had to fight my smile of triumph when she sucked in a breath. "So does this one."

She rolled her eyes, even as her face got darker and her breathing grew choppier. "Okay, Mr. Suds, I think they're clean enough now."

I said nothing and washed her belly and thighs. She wasn't the only one having trouble breathing normally. But as I was finishing up, I felt her weight lean on me more heavily, and I could feel her limbs trembling. She was exhausted, in pain, and I was in here feeling her up.

Fuck.

I quickly rinsed her down, switched off the water, and grabbed a towel. I slung it around her and picked her up, carrying her back to the bedroom. She didn't protest this time, and that told me more than anything just how tired she was.

Sitting her on the bed, I got one of my shirts and pulled it over her head, then used the towel to wring as much water from her hair as I could. I shoved back the covers and helped her lay back.

She opened her mouth, to argue about something, no doubt. "Sleep, Iris," I said, getting my words in first and started to pull away.

She grabbed my hand. "I'm scared to close my eyes," she whispered.

I could only imagine what they'd done to her in that cave, but it had to be bad for her to admit that to me. I could see the terror in her beautiful eyes. Horrors I could only imagine.

"Will you stay with me? Wake me if I look like I'm having a nightmare?"

"Yeah," I said before she even finished asking, because there was nowhere else I wanted to be. I'd planned on staying in here with her, anyway. My wolf wouldn't allow me to do anything else.

I climbed onto the bed beside her. That probably wasn't what she had in mind, there was a chair right there, but I needed to be closer to her than that.

She didn't tell me to back off, though. No, she pressed deeper into me when I moved in behind her. Giving in to the all-consuming force between us.

"Thank you, Draven," she said softly a few minutes later, her voice slightly slurred from fatigue. "I'll repay you for all you've done. F-for everything, I promise..."

"*Shh*, don't worry about any of that now, petal. Just close your eyes, I'm not going anywhere."

She nodded and her eyes were closed a moment later, her breath slowing, her body pressing deeper still into mine.

I watched her sleep.

There was nothing that could pull me from this room at that moment. It scared me and filled me up in a way I'd never experienced before. How could this little witch, this pain in my ass, the ancestor of my most hated enemies, be the one to bring me the kind of peace I'd only dreamed about while trapped in those woods for over three hundred years.

I didn't understand it. But it was fact.

She was mine.

When she woke with a scream an hour later, I pulled her into my arms and held her tight. "I'm here, go back to sleep. No one's going to hurt you here. I won't let them."

She was out again a moment later, but this time she hung onto me in return, like she had after I'd found her, as if seeking comfort from me was the most natural thing in the world—as if I was her lifeline.

Iris needed me. Almost as much as I needed her, of that, I was positive.

And I was keeping her.

No matter what.

Chapter Nineteen

Iris

I was so warm.

My sleepy brain cleared, and I became aware of the hard, naked flesh pressed against me.

Draven.

He was still there, like he'd promised. He'd held me tight all night as dreams of the caves and the crones, of Brody, had invaded my mind and tormented me all night long. But every time I woke, Draven was there. He'd never left me, not once.

I turned my head on the pillow, and blew out a shaky breath. He was brutally beautiful, raw, and untamed. The sexiest male I had ever laid eyes on.

He'd kissed me again in the shower.

And I'd liked it way too much.

My gaze moved over his chest. Claw and teeth marks, gouges, scarred his skin. Scars he'd gotten protecting his pack, fighting demons.

What would it be like to be one of the people he cared about, one of the people he loved? Sudden and fierce panic fired through me. I shouldn't be here. I couldn't do this. All the awful things Brody had said to me, done to me, shot through my mind.

There was no missing the connection between Draven and me, the obvious attraction, but I couldn't do this to myself again. I wouldn't. No, Draven wasn't Brody, but there was a whole lot of messed-up stuff between us that could not be ignored.

Biting back a groan, I eased carefully out of bed.

Draven muttered something and rolled to his back, and I froze in place. I bit my lip, then winced because they were still tender. He didn't wake, though, and my gaze skimmed over him again. Goddess, he was gorgeous, lying there. That richly tanned skin, the muscles on top of freaking muscles. And I liked his hands, a lot, they were large and rough and always warm.

Stop.

I tore my eyes from him and rushed to the other side of the room. This felt cowardly, but he looked so tired. Waking him would be a shitty thing to do, right?

Leaving without saying goodbye after he saved your ass would be an even shittier thing to do.

I ignored the voice in my head and listened to my heart that was currently beating out of my chest, telling me to run.

I found some workout shorts in his drawer and slipped them on, knotting them at the waist to hold them up, then grabbed my car keys and phone that were now sitting on his dresser, and with one last look at the sleeping alpha, got the hell out of there.

"Nice outfit," someone said as I hit the bottom of the stairs.

Asher. She was sitting in the great room.

"Yep, stunning," I said and held up my phone. "Can I have Draven's number?" I was running away, yes, but texting him a thank-you note would hopefully soften the blow of me taking off while he slept.

"Why don't you ask him for it yourself?"

"He's asleep, and I didn't want to wake him."

Asher started for the stairs.

"Please, don't wake him. He looked seriously wiped. And I need to get home, but I want to thank him again for everything he did...and you, too, of course. It's thanks to all of you that I'm going home to my family at all."

Asher watched me for several long seconds, then held out her hand. I gave her my phone, and she tapped in Draven's number. "He's going to be pissed you left," she said as she handed it back to me.

I knew that already. "I'm sure he'll get over it."

Her gold gaze stayed on me, and she tilted her head to the side. "He won't." Her lips curled up a little. "Don't be surprised if he comes for you as soon as he wakes."

Something sizzled inside me because I knew it, didn't I? That Draven would come after me, and deep inside I thought I might want him to. Yep, I was seriously messed up, which was exactly why I needed to get the hell out of here. I needed to get my head on straight, and fast.

I shoved my phone back in my pocket. "You guys are close, right? Make him see that chasing after me is a mistake. This obsession he has for me...it isn't good for either of us." Which was the truth, no matter how attracted I was to the alpha.

Asher tossed her head back and laughed.

"I don't see how that's funny."

She wiped a tear from her eye. "You will." She looked up at the ceiling and cocked her head. "You better get going. I can hear him stirring."

Shit.

I ran for the door, and Asher's laughter followed me. I flipped her off, which only made her laugh harder, and rushed out to my car.

The road was bumpy, and there were a bunch of potholes, but

I made it out to the main road without Draven catching up to me, then I floored it all the way home.

∼

Mags pulled the front door open before I could reach it, and Nia tore around her to get to me.

"What the hell are you wearing?" Magnolia said as I walked in, eyeing Draven's huge T-shirt and shorts. "Some wolf called and told us where you were, but they didn't...Oh, shit, what happened to your face?" Mags grabbed my hand. "And your arms!"

Nia whined, and I crouched down. "I'm okay, sweet girl. I promise." Nia said nothing, instead she pressed into my side, her body trembling. She was scared. I'd scared her.

I could only imagine how I looked. The rest of the family heard Magnolia and rushed into the entryway, including Willow.

"I'm okay." I had a lot to tell them, and I wasn't looking forward to it.

I was pulled into the kitchen, and Else pushed me into a seat. Rose was on the chaise, and her eyes filled with tears when she looked at me. "Iris," she whispered.

I buried my fingers in Nia's fur to calm my familiar. "I'm okay, Roe—"

Mom cried out. "Else! I need the healing balm."

"Already got it," my great aunt said, handing it to Mom.

"What did you do to yourself?" Mom said as she undid the bandages that Draven had put on me while I slept. She gasped. "W-why would you do this?"

Else froze and her gaze shot from my arms to me. "There's only one ritual that requires cuts like these."

I swallowed, my mouth suddenly dry, terror and pain washing over me all over again from just the memory of being in that place. "I have some things I need to tell you," I said.

I'd hoped, but taking Charity's remains to Shadow Falls wasn't the end of my task. But the vines twisting around my thigh, hadn't moved, I'd checked in the car before I came in, and Amy, Imogen, and Marina were still missing.

I looked up at my family, my heart in my throat. "The tree that fell...I felt a pull to go there. I found a box and there was a body... bones. Her name was Charity, and she was Selene's twin sister." Everyone stared at me with varying degrees of shock. I couldn't keep this from them any longer, not now. "I checked our records. Selene had crossed Charity's name out in blood. She'd been using dark magic. Selene killed her, buried her in a lead-lined box, but it was damaged." I turned to Mom. "Her bones were poisoning our cemetery."

"You took her to Shadow Falls," Else said, face draining of color.

"Yes."

Mom cried out and gripped the chair beside her.

Else moved to stand in front of me, then took my face in her hands, her eyes glistening with tears. "How are you still alive, Iris?"

Mom sobbed, and so did Rose. Magnolia and Willow lost it, Willow yelling and Mags cursing a blue streak.

"Draven," I whispered. My family's reaction making it hit home even harder that I almost died. "He came for me. He saved me."

I'd woken every half hour since I came to bed, the nightmares persistent and utterly terrifying. But that wasn't the reason I was awake this time.

Someone was in my bedroom with me.

I flicked on the lamp and froze, my heart damn near exploding in my chest.

Draven stood there in the dark.

Instead of barking or growling, Nia jumped off the bed and

trotted over to him, pleased to see him. Little traitor. She'd taken a shine to the alpha the moment they'd met.

"You left," he said.

I stared at him in disbelief. "I needed to get home, I told you that. What the hell are you doing in my room? And how did you get in? The house is warded."

He watched me with a look that was full of accusation, like I was the one in the wrong. "I wish you hadn't done that," he said ignoring me.

I couldn't believe this was happening. "Have you just been standing there watching me sleep? How long have you been here?"

He stepped forward, the light from the lamp finally revealing his handsome face. "A while."

"You're nuts, you know that, right?"

"Yes," he said.

"Okay, so how about telling me why you're in my room and how you got in?" My belly did this weird flip as something taunted me in the back of my mind, a feeling, a knowing. I didn't understand it, not fully, it was something I'd been afraid to examine too closely.

"I wanted to check on you," he said as if it were perfectly normal to come into a female's room and just stand there watching her sleep. "Willow let me in earlier when I told her the same thing. I guess she assumed you wanted me to stay. She didn't tell me to leave."

Oh my god! "Why would she do that?" Willow was just as certifiable as Draven was. I didn't understand her obsession with trying to find me a mate. After sharing what happened at Shadow Falls, how Draven had shown up and saved me after I sent rats to him for help, she'd obviously gotten the wrong idea.

"She thinks we're lovers," Draven said, confirming my own thoughts.

Nia was still at his side, and Draven patted her, his large rough hand running over her fur. My girl loved it. She loved him, I could feel it. And that only proved that he had no intention of harming me. Nia would be losing her mind if he was a threat to me in any way.

It wasn't just Nia who knew that, though.

No, he wouldn't hurt me, not now. He'd saved me multiple times. Taken care of me, and I appreciated it, but this still wasn't happening. It didn't matter that I was attracted to him. It would never work between us.

"You need to leave," I said. "I'm indebted to you for all you've done. I owe you so much, but you need to stop doing things like this. Stop following me. Whatever you think is happening here, it can't...it won't."

One moment he was across the room, and the next, he was in front of me. "You know what's happening here, Iris. If you would stop fucking running from me for five minutes and allow yourself to feel it, you'd know exactly why I'm here and why I can't just walk away."

I shook my head in denial. "I don't know what you're talking about. I don't want to know..."

"You were hurt by a male not worthy of you. I understand why this scares you, better than anyone. I know why you're afraid, but there is no fighting this. I've tried, believe me, but this is happening."

"No..."

"You're my mate, Iris."

I froze, my heart going wild in my chest. "You're wrong."

He held my gaze, then slowly, so damn slowly, dipped his head to the space between my shoulder and neck and breathed in deep. "I know your scent. Your voice, the warmth of your skin," he rasped against my ear. "The sound of your breathing when you sleep soothes me. Your body fits against mine like you were made to be there, because you were, little witch. You were made for me. I know it, my wolf knows it. You are mine, Iris Thornheart, and I've come to take you home."

~

Draven

Iris looked up at me with alarm. "You can't be serious."

I didn't answer. I didn't need to. She knew the truth as well as I did, she was just in deep denial. So much for easing her into it.

"You need to go back to your pack and get some help because you're wrong."

My pack was behind me in this. I'd done as Asher had suggested and taken it to a vote. Some weren't happy about it, but she'd been right, my people wanted their alpha happy and whole.

I brushed my thumb over her cheek, everything inside me calling out for her, roaring in my mind, my body. "I'm not wrong. It's impossible. This isn't something you can get wrong."

She pulled away from me and shook her head. "Well, I'm sorry, but I didn't choose it and I don't want it."

My wolf grew agitated, urging me to take her. To just pick her up and take her home to my keep. I was struggling not to listen to it as a panicky feeling rose inside me. I needed her. I needed her to be mine more than my next breath.

She stared up at me, eyes wide, the pulse in her throat throbbing. She was lying to me and herself. She felt it, too. I slid my fingers over her shoulder and lightly gripped the side of her throat. "Iris...Please." The words were dragged from me, desperate, needy, soul bearing.

She was trembling. "I...I can't."

"Please," I said again. Christ, begging her to accept me.

Her lip trembled, and I growled, pulled her in close and kissed her, kissing away her denials.

She whimpered against my lips and tried to pull away, but I held her tighter, claiming her mouth, kissing her deeper, harder. In moments, she went from shoving at my chest to yanking me closer. I growled and lifted her from her bed, then, taking two steps, pressed her against the wall.

"You may not want to give in to this," I said against her perfect, full lips, "but you need it. You need me as much as I do you." I kissed along her jaw. "Give in, petal."

"I can't," she said, panting. "We aren't good for each other."

I lifted my head and cupped her cheek, sliding my thumb between the flushed, heated skin and the cool, black markings there. "You don't know that."

"I know I remind you of Selene, the person you hate most in this world, the person who hurt you and your pack." She shook her head. "I'd have to be an idiot to get into any kind of relationship with you."

"If I can look past who you're related to, you can get over these fears you have. I don't look at you and see her, not anymore." That was mostly true. No, I didn't see Selene, but there was still wariness. It was hard to let go of three hundred years' worth of anger and hatred. I'd conquer it, though. We just needed time together.

She licked her lips, and her gaze slid from mine. "I said no."

Her words were final. She meant it. She wouldn't have me. "Denying me and our connection will have repercussions."

"I'm...I'm okay with that," she said and pushed at my chest.

Christ, I was close to dropping to my knees and begging for real, but there was fear, real and stark in her eyes. Iris wasn't afraid of me; she pushed and goaded me, fought with me. No, the male who had hurt her, he was behind that look in her eyes, and it was enough to make me take a step back, to let her go. "You're making a mistake."

"Maybe, but this is the way it has to be." Her lip trembled again. "Now, I need you to leave."

If she thought I'd just give up, she was wrong. I needed her...we needed each other. "I'll go," I said. "For now. But you need me for this task you're doing."

"I have no idea what my task is anymore. Nothing makes sense." She hugged herself and looked out the window to the night sky.

I could feel her frustration, that fear, even stronger now. It rolled off her, and I had to stop myself from pulling her back into my arms. My wolf wanted to comfort her badly. "Iris..."

"Please...just go."

I swallowed down my growl of frustration and did as she asked.

This isn't finished, little witch. I promise you that.

And as I walked away, I knew exactly what I had to do to get what I wanted, what we both wanted if she'd only allow herself to see it, to feel it. She was going to hate me for it, for a while at least, but she hadn't given me any other choice.

I needed to claim her.

And I couldn't wait any longer.

Chapter Twenty

Iris

I watched Draven go.

This couldn't be happening.

He believed what he'd said—that I was his mate.

My heart thundered in my chest. Could he be telling the truth?

There was no denying the incredibly strong pull I had to him. Against all my better judgment, I wanted him. I wanted to be close to him.

It was fucked up, wrong, illogical.

I paced to the other side of my room and back. Draven and I couldn't be more unsuited.

I looked down. My hands were shaking. Brody's hated face filled my mind again, as it did so often, and I shook my head, forcing the image away. He'd love this. Watching me squirm. And he'd love that I was scared out of my mind. Terrified of what this all meant.

Brody used to say he liked when I was scared because it gave him an excuse to hold me. But that wasn't it. No, he just liked me scared. Period. It turned him on, made him feel powerful.

What if Draven was right? Could we truly be mates? The answer echoed through my mind, and I grabbed for the doorframe.

My thigh tingled, the markings the mother gave me suddenly making themselves heard.

I closed my eyes. *Not again. Not now.*

But that feeling was there once more, and this time even stronger. I had no choice but to let it guide me. As much as I would rather stay in bed and pretend the last forty-eight hours hadn't happened, I had to go with this feeling. I needed to pass this goddamn task.

I looked down at my thigh. The markings were closer now than they'd been earlier today.

Time was running out.

Nia followed me out the door and down the stairs. I slid my feet into my boots, pulled on my coat, and walked out into the night. The moon was full and the air crisp. I almost expected to find Draven still here, but there was no sign of him, and I didn't feel him either.

The thought stopped me in my tracks. That wasn't freaking normal. Before he'd shown up, I hadn't gone around just sensing people willy-nilly.

He was right, wasn't he?

I'd tried to ignore the feeling building inside me, but I couldn't anymore.

We were...*shit*. We were mates.

I shoved it away.

Now was not the time to panic.

The tingling across my thigh increased, and I let it guide me. Nia and I rushed along the path toward our cemetery. I was being called back to the same place I'd found Charity, wasn't I? The feeling of urgency was overwhelming. Bram and Art had removed the tree, but the hole beside the path was still there. I walked around it, the feeling that this was where I needed to be reaching fever pitch. There was a small wooded area on either side of the path, and I moved deeper into it.

What felt like an alarm wailed in my head as my boots sank into soil that should be hard-packed like everywhere else but wasn't.

"Nia, stay on the path, keep watch."

Nia protect Iris. Nia keep watch.

"Good girl." I shone my phone's flashlight at the ground. The earth had recently been turned over. I crouched and propped my phone against a rock on the ground, then brushed away the dead leaves. My gut churned as I scraped some of the soil away. More. Until I was digging frantically with my bare hands. My stitches pulled, and my arms ached, but I didn't stop.

I touched something. Canvas?

I scraped away more dirt, exposing the corner of the heavy fabric, and pulled it back. The stench hit me before I saw her face.

I stumbled back, gasping for air.

But I knew this was what I'd find, hadn't I? As soon as I felt that soft soil, I knew another body was here. God, it was unrecognizable. Maggots had cleaned away most of the flesh on their face, but they were wearing woman's clothes. And these weren't old bones this time. Whoever this was hadn't been here that long.

I couldn't hide this. This was too big. It may be my task, but I needed to tell my family, and I needed to call the council. A witch had been murdered and somehow placed on our property without us knowing.

Hours later, the body had been removed by Ren's parents, who were both morticians, and identified through dental records. Imogen Lewis. One of the missing witches.

What the hell was going on? And why had she been buried on our property? A cold knot formed in my stomach. The mother had tasked me to find these girls, and I'd failed, I'd failed Imogen. I was failing everyone.

"It would be easier if you'd let us give you the serum. We can clear your names and start looking for the real culprits," Councilor Trotman was saying.

"What serum?"

The older Black man aimed his warm brown eyes at me. "It's essentially a truth serum, and the quickest and most effective way to eliminate you as suspects. I don't know why she was buried here, but I've known this family a long time, I don't think—"

"That they're capable of murder? They killed my son in cold blood," Sapphire said, walking up to join us. "They're capable of anything."

Isaac's mother hated us more than he did, and that was a whole lot of hate.

"That's not what happened and you know it, Sapphire," Councilor Trotman said. "Let's not dredge up the past."

She ran her hands down her cream slacks. "It was only a year ago, Nathan. It's still very much the present for my family."

"She needs to leave," Else said. "I don't trust her and her creepy son as far as I can throw them. They probably put that poor girl there as revenge."

Sapphire flushed. "How dare you."

"Don't try the Miss Innocent act with me, you old bag," Else fired at her.

Sapphire looked like she was about to tackle Else. Councilor Trotman stepped between them. "I think it's best if you leave, Sapphire. This is a sensitive issue, and the last thing we need is the two of you arguing." She marched off and he turned to Else and Mom. "Do you agree to take the serum? All of you?"

Else looked at Mom, who nodded. "But not Rose. She's too unwell and I won't put her through it."

"Of course," Trotman said. "She wouldn't be physically capable of this in her condition, anyway."

"Fine, when are we doing it?" Else asked.

"Today. The sooner the better."

The serum tasted like strawberry, something I hadn't expected but appreciated.

"Is your name Iris Endora Thornheart?" Councilor Trotman asked me.

"Yes." The truth was pulled from me all on its own. Even if I wanted to lie, I couldn't.

"Did you know Imogen Lewis?"

"Yes. But only as a passing acquaintance."

"Did you know her body was buried on your property?"

"No."

"Did you kill Imogen or know who did?"

"No."

The councilor stood back. "That's all of you, well, except for Rose. I'm satisfied that none of you were involved in this."

Nathan Trotman was a good man, unlike some on the council, and we were lucky he'd been the one who arrived on the scene first.

He gave us a sheepish look. "I need to warn you, the affects will take a few hours to wear off and will continue to grow stronger before it leaves your system. You may feel compelled to reveal things you ordinarily never would. So best you avoid going anywhere where there's a lot of people." He grinned. "Things could get awkward."

Awesome.

"Thanks, Nathan," Else said. "I'll see you out. You know, you have a great butt. Joan's a lucky lady."

"Why thank you, Else," Trotman said with a chuckle.

"No worries."

Mags giggled.

Okay, this stuff was no joke.

As intrusive as the serum was, I was glad we did it. We didn't need everyone thinking we were kidnapping and murdering witches. No one could question that now. That was the good news. The bad news was my task had just escalated from finding Amy and Marina and catching a kidnapper—to hunting down a cold-blooded killer.

Judging by the looks on my family's faces, they'd worked that out as well, and as much as they wanted to, they couldn't help me.

Else walked back in as Mom paced around, her face flushed, her eyes bright with fear, with anger. "Why? Why would she do this?"

"Who?" Willow asked.

Mom planted her hands on her hips. "The mother!"

The room went silent. We did not talk shit about the mother, not out loud. That was a risk none of us had ever been willing to take, but the serum was making it hard for Mom to keep how she was feeling inside.

"Mom..."

"I hate her," Mom cried. "I hate that bitch and what she's doing to us!"

Shit.

"I know she's a bitch, Daisy, but you can't say that." Else frowned, then cursed, then clamped her hand over her mouth.

"Everyone, stop talking!" Mags yelled.

I sure as hell wasn't feeling any love toward the goddess either. And I had a very strong urge to share as well. Willow clamped her hand over my mouth, stopping me as soon as my lips parted.

"This is going to get worse before it gets better," she said. "Everyone split up. Go to your rooms or for a drive, whatever, but somewhere no one will hear you."

In other words, if you want to keep your secrets a secret, then get the hell gone now. And I had a secret, a big one. Draven filled my head, and I knew I was minutes from spilling the beans. I was not ready to share this bit of information with my entire family yet.

Mom, Else, and Mags took off, going to their rooms, but that wasn't enough for me. I rushed outside and got in my car.

I didn't even know where I was going, just that I needed to make sure I didn't start telling everyone about Draven. As Nia and I hit the road, my stomach rumbled, which wasn't surprising. I'd found Imogen in the middle of the night; it was now late afternoon and I still hadn't eaten.

When I hit the city's outskirts, I took a detour through Big Sam's drive-through. That should be safe. Order, then get the hell gone. "Can I have a Sam's double cheese and bacon, fries, and a large Coke."

"Sure, anything else?" the guy asked.

"No, thank you. But I have to say, you have a great voice. Has anyone told you that?"

"Uh...no."

Shut up. "It's deep. It's actually quite sexy. I bet you get a lot of girls swooning over your voice. I'm not, I already like someone else, he has a sexy voice as well."

Silence.

My face flushed hot. I couldn't believe I had just said all of that. "Um...you can just go ahead and cancel that order."

More silence, then, "Okay."

I guess that meant I could never have a Sam's burger ever again for the rest of my life. I drove through and got the hell out of there. Driving to the city had been a huge mistake.

Everyone was still in their rooms when I arrived back at the house, thank the goddess, so I sent Nia to Rose's room, so she had someone with her, someone who wouldn't be tempted to spill all their secrets, and rushed back out of the house.

I took the path through the cemetery and out the other side to the field at the back.

The air was crisp, but the late afternoon sun had a little warmth in it. Exhaustion hit me, so I lay down on the grass. I'd just wait out the serum here.

I thought about Amy and Marina...of Imogen, as I stared up at the clouds.

My mind raced. So much had happened in such a short time. Already, I didn't recognize myself, my life, and this whole nightmare had barely just begun.

How was I going to do this? I felt inadequate and ill prepared. I was just me. I wasn't some crime-busting badass. I was definitely going to get myself killed. Something soft and furry brushed my hand. I glanced down. One of the little wild rabbits that lived in the field was pressed up against me. I gently stroked it. "Hello there." Several more hopped over.

Friend.

It was harder to read wild creatures, but that was the gist of what I was receiving from them. They considered me a friend; they trusted me. I lay still and closed my eyes, trying to control the rising fear.

Somehow, sheer exhaustion most likely, I drifted off.

"What the fuck are you doing now?" a familiar male voice snapped.

I jumped. I hadn't heard him approach. I kept my eyes closed. I'd known Draven would make an appearance when I came out here, hadn't I? That's the real reason I chose this place to rest, because this was the place where I first saw him. He'd approached in his wolf form then, and he'd made it very clear he hated me.

"I'm resting," I said, sounding as weary as I felt. "And you scared away the rabbits."

His boots thumped against the ground as he moved closer, and I heard the creak of leather as he sat.

"It's dangerous lying out here. You're still recovering." There was a pause. "And what is it with you and little furry animals?"

"They're drawn to me because of my power. They trust me

and feel a connection with me. And my arms are almost healed thanks to Else's balm," I said, opening an eye, then closing it again. "You're not naked. Shame, you look good with nothing on." I blushed, but there was no taking it back now.

He went silent.

"You'll have to excuse some of the shit that comes out of my mouth. I've had some truth serum because I found another dead body on our property. One of the missing witches. We took the serum to prove we didn't do it."

I heard him move closer. "And did it?"

"What?"

"Prove none of you did it?"

"Yep. We aren't murderers, Draven, despite what you think. And I have no plans to hurt you either, even though you're annoying."

He sat beside me. "You think I'm annoying?"

I opened my eyes and lifted to my elbows. "Yes. You're stubborn too."

He smirked. "I like this. What else?"

I could get up and leave. I could run away so he didn't hear all the things I thought about him, but this feeling was like being drunk, and no matter how hard I tried, I couldn't stop myself from saying all the things floating around my head. "You're hot, but you know that. How could you not? You have this wild look about you that's all sexy and growly, and I like your lips. You're a great kisser. When you kissed me, it was the best I've ever had in my life."

His throat worked. "Anything else?"

"You scare me," I said and felt my face burn hotter still. I wanted to shut myself up, but I couldn't. I sat up and tried to stand, but Draven grabbed me and pulled me onto his lap before I could run, holding me in place.

"Let me go," I whispered.

"How do I scare you, Iris?"

I tried to fight it, fight to get out of his lap, but again there was no escaping his hold, and no stopping the words from coming. "I'm scared of how I feel around you." I tried to get up again, but he wasn't going to let me. "Please, don't do this to me," I pleaded.

"I'm not doing this to be an asshole, Iris. I'm doing it to cut through all the bullshit. Tell me how you feel around me."

"I want you." My voice broke as the words tumbled out. "I feel this connection between us and it's...it's so big and terrifying. I want to reach out for it and run away from it at the same time."

"That's why you keep running from me?"

I nodded and bit my lower lip to stop myself from saying more.

Draven pressed his thumb on the stinging flesh, pulling my lip free. "Tell me."

I closed my eyes, looking into his was too much. "Yes," I rasped. "If I keep running, and if I keep pushing you to the limit of your control, then maybe you'll snap. Maybe you'll show yourself and all the darkness and hatred you really feel for me. It'll be easier not to care, then."

The sound of him swallowing was audible. "You don't want to care for me?"

I shook my head. "If I let myself care for you, it will hurt so much worse when you finally betray me, just like Brody did." My lips trembled. "I don't want to care for anyone like that again." I didn't even know I felt like that way, not until the words were pulled from me.

He cupped my face gently, his fingers swiping over the markings on my cheek. "Look at me."

I did, like I was a puppet on his string.

He looked into my eyes. "No matter how you feel about me, you won't ever allow yourself to give in to it, will you? You won't become my mate of your own free will?"

"You thought I was capable of murder a few minutes ago, why would you want that?"

"Answer me."

My heart raced, and I felt sick to my stomach. This was too much. Still, the words were forced from my lips. "I will never give in to another male, not ever again." It hurt, realizing that, but it was the truth.

"But you want me?"

"Yes." I was shaking so hard now with anger that he was making me say these things and at myself for being so damn broken.

"And deep down, you want me to take the choice from you, don't you, petal?" His voice was so low now, and husky.

I pressed my lips together, fighting the word trying to force its way past my lips. I blinked, and tears slid down my face. "Yes," I whispered. "I hate you so much right now."

He pressed a kiss to my forehead. "You'll get over it."

I felt out of control, small, and I hated that most of all. "Whatever you're planning, please, don't do it. Walk away from me, forget I exist. We're not good for each other." That was the truth as well. I wanted him, but my fear was greater.

"I know you believe that, Iris. But I've waited for you, waited to find you for close to four hundred years." He brushed my cheek with his thumb. "You've been honest with me..."

"I didn't have a choice."

He ignored that and carried on. "So I'm going to be honest with you. I didn't want to want you, little witch, not at first. I believed I hated you. But only because I thought you were Selene. I don't feel that way anymore. I want to make you mine. I want to protect you, possess you. I want to feed you and sleep beside you. I want to fuck you until neither of us can walk—"

"Stop." I tried to shove him away, even as my body reacted to his words, as the craving I felt for him grew even stronger.

He ignored my struggles and carried on. "And if I ignore all that, what I want and need from you, and walk away like you're asking me to...I *will* go insane. I will lose my mind, and my pack will either be forced to put me down or end your life to save me. Neither of those things work for me. There is only one option, and since I know you won't give in to me on your own, I'll do what I need to, to remove that choice from you. To make this easier on both of us."

He took my face in his large hands and kissed me, soft brushes of his lips against mine, almost—sweet, and it didn't matter how angry I was with him, I kissed him back, unable to stop myself.

Finally, he lifted his head and stood, putting me on my feet. "Go home, Iris."

"What are you going to do?"

He was already walking away.

"Draven! What the hell are you going to do?"

Then he was gone.

Chapter Twenty-One

Iris

I'd spent the morning walking our property, searching for any other patches of earth that had been recently overturned. Thankfully, I'd found none, but my heart had been in my throat the entire time, terrified I'd find another body.

Now I was back at the council building. This time I was searching the public records. It was something Else had said one morning, right after Amy and Imogen were taken, that had brought me here.

She'd said that last time something like this happened, *no one ever found those poor girls.* It popped into my head when I woke. I'd forgotten about it, and I'd wanted to ask her more, but that would be asking for help.

Mom and Else had already called the mother a bitch, I didn't think I should push it by asking Else anything that might remotely be related to my task. So now I was combing through old newspapers and written histories, looking for any crimes similar to what was happening here and now.

Honestly, I didn't know what else to do at this point.

Amy and Marina could still be alive, I had to believe that. But it was hard to think and focus when time was running out for all of us. What if I was too late? What if I never found them? I wanted to tear the city apart, but until I had a motive or a concrete suspect, I didn't know where to start.

I forced myself to focus on what was in front of me, then growled under my breath when Draven's face popped into my head. What the hell did he have planned for me? I shivered from the memory of his touch, even as my temper shot higher at the way he'd taken advantage of my situation.

Stop. I had more important things to worry about right now than an overbearing alpha.

I pushed the book in front of me aside. Most of the information had been transferred to their computer system, and I'd been given a tablet to search and read documents. The rest that hadn't yet been transferred had been collated into large books, much the same as the ones containing our private histories, only these were larger.

The grandfather clock on the other side of the large public space gonged nine times. It was getting late, and I'd been here for several hours. I'd usually be at the bar, but Warrick had given me some time off.

"I found another one!" Penny said, bustling into the room, Jasper scurrying along beside her.

No, I couldn't ask Else, but Penny was another story. I hadn't told her why I was doing all this research, but she knew this place and the secrets it held better than anyone, and she'd been more than enthusiastic about helping find what I was looking for. Nia jumped up and danced around Penny, then sniffed Jasper.

She plonked the book down in front of me and gave Nia a pat. "I've been slowly transferring all these documents to our council server, but I haven't loaded this one yet. I've read through most of what we have here, and I think this one might have what you're looking for." She beamed.

"Awesome, thanks so much, Pen. You're a lifesaver."

"I love helping. It's nice to be needed."

I pushed the tablet aside and slid the large tome closer. "I owe you."

The spine creaked as I opened it, the paper inside yellowed and brittle. This one went right back to Selene and Charity's time. They would have been in Roxburgh by now—while Draven was trapped in Salem.

I still struggled to believe that Selene had done that to him, but she had left Draven and his warriors trapped there. Draven said he was given a love draft, and I believed him. But if Selene was as bad as he said, then why weren't her bones resting at Shadow Falls as well? Or poisoning our cemetery?

Could Charity have used her twisted magic on her sister as well? Maybe she'd been controlling her in some way?

I didn't know, but if not, I guess being selfish and manipulative was a lot different than being evil and using dark magic.

"So, I texted you the other night," Penny said, startling me.

I'd momentarily forgotten she was standing there. "Did you?" I pulled out my phone and checked it. Crap, she had. "I'm sorry, Pen. This was the night we found Imogen, and my head was all over the place. I forgot to even check for messages."

"Oh! I didn't realize. It must've been so awful. Is that what this is all about? Are you looking for clues?" Pen was lovely, but her mother was a well-known busybody, and I wasn't going to risk sharing anything important.

I didn't want everyone to know about my task. We'd tried to keep that part quiet after Willow passed her task last year. "I was just curious, you know? This whole thing is so weird, and you're right, finding Imogen like that was horrible."

"I can only imagine." She bit her lip. "I mean, do you have any idea who did it? It's so scary they were at your house, Iris."

I studied her expression. There was nothing but concern in her wide eyes. "No." Though I wouldn't be excluding Sapphire, the female wanted to hurt us in a bad way. "I wouldn't like to accuse anyone of anything without evidence."

"Of course. You're right. I'm just worried for you all. You've always been so kind to me when others...weren't." She glanced away, looking embarrassed.

I took her hand. "There are a lot of assholes in this city, Pen. They're not worth your time."

She nodded, cheeks pink again. "You're right. Just, please, be careful."

"We will."

She brightened again. "Do you want a cup of coffee or something while you read? I'll be here until Dad leaves, so anything you want, just call."

"Thanks again, Pen, and I'm fine, you don't need to wait on me."

"No problem, let me know if you change your mind."

Penny and Jasper left, and I returned my focus to the book, turning the pages carefully, reading the immaculately printed accounts of what was happening in this area back then.

Then I found what I was looking for. It was on a sheet dated *March 15, 1705*. By then, Selene and Charity would have been in their mid to late thirties.

There were articles about witches going missing in a monthly news sheet. It spanned a twelve-month period. The Missing Maidens they'd started to call them as more and more witches vanished. The disappearances stopped, or at least no more were reported, after *March 1706*. There was no mention of them being found either.

I grabbed the tablet again and searched for The Missing Maidens.

A couple of articles popped up. The first was about a witch named Mary Eason, one of The Maidens, and the first to go missing. She'd been the daughter of some important witch, a Thomas Eason. The article had been marking the anniversary of Mary's disappearance. The next article was written by someone doing a study on The Maidens. It was dated 1992 and had a run-down of all the witches who had gone missing, the dates, places they were last seen, and the author's own theories. And that was all I could find.

But Oldwood Forest had been mentioned several times.

I did another search—this time on Thomas Eason.

His name popped up instantly. There was a lot written about him. I scrolled back to the earlier mentions. Thomas had been the very first elected member of the witch's council that we knew today. He helped draft our covenants and our laws. It was Thomas who had proposed outlawing dark magic, and the law was successfully passed.

If that wasn't a big old red flashing light, I didn't know what was. He'd outlawed dark magic, then within a couple of months his daughter vanished?

But whoever was responsible for The Maidens' disappearances would be dead and buried now—probably at Shadow Falls as well.

There was no denying the similarities, though.

Did this mean we were dealing with a copycat?

I took photos of everything I'd found. It was late, but Penny had let me stay since Gunther was stuck there working security for some unscheduled council meeting, and he was her ride home.

I quickly packed everything up and walked out into the hall. I rounded the corner, and I pulled up short.

Isaac stood in front of Penny, and he was holding her shoulders. His back was to me, and Penny gazed up at him wide-eyed. He said something and strode off. Penny turned and watched him walk away.

I rushed over. "Are you okay?"

Penny jumped and spun back to me, her face bright red. "It's... it's nothing."

"You looked freaked out, Pen. What did he say?"

She blinked rapidly, then looked up at me. "Isaac and I...we, um, we've been seeing each other."

I had to stop myself from recoiling. "What?" Why the hell would she want anything to do with that asshole?

She wrung her hands. "I know your families don't get along," she whispered, "but he's nice to me."

Penny was lovely, but not Isaac's type. I'd hate to think he was using her. "Have you told your dad?"

Her eyes filled with alarm. "No, I can't, he doesn't like Isaac. And Sapphire can't know, not yet. She'd never approve of me, and Isaac said she'd cause trouble for my dad or threaten his job to try to separate us. We have to keep this quiet for now. Please, promise me you won't tell anyone."

I didn't trust Isaac one bit, and what she was telling me sounded a lot like manipulation—something I was more than a little familiar with. Brody had been an expert.

Penny watched me, and I could tell she was on the verge of freaking out. I took her trembling hand. "I promise. But I don't trust that guy. He's threatened us." *He'd sent demons after me.* "I know you don't want to hear this, but he's capable of almost anything. He's done bad shit, Pen. He'll hurt you. That's what his family does."

She shook her head. "You don't know him like I do."

And I was glad. I knew the prick as intimately as I ever wanted to. "What I know is enough."

She sighed and pulled her hands from mine, twisting them in front of her. "I know you won't believe me, but he's changed."

"I don't believe people change, and I don't trust him. I won't get involved if you don't want me too, it's your life, but I'm here if you ever need to talk."

She offered me a wobbly smile. "Thank you, Iris."

"Stay safe, okay?"

"You as well," she said.

When Nia and I hit the hall, I was still in shock. I couldn't believe Penny would date Isaac. Literally, anyone would be a better choice. Male laughter rang out up ahead, a female voice joining in.

I glanced in one of the rooms as I walked by.

Chairs surrounded a long wooden table, and Cesare Sartori was there with a female I'd never seen before. A female who was not his wife.

Which would be fine, except he had his hands on her ass. Amy was still missing, and her father sure as hell didn't look like someone worried about her safety, especially since Imogen had just turned up dead.

I knew Cesare was an asshole, but this was next level. Keeping my head down, I rushed past before he saw me standing there watching him.

I'd called his secretary earlier that afternoon, trying to get a meeting with him. I was hoping to talk to him about Amy. I hadn't expected him to agree, but I needed as much information as I could get on the girls.

I'd been told he was in no state to talk to anyone. But, from what I'd just seen, the guy was doing just fine. Better than fine. I made a mental note to look more closely at Cesare, thanked Gunther as I passed him, and walked out.

It was dark and cloudy, and an ominous feeling settled over me. I rubbed a hand against one of my stitched-up forearms and looked around. Nia instantly went on full alert.

But there was no one in the vicinity, not even Draven. I thought I sensed him earlier, but I must have imagined it. Probably because I couldn't stop thinking about him and what he'd said to me in the field the day before. And Nia certainly would have already sniffed him out if he was here.

Rushing to my car, I did a quick check of my tires, still wary after what Isaac and his demons had done. But everything looked fine. My nerves grew and my pulse was racing faster than usual. I couldn't describe the feeling, but it was like my gut was telling me to brace, that something was coming.

I quickly got in and headed for home, trying to keep my mind focused on what I needed to do. I'd read over the documents I'd taken pictures of tonight and plan my next step. I needed to do a deep dive online and maybe ask around about Cesare Sartori. Something didn't feel right there, or maybe he was just an unfeeling asshole. Either way, I needed to take a closer look at him as well.

The drive home was uneventful, which was how I liked it.

Until I approached our driveway and saw a car parked out front. Big, black, and expensive. It belonged to Councilor Trotman.

What was he doing here this time of night? I quickly parked and hurried inside. Trotman was a good guy, but we weren't pals. He didn't just drop by for a friendly chit-chat or a cup of coffee.

Something had to be wrong. Like finding a dead body on your property, wrong. Maybe it had something to do with Imogen?

Voices carried down the hall from the living room. Nia and I rushed in and pulled to a stop at the look on everyone's faces. "What's going on?"

Mags looked like she was about to kill someone, her eyes bright with fury. Bram had his arm around her waist, holding her against him, but he wasn't comforting her, he was restraining her.

Mom was holding Art's hand, and she looked like she couldn't decide if she was going to scream or cry. Else had her hands planted on her hips, staring down Trotman. And Willow...well, I couldn't read her expression. She didn't look angry, though. Whatever this was hadn't pissed her off like it had the rest of my family.

"What's going on?" I asked.

No one said anything.

There was a knock at the door, and Willow rushed to answer it.

"Mom?"

"We're waiting on a witness, Iris," the councilor said.

"A witness? For what?"

The thud of boots echoed outside the door, then Rocco, one of the Knights of Hell, walked in. He and his mate were Willow's good friends, and they'd become friends to us as well.

Nia ran over to greet him, and the big half demon, half angel, gave her the pats she wanted as he took in the room. His brows lowered. "What's this about, Wills?"

Trotman stepped forward. "Thank you for coming in, Mr. Rocco."

Rocco frowned. "Just Rocco. Who the fuck are you?"

"I am Councilor Trotman from the Roxburgh witch's council," he added. "Something has come to light, and we've been told you might be able to help us confirm it."

What the fuck was this?

Roc crossed his arms and looked to Willow again. She said nothing. I assumed they weren't allowed to. I looked at Willow as well, and she couldn't hold my stare. My heart, which was already pounding, raced faster.

"Okay, I'm listening," Roc said.

"A year ago, you and your mate..."

Rocco snarled, looking pissed off now. "What the fuck is this?"

Trotman held up his hands. "I assure you we are no threat to your mate, Mr....er, Rocco. This is just a witness statement."

Rocco stared at the much smaller male, and he didn't look happy. He was extremely protective of his mate—all the knights were—they were like shifters that way, and he didn't like his mate being brought into this, whatever *this* was.

Councilor Trotman took Roc's silence as a get-the-hell-on-with-it and started again. "A year ago, you and your mate traveled to Salem, is that correct?"

Rocco looked to Willow again, and again she gave him nothing. His frown deepened. "Yes."

"Willow gave you a map, which led you to a rock? A rock holding a dagger that was being protected by wolf shifters?"

"Willow?" Roc said.

"It's okay, tell him," she said.

Roc frowned harder and turned back to Trotman. "Yeah, there were wolf shifters guarding it."

"What happened when you got there?" Trotman asked him.

"We got the dagger, and one of the wolves got me to hold the map up to the moon. Some kind of spell was broken."

"Did he say anything to you?" the councilor asked.

Rocco's jaw worked. "He said they'd been trapped there...by Willow's coven. I don't know how long for."

"Where's the dagger now?"

"Safe," Rocco said, and his eyes narrowed. "And if someone wants it, they'll have to go through Lucifer himself to get it."

"No, no, we're happy for the dagger to remain where it is." Trotman looked pale. "Thank you for your help."

Willow grabbed Roc's arm and led him back out. I could hear his deep voice as they left, wanting to know what the fuck was going on. He wasn't the only one.

They were talking about Draven and his warriors. They were the wolves guarding that rock.

This had something to do with me, it had to.

"You can't do this," Mags yelled at Trotman. "Females aren't chattel anymore, you sexist pig." Mags started fighting Bram's hold.

Chattel?

"Get her out of here," Willow said to Bram when she walked back in.

Bram picked Mags up and carried her out of the room.

"Can someone please tell me what the hell is going on here?" I said, dread thick in my veins.

"We'll fight this," Mom said. "I won't let this stand, I promise, sweetheart."

"Let what happen?"

Councilor Trotman turned to me, and there was sympathy in his gray eyes. "We had a meeting with the alpha of the Silver Claw pack tonight, Iris."

My stomach sank farther. "Okay."

"He made claims and backed it up with evidence. We just needed a witness statement, and Rocco gave that to us. He claimed abuse of magic by coven Thornheart and violation of the treaty between witches and shifters." Trotman cleared his throat several times. "He demanded restitution."

"What kind of restitution?"

"They lost pack members, elders, children, while their warriors were trapped. Selene and Charity wronged his pack in the worst way, there is no denying that now." Trotman looked uncomfortable. "He says you're his mate, Iris?"

"He's lying, isn't he?" Mom said. "You would have told us if that were true."

I turned to Mom and Art, hating the look on Mom's face. "He's not...he's not lying. I am his mate."

Willow's gaze was still unreadable. "What happens now?" she asked the councilor.

"He's willing to forget what was done to his pack...or at least not declare war on the witches in this city, if Iris agrees to become his mate in truth," Trotman said.

Draven told me what he wanted. And I understood why. He'd laid out what would happen if he didn't claim me. Still, I couldn't believe he'd actually done this. And I couldn't believe the council was considering it.

"We can fight him if you don't want this," Willow said. "But if he is your mate, if you run from this..."

"We are not forcing your sister to mate anyone," Mom said.

Willow kept her gaze steady, her emotions in check. "Arranged marriages happen all the time. This could be a good thing."

"Enough!" Mom yelled. "It is not a good thing, Willow. What

the hell are you thinking? Yes, he saved Iris and I'm so thankful for that, but to force her to do this? That's not okay. Not any way you look at it. Unless..." She turned to me. "Is this what you want, Iris? Do you want to be with Draven?"

My mind was racing—spinning—my heart thundered in my chest. Fear and longing were mixed up, battling inside me at her question.

"What are you going to do, honey?" Else asked when I didn't answer.

What could I do? He'd told me what would happen if I refused him. Either he'd go insane, or one of us would end up dead. This was always how it was going to end, wasn't it? I'd only delayed the inevitable when I turned him down. If I continued to fight this, his pack would declare war. People would lose their lives trying to protect me. I didn't have a choice.

I didn't want anyone fighting over this. This was messed up for so many reasons, but Draven and his pack were owed for what happened. He and his warriors had spent probably half their lives trapped in Salem, in those woods. I didn't want to be the thing to even that score, but someone in our coven had to pay the price for that wrong, and it looked like it was going to be me. "I'll go," I said.

Mom shook her head. "I'm not letting them force you into this, not if you don't want to be with him."

"Our coven caused their pack harm, Mom. And Draven is my mate, whether I wanted it or not, that's the truth. If I refuse, we'll just be causing more harm. A wolf denied by his mate can go insane. Draven's suffered enough." I didn't share the bit about them killing me to save him. There would most definitely be a war if I did, and I wouldn't be responsible for the people I loved getting hurt or worse.

"What happens now?" I asked Trotman.

"I need you to sign this declaration stating that you agree to the proposed restitution of your own free will. If you sign, I'll let the Silver Claw alpha know, and he'll be here to collect you in the morning," he said.

He took a small stack of papers from his briefcase and placed them on the coffee table. I sat on the couch and quickly read through everything—or tried to. It was all a blur.

Trotman handed me a pen. Nia whined and pawed at the floor, confused by the emotions she sensed coming from me.

I glanced up at my family. Mom was crying.

"The house won't be the same without you here," Else said and looked like she was about to cry as well.

Willow put her hand on my shoulder. "It's going to be okay. I believe that."

I nodded, even though I didn't exactly share her optimism, and signed my name. It didn't matter that I wanted Draven...god, craved him. Or that there was a deep, hidden part of me, a part I'd been afraid to look at too closely that wanted to belong to him, that exploded back to life when he was near—when I'd felt numb for so long. Because a relationship built on a foundation of hate, even if it had been misplaced, couldn't possibly work.

None of that mattered, though, because Draven was going to claim me as his mate, and I wasn't going to fight that. There was no point, no other option. But he wouldn't claim my heart. I would never give that to anyone ever again. It was locked up tight, and as long as I kept it that way, I'd be okay when it all went to hell.

Because it would.

How could it not?

Chapter Twenty-Two

Iris

Someone knocked on my door early the next morning, and before I could ask who it was, Willow walked in.

Nia immediately jumped down to greet her, and I sat up, resting against the headboard. I'd barely slept all night. I didn't know what to expect today, and I wasn't ashamed to admit, I was scared out of my mind.

"What's that?" I said, eyeing the garment bag my sister was carrying.

Her expression grew cautious. "A dress."

"Why do you have a dress with you?" She unzipped it and I saw a flash of white. "No. No freaking way."

Willow winced. "I know, I know. But Rowena's here...the whole coven is, actually."

"What? Why?" I scrambled out of bed and ran to the window. There were cars everywhere, and several people were gathered in the backyard, weaving what could only be a blessing arch.

"Else or Mom must have called them last night and told them what happened. They arrived in force this morning."

"I really don't need this shit today." I paced away from the window.

Willow's expression softened. "They want to show Draven and his pack how important you are to us, and in Rowena's words, 'let him know that if he hurts you, we will cut him down until there is nothing left.' She knows the sacrifice you're making for the coven, and she wants you to know she appreciates it."

Rowena was the head of our coven and Mom's second cousin. She was tough and smart and kind. She also didn't take shit from anyone.

I moved back to the window. One of my aunts was walking across the yard with a basket of flowers. *Goddammit.* We usually had a ceremony when a witch married or mated. Most wore a white dress and a floral wreath in their hair for the occasion. Willow never got to have one herself, and Mom and Else had been more than a little put out by it. The ceremony celebrated a female witch's womanhood and was performed to enhance her fertility and to call on the mother to ask for her blessings upon the union.

"This isn't a love match," I said. "Doing this is ridiculous. I don't want it. Plus, I have my task to complete. Amy and Marina are still missing, I don't have the time."

Willow chewed on her lip. "Rowena has her mind made up. They can't help you get out of this thing with Draven, not without bloodshed, and not without pissing off the council in a big way. This is their way of helping. Making sure the union has the mother's blessings is all they can do for you now. They want you to be safe and happy, and this is their way of stacking the odds in your favor."

"Fuck." I started pacing again. "I can't believe this is happening."

Willow pulled the garment bag away from the dress, and I

turned to look at it. It was long, made of soft, flowy muslin and lace. It looked vintage. "Was this Gran's?"

"Yep," Willow said, running her hand down the soft-looking fabric.

"I can't wear that. It should be saved for Mags or..." I was about to say Rose. But Rose wouldn't ever get to wear a dress like this. I swallowed back my emotions. I refused to cry.

"Just because you wear it doesn't mean someone else can't as well." Willow turned to me. "Look, I know this seems...insane. I know it's daunting and not what you wanted for yourself, especially after what happened with Brody."

I flinched. Just hearing his name sent tremors of revulsion through my body. "No, it isn't. But you don't have to worry, I'll suck it up. I'll do what I need to for the coven."

Willow's lips curled up gently. "You're attracted to Draven, though, yes?"

My face heated. I was no prude. Willow and I talked about most things, but for some reason, when it came to Draven, I struggled to find the words. "Yes, but that's fate's doing. I would never have chosen this. It doesn't matter how hot the guy is."

"I know, but the fates saw that you were made for each other and then did their thing. It may not seem like it now, but there's a reason you and Draven were brought together. Yes, you'll disagree on things and argue, but in the end, no one will take your back or protect and care for you like your mate will. I know that it seems impossible to have someone feel that way about you after what happened, but he will. The connection between mates is like nothing else."

"We hate each other," I said. Well, we had hated each other. I didn't know what I felt now, and I sure as hell had no idea what Draven felt.

Willow walked up to me and rested her hands on my shoulders. "I'm not gonna lie, it'll take time to get to know each other, and it won't be easy, but if you focus on that feeling in here"—she placed her fist against her sternum—"that feeling of rightness that sits right here when you're with him, it will guide you, both of you, and everything will work out. I promise."

I glanced out the window again and back. "I hope you're right, I do." I shrugged. "I don't know what Draven's thinking or what he wants, but my coven comes first, so I'll do my duty. But if nothing changes between us, I'll have a lot of shitty years ahead of me with a mate who doesn't trust me."

Willow's smile slipped. "Iris."

She looked pale all of a sudden. "What is it?"

"You know I've been pushing for you to find a mate, but what I didn't tell you—"

The door was thrown open, and Mags strode in. Bram followed, carrying Rose. He placed her on the bed and Mags got up beside her, Nia following and demanding attention.

"Right, if you're going through with this shit-show, let's get you ready," my baby sister said, sliding her arm around Roe so she could rest her head on Mags's shoulder.

Willow looked at Bram. "Did you search her for weapons?"

Bram's lips twitched. "She's clean."

We all sighed in relief, then he left us, heading back downstairs. The last thing we needed was Mags trying to stab Draven. We had enough to make up for already.

Mags rolled her eyes and ran her hand over Nia's fur. "I won't be so obvious when I take him out."

"You won't do a damned thing," Willow said.

"Fine, I won't," Mags agreed way too easily.

"Her fingers are crossed behind her back," Rose said.

Mags spun to her. "You little traitor."

"You can't do anything to him," Rose said, her voice weak, but there was conviction there, in spades. "You'll only cause trouble. I need to know that when I'm gone..."

"You're not going anywhere," Mags said.

Rose rested her hand on Mags and said nothing more.

Willow grabbed my hand and tugged me toward the door. "Right, go grab a shower and we'll get everything ready."

I stared at myself in the mirror. The dress draped over my curves, clinging in all the right places, and brushed the tops of my bare feet. My hair was down and slightly wavy, and Mom had come in a little while ago and placed a wreath made of jasmine on my head.

I'd been to ceremonies like this before. They were always fun, joyous occasions. I had no idea what Draven would think when he arrived to pick me up and saw all of this, and I decided I didn't care either. This was for my family, for my coven. If doing this ritual gave them some measure of peace, I wanted to give it to them.

"Have you packed everything you need?" Willow asked. "We can always bring the rest of your things to you."

"Yeah, I have everything I need." My bags were already downstairs. I rubbed Nia's head since she was pressed against me.

Nia make Iris feel better. Wolves make Iris feel better.

She could sense how I was feeling and was doing her best to help. I'd tried to explain what was happening, and she was having trouble understanding. But her excitement over seeing Draven again, and Ebony, of being with the wolves, was palpable. "You always make me feel better."

I tried to calm my nerves, for Nia's sake, but it was a struggle, especially with all the questions racing around in my head. Where would I be sleeping tonight? Would Draven expect us to have sex?

A little shiver moved through me as I remembered what he'd said in the field. I couldn't imagine him wanting some drawn-out courtship. He wanted me, he'd told me more than once, and in a short time, I'd be his, to do with as he wished.

"You may be his mate," Mags said, "but you're not his freaking prisoner. You can come and go as you please, right?"

"Of course." I wouldn't let him control me. I'd share his bed, but I wasn't his possession. I would not be controlled, not by anyone.

Mags huffed out a breath. "Good."

"You look beautiful," Rose said. "How do you feel?"

I looked over at her. She was propped up on my bed still. "Nervous...unsure."

Mags narrowed her eyes. "If he hurts you—"

"He won't. I've seen him with his pack, he loves them, and they love him back. He's a good male, Mags, I do believe that." I shrugged. "It's just that I wasn't looking for any male."

She moved up behind me and wrapped her arms around me, looking at our reflections. "You'll be his mate, but that's all. You'll still be you, and you'll still be ours. You sleep there, that's all."

I grinned at her. "Yeah, that's all."

She rested her chin on my shoulder. "I'm going to miss you."

"I'll miss you, too, all of you." Oh hell, my eyes started to sting. I ruthlessly fought back the tears. "But I'll still be here a lot. It'll be like I never left."

"I'm never doing this," Mags said. "I'm going to be single for the rest of my life. Guys suck."

"Some definitely do," I said. "But as long as there aren't any other packs out there with alphas we've pissed off in the past, you should be safe."

She nudged me. "You know what I mean, smart-ass."

"Bram doesn't suck," Willow said.

Mags glanced at Wills. "Well, obviously. But Bram's different, he's my best friend."

Poor Bram.

Mom walked into the room, Art behind her, and she was close to crying again. She'd been weepy most of the day. "It's time, sweetheart," she said.

The nerves in my belly exploded into a flurry, taking flight.

Draven was here.

I nodded, and Mom took my hand. We left the room, Nia at my side, my sisters following, and Art helping Rose down the stairs behind us.

Else was waiting at the bottom with Rowena.

The leader of our coven pulled me in for a tight hug. "If you don't want to do this…"

"It's okay, I promise," I said and hugged her back. "Thank you for everything."

She lifted her head. "If you need us for anything, just say the word."

Going by the look in her eyes, she meant *anything*, including breaking all the rules to get me back. I smiled up at her, it was shaky, but I was not going to freak out or lose my shit in front of everyone. They were here because they loved me. They already felt guilty that I had to do this, I wasn't going to make this harder on them by crying or screaming or fighting it every step of the way.

Else took my other hand, and Mom led us out to the backyard. There was no wind, but the air was cool, and goose bumps lifted over my skin. My entire coven stood behind the arch made of willow branches and covered in foliage and flowers. They looked at me now, love and light shining from them all. I could feel it, their strength, and it warmed me, surrounded me, protected me.

I felt Draven, too, but I hadn't sought him out yet. And it took every bit of my courage to finally lift my head.

The alpha of the Silver Claw pack stood on the other side of the arch, tall and strong and *intense*.

His warriors were gathered behind him. And if he was surprised by all of this, he didn't show it. His steady gaze was locked on me.

He took a step in my direction.

Warrick, who I only noticed was beside him now, stopped him, saying something I couldn't hear. No doubt Willow had sent her mate to explain how this worked.

I had to walk through the arch to him.

I had to offer myself, give myself to him.

A symbol of strength and a new beginning.

Rowena handed me a small terra-cotta pot. Inside, a wilted plant sat in the soil, the vervain's small purple flowers, dry and withered. The herb protected against evil spells and negative energy and could be used to purify sacred places and private dwellings. It was also used for medicinal purposes. Every bride was given one to take into her new home and was the first herb to be planted in her own herb garden.

When it was planted, depended on the witch.

I held it tightly in my hands as she started the chant. Else and Mom joined in next, then my sisters. The rest of the coven added their voices until they were one, calling on the mother for her blessings.

Else and Mom walked forward, taking my hands, and led me to the arch. I stopped in front of it and, as they let me go and stepped away, I turned back to my coven, my sisters, and I smiled. I didn't want them hurting or worrying. Of course, I was terrified, but I wasn't going to let them see it.

I turned back, and Draven was right there, waiting for me on the other side. All I had to do was walk through and take his hand and it would be done. His gaze was still intense, so much so, I was struggling to catch my breath, but there was something else there as well.

He was afraid.

Afraid that I'd change my mind, that I'd run away. He wanted me to walk to him of my own free will. I felt it now, just how much he wanted that from me.

And I won't lie; I did want to run. Draven scared me in so many ways, but running would cause harm. He was my future, my fate, whether I liked it or not, was irrelevant, and I had to find a way to make peace with that.

"Iris," he said, voice impossibly rough and full of so much trepidation and need...and hope. I responded to it as if he'd reached through the arch and taken my hand.

I took a steadying breath—

Nia barked and ran through, straight to Draven. His warriors chuckled, and Draven greeted her with a smile that stopped my heart. She pressed against his thigh and looked at me. There were more chuckles behind me, and I felt the tension break. My coven's relief. My familiar loving Draven could only be a good sign.

Iris come. We go with alpha. We run with wolves.

Nia couldn't contain her excitement any longer. She loved Draven, and she trusted him.

Draven held out his hand.

I walked through, finally, and took it. It didn't matter how I got here or how scared I was, I had to try to make the best of it.

He looked down at me. "Hey."

I smiled. "Hey there, alpha."

His nostrils flared. "You're beautiful."

"Thank you. You're utterly insane."

He flashed me his teeth in a wicked smile. "A little less, now you're here."

"So you think a relationship can work when both parties have been forced into it?" I said. My heart was pounding at the way he was looking at my mouth, at having him near, of thinking about what would happen when we got back to the keep.

"If I didn't, we wouldn't be standing here doing this now," he said.

In other words, one of us would be dead instead. Probably me.

"We can be good together, Iris."

I hoped like hell he was right and that I didn't grow to resent him. It didn't matter that neither of us had any real choice in this.

I'd just been torn from my home, my life. It would take time to get over that.

I gripped the small pot in my hand tighter as the wilted little herb transformed, becoming green and lush, as the little purple flowers unfurled, so many they overflowed the edges.

The mother had given us her blessing.

My coven cheered.

"Let's go home," Draven said.

Chapter Twenty-Three

Draven

Iris was quiet on the ride to the keep.

I glanced over at her again. She was looking out the side window, Nia's head in her lap. She had the fingers of one hand buried in her familiar's fur and the other held her little potted plant. My wolf chuffed at the sight of them, content for the first time in a long fucking time because she was coming home with me. Her bags were in the back of my truck, and she was sitting there in that white dress, flowers still in her hair, looking so beautiful I could barely control myself.

God, waiting on the other side of that arch for her had nearly killed me. But then she'd walked through, she'd taken my hand and smiled up at me with that fucking cute little lopsided grin, and my heart had started beating again.

"What are you thinking?" I asked before I could stop the words. I wanted her to want to be with me so badly. I knew that doing what I had, forcing her hand this way, was fucked up, but it had to be done, for both our sakes. She said herself that she wanted me. I just hoped she didn't hate me for it for the rest of our lives.

She turned from the window. "A lot of things."

"Like what?" I shouldn't push. She didn't owe me a damned thing, but I couldn't stop. I wanted to know everything she was thinking and feeling. I wanted to be inside her goddamn head. Obsessed wasn't strong enough a word for the way I felt about the female beside me. My female.

She ran her hand over Nia's fur. "Like I'm kind of surprised how well Warrick took this whole thing. He's usually protective of his new sisters."

"If you consider threatening to tear my dick off if I hurt you, well? Then I suppose he did."

"He said that?"

"Yeah, but he also wasn't going to get in my way. Warrick knows what it's like to pine for your mate and not be able to claim her."

She rubbed her lips together, her gaze darting from mine.

I wasn't letting her retreat. "What else are you thinking?"

She glanced back at me. "How does your pack feel about me coming to live with them? I know a lot of them don't like me."

"They will treat you with respect. You're my mate. They love me, and they'll grow to love you. What else?"

A small laugh escaped her, surprising me. "You're the most intense male I have ever met."

"I'm only this way around you." And that was the truth.

"I find that hard to believe."

"You'll see. Things will calm down now we're together."

Her gaze came to mine, then drifted away again. "You say we're together, what does that mean for you?"

I should hold back everything that welled up inside me at that moment, but she needed to know the truth. The sooner she understood the way things would be between us, the better. "It means you are mine, Iris. I will claim you in every way it's possible for a being to claim another. I'll take care of you, protect you, and I'll always be faithful to you." I glanced over at her, and she stared at me wide-eyed, her lips slightly parted. I couldn't read her expression. "And I'll belong to you," I added, wanting that so fucking badly. Wanting her to claim me as well, even if it all went to shit, even if this turned out to be a disaster. I still wanted that from her.

I heard her swallow in the now silent cab of the truck. "You can't just say stuff like that."

"Why not?" I couldn't not say stuff like that to her. I needed her to know it, to accept it.

"Because...this whole situation is insane. You just forced me into a relationship with you, Draven. What you just said scares the hell out of me. We barely know each other. It's too much, too soon."

I gripped the wheel tighter and tried to slow my breathing. "I've been free from my prison for just over a year, Iris. Almost everything I ever wanted is finally within my grasp. I don't know how to be subtle, I don't know how to *play it cool*. I wasn't born in your time, I feel like I've barely lived in it. I'm sorry if my intensity scares you, but I'm your mate, and as long as you're always honest with me, everything will be fine." I stared out the windshield, and I felt her watching me. I wanted to ask what she was thinking again but resisted, barely.

"And if I'm not honest with you?"

"Why wouldn't you be?" We needed to work on building trust between us, not cause more doubt.

She was quiet again for several long seconds, and again the urge to know what was going on in that head of hers was so fucking strong. "I'll be able to come and go as I please, right?" she finally asked. "You're not going to...to hold me there."

I *wanted* to lock her in my room and never let her out of my sight again. "You're not my prisoner, Iris. You can come and go all you like, but I need to know where you are. My wolf needs to know where you are when you're gone. And I need you back with me every night."

She nodded, her expression still so damned unreadable. "I still have my task; my coven is relying on me. That has to be my priority right now."

I knew that already, but things would go a lot differently from here on out. "Of course, but I'll be with you while you're working on it. Not Relic."

"I guess I can handle that," she said, surprising me. "And you know Relic's just a friend, right?"

My beast didn't give a fuck. Iris was mine, and I didn't want the male near her. Shifters were possessive, jealous, protective. I didn't say that, though. I needed to ease Iris into the way it would be between us.

I glanced at her again. "There's something else, something you're not telling me. I can sense it." And I could see it now in her eyes.

She ran her hand over her dress, and her fingers shook slightly. "Where will I be sleeping?"

I had to swallow down a snarl of hunger. "With me."

"You don't think we should take it slow? Get to know each other a little more before we take it...there?" Her voice was husky.

"You're my mate, Iris. That isn't going to change, no matter how much time passes. I *know* you, not in a conventional sense, but on a deeper level. We'll always have this connection. Everything else we'll learn about each other over time. If we sleep in separate rooms tonight, it will only make things more difficult tomorrow." I waited for her to protest, because Iris loved to argue with me. She pushed me as well, and fuck, after our talk in the field, I knew why.

She drew in a deep breath, and when she let it out, it shook. "Okay," she said.

My gaze shot back to her. "Okay?"

"You're right. I'll admit I'm nervous. Better to just get it over with, like tearing off a Band-Aid."

I gripped the steering wheel tighter. She wanted to get it over with? Fuck that, I'd make her crave me. I'd have her reaching for me night after night. She didn't understand this yet, what being mates meant, and she wouldn't, not until I claimed her. Soon she'd understand how intense things would become between us. But if it helped her tonight, I'd let her think this was something to get out of the way.

Tomorrow would be a different story.

I finally pulled up outside the keep, and Iris was out before I could get around the truck to open her door. She reached for her bags in the back, and I stopped her as the keep doors opened and my pack rushed out.

I brushed my fingers over her skin. "Someone else will bring those in." Then I took the plant from her hand, placed it back in the truck, and scooped her up in my arms, not just because I wanted her closer, and I did, but for my pack.

Her arms flew around my neck. "What are you doing?"

I pressed my mouth to her ear. "If they believe you care for me, petal, they'll warm to you a lot faster."

She stiffened for a moment, then tightened her arms around my neck and let me carry her inside.

The great room had been decorated, and Sally had gone all out with the food. I wanted to take my female upstairs and finally claim her, but they'd gone to all this trouble. I had to do this for my pack. Nothing about this was how we usually did things, but it was how it had to be done. I couldn't afford to take Iris away for a week—my pack needed me, and she had her task.

So I needed to show everyone that we were all in and that having Iris here was a good thing. Some would need more convincing than others. Many of them had been around when Selene did what she had, and it would take time for them to get used to having a witch living here, especially one who looked like her.

I put her on her feet, reluctantly letting her go as my people came up to congratulate us. Seeing Iris in her dress, the flowers still in her hair, I could tell it went a long way with some of the females. It looked like Iris had made an effort for me. They didn't need to know she'd done it for her coven or about the ritual.

Anything to help them accept her as fast as possible.

Now that I finally had her here, I wouldn't lose her, and the best way to keep her was for her to connect with the pack and make this place home.

My people could make that easy on her, or they could make it hard, depending on how she chose to look at her new situation.

Asher stood by Iris. I'd assigned her to my mate. At least if she was close, she could ensure Iris's transition here went smoothly, and if I wasn't around, step in if there were any issues.

I took Iris's hand. "You must be hungry." I led her to a table.

She sat, looking around the room, and Dirk brought her a drink. She smiled and thanked him, but going by the slight tremor in her voice, she was feeling overwhelmed.

My protective instincts went into overdrive.

I would make her love it here.

I had to.

"What happened to your arms?" Cleo, one of the older females, asked Iris when we finished eating.

Iris looked down at her forearms, then back up at Cleo. "I ah... had to perform a ritual."

Cleo's face screwed up. "You did that to yourself?"

Iris said nothing, just stared back.

The older wolf shook her head. "Why would you do that?"

"Cleo," I murmured, low but gentle, the warning clear.

She flushed. "I'm sorry, alpha, but why would the fates do this to you...to us? That's why I voted against this mating. You should be with your own kind, not—"

"That's enough," I said with more force, and this time there was no missing how over the line she'd stepped.

The room went silent, and all eyes turned our way. Cleo mumbled an apology and dipped her head. I understood their trepidation. I got why having a witch here would take some adjusting. Our pack didn't trust them, for good reason. Even I wasn't sure if I would ever trust Iris completely. That was something that would take time. But I couldn't let my pack see any doubts.

"Iris is a witch," I said, raising my voice so everyone could hear. "There are things you won't understand about her, and I'm sure that goes both ways. We'll all have to learn from each other. But Iris is my mate, and you will show her respect at all times."

Cleo's lips pressed into a thin line, not happy, and her expression was mirrored by several others in the room, but there were nods and, "Yes, alphas," muttered around us before everyone got back to eating and drinking.

Iris's discomfort was thick beside me. She didn't want to be here either. I felt her anger, her fear, it sat around her like a cloak, a wall. I rested my hand on her knee. "I'm sorry."

"The last twenty-four hours have been...they've been a lot," she said. "I'd like to go upstairs now."

"Of course." I curled my fingers around hers and stood. She let me lead her from the room and up the stairs. We hit the hall that led to my chambers and she pulled on my hand.

"I've changed my mind. I want my own room," she said, her eyes bright, that fear growing thicker by the moment.

This was all new, and she was afraid. How could she not be after how badly she'd been hurt in the past. Now she'd been forced from her home, her family as well. I stopped and turned to her. "Forget what Cleo said. They need time, that's all."

She wouldn't meet my eyes. "Well, I need time as well."

My wolf whined and clawed. I wasn't okay with that. And if I let her pull away from me now, if I allowed her fear and sadness to become a wall between us, adjusting to life here would be so much harder. I didn't like seeing her like this. Her fire was gone, and now more than ever, she needed it, that fight, her attitude, and her strength.

I needed to coax it back out to help her get through this, I knew that much. So I did what I had to, what was best for both of us. "No."

Fury flashed through her eyes instantly, and I almost smiled.

"What do you mean, no?"

"We are sleeping in the same bed tonight, and every night," I said, and there was a bit more growl in my voice than intended, but it was working.

I kept walking, towing her behind me.

"I don't want that," she said through gritted teeth.

She was lying to herself and to me. I spun, lifted her off her feet so we were eye-level, and held her furious stare as I breathed deep. "I can smell how wet you are, Iris. You want me as badly as I want you."

"I don't belong with you," she said, not denying it. "And I don't belong here."

"You will." I hooked my arm under her ass and hitched her higher. "And you belonged to me the moment the fates decided we should be together." I carried on down the hall toward my room. She started struggling. I ignored it and kept going, walking into the room and kicking the door shut behind us.

"I need to be with Nia," she said, looking for any excuse and shoving at my chest.

"Ebony will take good care of her."

Her jaw tightened. "Don't tell me what to do with my familiar."

"Stop trying to pick a fight."

"I'm not, you just really piss me off."

I gripped her tighter in my arms, my face close to hers. "And now I'm going to get you off."

She shoved at me again. "God, you are such an arrogant asshole."

"And you're a brat," I said because the more she yelled at me, the stronger her scent became.

"You're a goddamn control freak," she said and shoved again.

"I promise, you'll get off on that as well."

The fire ignited in her eyes again. "Arrogant, son of a..."

I slammed my mouth down on hers.

She gripped my shirt and tried to push me back, and I sucked on her sweet mouth and nipped her lower lip in return. She gasped, tried to shove me away once more, then changed her mind, and fisting my shirt, tugged me closer instead.

Her fingers thrust into my hair, holding me fast. *Fuck yes.* I groaned and claimed her mouth fully, making it mine.

Iris returned my kiss like we were in battle. "Asshole," she said against my lips and tore the front of my shirt open. The buttons *pinged* off the floor.

I snarled and had to fight the urge to throw her over my fucking knee and spank her round ass before I fucked her. "Stubborn, reckless, confusing..."

She sucked my lower lip into her mouth as her hand worked my belt. "You want a sweet, little mate who will do what you want, when you want? You have the wrong female," she said.

"Oh, I have the right female. And you make me fucking crazy." I lifted her higher off the ground and pressed her against the wall, feeling dizzy from how much I wanted her.

"You make *me* crazy!" she said, finally undoing the button of my jeans and sliding down the zipper.

She yanked down the front, and gripped my dick in her hot hand, and I growled as I shoved her dress up, then tugged her panties aside. "Celibacy's not looking so good anymore, Iris?"

She actually growled. "We're terrible together," she said, then moaned as I swiped my fingers over her pussy, testing how wet she was. Fucking drenched. "T-this will never work between us...you freaking *voted* on whether or not to mate with me."

Of course, she hadn't missed what Cleo said downstairs. My feisty witch missed nothing. I circled her slick little clit, and she moaned. "I'll make it work," I gritted out.

Her fingers dug into my shoulder. "What would you have done if they'd voted no?"

I held her brown gaze and circled her clit again, wringing a gasp from her. "I would have come for you anyway." I couldn't deny or fight what was between us, not anymore. I hadn't been strong enough.

"You might have my body, but that's all you'll ever have," she said as she guided the head of my cock to her opening.

I shifted my hips, pulling my dick from her hand. "Not yet." Her eyes spat fire, until I reached between us, took myself in hand, and dragged the head of my cock over her clit.

"*Oh god.*" Her nails dug into my skin.

I did it again, and again. "You're going to come for me first, Iris."

Her thighs shook and she whimpered as I tilted my hips and dragged the length of my cock through her slit. Her slick folds parted, spreading around my shaft and I dragged it up and back, covering myself in her juices, and pushing her closer to the edge at the same time.

Her forehead pressed against my shoulder, her desperate sounds, her pleas for me to take her, music to my ears.

I dipped my head, my mouth going to her ear. "I know you feel empty, petal, and I promise I'm going to make it better. I'm going to fill you up so good. As soon as you come for me, nice and hard, you'll get me."

She lifted her head, a desperate look in her beautiful eyes. "Draven..."

"Give it to me," I growled.

Then she finally let go, crying out, trembling against me. She tried to dip her head again, to hide from me, but I cupped her jaw and tilted her head back so I could see the pleasure I'd given her. I'd never witnessed anything more beautiful in my life.

Fuck knew how I'd held back, but I couldn't anymore. And as soon as she took her first shuddering breath, I slammed inside her, and all the tension, the hunger, the need I had for this female was delivered behind that first brutal thrust. She cried out, again, tightening her legs around my waist, and clawed at my back, holding me to her.

Oh fuck. She was so tight.

I slid out, and when I thrust back in, I shoved my hand behind her head before she could smack it against the wall as she arched against me. "You feel that? That's your mate finally taking you. I promise, petal, you'll crave this, you'll crave me, every day and every-fucking-night. Just me. Only me."

Then I lost control, taking her like the beast I was, claiming my mate because I was done waiting. Iris was mine, and she would be mine for as long as I lived and beyond. I didn't need trust or love, I just needed this.

I swiped my tongue over her shoulder, and she shuddered against me, her pussy clutching at me. "You going to come for me again already, little witch?"

Her fingernails dug deeper. "Don't stop."

I didn't want to stop, but she was so hot and wet around my dick, her pussy pulsing around me so damn tight, there would be no holding back.

I lifted my head and looked into her beautiful eyes. "I'm going to bite you now, Iris. I'm going to make you mine."

She started to shake her head, then she jolted in my arms and her cunt clamped down so hard on my cock I saw stars. I didn't wait, I sank my canines into the sweet spot between her neck and shoulder, claiming her, making her mine in the way my people had been doing for centuries. I marked her.

Iris screamed and shook in my arms, coming around me, becoming mine in truth, and I roared and went with her. Filling her up and becoming hers as well.

Chapter Twenty-Four

Iris

The keep was silent.

I looked at the sleeping wolf beside me, and somehow, I could feel the contentment rolling off him.

I wasn't sure how I felt.

Confusion was probably what was loudest in my mind. Draven infuriated and perplexed me. Pushed and goaded me. He'd known exactly what he was doing when he brought me in here. He knew what he needed to do to pull me from the despair I was sinking into.

The female downstairs hadn't hurt my feelings or upset me—a lot of beings didn't like witches or had trouble understanding the things we did. No, she hadn't upset me, but she had highlighted just how much I didn't belong here.

I knew, without a doubt, it was only a matter of time before Draven worked that out for himself as well. His craving for me would wane, and, mate or not, this would end.

But for now...I shivered. I couldn't stop thinking about what we did when he brought me into his room—I'd never experienced anything like it. When Brody was angry, the sex had been punishing, painful, often humiliating. I don't know if Draven had been truly angry or not. We'd definitely been arguing, but he hadn't once hurt me, and the only thing he'd wanted me to feel was pleasure.

My hand lifted to where he'd bitten me, marked me. There was no pain. It felt like it had almost healed. He'd licked and kissed it afterward, in a way that could only be described as reverent.

I glanced at my small potted plant that someone had brought up for me. The vervain flowers were a startling purple in the moonlight. Every witch's home had a flourishing patch of the herb because of what it represented. Home, family, love.

Mine represented a lie. I had none of those things here.

Maybe if I looked at this as some bizarre holiday? Great sex—understatement of the century. Good food—going by last night's offering. And an exotic location—if you liked living in woods crawling with demons.

Yep, that's exactly what I'd do. Not take any of this too seriously. I just had to make sure I didn't get attached to Draven, this place, or his people, and judging by the looks they gave me last night, that wasn't going to be a problem. They wanted me gone as much as I wanted to leave.

It was still dark outside, but I was too wired to sleep.

I slid my phone from the bedside table and checked it. There were several messages.

You still alive? That was Mags.

Willow's text was more restrained. *Let me know if you need anything.*

Rose's simple, *Miss you.* And Mom's, *I'm so proud of you.* Had had me fighting back tears.

Then I had to bite back a laugh when I read Else's. *Let me know if you want some of my castration elixir.*

Draven stirred, so I rolled to my side so my phone light didn't wake him, and he instantly rolled toward me in his sleep, pulling me into him. He was warm and muscled, and I could admit it was nice being held.

Brody hadn't liked to cuddle much—

That's because he was a freaking psychopath who'd planned to kill you.

God, I needed to get my head on straight. As distracting as this whole thing with Draven was, I had to focus on the most important thing happening in my life right then, my task, and finding Amy and Marina. The vines had been closer this morning, and I still had no idea who'd taken those females or why they'd buried Imogen's body on our property so close to Charity.

I opened my photos and clicked on the documents I'd taken pictures of at the council's public records library and read over them all again, but nothing new popped out at me. I opened Nightscape and searched Cesare Sartori's name.

Amy had no pictures of her father, and the only mention of him was a picture of a new Mercedes he'd gotten her for her twenty-second birthday a couple months ago. And soon after, it looked like Amy had moved out of the family home and into her own apartment in the city.

A lot of our histories weren't confined to "our world." We lived alongside humans, pretending we were the same as them, which meant there were alternate versions of a lot of things that happened to us, events, news, that were also recorded in their history books and in the human media.

I did a Google search for Cesare Sartori. He was lorded as a slick businessman, smart and wealthy. So, pretty much the same as in our world, only we knew he used magic to his advantage, that he'd used it to get ahead. The male was hungry for power in both ours and the human world, and he went after it with a single-minded focus.

Draven growled in his sleep and shoved one of his thighs

between mine. My breath escaped on a rush and my body, which was still recovering from what he'd done to me earlier, started to heat up all over again.

I did my best to ignore it and searched The Missing Maidens.

I got quite a few hits. Human experts, historians, amateur sleuths, and murder podcasts saying that whoever was behind The Maidens disappearances was the first serial killer ever documented.

There were debates over whether the perpetrator was a woman or a man and their possible motivations. Unfortunately, none of the human theories helped me.

Whoever was behind the original disappearances had a reason for doing it. Maybe some kind of power grab? A ritual? Sacrifice? That had to be the focus of my research next. There had to be a link to the disappearances happening now. I just had to find it. But first, there was somewhere I needed to go. I pulled back the covers.

"What are you doing?" Draven's sleepy, growly voice rumbled behind me.

I needed his help, and he'd already made it clear he would be going wherever I went when it came to my task. "Looking at some documents I got from the council library." I turned to him when something occurred to me. "Were you the reason they had a late meeting?"

He rested his head on his hand. "Yeah."

I was right, I had sensed him there. "I bet Sapphire Eldridge loved every moment of it."

Draven frowned.

"A small, angry woman with piercing blue eyes."

"She was the only one who didn't try to change my mind or seem the slightest bit outraged by it."

"I'm not surprised. She probably cracked open a bottle of bubbly tonight to celebrate. A Thornheart being torn from her family and taken to the big bad wolf's lair."

His gaze darkened. "My lair?"

I shrugged. "Sorry, your gothic castle on a hill surrounded by woods and demons who want to eat me."

He pushed me to my back, took my phone from my hand, and placed it on the bedside table. "It's not all that bad, is it?"

"Your keep is actually very cool."

His gaze moved over my face. "I won't let any demons eat you, by the way."

"I'd appreciate that."

His gaze went to my mouth, and he licked his lips. "I aim to please."

"I thought your aim was to drive me crazy."

He chuckled, and I couldn't look away. Who the hell was this? I felt like I was in bed with a different male than the one I'd walked into this room with.

"It was never the main goal."

His eyes were sleepy and sexy, his expression relaxed, and for the first time since I'd met him, his jaw wasn't clenched so tight I thought his teeth might shatter. He pushed my thighs apart and pressed his hips against mine. He was hard. A shiver ran through me.

"What's wrong with you? Where have you hidden the real Draven?" I said because I couldn't have this. This sexy, sleepy, easy-going version of Draven was dangerous. Where was my uptight, eternally pissed-off alpha?

His brows lowered. "There's nothing wrong with me. What are you talking about?"

"Why are you acting like this?"

"Like what?"

"Like this! Mr. Chill, all laid-back, happy-go-lucky."

He dragged his nose up the side of my throat, and I shivered. "Because I've eaten and I've slept. It's been a while." He lifted his head. "I've barely done either, not since I saw you. But mostly because I've finally been inside my mate. I know you're safe and I can keep you that way. I'm content, relaxed. Isn't that a good thing? We can't fight every moment of every day, can we?"

I didn't know what to say. No, I didn't want to fight all the time, but I didn't want to like him too much either.

He searched my gaze, and his head tilted to the side. "Don't worry, I'm sure you'll piss me off again, probably sooner rather than later."

He saw right through me, right to my coward's heart. I'd already told him all about my fear of letting him close in that field. But even if I hadn't, the male seemed to see everything when it came to me. But then I'd been having *feelings* when it came to him as well.

And right now, he was feeling affectionate and playful. I didn't need to tap into some mated couple thing to see that, though; it was plain on his handsome face.

"And what will you do when I piss you off again?" I asked, because I did love to push the guy.

He grinned. "I'll do what I did tonight. I'll bring you up here and fuck the angry right out of you."

I stared up at him. "You are unbelievable." And even more handsome when he grinned like that.

"Thanks."

"I didn't mean it as a compliment."

He shrugged a broad shoulder. "That's how I'm choosing to take it." His green eyes glowed in the shadowed room. "Are you pissed at me again, little witch?"

Yes, absolutely in a playful mood. "I'm not, *not* pissed off, wolf man."

He chuckled again. "Your smart mouth turns me on."

"I have a feeling turning you on isn't overly difficult." My pulse fluttered faster, my belly curling and heating.

"All I have to do is look at you, smell you, fucking think about you, and I'm hard for my mate," he said in a low, growly voice.

My mind scrambled at the way he said that. *His mate*. I was his mate. I knew it, but I hadn't really believed it, not until this moment. If he wasn't on top of me right then, I would have exploded out of this bed and run for the door because I knew, if I didn't guard my heart, I could fall for Draven Moreau.

I just had to fight it.

Fight fate.

Stronger people than you had tried, Willow for one, and failed.

Well, I'd be the exception.

"Don't think too hard about it, just go with it," he said, reading me again. "All we have to do is take it one day at a time, Iris, okay?"

I nodded. It was all I was capable of doing in my current state —turned on and kind of freaking out.

"Spread your legs wider for me, I'm going to eat your pussy until you come," he said.

He kissed me, one of his hard, overwhelming kisses that stole my breath, then moved down my body, pressing sucking kisses over my skin, playing with my nipples, teasing them, but not for long because Draven was on a mission. His mouth moved over my lower belly, and I spread wider for him instantly.

His mouth covered me, licking and kissing, fucking me with his eager tongue. His large hands wrapped around my thighs, and he held me open. His growls and groans filled the room, and all I could do was writhe under him.

I thrust my fingers in his hair and arched my hips, rubbing myself against his mouth, already out of control. He gripped me tighter, dragged his mouth to my clit, and sucked.

I screamed, shaking as I came. No one had ever gotten me there so easily. Draven barely touched me, and I was on the edge.

The aftershocks rocked through me, and my mind buzzed, my emotions all over the place. Draven rose over me, and when he sat back and rolled me to my stomach, I went willingly. Why would I stop him? He'd given me nothing but pleasure since he brought me up here.

And again, who was I to fight fate?

His hands moved to my hips, and he lifted them so I was up on my knees. A moment later, he was positioning himself behind me. "Ready?"

"Yes." I wanted him again so badly I shook.

He filled me with one smooth stroke before I finished getting the word out.

I groaned into the covers, fisting the sheets as he fucked me again. It was too much, every nerve ending oversensitive, overstimulated, but somehow, I wanted more. I was on a razor's edge already, and when he thrust back in, I couldn't stop myself from shoving back, and taking him deeper.

"That's it, take your mate, Iris. Take all of me."

His words turned me on more, and our bodies moved together, faster, harder, the slap of slick skin and Draven's grunts all I could hear. His fingers gripped me tighter, digging into my flesh, and he came down over me, his front to my back. One of his hands slid over my belly and across my chest, holding me tight to him, and his thrusts grew wilder, more punishing. His other hand went between my thighs, and I cried out when he rubbed his fingers over my clit.

"Come for me, let me feel you again, Iris. I need to feel you come around my cock one more time, petal," he said.

And with that, I came for him again, my body obeying his command like it was made to. Draven groaned against my ear, his cock pulsing deep inside me, coming with me. He stayed where he was, covering me, his big body quaking, rocking into me, working every last bit of pleasure from us both.

"One day soon, my seed will take root, Iris," he said against my ear.

I stiffened. "What?"

"Now we're mated, you can get pregnant."

"What?" I said again, my mind jumbled and still trembling

from the orgasm he'd just given me. I couldn't believe what I was hearing.

"What is it?" he said and rolled to his side, pulling me against him.

I pulled back. "We barely know each other. Having children is the last thing on my mind. What if I don't want kids?"

"Well, do you want kids?" he asked, looking way too relaxed.

"I don't know." That was a lie. I'd always wanted children, but I couldn't even think about that now. "Thankfully, I'm on the pill, so your attempt to *impregnate me* will be unsuccessful. You can use a condom next time. I can't believe I had sex with you without one."

"Shifters can't catch or carry sexually transmitted diseases, and if you're on the pill, then there's nothing to worry about." He dragged me back down with him. "We'll revisit the kids thing another time."

I lay there, silently fuming. He was infuriating and bossy and arrogant. And completely and utterly insane.

"You're pissed off with me again, aren't you?" he said.

"Yep."

"Give me a couple minutes and I'll fuck you again."

I shoved away from him and got out of bed.

"Come back here," he said.

"I have somewhere I need to be."

He was out of bed a second later. "If you think you're leaving me, Iris..."

"I'm not leaving you, that isn't an option since you went to the council and I was literally forced to sign my life away. We're stuck with each other." *For now, anyway.* As soon as he got tired of his new plaything, I'd be free to get on with my life. "But I have a task to pass, and time's running out."

His jaw tightened. "Wherever you're going, I'm coming with you."

I wanted to tell him no, but that would be reckless and point-less. Draven would come with me whether I said he could or not.

We dressed, headed downstairs, and out the door to his truck.

"Where are we going?" he asked as he opened his door.

"One of the missing witches has an apartment in the city. I want to search it while it's still dark."

He nodded and we climbed in. "Let's get this over with."

Chapter Twenty-Five

Iris

Draven was at my back, so close I could feel him as we walked through the foyer. I'd used a simple spell on the doorman, who'd forget we'd even been there within minutes of talking to us.

"Do you know which apartment we're looking for?" Draven asked me.

"Yep." I did, thanks to her oversharing on Nightscape. We climbed into the elevator, and I hit the button for the ninth floor. I would have hit up the other girl's apartments as well, but Imogen's family had already been in and cleared her place out, and Marina's family had security watching hers.

"I hate these things," he said when the doors closed and we shot upward.

Draven had been trapped for so long that I guess a lot of things were still new to him, like elevators. "It's safe."

"I still hate it."

He was in a bad mood. He had been since we left the keep. "We're nearly there."

He motioned to the camera in the corner. "And you're sure that thing's turned off?"

"Yes." I'd learned the spell to deactivate them from a witch who frequented the bar I used to work in. I didn't ask how he knew it, but I'd tried it afterward and it'd worked. It interfered with video and phone transmission. All you got was a lot of static. It was a simple but highly effective bit of blood magic.

He took my hand and lifted it, scowling at the slice I'd made on my palm. "You need to stop cutting yourself."

Electricity danced up my arm from that simple touch. I did my best to ignore it. "It's part of who I am, and something you'll have to get used to. Else makes a balm that speeds up healing. I have some back at the keep." Though I'd cut my palm so much it was permanently scarred, like all the witches in my coven.

He grumbled under his breath. Just another reason we were so unsuited. He wanted me to stop doing something that was a fundamental part of who I was and the way I used my magic. Him asking me not to cut myself to spell was like me asking him not to shift. But he didn't see it that way, obviously.

The doors slid open, and we strode out. It was the middle of the night, but you never knew who was around, so I hurried along the hall, checking room numbers.

"This one." Amy was a witch, which meant her place would be warded. I needed to break through it if I wanted to get inside. Not something I liked doing. It went against our covenants, our most basic laws, but I had no choice. I pulled my knife from my pocket. "Look away," I said to Draven.

He growled and did not look away, cursing under his breath as I cut a small X into the palm of my hand.

"My wolf doesn't like the smell of your blood," he growled.

He'd said that to me once before, and now I understood what he meant by it. He was breathing heavily and his jaw was tight. I didn't know how the whole inner-wolf thing worked, but it was obvious he was going through something on a base, animal level. When I cut myself, he felt it in some way.

I turned to him, rested my hand, the one not bleeding, on his shoulder, and looked into his eyes. Yep, his wolf was right there, I could see the change in that green gaze. "I've been doing this a long time. It's part of who I am. I'm sorry if it makes you unhappy," I said to him, "but I'm perfectly okay."

His gaze searched mine, wild and intense. "You can tell me you're okay a million times, Iris, but I'll never be okay with you hurting yourself, with you bleeding, no matter the reason. So let's get this over with. I want you back in my bed."

All righty then. I could admit I liked being in his bed as well. But I was a witch, and that would never change. I didn't want it to, and my task had to come first. "I'll move as quickly as I can."

"Good."

I pressed my hand to the door handle, tilted my head back, and closed my eyes. I felt the rush of power flow through me, Amy's ward. It had weakened while she'd been gone, which was what I'd been banking on. We needed to strengthen magic like this daily, which would make my job easier. I whispered the spell to breach it over and over again, faster and faster.

You needed a good reason to break a ward. If you had evil intent, it was impossible. The spell I was using could see into my heart. The words came from light and goodness and were the impartial judge that would grant the request or not. That's why blood was required. I was essentially giving the spell life, warmth, a beating heart for that moment in time.

I'd never used it before, and I didn't know if it would work now, but it was the only option we had, and I was highly motivated to get inside. Tingles danced from my chest along my arm and down to my hand that was wrapped around the door handle.

Another surge of power pulsed through me, and I had to hang on when it would have shoved me back. Draven was suddenly behind me, holding me there, even as he did some more unhappy growling. The power surge peaked, then flowed right through me before leaving through the hand that still gripped the door handle.

It clicked.

The ward breaking and the door unlocking.

I sagged against Draven, the spell taking my energy with it.

He hooked an arm around my waist, opened the door, and all but carried me in, shutting the door after us. "Okay?"

"Yeah, thanks. Some spells just take a lot out of you." I straightened, but he kept his arm around me for a long moment, his head bent, studying me before he finally released me. I stepped back before I was tempted to do something like kiss him. "Right... uh, we better get searching."

"What are we looking for?"

"I'm not entirely sure. But I'll know it when I see it." I hoped so, anyway.

It was a nice apartment, with more than enough room for one person. There was also no sign that Amy was a witch, which wasn't unusual, especially if you mixed with a lot of humans. Not everyone lived like my family.

But honestly, it didn't feel very...lived in. It was missing personality. Draven went to the kitchen to search, and I went to her bedroom.

The bed was in the middle, everything in shades of pinks and mauves, and she loved throw pillows. She'd made her bed the day she went missing, but that seemed to track, since the rest of her apartment was so perfectly presented. Amy liked every-thing in its place, apparently. I peeked into the en suite. Her cosmetics were still on the counter, and the drawer she kept them in, open. Had she been in a hurry to get to the club? This room didn't seem to match the rest of her extremely tidy apartment.

I checked the other drawers. Nothing of importance, just more makeup, hair care products, and a packet of condoms. I knew she'd been seeing someone, well, several someones. Again it was all over Nightscape. But as far as I could tell, no one seriously.

I went back into her bedroom and started going through the dresser. It didn't feel right, invading her privacy like this, but I was out of options.

"I think I found something," Draven said.

I turned, and he was at the door, holding a knife. "There was blood on this. They washed it, but I can still smell it."

"Hers?"

"I don't know, I'd have to smell her blood to compare it. But I can smell a lot of bleach, especially in the kitchen. Someone did a lot of cleaning in here recently."

Had someone hurt Amy with that knife, or worse, then cleaned away the blood? Was her body already buried somewhere as well? Dread crawled up my spine. What the hell kind of monster were we dealing with?

We checked the rest of the apartment, but there was nothing here, and after Draven's discovery, I wasn't surprised. Someone had been through this place and cleaned every surface, hiding any evidence that might have remained.

He held the door open, and we walked out and back down the hall to the elevator. My mind raced, the feeling of helplessness suddenly overwhelming. The doors slid closed.

"Iris?"

Draven's deep voice washed over me, offering me comfort without even realizing he was doing it. "I'm failing. My coven is relying on me. *Amy and Marina* are relying on me. No one else has any idea where they are or who's doing this. And if I don't pass this task, my coven will lose everything. And I don't know what to do next."

He closed the space between us. "We'll figure it out. Whoever took those females has slipped up somehow, they always do. We'll find them."

"I hope you're right." I bit my lip. Embarrassingly, it was quivering.

Draven's gaze slid over the star on my cheek, then dipped to my mouth.

"Draven—" One moment, he was staring down at me, the next, he hauled me off my feet, pressed me against the wall, and kissed me.

I clung to him as he plundered my mouth, owning it like only he could. How could I want that, *like it*, after everything that happened with Brody? After Draven had forced me into this messed-up relationship? But I did. I liked the way he kissed me, a lot. I couldn't get enough. And as far as distraction techniques went, it was highly successful.

The elevator doors dinged.

Someone laughed behind us. "Take your whore to a room already."

Draven stiffened, lowered me to the floor, and turned slowly. Two human males dressed in expensive clothes stood there grinning. I couldn't see Draven's face, but as soon as the humans got a look at him, their grins dropped and they stumbled back a step.

"What did you say?" Draven said, low and deadly.

I grabbed the back of his shirt when he strode toward them. "It's okay. Ignore them." He pulled me along with him.

"No, it's not," he said, sounding like the relentless predator he was.

One of them lifted his hands. "Hey, sorry. Didn't mean anything by it."

"Yes, you did," Draven said through gritted teeth. "You called my female a whore. You knew exactly what you were saying."

He took another step toward them, and I grabbed his arm, moving around to stand in front of him. *And wow*, he looked ready to literally tear them to pieces.

"Draven..." Nothing.

"Draven." Still nothing.

"*Draven.*" Finally, he looked down at me. "Let it go, okay? For me." I don't know why I said that or if it would make a difference, but it was all I could think of.

His eyes were wolf, and his chest heaved. My big bad wolf still had some serious anger issues, and after coming here where he thought I might be in danger, then seeing me cut myself when he was already in full-on protection mode—well, it seemed I'd pushed him to the very edge of his control.

These guys had just said the wrong thing at the wrong time.

Draven kept his eyes on me as the guys skirted us and rushed into the elevator, and as the doors closed, I released a breath and let go of his arm. He grabbed my hand, not letting me pull away, then led me across the foyer and out the door.

"Draven..."

"I need to get the fuck out of here before I turn around and hurt them."

Shit.

I let him lead me down the street and away from the building. "Are you okay?" I asked as we reached his truck.

He spun me and pressed me into the side of it. "No. My wolf wants to lock you up and keep you safe, Iris. And every time you're in danger, I struggle to keep control. I haven't forgotten the way you looked when I found you in the middle of that field, surrounded by demons, or in that fucking cave, unconscious and covered in blood. You have a habit of getting yourself hurt." He shook his head as if he were shaking back the beast and grappling for that control now. "You're my mate, and my need to protect you just got a whole lot more intense."

He was breathing heavily, and his wolf was still there. His beast hadn't retreated since we left the keep.

"I'll do my best not to get hurt again," I said, not sure what else to say, because I couldn't promise him it wouldn't happen.

His hand curled around the side of my throat, and his thumb brushed over my jaw. "You're a pain in my ass, little witch," he said, but there was no heat to his words, and something wild and exciting lit his gorgeous eyes.

"And you're unbelievably arrogant," I said, fighting a grin.

He tucked my hair behind my ear. "Get in the truck before I toss you in the back and fuck you on the street."

"I'll just...be getting in the truck, then."

He grinned, then, and opened the door for me. God, I loved that grin.

We both got in, and Draven started the truck. I glanced out the window as we pulled out onto the road.

A dark figure stood under a shop awning, and he was watching us.

Vampire.

And not just any vampire. It was Pretender.

Chapter Twenty-Six

Iris

The bell above the shop door rang, and I smiled when I saw it was Mags and Bram walking into The Cauldron. They were carrying boxes.

"Hey! What are you doing here?" Mags said as they put them on the counter.

"Wills went for lunch. I could hear her stomach growling, so took pity on her." I'd only stopped in to get some more of Else's healing balm. After last night, and the way Draven was with me cutting myself, I thought I should stock up. Hopefully, Willow wouldn't be long. I needed to get to the council building. I'd called Cesare Sartori's office again this morning, but he was hard to pin down, I thought maybe just showing up in the guy's office would be my best bet.

While I'd been waiting, I'd spent my time combing through Amy, Imogen and Marina's Nightscape pages again, going through their posts and pictures, reading the comments. Trying to find anything that might help. I'd also done a search on Pretender after seeing him last night, I was pretty sure he'd been following us, but he wasn't on the App.

"I didn't think I'd see you today." Mags eyes darkened. "I thought Draven would have you locked in his tower. You okay?"

I probably would be, if Draven had his way. He'd been more than a little reluctant for me to leave this morning, but had relented when I'd pushed. "I'm fine, I promise. So what's in the boxes?"

Mags studied me, worry in her eyes. "Else and I have been busy. After Rowena and the rest of the coven did their thing, the cemetery has improved, but there's still gonna be issues until Zinnia can come and cleanse it."

Our cousin Zinnia was our expert on all things death and the spirit world, and was exactly who we needed. "Mom told Rowena about Charity?"

"Yep, and when she found out you went to Shadow Falls she was pissed." Mags grinned. "She was proud of you, though, and now she thinks your new mate is the shit for coming to your rescue." Mags leaned on the counter and rested her chin in her hands. "So, did you have sex with him?" All humor had left her voice, and was replaced with something closer to fear.

Bram walked away, dissolving into the shadows as only he could.

"No comment," I said. I did not want to talk about this. I was still processing everything myself.

Her face turned pink, not from embarrassment, but from anger. "You slept with him? He forced you into this twisted relationship and dragged you to his castle of doom, and you just gave it up?"

"Mags..."

"He should be punished for what he did to you, not fucking rewarded!"

"Magnolia..."

"I can't believe you did that. What the hell is wrong with you?"

"This is one of your sisters?" a familiar voice said.

I looked up, and Asher strode to the counter. I hadn't even seen or heard her walk in. "What are you doing here?" She held my gaze, and I bit back a curse. "He sent you after me?" That explained why he relented and let me leave without him.

"I volunteered. He just wants to protect you—"

"Control," Mags interrupted. "Your nutjob of an alpha wants to control her."

"You have a very smart mouth for one so young and weak," Asher said.

Bram materialized out of the shadows. Tall, lean, and muscled, he stood several inches taller than Asher. His black eyes locked on her. He hadn't missed what Ash was, a warrior, making her a threat to Mags in his eyes. And he hadn't liked the way she'd just spoken to his best friend. He stared her down and shook his head, a silent warning.

Asher grinned up at him. "Oh, you could try it, shadow man." Then her golden eyes slid to Mags. "Our alpha is a good male. He'd never harm your sister. You have nothing to worry about." She winked. "The grown-ups have everything under control."

"Ash," I said as Mags surged forward.

Bram wrapped an arm around her, restraining her.

He seemed to be doing that a lot lately. She had trouble controlling her temper these days, and that was not my sister. She'd never tried to get physical with anyone before she went through what she had a year ago. We were all scarred in some way after Brody and Cora did what they had to us, and the scars Magnolia carried inside were just as brutal as the ones she carried on her skin. I worried that one day Bram wouldn't be there to stop her.

Asher looked up at Bram, ignoring Mags completely. "I haven't seen one of your kind in a long time, crow. If you ever want to spar with someone your own size, come by the keep."

Bram said nothing, but Mags's struggles renewed while she cursed at the warrior.

"Mags," I said and came around the counter.

Asher looked down at her and chuckled before her gaze slid back to me. "I'll be outside if you need me." Then she sauntered out.

"That bitch!" Mags shrieked. "I can't believe she said that!" She spun to Bram. "I can't believe she said that to you."

Bram's gaze was on the door, following Asher out. Then he looked down at Mags and again said nothing.

"She's one of Draven's warriors," I said to my sister. "By all accounts, one of his best, so taking her on would be a very stupid idea."

Mags didn't spare me a glance, her gaze was locked on her best friend. "You want her? Really? I thought you had better taste. If you sleep with that cow, I'll never speak to you again."

Bram's jaw tightened.

"I mean it," Mags said, breathing heavily, utterly furious.

They stared each other down, the tension so thick it filled the room.

"You done?" he finally said.

"Are you seriously telling me you're interested in *her*?" Mags flung an arm toward the door Asher had just walked out.

"I haven't told you anything," he said in his deep, yet quiet, voice. "You haven't let me get a fucking word in."

Uh-oh.

Mags stilled, staring up at him in shock. Bram never said a harsh word to her, or argued. She'd told me that herself. I'd never seen them like this.

Hurt transformed Mags's face, and she looked down, then quickly tugged at her sleeve that had ridden up, revealing one of her scars.

The muscle in Bram's jaw jumped again, then he hooked her around the back of the neck and pulled her against him.

Mags wrapped her arms around his waist. "I'm sorry."

"It's okay," he said.

But it wasn't. He wasn't. Mags couldn't see it then, but he was far from okay.

Mags finally pulled back and looked up at him. "She's all wrong for you." There was a note of desperation in her voice. "You see that, don't you?"

Bram just nodded.

She smiled, and it was strained as hell, then she looked at me. "We better get going, but you'll come by the house soon? Everyone misses you," she said, acting like nothing happened.

"I'll try," I said and made a mental note to have a talk with Willow about Mags. She was struggling, and we needed to find a way to help her. Bram shouldn't have to take the brunt of it.

They left, and I got to work stocking the shelves with the new supplies to kill time while I waited for Willow.

Asher walked back in. "I like your sister, she's feisty."

I ignored that. "I don't need a babysitter."

Asher picked up one of the herbal soaps Mom made for the store, sniffed it, and put it in her pocket. "You've almost died twice since Draven met you."

Okay, she got me there. "I told him I wouldn't do anything dangerous on my own."

Asher shrugged. "How much longer are you here for?"

I checked my phone. "As soon as Willow gets back, I'll head to the council building."

"Excellent. Then after that we can go for a drink?" She grinned. "I feel like getting tipsy and making bad choices."

I laughed. Yes, I was pissed that Draven had Asher shadowing me, but I was starting to seriously like the warrior. "And you think Draven would be okay with that?"

Her grin slipped. "Probably not. Raincheck on that." She pulled out her phone and started tapping at the screen.

"Are you texting Draven?"

"Yep," she said without looking up.

"I never took you for a snitch," I said.

"I am not." She winked. "I'm loyal."

Apparently, I wasn't trusted to get myself to the keep, or maybe he wanted to make sure I actually went back.

Asher stayed until Willow returned, then tailed me in her truck all the way to the council building. I waved and headed inside.

I stopped by Sartori's office first, but he wasn't available, so I sent a quick text to Asher, telling her to take off, that I'd hang here and do a little more research, and promised to go straight to the keep afterwards. She replied with a, thumbs-up. I lost time going through the old books, but came up with nothing new. I had no leads and nowhere to go. God, I felt lost. I needed another sign from the mother in a bad way.

Every day that passed, I feared the chances of finding those girls alive, lessened.

I left and headed back to the keep—and was halfway there when I spotted Asher following me. She'd waited all that time? Now I felt guilty as well.

My phone rang. Mom flashed on the screen. I answered on speaker. "Hey, mom."

"Are you okay? Is Draven treating you with respect?"

It had only been one day, but hearing her voice had my eyes stinging. "I'm fine, Mom. And yes, Draven is treating me with respect."

"If he does something..."

"He's not going to hurt me." Mom had taken some wrong turns in the relationship department before she and Art finally got it together. One of her exes, Mags's sperm donor, had been abusive, and I could hear the fear in her voice. "I promise, I'd tell you if I didn't feel safe. He's a good male."

"That's something at least. But I've been working on an appeal. This isn't right. You should've been given a choice. Every female should. And it's a precedent that could end in another witch being forced to mate someone who isn't so good, and who won't treat her with kindness or respect. I think we have a good case. I'm going to fight this."

"An appeal? Is that an option?" My stomach felt like I'd swallowed a lead pipe all of a sudden. "The council never goes back on a decision."

"I'm going to try. What they did, forcing this on you, is barbaric," Mom said. "You're not Selene or Charity, you shouldn't be made to pay for their crimes. There has to be another way."

"I'm not sure that's a good idea." No, this whole situation wasn't ideal, but fate had made any other option impossible. "There's more to this, and I think...I think it's only a matter of time before this all sorts itself out."

Mom was silent a beat. "Do you want to be mated to Draven?"

I opened my mouth, closed it.

"Would you have...if you'd been given the choice?" she asked gently.

A weird feeling curled in my chest. Would I? A short time ago, I wouldn't have even had to think about that answer. I gripped the wheel tighter. "There's a lot at stake. They could declare war if you try to take me back," I said instead of answering. "Draven wouldn't just let me go, Mom." My belly swirled at the thought of that, of him coming after me. God, I was messed up. Why the hell was I trying to talk my mother out of this? I was starting to like Draven, but that didn't mean I wanted to be mated. After Brody, I swore never to make myself so vulnerable again that my family was all I needed. That's still how I felt, right? Doubt filled me, and I quickly shook it off. "Let's just not talk about it now. We'll worry about the logistics of it all if it happens." And it wouldn't. Because again, the council never went back on a decision.

"If that's what you want." Mom said. "Will you come for dinner soon, sweetheart?"

"Try and stop me."

"Love you."

"Love you, too," I said, then ended the call.

As I drove up the road to the keep, goosebumps lifted all over my skin, because I *felt* him. His energy was thick, and kind of dark, and urgent. Somehow, I felt all that as well.

I had the sudden urge to turn around and drive home, to go to my family, to my old room, but I could admit there was a part of me that was excited to see Draven as well, and the heavy energy he was throwing out the closer I got to him, seemed to fill me, curling deep inside, heating me.

I'd left the keep hours ago, and knowing he was waiting for me had my heart rate spiking.

By the time I parked the car and shut off the engine, the air around me was electric. Draven's presence was everywhere. It seemed impossible that I could be the only one who felt it.

I shut the door behind me and walked toward the keep. The moon was high and the air crisp.

He stood at the front of the keep, his tall frame highlighted by the light shining from the windows behind him. He looked kind of wild, his green eyes watching me hungrily as I approached. The intensity of it was so strong I had to take a steadying breath.

"I'm back," I said stupidly when I reached him, suddenly feeling awkward. I was finding it hard to breathe all of a sudden.

He moved in, crowding me. His arm came around my waist and he pulled me in against his hard body.

"I didn't like being parted from you today," he said.

"It was only a few hours." But I'd felt it, too, this yearning I couldn't explain. I knew what it was now, it was Draven. The realization was so terrifying, I almost jerked back. Not that I could with the hold he had on me.

"Eleven hours, Iris. You've been away from me for eleven hours." His voice was rougher.

"We're mates, but this isn't some...love match. I have a life away from you, and that will never change."

"We mated yesterday," he said and dipped his head, his mouth an inch from mine. "A wolf is at his most volatile after taking his mate for the first time. Today has been torture for me."

I didn't know what to say, and I didn't want to admit that it had been kind of hard for me as well. Not torture, but it had been weird. All day I'd felt like something...someone was missing.

His nostrils flared, and his grip on me tightened. "Do you wish you hadn't come back? That tonight you could crawl into your old bed, in your old room, alone?"

I'd thought that, hadn't I? A short time ago, but I could admit that maybe that hadn't felt right either. I didn't want to encourage this connection between us, though. It was a one-way road to heartache. We were nothing but fate's puppets. But the way he was looking at me, the desperate hunger, the need, god, the vulnerability, I couldn't bring myself to lie. "No."

He dipped his head closer, so his lips brushed mine when he spoke next. "I'm going to fuck you all night, Iris."

I dug my fingers into his biceps—

The door opened behind us.

"Dinner's ready! Come get it while it's hot," Sally called.

Draven

Iris was sitting at one of the tables, her plate piled high with food. Maybe I went a little overboard, but caring for my mate was ingrained, and that meant making sure all her needs were satisfied.

Asher was sitting with her, and whatever my warrior had just said had my new mate laughing.

I couldn't take my eyes off her.

My little witch had fallen asleep on the way home from the city last night, after breaking into that witch's apartment, and I'd carried her upstairs and back to our bed.

My gaze moved over her delicate features, and something clutched me tight behind my ribs. I craved her constantly, her touch, her scent, the sound of her voice. Christ, I loved talking to her...even when we were arguing. I wanted to know what she was thinking all the time, listen to what she had to say—

"I think Ash likes your mate," Dirk said. "She's a good judge of character, and she doesn't suffer fools. The pack will follow her lead."

That was why I'd put them together, that and Asher had always had more of a level head when it came to Iris, and thankfully, it looked like it was working. "I hope so." I turned to Dirk. "How did the patrol go tonight?"

"There were several demon clusters close by, but they stayed back." Dirk did not look happy.

I understood why. Our pups and adolescent pack members needed to be watched closely whenever they were outside. The risk of them being snatched by a demon was still too damn high. I wanted my people to be able to run these forests freely, and one day, my own children, but that wasn't an option yet.

I glanced at Iris again, and my territorial instincts skyrocketed. She was reluctant to have my pups now, but she'd change her mind. I shouldn't have mentioned getting her pregnant so soon, but the words had slipped out before I could stop them. My wolf had rushed forward, and I'd wanted to claim her in every way possible. And selfishly, I thought getting her pregnant would make her more likely to fit in here—and more likely to stay.

Dirk's youngest son Wren ran up to his dad, and the warrior lifted him to his shoulders. "We'll take another look tonight. We'll find them, wherever they're hiding."

"Good, keep me posted."

"Hey, Dirk," Iris said, joining us.

Dirk grinned and inclined his head. "Iris."

The urge to kiss her was great, so great I didn't even try to resist.

She was mine, in every way now, and she'd been gone all fucking day. I needed to be close to her now. Hooking her around the waist, I hauled her to me and sucked on her perfect lips, and when she didn't open for me fast enough, I took her chin, opened her mouth, and swiped my tongue inside, desperate for the taste of her again. I couldn't get enough. If she'd been here, I wouldn't have been able to stop kissing her.

When I finally lifted my head, she blinked up at me, her cheeks turning pink before her gaze shot around the room.

"They don't care," I said, dragging my nose up her throat, breathing in her scent, it was now mixed with mine. I held in my snarl of possessiveness. Fuck, I could smell how ripe for fucking she was. "You're my mate, petal. Mate's kiss."

She nodded but still looked unsure. *Fuck.*

I didn't want to hold back, I couldn't when I was with her. But then, I'd known she was mine a lot longer than she had. I was ten steps ahead of her, and maybe I needed to give her some time to catch up. "You had enough to eat?"

"Yeah, I'm stuffed." Then Iris smiled her sweet crooked smile up at Wren, her cheeks still pink. "And who's this?"

The boy smiled back as Dirk's mate, Belinda, rushed over, and ignoring Iris, inclined her head to me, lifted Wren from his father's shoulders, and rushed away.

I frowned, and Dirk winced a little.

"Do we have a problem?"

"I'll talk to her," Dirk said, looking uncomfortable.

"Oh," Iris said, looking between us and then at Belinda's retreating back, working out for herself what had just happened. "No, please, don't," she said to Dirk, then looked at me. "It's fine. I get why some of your people are wary of me."

"Sort your female out," Asher said to Dirk, joining us and also not missing what just happened. "She disrespected the alpha's female right in front of him. Not cool."

Iris looked anxious. "Ash, it's fine."

"Nope, not even a little bit. She knows better."

Dirk scowled at Asher, and she scowled back.

Iris's hands were clutched in front of her, her discomfort obvious. Fucking hell. "Ash is right," I said to Dirk. "If Belinda has a problem with my mate, she can come to me, or complain to you about it, but it does not touch Iris, understand?"

"Yeah, Drave, of course."

Iris's gaze shot to me. "You can't make people like me, Draven. I'm a big girl, I can take a little rejection."

"No disrespect, Iris," Asher said, "but we don't do that shit, not to our alpha and sure as fuck, not to his mate. Belinda needs an attitude adjustment, and fast."

Iris nodded, but she still wasn't happy. She turned to me. "I might go for a walk or something, is it safe? Just outside the keep? I need some air...and I'm thinking your pack might need a little break from me as well."

"No, they don't," I growled out.

"It's okay, Draven." There was a desperation in her eyes. She was escaping, even if it was just for a short time. She wanted to escape us, escape me.

She walked away and I felt it, her relief, but what I felt most, was her absence. She was literally just outside, but we were newly mated, the tie between us wild and untamed. I was hungry for her all the time. I should give her the space she needed, but I couldn't do, not after being without her all day.

Fuck that. She was my mate, mine to protect however I saw fit. I strode out after her. She hadn't gotten far. I caught up to her.

She turned, looking up at me, her eyes wide, glossy. "I'm okay." She wasn't. "I know this is a lot—"

A scrape sounded behind us, and I spun around, a vicious growl tore from me as a dark figure took off through the trees.

Chapter Twenty-Seven

Iris

D raven exploded into action, sprinting after the vampire. The same vampire who I saw watching us after we'd searched Amy's apartment. I ran after them and burst through the trees in time to see Draven tackle him to the ground. He had to still be young, as far as vampires went. They weren't easy to catch, and the older they got the faster and stronger they were.

He was wearing a hoodie, and it fell back as Draven stood, dragging him to his feet.

"Pretender," I said to the cursing vampire.

His vibrant purple gaze shot to me. "Ender," he corrected.

"You know this fucker?" Draven bit out.

"He was at The Bank. He stopped a demon from hurting me."

My alpha looked down at the male, expression like thunder. "What the fuck are you doing in my territory? Are you spying on my mate, vamp?"

Ender started up at him, seemingly unfazed. "My master has

taken an interest in your mate." His lips curled. "But he won't take her from you unless she wants to be taken." Ender turned my way. "Do you want to be taken, Iris?"

Was he serious? "No, I don't want to be taken. What the hell?"

"Your master?" Draven snarled.

"A vampire named Nero," I said.

Draven growled viciously. "You tell him to stay away from her. I don't give a fuck what he is, I'll kill him if he comes near her. And if he sends anyone else into my territory, I'll tear them to shreds and send them back to him in little pieces."

"Are you sure?" Ender said to me, ignoring the snarling wolf shifter shaking the shit out of him. "There are plenty of witches who'd jump at the chance to be with one such as him."

"Your master told me witches weren't to his taste," I said, and hoped he couldn't see the way my heart was trying to pound out of my chest.

"They're not, usually, but still they come, and when he turns them down, they turn to any that will have them. But you're different. He liked your...candor."

"So there're other vampires? And witches offer to feed them?"

"Yes."

Shit. "Somewhere at the club?"

"Below it. The Vault. It's where people come to feed and be fed from," Ender said.

The last place I wanted to go was back to that club. "Are you sure they're witches?"

"Yes." He grinned, flashing a whole lot of fang.

I pulled my phone from my pocket and opened Nightscape, pulling Amy Sartori's page up. "Have you seen her?" I held up her picture.

He said nothing.

"What about her?" I said, doing the same with Marina's page, then Imogen's. "They're missing, all of them witches, and I'm guessing, all visitors at your master's blood bank."

His mouth flattened. "No one at The Vault had anything to do with their disappearances. They left in one piece, all of them."

I looked up at Draven, then back to Ender. "Take us there."

"Iris," Draven said, expression hard.

"Time's running out. I can't ignore this."

Draven cursed and dragged the vampire over to my car. "Fine, but this fucker will be giving us a guided tour."

We followed Ender through The Bank. It was full and loud.

I glanced up, but the big viewing window was dark. Nero, the ancient and terrifying vamp, wasn't there watching over his domain tonight. Or at least I didn't think he was.

We reached the back of the club, and Ender punched a code into a keypad by the door. It swung open and we took the stairs down to the basement and were greeted with another door, this one massive and made of steel.

A vault.

The Vault.

He swung the thick steel rods, and the *clunk* of the door unlocking filled the small space.

Draven looked down at me, brow raised and on full alert.

"I have no idea what's behind that door," I said, because I didn't want my surly new mate to hold this against me later. I was far too tired to argue.

The door opened a crack, and music drifted out.

Draven curled his fingers around the back of my neck. "Stay close."

"I plan on it." I felt a hell of a lot safer next to a guy who could shift into an alpha wolf at any moment and easily tear someone apart.

We stepped through the door and into another club. It was a

big space. The walls were red brick, and the furnishings were mainly dark wood. The color palette was rich and lush.

And holy shit.

I was not prepared for what was going on around me. I was no animal, but even I could smell the sex and blood. I looked up at Draven, and his eyes had changed, his entire body held ridged.

"What the fuck is this?" he growled.

"Like I said, this is where the local blood drinkers come to feed. This way no one dies, and the donors enjoy quality time with a vamp or...whatever," Ender said.

Whatever? What else was there?

I turned and spotted several witches I knew doing things I'd never wanted to see them doing. I couldn't believe it. They actually came here *voluntarily.*

"If you tell anyone about this place, or who you saw here, we will have to kill you," Ender said. "Everyone who walks through that door signs a nondisclosure, which is why they feel comfortable doing..." He motioned to a couple sitting on a couch beside us. A female sat in a male's lap, his arms were around her, hands on her breasts, and he was drinking from her neck. Another male was between her spread thighs.

His head turned, and he bit into her inner thigh. She screamed, writhing, coming in front of everyone.

Draven growled under his breath, then pulled me closer.

Okay, I needed to find someone to talk to who wasn't...busy and then get the hell out of here. I searched the room.

Whoa.

Lauren Beegan.

The last person I would have ever expected to see here. Coven Beegan was old and rich and acted like they were above everyone. Lauren had bullied Willow in middle school and was still a bully now. She was currently straddling a vampire, humping against him wildly, like she'd lost her damn mind, while he drank from her exposed breast, his fangs sunk deep into her flesh.

Lauren was absolutely the person I needed to talk to. She had a lot to lose if her coven—if any of the covens—found out she came here. Not to mention her fiancé. This most certainly wasn't the image she'd spent her life cultivating. She was also friendly with Amy and the others.

"Can I go?" Ender said, looking antsy.

"Yes," Draven said.

"We need to stay for a while. Is that all right?"

Ender shrugged. "If anyone asks, you don't know me."

He turned to walk away, and Draven stopped him. "If I see you again anywhere near my mate, I will kill you."

Ender saluted my wolf and walked away.

My wolf.

Where had that come from? I'd thought it more than once, though, hadn't I?

"So what's the plan?" Draven asked.

I motioned to Lauren. "We need to wait for her to, ah...finish."

"Jesus," he muttered.

A few people glanced our way, and I realized how out of place we looked just standing there like voyeurs. More than one female was gazing longingly at Draven, and no, I wasn't a wolf, but my hackles rose. I didn't like it. Not one bit. Being mated was seriously messing with me because irrational jealousy fired through me hard and fast.

"Sit in that chair." I pointed to the one near us.

He looked at it with a scowl, then back at me. "I'd rather not."

"I don't want to get kicked out of here before I talk to Lauren." And for all we knew, Ender could be calling security to do just that despite what he said, we needed to try and blend in, but mostly, I wanted to show every female in this room that Draven was mine. That wasn't me, I wasn't that person, but there was no fighting the impulse.

Draven grumbled but did as I asked.

I climbed into his lap, and his hands went to my thighs and

dug in instantly. I looked down at him. "Now we look like we belong here," I said low because although there was music, vampires had excellent hearing, even better than wolves.

"You have it all figured out, don't you, little witch?" His voice had grown deeper while he studied me too damn closely.

The way he said it, I wasn't sure he considered that a good thing or not.

The room went dark.

Draven's hold on me tightened to almost painful. The music stopped, everyone went quiet. I could hear movement but couldn't see a thing.

"I don't fucking like this," Draven said against my ear.

He wasn't the only one.

"We're leaving." His thighs tensed, about to stand—

The lights came back on. But this time only in the center of the room.

Nero stood there in a pair of trousers and no shirt. His skin was impossibly pale, his chest muscled and hairless. His hair was combed back, and his deep purple eyes regarded the room with a stare that sent a shiver down my spine.

He nodded and chains slowly lowered from the ceiling as he turned slowly, taking in everyone in the room.

His gaze slid to me and paused.

I sucked in a breath.

Draven growled, baring his teeth.

Nero turned his attention to Draven, and the males stared each other down for long, tense seconds.

"Draven..."

With a snarl, Draven slid his hand up my chest, curling his fingers around my throat, displaying his ownership of me to Nero in the most obvious and animalistic of ways.

Brody had liked doing that when he was punishing me, wrapping his hand around my throat, but this didn't feel anything like that. Brody did it to scare me, Draven did it to claim and protect me. Goddess, I *liked* it when my alpha did it.

So I relaxed into his hold, showing Nero this was where I wanted to be, as the ancient vampire regarded us for another long moment, then finally his gaze slid away, moving to the woman beside us.

A witch. One I didn't know.

He crooked his finger at her, and she stood, walking to him as if she were connected to a rope that he was pulling.

Nero didn't drink from witches, he'd told me himself, and so had Ender. So was this little display for me? Did he think I'd get jealous and offer him my blood? I had no idea how a predator like him thought.

And the way Draven had tensed beneath me, he'd probably come to the same conclusion.

The witch stood there as he moved around her, her breath rushing past her lips, her eyes closed as if already in ecstasy.

Nero finally stood in front of her, his hands going to the neckline of her dress, then in one violent move, he tore it off her body, followed by her underwear, exposing her body to everyone in the room.

"Arms," he said smoothly.

She lifted them, and he took her wrists, shackling them to the chains above her, leaving her exposed and vulnerable.

What the hell was this?

Nero turned back to the crowd. "Donte, Cassius, Ensio."

The crowd shuffled around, and three males came forward, all vampires going by their extended fangs. The witch quivered, not from fear but excitement.

They moved in, surrounding her, and I watched in fascinated horror as all four males pounced on her. They bit into her flesh, drinking from different parts of her body, their hands in action the whole time, pleasuring her as they fed.

The witch begged for more, writhing, sobbing.

And one by one, the vampires gave her what she begged for, moving in front of her or behind her, forcing her legs wide, they each fucked her. I lost count of how many times she orgasmed. She was a trembling, limp mess by the time they finished with her, and judging by the envious looks around the room, this was a coveted position to be in.

It was my worst nightmare.

Nero finally unchained her and held her upright like a limp doll in front of him, his arms, one around her waist, the other across her chest, so he could grip her jaw to hold her head up.

He turned slowly, until he was looking at me again, then he dragged his tongue up the side of her throat, cleaning up the blood still on her skin.

I swallowed and sank deeper into Draven, and the tension in his body beneath me told me he was ready to explode out of his seat at any moment and take on the powerful vampire in front of everyone. Draven was incredibly strong, a warrior, but vamps were on another level, the old ones anyway, and Nero was definitely old.

I turned away from the vampire, giving him my back, not giving him the attention he seemed to want from me for some messed-up reason, and took Draven's jaw in my hand.

His incisors were extended, and his eyes were glowing with rage. "Look at me." His eyes didn't shift from Nero. "Draven, *look at me.*"

His green gaze finally shifted to mine.

"He doesn't matter," I said. "I don't want him."

"Who do you want, Iris?" His voice was so low and full of grit it lifted goose bumps all over my body. "I can smell you, little witch, your pussy is drenched."

"You made me this way. You did this to me. I climbed on your lap because I needed every female in this room to know that you are mine, Draven." I leaned in and pressed my face to the side of his throat and kissed my way to his ear. "I want you. I want my mate inside me." I told myself I said it to defuse the volatile situation we were in, but that wasn't the truth. "Watching that witch being fucked and fed from didn't turn me on, sitting on my mate's lap while it happened, feeling your hard body under me, hot and strong, that's what turned me on."

The lights came back on, and I knew that all participants in the little scene that had just played out behind me had gone, or at least I hoped so. I'd probably made a powerful enemy tonight, turning my back on Nero, but I wasn't going to encourage that monster in any way.

Draven watched me silently, hungrily, and I had no clue what he was thinking. His nostrils flared, and his fingers dug into my flesh.

He was ready to jump out of his skin, and I wouldn't be able to contain him for much longer. "Let's talk to Lauren, then you can take me home."

Draven's eyes grew darker, hungrier. "Be quick."

I nodded and climbed off his lap. Lauren was on the other side of the room. She was still with her vampire and turned when he said something against her ear.

Her spine stiffened as we approached.

"Hi, Lauren," I said, smiling.

"Sorry, who are you...and what the hell is that on your face?" she said, managing to look down her nose at me even though I was the one standing.

I ignored her rudeness, and Draven's furious growl. Her words didn't hurt me. I'd certainly dealt with bigger assholes than her. "Iris Thornheart, we've met a few times at different gatherings." She'd ignored me then as well.

"Thornheart?" She smirked. "You must be one of Willow's sister."

"Yep, that's me." Bitch. Willow could take her down without even losing her breath these days. "I'd like a quick word, actually."

"I'm a bit busy at the moment," she said and turned away, dismissing me.

"Oh, I think you'd be interested in what I have to say," I said and held her gaze when she glanced back at me, letting her see I wasn't in the mood for her bullshit.

Her gaze moved over my face again, and knew she saw something there, besides the obvious, because she whispered to her vamp friend and stood. "Fine, I'll bite. What do you want?"

"What do you know about Amy Sartori, Imogen Lewis, and Marina Leone?" I asked.

She stilled, her gaze darting away and back. "Why would I know anything?"

Oh, yeah, she knew something. "Because they came here as well, and you guys were friendly."

Her gaze sharpened, trying to figure out why it was me asking these questions. "I have nothing to say. I'm done with this conversation."

"If you know anything, Lauren, it would be in your best interests to share it with me." She started to turn, dismissing me, and I grabbed her arm. "I know you're worried people will find out you come here, but keeping any information to yourself about those girls to save your own ass is seriously shitty. Imogen is dead, Lauren. If you know something, you need to talk."

Her gaze spat fire. "You and your friend don't intimidate me. I said I'm done."

"Draven is the alpha of the Silver Claw pack, and my family is powerful. You know, people are interested in what we do and say —and neither of us have signed a nondisclosure."

She stilled.

"So, unless you want your fiancé and your coven to find out what you get up to on Thursday nights, I'd suggest you start talking."

"I'm not doing anything wrong," she said, face flushing. "It's mutually beneficial, and I'm allowed some pleasure in my life."

"I agree, you are. And you can carry on enjoying yourself if you tell me whatever it is you know. You have to have seen or heard something. Maybe you talked to them?"

She crossed her arms over her chest.

"Anything could be helpful, Lauren."

If her eyes were daggers, I'd look like a bleeding pincushion about now. "I heard them talking about Oldwood Forest, some ritual they wanted to do out there."

"A ritual? What kind of ritual?"

"No clue, but they said they were meeting someone there."

"Who?" I needed to know who it was.

"I don't know."

The offhand way she said it, the almost bored expression, I believed her. "Oldwood's where Amy and Marina were last seen before they vanished."

She shrugged. "It's nothing to do with me."

Lovely.

I had to assume whoever they went to meet was behind their disappearances, and it sounded like they went willingly. Did that mean it was someone they knew?

"Can I go now?" she said.

Draven had remained quiet behind me, letting me do my thing. He moved in now, so I could feel the heat of his body behind me. "Sure, enjoy your night. I guarantee you're having a lot more fun than Amy and Marina right now."

She ignored that. "You said you'd keep your mouth shut."

"I will."

"Blood oath," she bit out.

Draven grabbed my wrist. "No more fucking blood."

"I have to." I pulled free, then took the small knife from my pocket. I nicked my skin, and several vampires instantly turned my way, eyes bright. Draven made a furious sound. If we didn't get out of there soon, he was going to tear this room apart.

Lauren did the same, and I swore to keep my mouth shut.

As soon as it was done, we headed for the door.

Movement on the couch beside the exit caught my eye.

A male sat shrouded in shadow, a female, blond and delicate, lay across it. Her head was in his lap, and she was looking up at him while her hand worked between her thighs. He held her hand and forearm carefully, and eyes closed, he fed from her wrist. But he sat impossibly still, not in a frenzy like the others in the room.

I recognized him even before his violet eyes opened and caught mine.

Ronan.

I glanced back at the female. In the shadows, she could have passed for Rose, at least a year or two ago, before she got as sick as she was.

My gaze sliced back up to Ronan. His eyes were closed again.

He needed this, this place, I realized. He needed to feed. I'd noticed he hadn't looked himself for the last couple of weeks. Kind of unwell.

I wanted to say something to him, but him closing his eyes again, closing us out, told me how much he didn't want that.

Ronan was a dhampir, half vamp, but I'd never thought about how he fed. His sister Luna had her mate Gunner to sustain her. Ronan had no one.

I quickly looked away, and Draven ushered me out the door.

Chapter Twenty-Eight

Iris

D raven led me out the door and away from the club.

"I hope you got what you wanted because we're not going back there, Iris, never again," he said.

He wrapped his hand tightly around mine, and I tried to pull away, but he didn't let go and kept moving toward my car.

"Draven." I tried to pull free again. "Can you ease up a bit? Draven?" He ignored me and kept walking. "Why are you pissed off right now?"

He snarled. "That fucking vamp, he wants you. He wants to take you from me. I'll kill him first."

I could feel the rage rolling off him. "You don't need to be like this, so...territorial."

He stopped suddenly and turned. "I'm a fucking animal, Iris. *I am* territorial, it's in my DNA, especially when it comes to you. I'm also newly mated. You thought I was crazy before, wait and see what happens when another male dares to lay a hand on you, and god help them if they try to take you from me."

I stared up at him, shocked and not sure what to say. "I know this whole thing will take some getting used to...for both of us, but I don't think you understand."

"No, little witch, it's you who doesn't understand. We mated less than forty-eight hours ago." His grip on me tightened. "When my people mate, the male locks his female away with him and they fuck for a week. We need that, not only to claim our females and to work out all the intense...the fucking *violent* hunger we have for them, but to strengthen the bond between us." He slid his fingers into my hair and fisted, tilting my head back. "I need that, Iris. My wolf needs it. We need it."

Jesus. This was too much, too intense, like everything between us. I craved him, too, but he was right. The way he wanted me was most definitely violent. I'd been with a violent male before, and I didn't want that again. I could lie and pretend I was fine. I could let him have me the way he described, the way Brody used to take me when he felt particularly hateful. I could put up with it while I bided my time until this was over because it would end in spectacular disaster. How else could it end? We were virtual strangers forced together.

But I wasn't that female anymore, the one Brody had shaped and molded, and I wouldn't let anyone hurt me again. I wouldn't put my wants and needs aside for what someone else wanted from me. "No," I said. "I don't want that."

He jolted as if I'd slapped him. Confusion filled his gaze. "No? You're denying me?" His hold on my hair wasn't painful, it was possessive, and he kept hold of me as he lowered his head closer to mine. "You want me, too, Iris, I know you do."

I wasn't going to lie about that. "I do, but I don't want what you just described. I don't want violence." I lifted my hand to the cold, marked skin of my cheek. "I've had violent, Draven."

His hold on me immediately eased up, and he paled. "I would never hurt you."

"You hated me," I said, unable to pretend that everything that happened between us hadn't. "That much hate doesn't just vanish."

His breathing grew ragged. "I don't hate you. I hate Selene."

"Pretending you don't hate someone is easy with the right motivation." Like how Brody pretended to love me to get access to my family, to hurt us. "Until things get quiet, and you're looking into the face of the person you believed hurt you. There's no hiding the hate then. The urge to punish them, to make them pay for whatever it is you blame them for, is too hard to resist."

His brows lowered, and his head jerked back.

Where the hell had that come from? My hand shook, and I curled my fingers into a fist to stop it.

"You think I'd do that, that I'd treat you that way?" he asked, his voice impossibly rough.

"I think you're capable of anything. Most beings are." I looked into his wild stare. "Myself included."

I expected him to get angry, to shove me away, or yell. Instead, his fingers, still in my hair, gently massaged my scalp. "He did that to you? The fucker who marked your face?"

A sob burst from my throat, surprising me. That pain was never far away, and Draven's sudden kindness had thrown me, allowing it to roar to the surface. I'd told Draven that Brody had used me to come after my family, but I'd kept the rest of the ugly truth to myself. Why lie? Why hide the truth? He already saw it in my face, heard it in my voice. "Yes, he hurt me...in a lot of ways." I took a shuddering breath. "But he's dead now, so he can't hurt anyone else ever again."

He shook his head. "If it were possible, I would bring him back to life so I could destroy him in every way possible for hurting my mate, for causing you pain."

I laughed, the sound coming out of nowhere. I felt freaking

manic. "God, I can never predict what you'll say next or how you'll react to anything."

He did that thing he did often, rubbing his thumb over my cheek. "The violence I'm speaking of, Iris, is not born of anger or hatred or selfishness. It's born of passion, of wanting to please your mate above anything else. For that week, when it's just the two of them, it's all about her. Nothing else matters, not food, not sleep, only pleasing and caring for our females. I don't hate you. I want to give you that. I want this to work between us, petal, and I want you to be happy with me and my pack."

My body reacted to his words despite myself. My track record when it came to judging a male's character had been proven seriously deficient, but I thought I might believe him.

He pressed a firm hand to my lower back and opened the passenger door of the car. "Let me take you home. We can talk more there."

My emotions were raw, confused. This whole night had been insane. And I was so damned exhausted. Just thinking of Brody made me weary to my bones. I got in. I'd given myself to this male. Yes, the council would hold me to it, but I didn't think I could go anywhere else but with him, even if I had the choice because he wasn't the only one affected by us mating. It was a powerful thing. Like a part of me I never knew existed had been brought to life, a part of me that knew him as well.

It was all just some trick created by the fates, though, wasn't it? I had to keep reminding myself of that. We were their playthings, even if it felt real.

So impossibly real.

I'd seen how mating Warrick had affected Willow, how she and Warrick were with each other, but they had history, they'd known each other for a year before they mated. They chose to be together.

I hadn't had that choice.

Unless deciding between letting Draven go mad or me getting murdered by his pack to save him was a choice. Now, I felt like I was on a runaway train and there was no stopping it. This deep, weird, confusing connection was slowly but surely tying me tighter and tighter to Draven, and I didn't know if I could stop it.

Or if I even wanted to, anymore.

My brain screeched to a halt at that thought, and I made myself focus on why we were here in the first place.

Draven climbed in the car and started it.

"If we get something of Amy's from her apartment, do you think you'd be able to track her scent through Oldwood Forest?"

"Yeah, if her scent's still there, I'll find it."

"Right, let's go to her place."

"We're going home. I'll send Asher to get it. Can she get in past the ward?"

"Yes." Since the ward had been broken, Asher would have no trouble getting in. Maybe I should insist on going myself, but I was tired, no, exhausted, and there was nothing else we could do tonight.

He sent his warrior a text and pulled out onto the street, heading for the keep.

Everyone was already in bed when we arrived, not surprising considering how late it was. As we approached the stairs, Draven took my hand. His palm was hot and dry, rough, comforting, and he led me up the stairs to his bedroom, closing us in.

I couldn't look away as he reached back and tugged off his shirt, tossing it aside, and my breath caught when he closed the space between us. He gazed down at me as he slid his hands around my waist, then took my shirt in his hands. He waited, silently asking me for permission. I nodded and he lifted it over my head. Then kept on going, undressing me completely.

"I'm going to show you what violent hunger means to me, petal," he said. "It's powerful, and urgent, and out of control, but never about inflicting pain, never fueled by hatred."

My breathing was choppy, and my skin felt hot and achy, his

words hitting me and sinking deep. I wanted that; I wanted him to prove it to me, to show me so badly. I needed it to be true.

He regarded me, gaze on the wild side, and I expected him to lead me to his bed. Instead, he pulled me to him, lifted me, and kissed me.

He kissed me like he was dying and I was the only thing that could save him.

I wrapped my legs around his waist as he walked across the room to the large window and pressed me to the wall. The kiss grew more frantic, and his hands cupped my butt and squeezed. He moved me against him, working me up against the hardness of his cock that strained against his jeans.

I rolled my hips, and he pulled his mouth from mine with a snarl, forcing a whimper from me. I didn't want him to stop. I was already close to coming.

But he put me down and spun me so I was facing the window. The moonlight shone in, and I could see our reflections clearly in the glass—me, naked, and Draven, tall and muscled behind me.

He shucked off his jeans, his boots, and socks as well, then he pressed in against me once more. I could feel his heart pounding against my back as his dark gaze slid over the bite mark he'd made on my shoulder, a permanent scar I'd carry always, marking me as his.

And I could admit when I looked at that mark in the mirror, I liked the way it made me feel.

Wanted, safe...his.

Dipping his head, he kissed the scarred skin and lifted his gaze to me as his palms slid up my hips to my waist. "Watch." He kissed along my throat. "Watch what I do to you, Iris, how I worship you. See how much I want you."

His hands moved over my body, his lips following along in their wake. I couldn't take my eyes off him, us. His body shook as he did what he said, as he *worshiped* me. I could barely believe it. This powerful male actually shook from wanting me.

He moved around my body, sucking and kissing, marking my skin with his whiskered jaw and the roughened skin of his hands. Finally, he took a nipple into his mouth while his hands curled around my hips, working me into a frenzy just from his teasing.

By the time he dropped to his knees in front of me, I was slick and panting. Draven threw my leg over his shoulder, opening me wide for his mouth. His hands gripped my hips tighter, holding me up, and pressed his lips to me, dragging his tongue through my folds. A moment later, his growls and groans filled the room.

It didn't take long before I was trembling. On the precipice and unable to stop it when he drew my clit into his mouth and sucked.

My hips jerked, and his fingers dug in, holding me still as I came against his mouth.

"Fuck, that's it," he growled.

I'd barely recovered when he stood and moved behind me. He banded his arm around my middle and lifted me so my feet were on top of his. Like this, I was forced to lean forward, causing Draven to support my weight fully. He took himself in hand and rubbed the head of his cock along my slit from behind.

I quivered, desperate for him. "P-please."

"Never need to beg me to fuck you, petal." He slid into me with a groan.

I gasped, lifting to my tiptoes as I spasmed around his long, thick cock.

"Watch," he said again. "Watch what you do to me, Iris." One of his arms was across my chest, between my breasts, and he gripped my shoulder, the other moving so it was across my hips.

As soon as my hands rested on his forearm, he slid free and slammed back in.

"*Oh god.*" He went so deep, and there was nothing I could do but take it. My eyes drifted closed.

"No, open your eyes. Look at yourself," he said harshly, then he took me, thrusting into me with force.

I did. I opened my eyes and gasped. My hair was wild and my face was flushed. My breasts were full, nipples taut and dark, and my inner thighs glistened from my need. I was wild in my hunger for him, pushing back against him with each of his brutal thrusts, my body begging for more, and Draven was answering, giving everything to me.

No, this didn't feel like punishment. There was no resemblance between what Draven and I were doing and what Brody had done to me. This was about giving and receiving pleasure, not taking, not inflicting.

There was no pain, no hatred. I felt powerful.

Draven moved faster, harder, his face twisted with...god, with *violent* pleasure. The same thing he was giving to me. The same thing I saw on my face.

"You see?" he growled, his hand moving to my throat. He pressed his cheek to my cold one, his eyes meeting mine in our reflections. "Do you see it, Iris?"

I whimpered. "Yes."

"I want to be all you can think about, all you dream about. I want you to wake up craving me and go to sleep sated after letting me give you everything you've ached for during the day."

Oh god.

"Do you understand now?" he gritted out against the corner of my mouth.

I nodded, panting, so close.

His other hand went between my thighs, and he rubbed my clit. "Now let me feel you come. Come for your mate."

I ignited, coming for him a second time.

Draven made a sound that was raw and animal and pulsed inside me, pumping me full of his seed. His wild growls and snarls filled my head, sending my release higher.

He dragged his mouth over my skin, anywhere he could reach, as he finally slowed his thrusts. We stared at each other in the window, something moving between us that felt new and wonderful and terrifying all at the same time. I'd never felt so exposed, so vulnerable. So safe.

He grasped my chin, turning my head, and kissed me, full of hunger and longing, of passion. Then he held my gaze as he carefully eased out and lifted me, carrying me to his bed.

Laying me down, he climbed up beside me, running his hand down my side. "Rest now, because I'll be reaching for you again soon, petal. I need to pleasure my mate all night. I need to make you feel good."

I could see in his eyes that he meant it and just how much he needed me. "Is that what it's supposed to be like when you're mated? Because I...I've never experienced anything like that before," I said, telling him exactly what I was thinking. He seemed to have that effect on me.

"Yes." He tucked me in tight against him. "And me either."

I don't know how long I slept, but I woke to his kisses again sometime during the night. This time, he took me slow and deep, bringing me to several more earth-shattering orgasms before I passed out again.

And later, when the early tendrils of light were peeking through the window, it was me who reached for him. My body called out for his, and I didn't fight it. Draven flipped me onto my belly, made me come with his mouth, then fucked me from behind. It was wild and out of control, and he told me and showed me how much he liked that I'd woken him, that I'd asked for what I needed.

And it wouldn't be the last time. Because I ached for him so badly. I never knew a need like this existed, and not just the sex, his touch, the warmth of his skin against mine, the sound of his voice. God, I needed him, too.

Draven wrapped me in his arms and kissed my throat, my jaw. "We'll make this work, Iris," he said. "I want this, I need you. Will you try, petal? Will you give us that?"

How could I say no? I didn't want to. After Brody, I hadn't

A VOW OF RUIN

wanted anything to do with love and relationships, but I could fall
for Draven. If I dropped the walls I'd built around myself, I could
fall for the male holding me tight. So I said what was in my shriveled little heart. "I want to try."

He rolled me onto my back and looked down at me. "You
don't know how happy that makes me," he said, and the smile he
gave me ninja-kicked down the first brick in my emotional wall.
"As long as there is honesty between us, as long as we talk about
how we're feeling, we can make this work. Nothing can get in our
way. Not Selene, and not how we got here."

I cupped his whiskered jaw and smiled up at him. "Okay."

He grinned wider, and then he kissed me again.

Maybe I'd lost my mind, but there was no getting off this train.

I just hoped this didn't all end in a fiery wreck.

Chapter Twenty-Nine

Draven

My gaze was instantly drawn to Iris as she walked down the stairs, Nia at her side. She was chatting to her familiar, having a conversation with her dog like you would with another person.

The great room was bustling, people eating and talking, but my mate was all I could see. She fascinated me in every way. Iris's abilities, her magic, it wasn't something I'd allowed myself to think about when it wasn't right in my face. It was easy to forget what she was capable of.

I'd hated all witches. After what Selene and her sister had done, I'd no longer trusted magic, and honestly, I was still wary.

And now, I had a mate who could communicate with animals. She'd sent fifty rats to find me, to lead me back to her. I'd once seen Charity do it with a horse. She'd whispered something to the beast, and it had taken off. The human male riding it had been thrown and killed, all because he'd dared to reject her.

My mate had inherited her looks from Selene but her powers from Charity.

Something sunk its claws low in my gut, and I shoved it aside as I glanced up at Iris. She was smiling at Asher, who had just walked in. Light streamed through the windows, and it made Iris's hair look several shades lighter, so much like Selene's.

But they were not the same person.

Inside, they were nothing alike.

I'd sure as hell never wanted Selene the way I wanted Iris. What I'd felt for Selene hadn't been real. Selene hadn't been my mate. Iris was. Why the hell was I thinking about this?

The more I got to know Iris and every day I spent in her company, the resemblance between my mate and Selene became less and less.

I had to find a way to let go of my hatred and my thirst for revenge because I had nowhere to direct it, not anymore.

Nia trotted down the stairs and ran right to me. I crouched and rubbed her head. "Hey, Nia, how's my good girl?"

"Nia says, that yes, you're right, she has been a very good girl, and she'd like to know if she gets a treat now?" Iris said, that smile in her voice as well.

I swiped a piece of bacon from the middle of the closest table and gave it to her. Nia swallowed it in one bite, then danced around me before pushing her head against my hand and demanding more pats.

"You have a friend for life," Iris said, chuckling.

I looked up from Nia. "Glad to hear it." I held her gaze, searching for any sign of how she was feeling after last night. It felt like a breakthrough to me, like a massive step in the right direction, and I hoped Iris felt that way too. I took her hand and pulled her to me, then cupped the back of her head and kissed her. "Good morning," I said against her lips. I felt starved of her already.

"Morning," she said, her eyes dancing. "Didn't we just do this upstairs?"

I massaged the back of her neck, then kissed my way along her jaw, so what I said next would be for her ears only. "I ate your pussy, then fucked you upstairs, but I didn't say good morning." I lifted my head so I could see her face.

Her cheeks turned pink. "That filthy mouth of yours...I think you love to shock me."

"I could put it to better use if you'd like?"

For once, she didn't have a smart comeback at the ready, something I was starting to think she used to keep herself distant. No, her brown eyes heated.

"I have what you wanted," Asher said, breaking the moment and shoving a bag at me.

"What's this?"

"A sweater from that witch's laundry hamper," Ash said.

After the night I'd had with Iris, I'd almost forgotten about it. I hated this wild goose chase she was on at the mother's whim. I wanted Iris to myself. I wanted to take her back upstairs and keep her there.

"Thanks, Ash. I owe you," Iris said, taking it from her.

"Nah, it's all part of the job," she said, then tilted her head to the side. "Unless you have a spell or potion for sexual stamina? Bears are good in the sack, but they tire easily."

I chuckled at the look on Iris's face.

"This is not a laughing matter," Ash said to me. "He's good for two rounds, then he's out for the count."

"Um..." Iris said.

"You don't have anything like that? Nothing at all?" Asher said hopefully.

I laughed harder, and Iris waved a hand at me to shut up. "Ignore him. I'll ask my aunt Else. She's the best herbal and potion specialist I know. If anyone can get you what you want, it's her."

All my humor vanished at her words.

Is that what Selene was? A herbal and potion specialist? Yes, she'd had an affinity with animals, but she'd always been out harvesting herbs and other things as well. Is that how she created her love draft to control me? The reminder of what Iris's family was capable of had me freezing in place—

A memory flashed through my mind. Charity, her blood smeared on my chest where she'd planted her sliced palm, calling out her spell that destroyed so many lives. My warriors and I were unable to move as Selene and Charity walked away that last time.

I shook my head. I didn't need to be thinking about that now. I needed to put it back in the past, where it belonged.

"Draven?"

I looked down at Iris. She was frowning. "Sorry, what?"

"Where did you go? I called your name three times."

"I was trying to work out our next move," I said, lying, and motioned to the sweater she held.

"Well, I'm ready when you are." Her smile vanished, replaced by tension. "My time is running out. I don't know how much longer I have to find Amy and Marina, but it can't be long."

"Let's go now, then," I said.

The sooner this was over, the sooner I could bury the past where it belonged.

"Stay close," Iris said to Nia when we got out of the car.

Oldwood Forest was at the southernmost end of Roxburgh State Forest, and from what Iris had told me, two of the three witches missing were last seen on this stretch of road. Amy Sartori had been seen wandering along here.

Nia sat and looked up at Iris, her expression one of concentration as she listened and, I assumed, replied to Iris.

"No chasing today," Iris said. "Stay close to me, and if you sense a demon, you run the other way." Iris paused and shook her head at whatever her familiar was telling her. "No, you will not fight them. Remember the rules: if there's more than one, even if they are trying to hurt me, you run."

"You're wasting your breath," I said and scratched Nia behind the ears. "You didn't see her standing over your unconscious body. You were surrounded by demons, and there was no way she was abandoning you. You're asking her to go against every one of her instincts. She'll protect you no matter what you say. She loves you. I don't need to understand what she's saying to see that."

Worry filled her gaze. "I just...I can't bear to think of her getting hurt."

"She feels the same way about you." Nia ran around my legs and licked my hand. "Does she understand me, or is it only you?"

"With the way she and I communicate, just me, but animals, especially domesticated ones like cats and dogs, can pick up on a lot of what people are trying to say, they sense it, when we're happy with them or annoyed or whatever. Like when you called her a good girl, she picked up on it easily." Iris looked up at me. "She said that you're with us now, so no demon will hurt me."

"She's right," I said. "I'll never let anything hurt you."

Iris held my gaze and licked her lips, then quickly looked away, grabbed Amy's sweater, and held it out for me. "I guess you better sniff this."

My new mate was thawing, but that fear was still there, and at times she still hid behind it. For some reason, she was still holding back, despite saying she wanted to try to make it work between us. It probably had more to do with her ex-boyfriend than anything else. I hoped that's all it was. I could show her I wasn't like him over and over again, and hopefully, one day, she'd finally believe it. I couldn't fight blind, though.

I'd let her have her little bit of distance for now—there would be none later tonight when I got her alone and in our bed again.

"Why don't you and Nia stay here? I'll be able to move faster." *And get you back to safety quicker.*

"I'm coming," she said. "I know I'm not as fast as you, but I can move quickly when I go into my animal state."

She closed her eyes and started breathing slow and steady. "What are you talking about?"

"I'm about to show you, but I need to concentrate."

Iris kept her eyes closed, and Nia danced around her, the dog quivering with excitement. I froze, sensing the change before I saw it.

Wolf.

Iris was turning into a fucking *wolf*.

I could still see her. Iris was still there, but there was this shadow of a wolf surrounding her. "What the fuck is this?" She turned to me, and her eyes were different. Jesus fucking Christ, they were arctic blue, and yeah, all animal.

"This is part of my magic," she said. "I can call on different animals, and when I do, I take on some of their abilities. I can run faster as a wolf, see and hear better too."

I stood fucking statue still, my mind scrambling.

"How does she feel to you?" Iris asked. "I don't know if she's the spirit of a wolf or part of me, but she's the same wolf who comes whenever I call."

Goose bumps rose all over my skin as I took her in. "It's you," I rasped. "She's you. You are one and the same." I didn't know how to describe it. If Iris had been born a wolf or a shifter, the ghostly figure surrounding her is how she would've looked, how she would have *felt*. I knew it with certainty.

She smiled. "I did wonder. I've always had this incredible connection to animals, like I was one of them, even though I'm not."

"You never told me about this. I had no idea." My heart was fucking racing. She was so fucking powerful—and she'd kept it from me, hidden it. "Why didn't you tell me you could do this?"

She frowned. "I don't know...I didn't think it was important."

"What else can you do that you haven't told me?" A feeling I didn't like shifted through me.

"Nothing. Draven, are you...are you seriously angry at me right now?" Her *blue* wolf's eyes were full of fire.

I shoved my fingers through my hair. I didn't know what I was, but I didn't like secrets, especially when it came to her magic. "Is there more, Iris? You promised to be honest with me."

"No, there isn't, and I didn't think you meant about this. Why the hell does it matter?" she said, spine stiffening.

"It just does. We're mates. I should know who the fuck I'm sleeping beside," I bit out.

She stilled, watching me with those eerie fucking eyes that weren't hers, but also were. "You don't trust me."

Not a question. I gritted my teeth. *Shit.* No, I realized, I didn't, not fully, not yet. I wanted to, so badly, but I had three hundred years of resentment, of mistrust and fear, to work through. "We all have shit we're working through, which is why I demand complete honesty," I said instead.

Iris pressed her mouth into a flat line, but she dipped her chin. "I've not purposely kept anything from you. Is there anything you need to tell me?"

I shook my head, still struggling with this, with the way she fucking looked.

She held herself rigid, distant. "Cool, then let's get this over with."

I inwardly cursed. I didn't know what else to say to her. So I sniffed the damned sweater, tossed it back in the truck, and moved to the entrance of the forest.

I paced back and forth, scenting the air. It didn't take long. A scent, sweet and floral, reached me. "Got it." I stayed in my human form. I didn't need to go wolf to follow the trail, and I needed to be able to communicate with Iris. "You can manage a jog?" I asked her as we headed into the forest.

"I'm a runner, even before I knew I could do this." Her color was high, her wolf's eyes bright with pleasure. "Start running, I'll keep up."

Nia looked ready to explode out of her skin.

I started slow and Iris kept up easily, so I picked up the pace. Again, my mate had no trouble keeping up with me in her wolf form. Exhilaration filled me out of nowhere.

"Is that all you've got?" she called from behind, pushing me like she loved to.

I glanced back at her and bared my teeth in a grin, then accelerated. The pounding of her feet hitting the forest floor stayed close behind me. Her laughter, the pure joy I heard, filled me with the same. I jumped a creek, and she was right there with me.

I never imagined we could have this. That we'd ever be able to run together like this. Her magic had given this to us. The realization twisted all up inside me. How could you fear something and be thankful for it at the same time? But that's exactly how I was feeling.

She was beside me now, and I glanced at her again. Fuck, she was gorgeous—

A growl ripped through the woods, and I spun back.

Demons, several of them, moved out from behind the trees ahead of us. Nia snarled, baring her teeth.

"Go back," I said to Iris. "Get out of the woods."

Then I dug my feet into the packed earth and ran at them, holding nothing back.

More demons, more than I could fight alone, moved to block our way.

Fuck. I needed to hold them off until Iris got to safety. They weren't getting to my mate. Nothing else mattered except keeping her safe.

I exploded into my wolf, my clothes shredding to the forest floor around me.

Then I ran at them.

Chapter Thirty

Iris

Demons surrounded Draven.

     Nia jumped in front of me, barking and growling.

Nia help alpha. Nia fight.

She'd be killed. "No, Nia stay."

Draven tore into a demon, but there were too many. One clawed him, another trying to take a bite out of his side.

I had to do something. There was no way I was going to just leave him here to be torn to shreds. Up until we were ambushed, the forest had been alive with the sounds of animals and birds, of the wildlife that lived here.

I closed my eyes and called on my power, trying to reach out to every beating heart around me. I knew I could control more than one animal after the rats. I'd never tried to call on more than one species, though. Kicking off my shoes, I dug my toes into the dirt and made a slice in my hand.

The growls and snarls grew. Draven was fighting for his life to protect me.

I smeared blood over my palms and pressed my hands to my face, then lifted my hands in the air, something I'd never done before, but it felt right. My power grew and expanded, thickening, reaching out.

Come to me. Come to me, all of you. From the forest floor and perched in the trees above, come to me.

It didn't take long. I heard them before I saw them, a sound that grew in intensity by the second.

Thousands of small feet, flapping wings, chirping and squawking, squeaks and growls and hisses.

The forest floor and the canopy above were alive, moving as one as they came. Squirrels and rats and snakes, birds of all kinds. Possums and foxes, they ran to me, surrounding Nia and I.

My heart pounded as I took them in. "Thank you for coming, friends. I need your help," I called out. "I know it's scary, but I need you to show me how brave you are. Who will help me save the wolf?"

My mind was filled with their small voices, their eagerness to help Draven, to do my bidding. They'd seen the wolves here fighting the demons, and they appreciated it. They turned as one and swarmed toward the demons; the ground made of fur and scales; the sky made of feathers.

They attacked, and the demon's screams echoed around us as teeth and claws and talons tore at the evil invading their world.

It was like the demons were swallowed whole, ripped to pieces by the animals in the forest. Draven stood in the middle, watching as the animals I'd summoned devoured the demons until there was nothing left but ash.

And when they were done, thousands of little eyes turned to me, waiting for my next command. I had full control over them, all of them. It was incredible—and terrifying.

"Thank you," I said. "All of you. They were bad, and you did a very good thing. We'll forever be grateful, but you can go now." I scooped up some of the dirt at my feet, rubbed it between my palms, then over my face, breaking the magic of my blood and releasing the creatures to the forest, something else I just instinctively knew to do.

They left as fast as they'd come, returning to their homes.

My heart was still racing as I turned back to Draven.

He'd shifted back to his human form and was watching me like he had earlier, warily, like he expected me to send the animals after him as well. He didn't trust me, and I realized that he may never, that he'd forever be waiting for me to turn on him, like Selene and Charity had. I didn't know what to do about that—except protect my heart even more fiercely.

"Fucking hell, Iris," he finally rasped.

I didn't want to talk about it. I didn't want to see that look on his face another moment. "Do you still have Amy's scent?"

He nodded and thankfully said no more about what had just happened.

"Are you okay to carry on?" He had a couple of bite marks and deep scratches from the demons, but it didn't look serious.

"Yeah." He picked up what was left of his jeans and pulled them on. "Let's go."

I got the feeling that he wasn't ready to talk about what just happened either.

He ran at a slower pace this time, and Nia and I followed. We went deeper into the woods, to a part I'd never been to before.

Then Draven stopped.

"What is it?"

"The scent, it ends here." He frowned and turned in a slow circle.

I did the same, but there was nothing there. Just a small clearing surrounded by trees. "What's that?" I pointed to a rocky pile on the ground.

Draven strode over and crouched down to check it out.

"What's left of a stone structure of some kind, maybe a small cabin or a cottage?"

I'd never heard of anyone living in these woods. I turned in a slow circle. Looking for something, anything. But there was nothing.

"Still no scent?" I asked Draven.

"Nothing. It's gone."

We searched the area for another hour. There was no recently disturbed dirt, no sign that anyone had been here in years. "What the hell is going on here?"

"Fucked if I know, but it's going to be dark soon. We need to get out of the woods."

He was right, there were more demons here, a lot more.

We ran back the way we came, and Draven didn't say anything as we reached the ashy pile that was all that was left of the demons who'd tried to attack us. He did falter as we passed, though.

He was quiet on the drive home as well. And when he finally closed the bedroom door behind us, he led me to the bathroom, undressed me, and pulled me into the shower with him.

He washed my face, carefully scrubbing away the blood and remaining dirt without a word, without mentioning what had happened.

Washing away what remained of the magic I'd used, of what I'd done in the woods.

Then he dried me off and took me to bed.

Chapter Thirty-One

Iris

I gently ran the brush through Rose's hair.

"So why are you here?" she asked.

"Rude. I thought you'd be pleased to see me." I smoothed my hand over her freshly washed locks. They used to be so thick. I'd stopped in before I headed to the city. I had people to question and a few leads to follow. Ash was still following me, and I hoped she'd be up for searching Marina's place with me today. The security her family had hired had left, which probably meant they'd already been through the place, but it was still worth a shot.

Rose laughed. It was soft and sweet. "I am, and you know it. I'm just surprised. I thought you'd be all loved up with your mate."

My mate was still being weird. We'd reached for each other in the dark, and he'd taken me several times in the night. But there was a distance when we woke this morning, when the dark was gone, and the room was bathed in light. There was only one explanation. He'd seen me use my magic yesterday, and it had freaked him out.

"He's busy with his warriors this morning, patrolling for demons." He was taking them back to Oldwood, determined to clear the entire State Forest, it seemed, and take as much territory as he could. At least what he and the hounds had agreed on, anyway.

"Well, that's good, the fewer demons in those woods, the better. When it's Mags' turn, she'll have less to worry about." She never mentioned her own task. Rose had accepted her time left was short, and she didn't mind talking about it. Her family, however, had not accepted it and never would.

"Could you pass my water?" she asked.

The glass was empty. "Let me get you a refill. Be right back." I headed downstairs and had just reached the bottom when Ronan walked out of the kitchen. He was carrying a packet of cookies.

His violet gaze met mine, and, as always, he gave away nothing. "Iris," he said in greeting. "How is Rose this morning?"

"She's much the same, but seems in good spirits." The male in front of me looked different. The last time he was here visiting Rose, he'd been thinner, paler, the violet of his eyes duller. This transformation was a result of him feeding at The Vault. Had he been starving himself?

He inclined his head. "I'll go up now and visit with her, if you're agreeable?"

"Of course." He started up the stairs, but I grabbed his arm, stopping him. He stilled, the muscle under my hand tensing, and he turned back. "The other night, at The Vault. I haven't told anyone. I haven't told Rose," I said.

He blinked down at me but said nothing.

"How long have you been going there?" His gaze didn't falter, and I struggled to hold it.

"A while," he finally said.

I didn't want to, but I had to ask. "Did you know the girls who went missing?"

"Know them?"

I'd have to spell it out. "Did you feed from them?"

"I don't know," he said.

"You don't know?"

He just stared at me and said no more.

He wasn't there to get up close and personal with anyone. Ronan went there for one thing, and only when he was desperate. To feed. "Why did you wait so long, Ronan? You look so much healthier now. Why don't you feed more regularly?" Maybe that was intrusive, but Ronan preferred people to be as blunt as he was. He didn't understand subtext or nuance or teasing.

But right now, his gaze bore into me in a way it never had before. It was almost like he was angry, but that was impossible. Ronan didn't get angry. "I don't talk about that, Iris."

Okay, I hadn't expected that. "I'm sorry. I shouldn't have asked."

Without another word, he turned and disappeared upstairs.

I got Rose's water and headed back up, and when I walked in, she was lying there, her large blue eyes on Ronan, who was sitting by the bed reading to her in his deep yet smooth voice. *Jane Eyre* was held loosely in one of his long-fingered hands. One of Rose's favorites. According to Mags, they'd been working their way through Rose's bookshelf. The packet of biscuits was open on her bedside table, half of one laying beside it, which was probably all she'd managed to eat.

I helped Rose take a sip of water, placed the cup on her bedside table, kissed her cheek, and left them to it. Rose barely noticed I'd returned now that Ronan was there. I didn't understand why he kept coming back. But every day, without fail, he showed up, even if it was only for a short time.

I'd think he was in love with her if I didn't know he wasn't capable of feeling anything at all.

~

It was late evening when I pulled up outside the keep. Asher a few minutes after me. She'd been following me around all day, like I knew she would be, and she'd been more than happy to help me search Marina's place. The ward on her apartment had already been broken by her family, which made things easier, but like Amy's place, we'd found nothing.

Nia and I got out of my car.

"Maybe tomorrow you could just ride with me," I said to Ash when she leaned on the car beside me.

Music drifted out from the keep.

"As long as I can drive," she said and grinned.

"Fine." I motioned to the keep. "What's going on?"

"Mating party. Hannah and Linus were due back tonight."

"They've been away? Like a honeymoon?"

She glanced away into the forest. "Yes and no. It's this...special place we go when we mate. Every pack has something like it. The one here was created when the previous pack made a deal with one of the local covens. It's this enchanted oasis, safe and secluded. The couple goes there to screw each other's brains out for a week without interruption." She winked. "Oh, and it's all deep and spiritual and blah, blah, blah."

"Oh, I...yeah, I've heard of it. I've never seen it, though, I just assumed...I thought you must not use it, or only the previous pack could." Because Draven hadn't mentioned it. I understood why, of course. Neither of us had wanted this, for one thing. And I'm sure "spiritual" was the last thing he'd wanted with me.

When he said they usually take their mates away for a week, I hadn't put two and two together. He'd meant this oasis Ash was talking about.

"Did I just fuck up? You look like someone pulled your pants down in front of the whole class." Her brows shot up, realization in her eyes. "You know why Draven didn't take you, right? Besides your task, he didn't know what would happen when he got you here. He had to do things differently."

"It's fine." What Asher said made sense, of course. So why did I have this feeling of disappointment? God, I was so sick of all this uncertainty. My life felt like it was in constant chaos. And I didn't know what to do next with my task. I should be out now searching for Amy and Marina, but I didn't know where to look next. "Come on, I need a drink."

Asher slung an arm around my shoulders. "Now you're talking."

Draven was deep in conversation with several of his warriors when we walked in. His head came up instantly, as if he sensed me enter the room, his gaze slicing right to me. My belly curled and warmed, and I waved before Ash directed me to the bar.

People were still getting things ready, food was being brought out, and decorations received their finishing touches. But we weren't the only ones early to the bar. The pack was ready to blow off some steam. Ebony ran over. "Can I play with Nia?"

Nia play!

I laughed. Nia loved Ebony. "She'd love to." I crouched down. "You stay with Ebony, okay? You keep her safe."

Nia grinned, licked my face, and ran outside with the younger wolf.

Someone turned up the music, and Asher took my hand, dragging me over to a group of females. Bridget was among them, and I inwardly winced. They froze when we joined them, the conversation screeching to an obvious halt.

"Hey," I said. "Sorry, if we're interrupting, I just thought..."

"Screw that," Asher said to the small group. "Stop being fucking weird. Iris is the shit, and if you'd get your heads out of your asses long enough, you'd see that for yourself."

Bridget colored and stepped forward. "Hey...so I've been meaning to talk to you about the other day. What I did, it was a dick move. I'm sorry. You seem cool. But some of us still remember what happened with Draven and the others back then...all the things that happened after, and I took that out on you. Start again?"

I smiled. "I'd like that."

And just like that, the ice broke.

Three hours later, the room was full. Hannah and Linus were back, and I was dancing with all my new friends. We'd had a few drinks, but I wasn't drunk, just tipsy. I thought it wise to keep a clear head. I looked over at Hannah and Linus again. Draven had brought them over to meet me after they'd arrived, and the way they were with each other made my heart hurt.

I'd wanted that once, that kind of love.

Hannah was sitting in Linus's lap, and they couldn't keep their hands off each other. Hannah was glowing, and Linus looked as if he'd won the lottery.

"Sickening, right?" Ash said, grabbing my hand and spinning me.

I laughed. "You're the most cynical person I've ever met."

Her smile slipped.

"Ash? What is it?"

Her gaze came back to me. "I was mated once."

I stared at her in shock. "What?"

"He died," she said. "While I was trapped with Draven and the others. Boone was one of only a couple of fighting-age males left with the pack. He was trying to keep everyone safe. Demons came, a lot of them." Her jaw tightened, and she looked away. "You want another drink?" She strode to the bar.

I followed and grabbed her arm. "I'm so sorry, Ash. I had no idea. God, you must...you must hate me."

"Nah, unlike some of the idiots here, I know you're not a crazy bitch like Selene or her nutbag sister."

"But still, just looking at me must remind you of what happened."

"It's okay, Iris." She smiled gently. "I miss him every fucking day, and I wish he was here with me now, but life can be shitty sometimes, you know that as well as I do. We either roll with it or get flattened. We're rollers, yeah?"

"Yeah." I smiled back, but I ached for her. And even though I wasn't the one who'd hurt this pack, I still felt that guilt. My family was the reason she'd lost her mate.

A hard, warm body pressed into my back, and a muscled arm snaked around my waist. Draven pressed his face into the crook of my neck. "Hey," he said against my skin. Asher winked and went back to the dance floor.

"Hey." I turned in his arms and looked up at him. "Are you enjoying yourself?"

"A lot more now," he said, his gaze searching mine. "You wanna go for a walk?" There was no missing the rough yet hopeful note to his voice.

"Where are you taking me?"

"You'll see." He grabbed a couple of beers in one hand, wrapped his fingers around mine with the other, then led me from the room.

His grip was gentle yet sure, and I found myself clinging to him, soaking in his warmth. There was a full moon, and Draven led me along a pebbled path around the side of the keep and into a small wooded area.

I'd never been back here. "Is it safe?"

"Yeah, it's demon free and patrolled regularly." He glanced down at me. "I told you I'd keep you safe, Iris. You didn't believe me?"

"I believed you," I said and meant it. I knew he'd keep me safe. I just wish I knew how he felt about me. I wasn't the mate he would have wished for himself; I knew that much. And although he might want to, he didn't trust me, not fully.

We broke through the trees, and I stopped in my tracks. "Wow, this is...beautiful." A small lake surrounded by trees glistened as moonlight danced across the surface.

"You really like it?"

I turned back to him. He sounded...unsure. "I really do."

His head was dipped, and he looked up from under his thick lashes. "Good, because I want you to love it here, Iris." His throat worked. "I want you to love it here...with me."

My pulse thudded at my throat. "Well, this definitely helps."

He grinned, flashing his white teeth. The male continually threw me off balance.

Goddess, I loved that grin.

"Can you swim?" he asked.

"Um...yes, but in case you haven't noticed, because you shifters run hot, it's freaking autumn. That water has to be freezing."

The grin grew wider, and he shook his head as he tugged off his shirt. "It's warm. Test it."

I kicked off my shoes, pulled off my socks, and walked to the edge to dip my toes in.

"Another deal the previous pack made with one of the older covens from around here. It's cool in summer and warm in winter."

I stared out at the lake in awe. "That's some impressive magic. Do you know which coven did this?"

He shook his head, and that grin widened. "But I'm not unhappy about it, especially now."

I turned to him. "Why especially now?"

"Because I'm about to go skinny dipping with my hot as fuck mate."

I laughed.

"What?" he asked, closing the space between us.

"I never know what will come out of your mouth."

He grinned and slid his hands up under my sweater, pulling it over my head and placing it on a rock. "I'm full of surprises. Now take off your pants."

Who was I to argue? "I will, if you will."

He stepped back and undid his jeans. I quickly shoved mine

down, my underwear with them, then my shirt and bra. Once everything was tossed aside, I ran straight into the warm water.

Draven's growl and the sound of him chasing me had me laughing and spinning to splash him. He spluttered, then caught me up in his arms, his laughter deep and throaty. I'd never heard him laugh like that before. It was sexy and lifted goose bumps all over my body, even in the warm water.

Steam rose around us, and he pulled me closer, guiding my legs around his waist. "I didn't like being apart from you today, petal."

"I'm here now," I said, because I didn't want to go into why I'd stayed away all day. That I'd felt the distance between us even while I lay in his arms during the night. "Draven?"

"Yeah?"

I should keep my mouth shut, but that wasn't how it was between us. I couldn't help but say what was on my mind. "I know you're disappointed with all of this..."

"With what?"

"Having a witch for a mate, especially from my coven. Not being able to do what Hannah and Linus did and go to your hidden oasis to consummate our mating. You already missed out on so much."

This had been a no-win situation for both of us. That's how I'd felt at first, anyway.

His fingers flexed against my skin. "Not disappointed...but I was afraid." He tucked my hair behind my ear. "You scared the fuck out of me, little witch."

"Are you still scared?"

His throat worked. "No."

He was lying. Of course, he was. Again, it all boiled down to trust, and he didn't trust me. Lust wasn't enough to hold a relationship together, and I still reminded him of Selene and Charity, of their betrayal. Did he truly think I was capable of turning on him like that? I slipped my arms around his neck because I didn't want to think about this anymore and kissed him.

His arms banded more tightly around me, and he kissed me back fiercely. I reached between us, took his cock in my hand, and led him right where I needed him most.

Draven groaned as he filled me, holding me tighter to him as we rocked against each other. Our mouths never separated, even when the kissing slowed, our lips brushing, hovering, breathing in each other as we moved together.

Time meant nothing as we took pleasure in each other. He slid his hand between our bodies and circled my clit as he filled me over and over again.

He kissed his way up my throat. "So fucking perfect. My beautiful mate." There was a reverence in his voice that made my body tremble and my heart grip tight. He pressed his forehead to mine. "Let me feel you, petal. Come for me."

He thrust deep and held there, grinding against me, causing fire to roll through me. Until I came with a cry, trembling against him.

Draven was breathing heavily, but he hadn't come yet. "Take me to shore," I said against his gorgeous mouth.

"Why?"

"I haven't taken you in my mouth yet, and I really want to. I need to know how you taste," I said, needing that, to give him that, so badly.

His arms tightened around me, and he nodded with a groan.

A second later, he slid from me, and we were moving back through the water to where we'd taken off our clothes. But he didn't go all the way, he stopped when the water reached just below his fine ass.

He lowered me to my feet, looking down at me, his chest pumping, nostrils flared, cock hard and jutting from his body as I lowered myself to my knees and realized why he'd stopped where he had. I was warm in water up to my shoulders. He was always ensuring my comfort, always putting me first.

Taking him in hand, I looked up at him. "You're beautiful as well."

His breath shuddered out of him, and he watched as I leaned in and wrapped my lips around the head of his cock. Draven hissed through clenched teeth, then gripped the back of my head with one hand and cupped the side of my face with the other.

"Suck me, petal," he said, demand, hunger, desperation all there.

I did. I sucked him down as deep as I could, then I kept going. I didn't tease. I took him in my mouth over and over again. His thumb slid along my jaw, then traced the side of my mouth.

"Do you like the way your mate tastes?" he asked, and god, that vulnerability was back in his eyes and in his incredibly deep voice.

I nodded up at him. I loved it. I couldn't get enough of him. I moved faster, sucked harder, and his fingers fisted my hair tighter.

"I'm the only male you'll ever get on your knees for, isn't that right, Iris? It'll only be me?" He thrust his hips as if he couldn't stop himself. "You are mine, my female, my mate, for the rest of our lives. I'm never letting you go." He brushed his thumb over my cold cheek. "And I'm yours. Only ever yours. You know that, don't you, petal?"

His words should have scared me, but they didn't. I liked them, liked the way that sounded. I was broken, and so was he, but maybe if we tried, we could be less broken together?

"Oh, fuck." He groaned. "You gonna swallow for me?"

I shivered at the dirty growl in his voice, the dominance, the ownership, and yeah, the longing. I liked it all, and I gave him what he wanted. When he threw his head back and groaned with his release, I stayed right where I was, and I took all of him.

Finally, he eased from my mouth and lowered himself into the water beside me, pulling me into his lap, the water skimming both of our shoulders.

He swiped his thumb over my swollen lips. "Thank you, petal."

"You don't need to thank me. I liked it. I like you," I said and smiled up at him.

His gaze darkened, growing so much more intense. "I like you too."

My heart fluttered.

He wrapped his arms tighter around me then kissed my shoulder, right over the mark he'd given me. "Are you warm enough? Do you want to go back to the party?"

I shook my head. "Can we stay here a little longer?" Where the real world didn't exist, at least for a little while.

He nodded, then leaned in and kissed me again.

Chapter Thirty-Two

Iris

The world swayed around me, everything muted, as if I were walking on the sea floor in stormy weather. The voices called to me again, voices that were impossible to ignore. They reached deep down inside, taking control of every part of me. I was helpless against it.

Icy coldness soaked through the T-shirt I was wearing. My bare legs, my feet, numb and throbbing.

I'd been walking for a long time. It was dark, the forest around me quiet, eerie. And all the while, they called out to me, their voices desperate and mournful.

Something moved to my right.

A large, cloaked figure stood among the shadows in the distance, a long staff of twisted branches in his hand. His face was covered with a hood, and he didn't come closer, but I knew he was watching me, and the coldness that flowed from him turned my bones to ice.

Then he was gone.

I'd seen him before, hadn't I? In my vision at Shadow Falls.

The trees ahead parted, and I rushed through, terrified he was coming after me, then they closed behind me, the branches twisting together and sealing me in.

A cottage.

It was made of stone, and light shone from inside through the small windows while smoke drifted lazily from its chimney. The scents of rich stew, of the herbs that grew in abundance in the gardens, surrounded it.

The voices stopped.

I was all alone and frozen to the bone. I tried to walk to the door, to the little house that looked warm and inviting, but I couldn't get any closer. I tried to run to it, but still, I couldn't reach it.

The voices started again, louder, more urgent, until they were screaming at me.

Come inside!

Now, Iris!

I sobbed. That feeling of being torn in two that I'd felt in the cave came over me again with force.

I changed my mind. No, I didn't want to go into that cottage. I wanted to get away from it. I *needed* to get away from it.

"No. Please...let me go."

Someone moved inside, walking past the window.

The door handle turned, the door started to open—

Draven

I ran through the forest at full speed, chasing Iris's scent. I'd woken and found her gone from our bed. Her scent grew stronger as I went deeper into the woods.

I didn't know what the fuck was going on, but she had to have left as soon as I'd gone to sleep. Her scent was several hours old. I was in my human form so I could call for her, but so far, there was no sign of her.

Doubt tried to creep forward, and I gritted my teeth and shoved it down. Whatever this was, Iris would explain—after I shook the fuck out of her for coming here on her own. She hadn't even brought Nia with her, for fuck's sake.

If anything had happened to her—

Iris screamed in the distance. "No!"

Fear spiked through me and I ran faster.

Moonlight filtered through the trees, making the forest dark and shadowy, dappled light trying to break through. I recognized it. We'd been here before.

She screamed again and the fear gripped tighter.

Then I saw her.

She stood in a small clearing, in only my shirt. She'd put it on before she'd gone downstairs to get a snack. Had she left then? I'd been wiped. Christ, I hadn't even known she was gone.

I rushed for her, searching the shadows for demons, scenting the air for danger. But there was nothing.

I grabbed her arm and spun her to face me. "Iris..." Her eyes were rolled back in her head, only the whites showing. "Iris?" Nothing. "Iris," I said again, louder this time.

But she couldn't see or hear me.

"No," she screamed again. "Let me go!" Her hands lifted, and she covered her ears.

I shook her. "Iris! Look at me. Fucking wake up."

Her arms fell to her sides, and her mouth opened, a scream of agony was ripped from her throat, and I watched in horror as the now healed slices in her forearms tore open. Blood instantly pumped from the fresh wounds.

"Oh fuck." I shook her harder. "Iris."

Nothing.

Fuck this.

I snatched her up in my arms and started running. I needed to call for help, and I couldn't carry her if I went wolf. I needed to partially shift, something that was painful and only the strongest of the pack could do. I felt my head contort as I called the shift forward, bone crunching, reshaping into my wolf, while my body remained in my human form.

As soon as my muzzle elongated, I tilted my head back and howled.

The call was answered a moment later. They were on their way.

Fuck, she was losing too much blood. I stopped, lay her carefully on the ground, yanked off my shirt, and quickly tore it up. I wrapped her arms, trying to staunch the blood, then lifted her and started running again toward the road. She'd walked so far, if I carried her back by foot, I was afraid she wouldn't make it.

Ash was waiting with the truck when I burst through the tree line. I jumped in the back, and Asher took off immediately. There was a tarp back here, and I pulled it over Iris to keep her warm and held her tight to my chest.

Her skin was fucking freezing. She could have hypothermia in this weather, walking around in only one of my shirts. "Stay with me, petal. I need you to stay with me." Her eyes were closed, her skin white, lips bloodless. "Iris, open your eyes."

She didn't move.

"Iris!" I barked at her.

Her lashes fluttered, her eyes rolling back down before they slowly opened.

Whatever that was, she was back now. Her eyes were wide and

deep brown again, and there was recognition in her gaze. "D-Draven?"

I held her tighter to me. "Don't try to speak, okay? Just stay right here with me. Look at me."

She nodded, her gaze not leaving mine, but she was scared out of her fucking mind, and I wanted to tear this forest apart and find whoever was doing this to her—and when I did, I would fucking destroy them.

~

Iris

I lifted my arms and stared down at them groggily. They were wrapped again, and I assumed stitched. Last night hadn't been a dream.

"You're awake."

I turned my head on the pillow. Draven sat by the bed. He looked tired.

His eyes were darker than I'd ever seen them, and stress lined his face. "What the fuck was that? What happened last night?"

I closed my eyes and tried to think. It was hazy. "I don't... know. One moment I was downstairs getting food, the next I was walking through the woods."

He shoved his fingers through his hair. "You could have been killed. It's a fucking miracle demons didn't get to you first. Fuck." He shot out of his chair. "So you're telling me you have no idea why you left the keep?"

His body was rigid. "That's what I'm telling you. I heard... voices. I can't remember what they said, but whatever it was made it impossible for me to resist, to fight it. Until I reached the cottage."

"Cottage?"

"There was a stone cottage. Someone was inside. They were trying to get me to come in, but I couldn't reach it, and then I didn't want to, so I tried to fight it." I looked up at him. "Then you were there, and I was in the truck." He was breathing heavily, and the veins and tendons in his forearms bulged.

He said nothing.

"You're angry. You think I'm lying," I whispered.

He sat on the edge of the bed and carefully cupped my newly bandaged arms. "I don't think you're lying. I saw you, I saw what they did to you, whatever the hell evil that was. I'm angry because I promised to protect you and they got to you in my territory, in *my* fucking keep. Christ, you could've...." He cursed again. "How am I supposed to keep you safe when they're using dark magic to get to you?" He rubbed his thumb over the scar on the palm of my hand, then kissed me there. "I don't know what to do," he rasped.

I covered his hand with mine. "We'll work this out." I shook my head. "I won't let them win, Draven."

Without a word, he climbed into bed beside me and carefully pulled me into his arms.

I woke again a couple of hours later when my phone beeped, letting me know I had a Nightscape notification. I checked the screen.

No.

"What is it?" Draven asked.

My heart thundered in my chest. "Another witch is missing." I looked up at him. "Somehow, they got to Kristi."

Chapter Thirty-Three

Iris

I tugged the sleeves of my shirt down to cover the bandages, and glanced around the room.

The bar was intimate and dimly lit.

A perfect spot for a clandestine dinner date with your secret lover.

Cesare Sartori sat in a booth in one of the darker corners, the female I'd seen him with in that council meeting room, pressed against his side. He was holding her hand under the table—well, I hoped that's what was happening under there.

I shuddered.

Cesare wore an expensive suit, nothing out of place. His hair was combed carefully, brows shaped, and a fresh fake tan made his skin look more orange than golden. He had on a gold watch and gold cuff links, and as he tucked a loose strand of hair behind his companion's ear, the huge emerald in the pinky ring, glinted in the light.

"Are you sure you're all right?" Draven asked. "Are your arms causing you pain?"

That was the second time he'd asked since we got here. "Between Mari's numbing cream and Else's healing balm, I can't feel a thing." He watched me for several long seconds and I could tell he was about to try and convince me to go back to the keep again. "I'm not in any pain, Draven, I promise."

He made a rough sound from across the table, and thankfully dropped it. "So how do you want to do this?" His gaze darkened. "You want me to make him talk?"

"I don't need you to beat a confession out of him just yet. I honestly don't know if he's capable of kidnapping and murder or if he's just an unfeeling piece of shit. I'm hoping today I can either rule him out or get some kind of evidence."

Draven took my hand and gently slid his fingers over my bandaged forearm. "It'd be faster if I just beat him."

"I won't pretend I wouldn't love to see that. The guy's an asshole, but we should probably go for a subtler approach."

So much had changed between us over the last couple of days. I didn't know how to explain it, but something had shifted.

Whatever it was, he'd stopped looking at me as if he were waiting for the other shoe to drop. He'd been sharing with me, telling me about himself, his family, his pack. I thought he might be starting to trust me.

And for me, that change in him, seeing it, feeling it, was causing a change in me as well. That wall around my heart was falling down brick by brick. We'd been together for such a short time, but the connection between us, it made it feel so much longer, especially with everything we'd been through. The *knowing* he'd told me he felt when it came to me, I felt it too. And maybe it was stupid, but I had hope that maybe I'd have something wonderful waiting at the other end of all this.

That Draven and I could build a life together.

That we could be—happy.

Draven didn't reply, he eyed the other male with distaste and growled under his breath. He may be starting to trust me, but he still didn't love my kind, and that might never change.

I made myself focus on why I was here. I'd asked Penny to look into the historical records and let me know if there was mention of any old cottages in that area of the woods I'd been compelled to go to. She'd called, and not only did she have something, she'd told me where I'd find Sartori. His secretary liked to gossip. And with Kristi Charles missing now as well, I wanted to question the guy. I didn't trust him. And since he was currently here cheating on his wife, I'd say my character assessment was spot on.

The female with him said something then stood, and headed for the bathroom.

"Let's go."

Cesare looked up and stilled as we approached, his gaze narrowing. "I know you." He looked me up and down. "You're a Thornheart, yes? What on earth do you want?"

Draven growled again.

Not surprising, when somehow, Cesare had managed to inject a huge amount of arrogance into every single word.

"Yep, that's me."

His gaze slid to Draven, then darted to the bathroom. "If you think you can intimidate me into rubber stamping your mother's request, you're wasting your breath. It's not up to me. Forcing my hand won't get you anywhere."

Draven frowned. "What's he talking about?"

This sure as hell wasn't the place to talk about this. I studiously avoided Draven's stare and looked back at Sartori. "That's not why I'm here. But I'd like a few minutes of your time."

"I'm busy. You're interrupting my evening."

My temper flared. I was so done. I'd be subtler if I believed this asshole had feelings, but he didn't, and I couldn't afford to be cautious anymore. "Did you have anything to do with Amy's disappearance, councilor?"

He jerked back in his seat, and his face reddened.

"I beg your pardon?" A twitch started just below his eye.

"I need to find who's behind the disappearances, and you're on my list."

He shot out of his seat, and Draven stepped forward, pulling me behind him with a snarl.

"It's okay, he can't hurt me, not in here," I said. "The bar's witch owned and warded in a way that prevents people from using spells to harm." A lot of witch owned bars did the same, mainly to stop people from drunk spelling.

Sartori planted his hands on the table and leaned forward. "Leave," he bit out.

Draven took another step forward, and I grabbed on to his arm again, but there was no stopping him, and he dragged me along with him. Might as well go with it.

"Either you talk or Draven makes you talk."

Sartori stumbled back several steps. "You dare to threaten me?"

"Yes, I dare. Now talk." Though spending even this short amount of time with the guy had changed my mind. I couldn't imagine him doing anything that would get his hands dirty. And he was too vain to do anything that big, that monumental, and not let everyone know about it.

His gaze moved back to Draven, and he wisely decided to start talking. Not surprising, this man would throw his own mother in front of a bus rather than get a hair out of place.

"I don't know where Amy is, and I have a witness to prove my whereabouts the night she was taken, the nights the others were taken as well."

"Your wife?" I asked.

He flushed. "No."

"Ah...your mistress then."

His eyes spat fire. "You would be wise to keep whatever you think you know to yourself."

"Or what?" Draven snarled.

Sartori flinched.

"And your witness? They'd confirm this?" I asked and motioned to the bathroom, she was currently in.

He looked furious. "If it came down to it, but your accusations are baseless and ridiculous. I want my daughter back, Miss Thornheart."

"But screwing your mistress is more important than looking for Amy, or I don't know, actually giving a shit." This guy was a giant asshole, but he wasn't a killer or even a kidnapper. I couldn't see him planning an abduction between tanning sessions, and he had his hands full with a wife and mistress.

"Are we done here?" he bit out.

"We sure are."

"You'll pay for this outrage," he spat.

I spun back to him. "If you do anything, anything at all against my coven or my pack, I will make sure your wife knows what a pig you really are. Though I suspect she knows that already." Then I walked away.

I cursed several times. I was furious that I still didn't have any answers, and I was pissed off on Amy and her mother's behalf.

"Iris." Draven grabbed my hand.

I shoved the door open and walked out onto the street. "How fucking dare he threaten us? Who the hell does he think he is? People like him make me sick. They don't know the meaning of the word family. By blood or by choice, you take care of the people you love. You don't do what that selfish fucker is doing. Jesus, his daughter is missing and all he cares about is keeping his affair a secret."

Draven gave my hand a squeeze. "Iris."

I stopped my angry march down the sidewalk and turned to him.

"Your pack?" he said in a way I couldn't read.

My face heated, I had said that, hadn't I? "I-I just meant...I didn't mean..." He cupped the side of my face and pressed his thumb to my lips, shutting down my stuttering.

"That's the first time you've said that...your pack." His gaze searched mine, and my heart raced. "I love that you feel that way, petal. A whole fucking lot."

I didn't know what I'd say, even if I could speak, but I didn't have to worry about that because he kissed me, soft and intense and packed with emotion. When he lifted his head again, I struggled to look him in the eyes, but Draven wouldn't allow anything else. He took my chin between his fingers, his stare locking on mine.

I wasn't a wolf shifter, but even I found it hard to disobey him when he was intense like this. And, right now, he wanted my gaze on his. He wanted to see right into my soul, and the way the green of his eyes darkened, I thought he might actually be able to.

I was starting to think there wasn't anything this male couldn't do when he decided on it.

He tucked my hair behind my ear. "Let's go see your friend, then I want to take you home," he said in a rough voice.

"Okay." If he'd said, let's go to the moon right then, with that voice and that look in his eyes, I would have jumped on board his rocket ship and waited for him to call out the countdown.

He took my hand, the hold possessive, protective, reassuring, and he led me to his truck.

Draven held my hand the whole drive to the council building, and as we strode across the foyer and down the hall.

"Why won't you listen to me?" I heard Penny say ahead of us.

We rounded the corner, and on the other side of the large room was Penny's desk. She stood behind it, Isaac Eldridge right there in her space. He loomed over her, his hands on her upper arms. She was upset. He leaned in and said something I couldn't hear.

I started toward them. I knew that asshole would hurt her.

Isaac glanced over his shoulder at us, released her, and with a scowl, took off.

I rushed to Penny. "Are you okay?"

She was trembling, her eyes glistening with unshed tears.

"I'll deal with him," Draven said, about to go after Isaac.

"No, please," Penny said. "I promise, I'm okay."

"You're not." I put my arm around her shoulders when a tear streaked down her face.

She swiped it away, and Jasper made a chattering sound from her desk. He was worried, that's what I was getting from him. Pen ran her hand down her familiar's back. "Sapphire found out about us, but it's...it's going to be okay."

She was lying. "You don't need to pretend with us."

Her fingers curled around the edge of the desk. "She threatened me, Iris." Her lips trembled. "I'm...I'm scared." She chewed her lip and looked away, her eyes filling with tears. "Isaac said he'd handle it, but she...she hates me."

Sapphire hated most people, but Isaac was her only child now, and she'd already have his future mapped out, and there was no way she'd allow Penny to be part of it.

Her gaze met mine. "S-she threatened to...she said she'd go after my dad if I don't give Isaac up."

Draven growled.

"What are you going to do?"

She shook her head. "She's rich and powerful, she has a lot of influence here. If my dad finds out about any of this, he'll lose his mind. He'll confront her and he'll lose his job."

Nothing about this was okay. Coven Eldridge had lost a lot of their power last year when Isaac's twin, Elmer, lost his trial against Willow, and it had obviously sent the old bat off the deep end. Maybe this was how she made herself feel powerful now, terrorizing innocent people.

"I don't like this. Sapphire shouldn't be allowed to throw around threats like that, and if Isaac cares for you, he'll shut her down." I wasn't confident he would, though. The only person Isaac cared about was himself.

I glanced at Draven. He was gritting his teeth, his gaze darting to the door Isaac had walked out of.

Pen hugged herself. "I'm sure he will."

I didn't believe that for a second.

We finally left after I'd made sure she was going to be okay.

Draven glanced down at me, with fire burning in his gaze. "Isaac's the asshole who sent those demons after you, yes?"

"There's no proof of that," I said, instead of answering him.

"That's a yes, then?" Draven said, fingers curled into tight fists. *Shit.*

Chapter Thirty-Four

Iris

T he way Draven was gripping the wheel of his truck as we drove out of the city made it obvious he was still worked up over Isaac. Penny had handed me a folder with the information she'd copied from the city records. She wasn't sure if it was anything, but something was better than nothing at this point, and I'd made Penny promise to let me know if she needed anything. She'd looked terrified as we'd walked away. And I didn't blame her. Sapphire was pure evil.

"Maybe Isaac will do the right thing and tell his mother to back off," I said into the silent cab.

Draven's fingers clenched around the wheel. "The guy's a piece of shit. I should've already ended him for coming after you like he did."

"You can't do that. We don't have any proof it was him, and the last thing my family needs is the council breathing down our necks. Between Warrick killing Elmer last year, then finding a dead witch on our land, we've had more attention from them than we've ever had."

"He ordered them to hurt you," Draven ground out.

I touched his arm. "And you saved me."

"I acted like a dick."

I chuckled. "Yes, you did, but it wasn't your fault, and you still saved me."

He glanced at me, his throat working. "The way I treated you... I'm so fucking sorry, petal. You didn't deserve that."

My heart did a little flutter. "Thanks, but you don't need to apologize. You thought I was...Selene. I understand why you did and said the things you did."

He groaned. "Don't remind me of the shit I said to you. It makes me sick to my stomach."

I slid closer to him and ran my hand down his muscled forearm. "It's okay."

He said nothing for a few minutes, his breathing rough like he was trying to regain his control.

"Are you okay?"

"No." He glanced at me. "I'll never forgive myself for the way I treated you."

My heart beat harder, faster. The way he looked at me, the things he was saying. He cared. He did. There was no mistaking it for anything else. "Well, I forgive you."

The muscles in his jaw clenched. "I don't deserve it, but I'll take it, Iris, and be fucking thankful."

The cab grew quiet again. I kept my hand on his arm. I couldn't quite seem to let him go.

"So, what was Sartori talking about back there?" he asked after several more minutes. "Your mother's request?"

Crap. I'd forgotten all about that. I had no option but to tell him the truth. "Mom appealed the council's decision. She requested they revoke their approval of your request for restitution."

The muscle under my hand went rock solid.

"It was the day after we mated. I didn't know she was going to do it."

"They're going to try to take you away from me?"

I thought I knew how he sounded when he was angry, but I'd been wrong. Rage rolled off him now, thick and brutal.

"Draven..."

He jerked the wheel to the right, leaving the tree-lined road and swerving into a shadowed area surrounded by towering pines that blocked out the moon. He turned to me, and I could barely see his face, but his eyes glowed bright green and were utterly fierce.

"I will kill the entire council before I let them take you away from me," he said, and the way he sounded, I knew his canines had extended.

I swallowed, my mouth dry, my pulse thudding wildly at my throat. "Draven..."

"Do you want that, Iris? Do you want them to take you away from me?" The fierceness in his voice lifted goose bumps all over my skin. "Do you want to return to your old life, one without me in it?"

As he said those words, my heart screamed out what my mind had been trying desperately to suppress.

Against all odds and everything we'd been through, I'd fallen for the broken male staring at me like his life depended on my answer, and there was no way I could say anything but the truth. "No, I don't want to leave you." I shook my head. "My mother only appealed the council's decision because she thought she was protecting me from something I didn't want."

What I'd felt for Brody was *nothing* compared to how I felt about the male sitting across from me. Because this was real. How Draven treated me, the way he touched me, and spoke to me, looked at me, *was real.* My heart raced faster. "But even if they approved it tomorrow, I wouldn't leave you, because I choose you,

Draven, as my mate, and because I...I've fallen for you," I said, laying myself bare. "I'm in love with you."

He stared at me, eyes wild, breathing hard, but said nothing.

Oh god.

I couldn't believe I'd said it out loud. The realization had hit so hard, the words had just poured out. What was I thinking? I dropped my gaze, unable to hold his another moment.

He made a sound that was raw and full of desperate need. A sound that came straight from his beast. My gaze shot back to his, and he hooked me around the back of the neck, fingers delving into my hair, and his mouth came down hard on mine. He kissed me like the world was about to end. Like a male kissed the female he loved and wouldn't survive being parted from.

I whimpered into his mouth.

Draven undid his seat belt and mine, then reached down to the latch that slid the seat back, giving us more room, and hauled me across his lap. His fingers tore at the front of my pants, and he yanked them down my legs. It was cold enough to frost up the windows, but I barely noticed the chilled air as I straddled him and frantically yanked at the front of his jeans. Finally, I got them open, and he lifted his ass so I could pull them down enough to free his thick, impossibly hard cock.

He yanked my panties aside and rubbed his thumb along my slit. "So wet, Iris. Always so wet for me. Because you were made for me, petal. We were made for each other." He gripped the side of my throat. "Who do you belong to?"

"You," I choked out.

"Show me," he said, so rough and full of need that my inner muscles clenched.

I shook as I positioned him at my opening, then with a violent sound, a sound I'd never heard before from him, he jerked me down on his cock as he thrust inside me deep. I cried out, shaking, and started rocking against him instantly. I doubted it was possible to take him any deeper, but I couldn't get enough. I gripped his neck with one hand and his shoulder with the other and fucked him like my life depended on it as well.

Draven's fingers dug into my skin, and every time I rose up, he pulled me back down hard, filling me to my limits, giving me exactly what I needed. His hand slid into my hair, and he gripped it and dragged my face close to his, licking and sucking my jaw, my throat, nipping my hot, tingling skin.

He held me more firmly, his mouth against the corner of mine. "I won't ever let you go, not now, you know that, don't you, petal?"

The rough possessiveness in his voice thrilled me in a way I never dreamed possible. Having someone claim me in that way wasn't something I'd ever wanted—I wanted that from Draven. I needed it.

I shook harder, zaps of pleasure shooting through me. "Yes," I gasped out.

"You won't ever try and leave me, will you, sweetheart?"

Draven had slowly but surely shattered my walls, and the vulnerability in his words, in his voice, went straight to my defenseless heart. "I won't leave you," I promised. Then, hooking his arm around my waist, he brought me down hard again, planting himself deep, and I came, crying, sobbing against his shoulder. He throbbed inside me, his growls filling the cab as he came as well. All I could do was cling to him, rocking as best I could with the tight hold he had on me that somehow increased my pleasure, taking it to even greater heights.

We hung on to one another until I finally collapsed against him, still trembling as he smoothed his hand up and down my back.

I felt as if my world had just changed, and in the last year, it had already changed so much. But for once, it had changed for the better.

Draven was asleep, and I was sitting by the fire in our room, reading over the information Pen had given me. The ticking time bomb on my thigh made it impossible to rest. My mind wouldn't quiet.

I scanned the computer screen. There had been a cottage on that site a very long time ago, and the place had eventually been torn down after the witch who'd lived there died.

Ortus Cottage.

Why did that sound familiar? There was no information in the files about who the witch was, but the place had leveled after all kinds of unpleasant things happened out there. What those unpleasant things were, it didn't say.

I opened my laptop, logged into the council's public files, and typed in the cottage name. Nothing more came up than what Penny had given me. I tried a web search next. Nothing there either.

Ortus. I was sure I'd heard that word before. I typed that in on its own. It was Latin.

Beginning. Dawning. Coming into being. Rising. Birth.

Maybe the witch had been a midwife?

I yawned and glanced at the bed.

Draven was propped up on his pillow, his hands behind his head, biceps bulging. The sheet was low, resting on his hips, and the light from the fire danced over the rigid muscles of his chest and abs. His eyes were open, and he was watching me.

"How long have you been awake?" I asked, my breath catching from just the sight of him like that. Goddess, he was beautiful.

"I haven't been to sleep."

I shut the laptop and placed it on the small table by my chair. "So you've just been sitting there watching me?"

"Yes, it's one of my new favorite things to do."

I walked over and climbed onto the mattress, curling into his side. How had this happened? This level of intimacy? It felt easy, right to seek comfort from him now. Draven immediately welcomed me, pulling me in close, then he kissed me, slow and deep, and somehow sweet at the same time.

When he lifted his head, I smiled. "You know, you really are an excellent kisser. Have I ever told you that?"

"Yes, as a matter of fact," I said, grinning back.

"Well, it can't be overstated. So they really kissed like that in the olden days, huh? I assumed it'd be all cheek pecking and hand holding." I shook my head. "Who's the hussy I need to take out for teaching my mate to French like a beast?"

He threw his head back and laughed, wrapping his hand around the side of my neck and pressed his face to my throat. "Your mate *is* a beast," he said against my ear and growled when I shivered. He lifted his head. "And you'd be surprised what people got up to in the *olden days*. I can assure you it wasn't all pecks on the cheek and fucking with the candles out."

I chuckled and he wrapped me tighter in his arms, pressing his lips to the top of my head.

I glanced at my little vervain, still thriving on the window ledge, and nerves ignited in my belly. "Hey...so do you have somewhere I can plant a herb garden? I thought it was time I planted that." I motioned to the vervain.

"You can make a garden wherever you'd like, petal."

He started tracing the vines on my thigh, and I could tell he was measuring the distance between the two. Yesterday, the space between them had been three of his fingers wide. Today it was only two.

"What if I fail?" I whispered against his chest.

He pressed his mouth to the top of my head. "You were given an impossible task. The fact you've gotten this far shows how strong and resilient you are. Christ, you're so goddamn brave. If anyone can succeed in this, it's you."

I tilted my head back and looked up at him. "You think I'm brave?"

"It doesn't matter what's thrown at you or how many times

you get knocked down, you keep on getting back up, you keep fighting." He tucked my hair behind my ear. "Female, you are the bravest warrior I know."

Those roughly spoken words meant everything. "And if I don't succeed?"

His penetrating gaze held mine. "Life will continue on. Your family will still love you, Iris, no matter what."

"But we won't be the same. We'll lose so much, all of us. I'd never be able to forgive myself for that." If I failed, the devastation to my coven would be immeasurable.

"Then we'll just have to make sure you don't fail." He slid his fingers under my chin. "But if the worst should happen, you'll still have me, you'll have this pack. Nothing will change that."

I clung tighter to him and squeezed my eyes closed.

A scream came from outside.

I ran out of the bathroom just as Draven was yanking the bedroom door open to whoever was pounding on it.

"A feral," Dirk said and took off.

Draven cursed and ran after him.

I was wearing Draven's shirt, and I grabbed my pants, hopping around, trying to quickly tug them on, then ran after him.

It was mid-morning and the great hall was full of pack members, mainly females and children. It was usually the quietest time in the keep. "What's going on?" I asked Jennifer, one of the females I'd gotten to know recently. "Where's Draven?"

This pack was strong and brave, but there was genuine fear in her eyes. "A feral wolf shifter's wandered into our territory. They've gone after it."

Shit.

Once feral, there was no coming back. The shifter became

vicious and fueled by blood lust. They became cold-blooded killers.

"Wren!" Bridget screamed out. "Has anyone seen him?" She spun around. "Wren!"

Oh fuck.

Everyone searched the room, calling his name.

"I see him. He's outside!" Ebony cried.

Bridget ran out the door, and I ran after her. We tore around the side of the keep, and Wren was sitting on the ground across the yard, playing with his toy cars.

Bridget called his name as a vicious growl rang out across the yard. The feral entered the grounds from the opposite side. I'd never seen anything like it. Not fully man, and not all wolf, the beast was hideous. It had fur missing in patches, and its foaming maw hung open. Crazed eyes swung to Wren.

Bridget screamed.

I grabbed her arm. "As soon as he's focused on me, run to Wren and get him inside."

She nodded, horror and fear transforming her face.

"Hey!" I called out as I pulled my blade from my pocket. Its head swung back to me, and I held up my hand and sliced my palm, once, twice, making an *X*. I had the feral's complete attention now that he could smell my blood. He stalked me.

"Back away slowly, Bridget."

"He'll kill you," she whispered.

"Just get Wren inside, I'll be okay. Trust me." I had no idea if that was true. I had to get close to the beast if I was going to immobilize him, like within touching distance close, which gave me a fifty-fifty chance of getting out of this alive, but I wasn't letting him hurt Wren.

Bridget backed away, moving silently along the edge of the keep, then sprinted to Wren, scooped him up, and ran for the door. Now it was just me and the drooling, feral beast closing in on me.

A child screamed, then started crying inside, and the feral turned that way, the hunger in his eyes increasing. If I failed, he would do everything he could to get inside, and even if they over-powered him, someone would get hurt. The females in there were vicious. They would fight to the death to protect their pups, but like me, they weren't warriors. And now I was all that stood between them and this monster now.

I wouldn't let anyone hurt them.

The feral roared, foam flying from its mouth—and then he charged.

My instincts told me to run. Instead, I planted my feet, and as his body smashed into mine, I slapped my hand against the center of his forehead as we went down, momentarily stopping him from taking a bite out of me. "In this spot, you will rot!" I screamed.

The feral froze, just like the demon had in the nightclub, and rolled to his side, unable to move. He stared up at me with fury in his crazed eyes. I didn't waste time, not sure how long the spell would hold, and scrambled to my feet. I pulled my blade free, and stabbed it into the artery in his throat, then sliced across. His blood gushed out, spraying me. The feral twitched and went limp, bleeding out on the grass.

Panting, I straightened.

That's when I saw Draven.

He stood on the other side of the yard, Asher and the other warriors behind him. And there was no missing the look of horror on their faces.

Chapter Thirty-Five

Iris

Dirk ran for the keep, carrying Tammy, one of their females, her leg badly mauled. And a couple of his warriors tossed a second dead feral on the ground. There'd been two of them.

My gaze flew over to Draven. Gouges covered his chest, a vicious bite mark at his side, blood oozing out.

"Draven..." I started toward him.

He took a step back.

I froze, my heart seizing in my chest. "What do you think I'm going to do?" I whispered, but I already knew, didn't I? He was looking at me like he didn't know me, like the last few weeks had never happened.

His warriors dropped their gazes and hurried away, going into the keep.

"Draven?"

He planted his hands on his hips. "It's okay," he said, but I wasn't sure who he was trying to reassure, him or me.

"You're hurt. Let me check your wounds," I rasped.

His jaw worked. "You never told me you could do that. You overpowered him with your magic. He was frozen, helpless against you."

I stayed where I was. If he took another step away from me, I didn't think my heart could handle it. "It's new."

"Have you done that before? That spell?"

"Yes."

His chest heaved with each agitated breath. "When?"

"On a demon in the nightclub the first night you kissed me."

His gaze slid away from me, that strong jaw still working, every muscle rock solid.

Oh god. "You still don't trust me."

His gaze sliced back to me, and his throat worked. "Of course I do."

I didn't believe him.

"You saved Wren," he said, but there was a distance in his gaze that cut me to the quick. He was trying to hide it, fight it, but I saw it, stark in his eyes. "You could have been killed." There was a moment, just a split-second, of hesitancy, his step faltering before he strode toward me and pulled me into his arms, but I didn't miss that either. "Thank fuck you're all right."

Despite his arms around me and the words he'd just said, I felt the trust we'd worked so hard to build shattering around us. "Draven—"

"It's okay," he said again.

Why did he keep saying that? I stared up at him, my heart pounding in my chest. God, was he...afraid of me?

He held me a little too tightly and a little too desperately. "I need to make sure everyone else is okay. You're sure you're not hurt?"

"I'm fine."

He released me. "Go clean up, okay? Then come find me."

"All right."

Then I watched as he strode away, inside the keep to check on his people.

Ebony stood at the door watching, with Nia beside her, and my familiar ran to me, sensing my distress.

I forced a smile, swiping away the hot tear that streaked down my cheek. "Everything's okay, Ebs," I lied. "Go inside. I'll be right in."

I felt as if I were back at Shadow Falls, trapped in my worst nightmare. I'd worked so hard to earn his trust, but I was never going to have it.

I couldn't stay here. Not after that.

He'd been afraid of me. He'd *backed away* from me.

Ebs ran inside, and I pulled my keys from my pocket and strode to my car.

I'd never learned my lesson with Brody. I'd stayed when I shouldn't have, and my family had suffered for it. I wouldn't make the same mistake again, and this time, at least, the only person who would suffer—would be me.

I'd seen this coming from the start, and, still, I'd dropped my guard. I'd risked my heart again and lost.

I'd told him I loved him, but he hadn't said it back, had he? Nausea washed through me. I'd been so caught up in him, in the wildness of the moment, the fierceness of his need for me, that I'd convinced myself he had.

But he hadn't said the words.

I covered my face with trembling hands, but refused to give vent to the agony and loss I felt. Being betrayed and attacked by Brody was nothing compared to the pain I felt now.

I drove away and headed for home.

Draven

I strode through the keep, calling for Iris. I'd been out with my warriors all night, and I hadn't gotten back to my mate like I'd planned. There was no sign of her, and I was starting to panic. "Ebony!" I tried instead.

Ebs would know where Iris was. The pup had taken a shine to my mate and Nia, but she didn't come running, not even when I called her a second time. I strode down the hall, checking the rooms beside mine—no Iris.

I took the stairs to the great room and searched the tables. The room was fairly full. It was Sunday, and Sally made a big breakfast for the whole pack on Sunday. "Have you seen Iris?" I asked Ash.

Asher looked up at me and frowned. "She's gone."

"What do you mean, gone?"

"Ebs saw her get in her car and leave right after she took out that feral."

What the fuck? I pulled out my phone and checked for messages or missed calls. Nothing. "Why would she do that?"

Ash tilted her head to the side, her expression gentling. "You know why."

"The hell I do." But even as I said it, my gut twisted tight.

"Drave, you looked at her like you thought she was coming for you next." Ash's gaze grew sympathetic. "You lost it there for a moment, I saw it in your eyes. You were back there, in Salem, in that woods. I get why it happened, but your mate won't."

Oh fuck. Ash told me I needed to work through what had happened since we got free. I hadn't, desperately holding onto my hate, and now I'd hurt Iris.

I knew she wasn't anything like Charity or Selene, I did. I'd just...I'd lost my damn mind for a few moments. I'd been so on edge for days. I hadn't slept, afraid whoever was behind all of this would try to snatch Iris from my bed again. My adrenaline had been through the roof, and we'd almost lost Tammy to one of those ferals. I hadn't been thinking straight; I hadn't been thinking at all.

Seeing her use the same spell Charity had used to trap me and my warriors had shocked the fuck out of me. Ash was right, I'd been slammed back to that time, trapped, filled with hopelessness. It took me a moment to shake that off.

Ebony marched over and scowled up at me, her face reddened with fury. "You made Iris cry."

I'd made her cry? *Oh fuck.* I felt sick to my stomach. "Ebs—"

She stormed off.

Goddammit. I strode away, out the door, trying to call Iris as I went. She didn't pick up. I jumped in my truck and headed down the mountain.

My wolf paced and whined on the drive to her mother's house, feeling Iris's absence strongly. Her words from the day in the field, when she'd been unable to tell me anything but the truth, were on repeat in my head.

"If I let myself care for you, it will hurt so much worse when you finally betray me, just like Brody did." Her lips trembled. *"I don't want to care for anyone like that again."*

I'd done what she'd been most afraid of. I'd betrayed her trust.

Every day Iris had been growing closer to the pack. My pack mates were more welcoming, including her more often.

And she and I... During the night, we fucked and talked, and she'd nap, then I'd reach for her or she for me and it started all over again.

I'd grown to love the talking part of our night as much as I loved being inside her.

Fuck, I'd held myself back, hadn't I? Waiting for something to happen, expecting it because I was a fucking idiot.

But Iris was goodness and light. She was giving and strong and loyal. I knew she was all those things, because she showed us every day.

She never asked me for anything. She never offered false smiles or faked her true feelings. When she was pissed off, she told me, showed me, and when she was happy, her entire face lit up.

Iris was exactly what she put out to the world.

I hit the steering wheel hard, so fucking angry with myself.

Christ, furry little animals were drawn to her, trusted her, wanted to be close to her. Charity had never had that. She may have had an affinity with animals, but they didn't come to her of their own free will, she demanded it of them. My petal had stray cats following her, wild rabbits lying against her—birds flying around her head like she was a princess from a goddamn fairy story. How could I not have seen that? Seen her? Seen Iris for all she was.

How could I have allowed, even one moment of doubt, to creep into my mind?

I needed her back. I needed her with me.

The truck rolled to a stop outside the house, and I jumped out, strode to the front door, and banged on it. It opened a second later as if someone had been there waiting.

Daisy. Iris's mother looked up at me, and she wasn't happy.

"I need to speak with Iris."

"She doesn't want to see you."

"I need to speak with my mate, Daisy. You can't stop me from taking her home," I said as calmly as I could, though with a lot more growl than I'd intended.

Daisy shook her head. "You're not taking her anywhere. She is home."

If I had to drag my mate out of there, kicking and screaming, I would. If that's what it would take for her to listen to me, I'd do it. "She's mine and you know it, the council—"

"You had your chance, and you blew it. You don't get another one, alpha. You put her through all of that, then you just...tossed her aside."

"That's not what happened."

"I don't need all the details. I know how she looked when she walked in here last night. I never want to see pain like that in her eyes ever again." She started to shut the door.

I shoved my hand against it. "She's my mate. Nothing you or the council say can change that. We're bound in a way that is irrevocable."

"I'll see about that."

"No. You won't do a damned thing. There's nothing you can do."

Daisy stared up at me with contempt. "Has she planted the vervain?"

"What?" I growled. "What the fuck are you talking about?"

"The little pot she got before she left. Has she planted it at the keep yet?"

I wanted to fucking snarl. What did that have to do with my mate coming home? "No."

Daisy seemed to breathe a sigh of relief.

Why was she wasting my time with this? "Just get Iris."

Daisy crossed her arms. "No. If she wanted to be with you, she would have planted the herb."

"I don't know what the hell you're talking about."

"A witch plants it when she moves into her new home. But more importantly, when she *feels* like she's home. That herb gives us everything we need to take care of our families. She didn't plant it, Draven, because you are not her family."

I stared down at her, wanting to fucking roar in pain and frustration.

"It's okay, Mom," Iris said from behind her mother.

My gaze shot to my mate, and it took everything in me not to shove my way inside and snatch her up.

Daisy stiffened, then finally made eye contact with her daughter. At Iris's nod, she backed away. "I'll be in the kitchen if you need me." Then she left us alone, after sending one last scowl my way.

I took Iris in, and my fucking legs almost gave out. The relief at seeing her was so fierce. "Iris...please. I need you to listen to me. I wasn't thinking clearly. It was just a shock, seeing what you did. That spell, it's what Charity used on me...back then, and I just..."

"Stop," Iris said, her expression blank. "I saw your face after it happened. You were afraid I'd turn on you as well."

"No...no, that's not true..."

"You took a *step back* from me, Draven. God, how else am I supposed to interpret that?"

"I didn't mean it. I just...I reacted, I..."

"Yeah, you did. You showed me how you truly felt." She crossed her arms, putting up her walls. "For the record, I trusted you. After what happened with Brody, I'd lost sight of who I was. You made me want to live again, for myself, and...for you. You made me care." She shook her head. "Somehow, I'd convinced myself that we could work, that we could be together. But you can't let the past go, and I understand why, I do. But every time you doubt me, it hurts like hell. And I can't do it anymore."

"It won't ever happen again—"

"That's what Brody used to say after he hurt me, every single time."

"I'm nothing like that piece of shit, and you know it."

"I know you're not like him. You're a good male, Draven, and I wish I could believe something like this won't happen again, but it will, and I'm not strong enough to keep putting my heart on the line only to get it stomped on. I won't do it. We both have a whole truckload of baggage that we can't seem to get past." Her gaze hit mine. "We'll just keep hurting each other if we try to stick this out."

"For fuck's sake, Iris. This isn't ending." I reached for her, and she didn't step back. She let me grip the side of her throat. She was trembling. "Please, petal."

"I know your wolf will need to be near me sometimes. So if you need me close for your sanity, I won't deny you. But we can't have more than that."

No. My heart smacked against the back of my ribs. "You don't mean that."

"Yes, I do."

I stared at her, waiting for her to say something more, something that could make this right. She didn't. She was trying to hide it, but she felt as fucking awful as I did. I could see it, the hurt and longing lay naked in her eyes. But ever since that fucker Brody did what he had to her and her family, she'd stopped trusting her own instincts. I'd gotten through to her, though—then I'd fucking destroyed her trust all over again.

I needed her back with me. If I had her with me, I could fix this. I knew it with everything in me. She was my mate, and she belonged with me.

A memory pushed forward, hitting me out of nowhere.

"Hey...so do you have somewhere I can plant a herb garden? I thought it was time I planted that..." She motioned to the little herb *she'd brought with her.*

"You can make a garden wherever you'd like, petal."

Hope surged through me. She had planned to plant it, the vervain.

She'd decided to make the keep her home.

I was her family.

No fucking way would I give up on her, on us. She wasn't going to back down, though, not right now with the pain I'd caused her so fresh. So I'd give my little witch a day or two, even though it would kill me, then I was coming back, and I was taking her home.

And if she still refused, I'd snatch her off the damn street if I had to—my mate belonged with me, and I would find a way to earn her forgiveness.

Chapter Thirty-Six

Iris

I turned the page of the book I was reading as quietly as I could, not wanting to wake Rose.

I'd dragged a few books up from our library. I'd been looking for one in particular. One I hadn't looked at since I was a kid. It was filled with some of our more horrific histories. There was nothing in it about The Maidens, I remembered that much, but I wondered if it had anything about Ortus Cottage? Willow and I used to read it when Rose and Mags were asleep. We'd scare the hell out of ourselves. The name of the cottage was still so familiar, but I couldn't place where I'd seen it. Now I thought it might be that book.

If only I could remember what was on the cover, or what it was called. My terrified young brain must have blocked it out. So far, none of the ones I'd brought up were it.

I glanced at Rose again, and smiled when I saw she was awake. "Hey." And did my best to hide the fact that what I wanted to do, was crawl into bed and cry for a week, or a month…maybe a year. I didn't have that luxury, though, so my broken heart would have to wait because there was still a killer out there somewhere. "Good sleep?"

Rose didn't answer, staring ahead blindly.

"Rose?"

She said nothing, then drew in a shuddering breath and shook her head, anger flashing through her eyes, real and fierce. "All my body wants to do is sleep."

Rose never got angry, at least not in front of us.

Her eyes slid shut. "I wish…"

"What?"

She said nothing.

"Talk to me, Roe?"

Her gaze locked on mine. "I don't want to do this anymore. I don't want…*this*, anymore. I'm worse, Iris, and I've…I've had enough."

I didn't know if something had caused this or if my sister was just tired, too tired to fight her emotions today, to put on the brave face she always presented to us—but seeing her like this destroyed me.

I went to her, pulling her into my arms, and the floodgates opened, the last shreds of her control shattering. Rose cried, her frail body shaking so hard I thought she'd hurt herself.

"It's not fair," she choked out. "It's not fucking fair."

Grief and despair tore at my heart. Rose never let us see her like this. She bottled it all up for her and us.

And not for the first time, I prayed to the goddess, asking her to spare Rose, to make her well, but in my heart, I knew my plea fell on deaf ears. There was nothing anyone could do for her. We'd tried everything over the years.

We clung to each other, and I cried with her, shaking with rage of my own, that this was happening to her, to us. Rose was right, none of this was fucking fair.

I stayed with her until she cried herself out and collapsed into a deep sleep.

Wiping my eyes, I instructed Nia to stay with her.

I headed downstairs, and Ronan stood in the doorway, a pack of gummy bears in his hand. "Hey, Ronan."

"I came up," he said. "But I didn't want to disturb you both. Why was Rose crying?" he asked instead of his usual greeting.

I shook my head. "She's just...having a bad day." I didn't know how else to explain it to him.

He frowned, then started for the stairs.

"Please, don't wake her. She wore herself out. She needs rest."

Ronan turned to me. "I would never wake Rose. I would never do anything to hurt her."

"Of course. I know you wouldn't." The way he said it gutted me, as if I didn't trust him anymore. As if me seeing him feeding at The Vault had changed my opinion of him.

He inclined his head and headed upstairs and I made my way to the library to search for that book. But after another good look, I was positive it wasn't there. Several other books were missing as well, which usually meant Willow had been here.

I quickly sent her a text, explaining the book I was looking for.

She replied immediately.

Willow: *It's at the shop. I don't need it anymore, if you want to pick it up.*

I rushed upstairs and faltered at the door when I saw Ronan sitting by Roe's bed. My sister had rolled to her side while she slept, and her hand was on top of Ronan's. The male was looking down at it, his lavender gaze locked onto her frail hand, his entire body motionless.

"Ronan?"

He looked up.

"I have to leave for a bit. Are you okay to stay with Rose for a while longer? I don't want to leave her on her own."

He nodded and then looked back down at Rose's hand. I had

no idea what was going on in his head, and I didn't have time to question him. The only thing that mattered was that Roe was safe with him. I rushed back down, snatched up my keys, and headed out.

I spotted Asher behind me in her truck about fifteen minutes later. I thought she'd approach when we reached Willow's store, but she didn't. Draven still had her following me, but she must have been instructed to stay back.

I unlocked the store and let myself in.

Sure enough, there was a stack of books in the kitchen. She often needed the books for research or different things to do with the store.

I sat at the table, and quickly found the book I was looking for. I remembered the heavily engraved cover as soon as I saw it. I ran my finger down the index, searching for the section on dwellings.

I opened to the section and scanned the thick pages, looking for information on all the cursed, enchanted, and hexed buildings in the area, past and present. Several haunted houses, an asylum, an abandoned private girl's school...

Ortus Cottage.

I knew I'd seen the name. I quickly read the passages, and my heart beat faster, my palms growing sweaty. *Where the living and the dead walk side by side.*

It told the story of a dark witch who had lived in the cottage. The nameless monster had murdered a bunch of witches, and they'd never been found. She'd used them as practice, to master her reanimation spell. Once perfected, she planned to bring back the three elder crones of Shadow Falls, in one hell of a power grab.

I cursed.

The Maidens—it had to be them—the murdered witches mentioned in this book. Who else could it be?

I'd seen the cottage, and whoever was behind these new disappearances had called me there. Did this mean they wanted to reanimate the crones as well?

Pieces of the puzzle snapped together in my mind. I snatched up my phone and opened the photos I'd taken at the council building. I scrolled to the news sheets I'd read, and checked the date the last missing witch had been recorded. *March 1706.* I scrolled back farther to the pictures I'd taken when I first came to the council, searching coven Thornheart's histories.

There, Selene's entry, after they'd been forced to kill Charity. *March 1706.*

"Fuck." Charity was the witch of Ortus cottage, of course she was. She'd killed all those witches and Selene had killed her before she could reanimate the crones.

Now, somehow, Charity was trying to do it again.

Oh goddess.

This was huge, too big for just me. I was pretty sure I was about to hyperventilate. What the fuck did I do with this? How could *I* save those girls?

Nia whined.

Nia miss wolves. Nia miss alpha. Nia want to go home.

I patted her head, my mind in a spin. "You're not the only one." To her, home was with the wolves now. She wanted to go to the keep.

My hand lifted to the mark Draven had given me the night we mated, and I realized I felt the same way.

Draven had reacted badly when he'd seen what I could do. He'd let the past resurface and cloud his judgment. But so had I. I'd let my fear rule me, and I'd thrown my wall back up.

Brody might be dead, but I was still letting him win. Back then, I'd clung to him when I should have run the hell away. I'd lived with the guilt of staying with him for so long that my first instinct had been to run from Draven. God, my mate had been to hell and back.

When he'd come for me, he'd told me the spell I'd used was the same one Charity used to trap him, and still let him walk away. I covered my face with my hands and tried to breathe.

His reaction hadn't been about me.

Goddess, seeing me do that, it must have taken him right back to that awful time, to what happened to him and his warriors.

Instead of running, I should have stayed and talked to him, I should have helped him through it. I should have fought for us. I should have held on tight.

I didn't know what a future with Draven looked like, but I realized I wanted it, anyway.

I'd promised him I'd try, and at the first hurdle, I'd run.

I missed my mate.

I couldn't sleep without him.

And I couldn't succeed in this task without him.

I needed Draven. I wanted to be with him. Maybe it was a bad idea. Maybe he'd never fully trust me again, but I had to try. "Come on, sweet girl. Let's go."

My phone rang as I was locking up.

Penny.

"Hey, Pen, everything okay?"

Silence.

"Pen?"

"I-Iris...oh goddess. Sapphire's here. She's at the front door. I told her to leave, but she won't go."

Fuck. "Is your dad home?"

"No."

"When did you last strengthen your wards?"

"I...I don't know."

Not good. "Lock yourself in a room and start warding it, Pen. Over and over again, make it as strong as you can." Nia and I jumped into my car. "I'm on my way."

"No, just, I need someone to talk to until Isaac gets here. He's on the way."

I got in my car and headed for her house, anyway. I didn't trust Isaac to protect Penny from his psycho mother. Gunther lived near the council buildings for an easier commute, and not far from Willow's shop. "I can be there in a few minutes."

"No, it's too dangerous," she said.

I turned onto Casper Road, where there were several cafés and bars and where all the council members often came to lunch. It was busy, people filling the outdoor tables—

I did a double take.

Isaac Eldridge *and Sapphire* were sitting outside a cafe.

Where they weren't was at Penny's house.

What the actual fuck was going on?

I slammed on the brakes, pulling into the nearest park.

Penny said Sapphire was at the door, that she'd talked to her, but she couldn't have done that because Sapphire was sitting right there. Penny had lied to me.

"Iris?" Penny said.

"Is Sapphire still there, Pen?"

"Yes."

"And you're sure it's her?"

Silence. "Yes." Her voice sounded weird.

"Are you absolutely sure?"

"Yes...I'm so scared, Iris."

For some reason, Penny wanted me to think Sapphire wanted to hurt her.

"Um...Isaac just arrived. I need to go." She hung up.

I didn't know what the hell was going on, but I was going to find out.

Sapphire stood, kissed her son's cheek, got into the town car that had just pulled up, and left. Isaac stayed, sipping his coffee.

"Stay, Nia." I shoved my door open and strode across the street. Isaac looked up as I took the chair his mother had just vacated. We were in a public place, so even if he wanted to hurt me, he couldn't. Not out in the open.

He sipped his coffee. "What the fuck do you want?"

Fine. I didn't have time for small talk either. "What's going on between you and Penny Morgans?"

His eyes narrowed. "Why would I tell you a damned thing?"

"Because, apparently, the two of you are in a secret relationship. And she just called and told me your mother was at her house, threatening to hurt her, and you'd just arrived to save the day. But you're not, you're here, and so was Sapphire up until a moment ago."

Fury and confusion filled his gaze. "What the fuck?"

"Are you in some kind of relationship with her?"

He curled his fingers into a fist. "I don't know what the fuck she's playing at, but we are not seeing each other, not anymore," he bit out.

"Not anymore?"

"We used to fuck," he said. "But I haven't touched her for over a year."

He'd been sleeping with Penny? Innocent, shy, sweet, little Penny. "But Penny said...she's..."

"An excellent actress." Isaac sat forward. "I don't owe you anything, but I won't have that bitch saying shit about my family." He ground his teeth. "Penny was intimately involved with me and Elmer, but that was a long time ago."

"Both of you?"

He bared his teeth, a shark's smile. "We liked to share, and she was all for it."

Fuck, this guy was a major asshole, but I didn't think he was lying. How could I not believe him? Penny had just called with a fake SOS. What reason would she have for any of this? "You two looked close at the council chambers."

"She's been trying to start something up again. Constantly calling, following me, trying to get me to meet with her. I shared with Elmer, but he was more into her than I was. She favored my brother, anyway, says she was in love with him." He sat back. "I'm not interested anymore, and that's what I've been telling her."

What the hell was going on?

"You didn't send those demons after me, did you?"

"No," he ground out. "I've been trying to get on with my life, but you won't stay the fuck out of it."

"Was Penny with you that day? The day I came to your offices with the hellhound?"

His brows lowered. "Yes, but I sent her away."

Fuck. It was Penny. She'd seen me there and sent the demons after me. Why? Why the hell would she do that? And why was she trying to make me believe Sapphire was threatening her?

Isaac's expression changed to one of fury. "She actually suggested we *reanimate* my brother, that we dabble in the foulest of magic to bring him back. As if I would ever do that to him, bring Elmer back as some fucked-up, twisted version of himself."

Oh goddess.

Reanimate.

The description of Ortus Cottage filled my head.

Where the living and the dead walk side by side.

It was Penny. She'd taken those witches. She'd fooled everyone.

To get Elmer back—she was helping Charity from the grave. And that cottage was the key.

His gaze hardened and he sat forward again. "What's she up to? Do you think she's still trying to reanimate my brother? She contacted my mother, threatening to share a picture she took of him, one we don't want getting out. She told Mom not to tell me, that she wants to meet with her tonight to discuss payment."

"It's not money she wants. Neither of you should meet with her, it's too dangerous. She's been manipulating us. She wanted me to believe Sapphire wants to hurt her. And she knew I'd assume you sent those demons after me. She did it to keep the tensions high between our families, to keep us focused on each other and not what she was scheming." I shot to my feet and Isaac did as well. "I need to go, but you need to stay away from Penny."

He called my name as I ran back to my car and got in.

I had to stop her.

Chapter Thirty-Seven

Iris

I hit Penny's number and waited.

It rang four times then went to voicemail.

I hit it again.

It rang twice—and this time she answered, but she said nothing, and neither did I. I waited.

Finally, she sighed. "You know I was lying, huh?"

"Yes." Fear and anger knotted inside me.

"I can explain. You see, I thought..."

"Stop, Penny. No more lies."

Silence.

I had to tread very carefully here. "I think I know what you're doing and I think you're in over your head. Let me help you."

More silence.

"Penny..."

"Don't pretend you're my friend now, Iris." The change in her voice sent icy shards down my spine. "You're such a stupid bitch.

You have all this power, and you choose to be nothing. Charity would be ashamed of you, of all of you, in your pathetic coven."

Even though I knew what Penny was doing, but the conformation had me gripping my phone tighter. "How did Charity reach out to you, Pen?"

I could almost hear her mind ticking over, deciding what she should tell me. Again, I said nothing and waited.

"I've been stuck working with all those dusty books for years," she finally said. "Forgotten, always overlooked, but there's so much power in them, you know? So one night, I tried to tap into it. I did a séance, but instead of reaching the person I wanted...Charity reached out to me."

"You were trying to reach Elmer? Isaac told me the truth about you and his brother. You loved him?"

"Charity called out to *me*. She chose *me*. And she told me a way to get him back," she said, excitement in her voice now.

"You're going to reanimate him."

"That's not possible, sadly, but there's another way."

She'd lost her damn mind. "If you do this, Penny, however you do this, you won't be bringing him back. He won't be the man you loved, he'll be a mindless monster."

"No! You're wrong," she hissed. "Charity knows how to do it."

Things were clicking into place. When Thomas Eason outlawed dark magic, Charity knew she had to make her move. She took his daughter first, maybe as a warning, or maybe it was revenge. Then all those other innocent witches followed, murdered during her attempts to bring back the three elder crones of Shadow Falls. If she'd been successful, she would have taken over this city. How many covens would have been wiped out in her bid for power? I shuddered at the thought of what could have been. "She practiced on The Missing Maidens, didn't she? All those years ago." Then Selene killed her before she could bring the crones back.

Penny laughed again. "You're such an idiot, watching you

stumble around trying to figure this all out has been hilarious. I even helped you, and still you couldn't work it out." The laughter in her voice died. "It was me who unearthed Charity's remains. She told me where she'd been buried, but you showed up before I could take her bones."

And once I had them in our cemetery, she couldn't get to them. "So the crones reached out to me."

"And you took Charity's remains right to them." A pause. "They weren't happy when you got away."

I couldn't believe what I was hearing, that Penny was capable of this. "Are the girls alive?"

"For now."

My pulse thundered in my ears. "Did you kill Imogen?"

"I hadn't planned on it, but Death had Charity locked in her cottage and she needed a sacrifice to open the door. Imogen walked in while I was putting Amy in a trance after a night out at The Vault." Penny huffed. "It all worked out in the end, though. Those idiots were so easy to overpower after they'd let vamps feed on them. I just had to hang around and wait for them to stumble out of the club. Kristi was a little more difficult to get to, but again, I was underestimated. No one would ever suspect me." She outright laughed. "Sweet little Penny wouldn't hurt a fly."

She was a monster. Helping Charity in exchange for bringing Elmer back was bad enough, but murder? There was no saving her now. "You stabbed Imogen in Amy's apartment."

"I'm not going to feel bad about it," she spat. "They made a fool of me at The Vault, turning their backs on me, rejecting me. They called themselves the *specials*, because of their extra gifts, and I wasn't special enough for them…Well, who's the special one now?"

If Death was involved, that meant Charity was in limbo. She was in Death's realm, and still, she'd found a way to pull souls through to the other side.

Even dead, she was incredibly powerful, and now the crones and Charity were channeling what power they could access through Penny to get what they wanted, and it was working.

Death was all about checks and balances, and if a soul escaped his realm, he hunted them down and dragged them back. But that was the same for any realm, balance must always be maintained.

Charity hadn't taken those girls to practice on, not this time, she needed their souls to replace her and the crones when they were reanimated, to maintain that balance. They had three, but they need a fourth.

They'd almost taken my soul at Shadow Falls, and then they'd tried again when they'd called me to Charity's cottage.

"Charity wants my soul, doesn't she?"

"Yes."

"Why me?"

"Because Death's keeping a close eye on her. She needed a soul from the same bloodline with similar powers."

If Charity thought she could fool Death, she was wrong. From what I'd read about him, he knew every soul in limbo, and he presided over the land of nothing and nowhere with an iron fist. "We've been alone several times, Penny, why didn't you try and take me then?"

"You were never really alone, were you? If you weren't with your wolf, he was following you or had another doing it for him. After our last failed attempt, we decided to change tactics. The ritual is time sensitive, and I was concerned that if I did manage to get to you, your mate would get your coven involved and try and ruin everything."

Even without knowing he was doing it, Draven had saved me. I needed to keep her talking. I had to find those girls before it was too late. "And what does Isaac have to do with all of this?"

"I need his body. Elmer's bones are warded in his family cemetery, so Isaac will have to host Elmer's spirit instead," she said, a

361

smile in her voice. "I'm going to kill Sapphire, say it's self-defense, then nothing will get in our way when Elmer comes back. Everyone will believe he's Isaac...you're not the only one I told about my *secret* relationship or how Sapphire had it in for me. They'll believe her murder was self-defense, then once Charity and the crones are reanimated, they'll bring my Elmer back to me, like they promised."

My mind was spinning, and my heart was racing. "You just admitted everything to me, Penny. You know I can't let you get away with it."

She laughed, a grating giggle. "Oh, you can't stop me, Iris, and you won't tell anyone what I've told you."

"And why is that?"

"Because if you do, your whole family will die, screaming in agony. It's just a little spell Charity taught me. She's taught me lots of spells." She sounded giddy, she was so pleased with herself.

She was willing to kill my entire family to get what she wanted. "Penny..."

"Discussion time is over. I have somewhere to be...oh, and so do you. We require your presence at Ortus Cottage, Iris. And if you're not there by dawn, a hoard of demons will descend on Silver Claw's keep and tear them all to shreds. The demons in that forest answer to me now, thanks to Charity."

I gripped the wheel tighter, nausea swirling in my belly. She could be lying, but I couldn't risk it. Draven and his warriors were strong, strong enough to take on a hoard of demons, but they had elders and pups there. I'd never forgive myself if anyone was hurt because of me. "I will find a way to stop you."

She laughed. "No, you won't."

Draven

I yanked on some shorts and strode toward the keep. Ebony ran out and handed me a bottle of water. Taking a deep pull, I spat out the demon blood, then poured the rest over my head, trying to wash the rest off my chest.

The demon population around the keep had increased to worrying levels the last couple of days. I didn't know what the hell was going on, but we'd moved the females and pups into the keep, with Kenric and the other elder males protecting them, and everyone else who could fight had spent the last two nights killing as many demons as we could.

I hadn't been able to get back to Iris because of it, and I was seriously struggling without her.

The sound of a car echoed in the distance.

I tilted my head to listen, and my heart immediately beat harder.

Handing Ebs the water bottle, I jogged to the parking area. Electricity sizzled over my skin, and heat licked through my veins before I even saw her car.

Iris parked, and I was there, pulling her door open before she'd turned off the engine. I stared down at her, fighting not to grab her up into my arms. She hadn't looked up at me yet. "Petal?"

Her hands shook as she undid her seat belt.

"Iris." I conveyed all the yearning and hunger I felt in that one precious word.

Her head tilted back, and tears streaked down her cheeks. Her lips trembled. "I...I need you."

I didn't need to hear another word. I hauled her out of her seat, and she wrapped herself around me. "I'm sorry. I'm so fucking sorry," I said, lips pressed against her soft hair. "I was wrong. I fucked everything up. I let the past cloud my head. I can't be without you."

Her small frame trembled in my arms, and then she looked up at me. "I did the same. I let my fears stop me from reaching for you instead of running. I was so afraid."

Selene had fucked me up like Brody had Iris, and we'd been too scared to allow ourselves to fully trust each other. I refused to let Selene fuck up my future as well. I was done letting her dictate my life.

My mouth came down on Iris's as I tightened my arms around her and headed for the keep. The chatter stopped when we walked in, and I kept moving, carrying my mate up the stairs and to our room.

Kicking the door shut, I walked to the bathroom. "Shower," I said against her lips. I was covered in demon blood, and I didn't want it all over my precious female.

I quickly undressed her, and she shoved down my shorts.

The water hit us, and I lifted her again, pressing her to the wall. "Tell me you'll stay, petal?"

Her fingers thrust into my hair. "I don't want to be anywhere but with you."

My cock was pressed between our slippery bodies, and I dragged my length through her slit, wringing a moan from her.

Her nails dug into my back. "Don't make me wait," she gasped out.

I couldn't. I needed to be inside her right the fuck now. Tilting my hips, I lined the head of my cock up and thrust home, filling her. We clung to each other, eyes locked, bodies sliding together as I claimed what was mine, and she did the same in return.

"I'm sorry," I said again, panting against her lips. "I fucking hate that I hurt you."

She cupped my face. "It's okay. I'm back, and I'll never leave you again."

I groaned, happiness and pleasure overwhelming me. "I fucking love you, Iris." I groaned, pressing my forehead to hers. "God, petal, so much." The words spilled from me easily. Words that my strong, fierce, beautiful female deserved to hear from her male.

I'd been so damn afraid to let her in, to bare my soul. I wasn't afraid anymore.

I took her faster, harder. My lower gut ached, my heart raced, and tingles danced up my spine. "Gonna come...can't hold back, Iris. Come with me."

She gazed up at me with heavy lids and lips parted. My female was right there with me. I could feel her clenching, fluttering around me. I gripped her hair and pressed my forehead to hers as I fucked her harder against the shower wall. She bit her lip, then cried out, coming around my cock. I covered her mouth with mine, swallowing down her cries, and then pulled my mouth from hers and roared as my orgasm slammed through me.

I stayed inside her, still moving, slowing my pace as I kissed her, drinking her in. Her warmth, her scent—every fucking thing about her.

I felt as if I'd been separated from her for months, not days.

Because I loved her.

I was so deeply in love with my mate that being apart from her had felt as if my heart had been torn from my chest.

I kissed her again and lifted my head as I reluctantly slid from her body.

She ran her hand over my chest, over the wounds still healing. "What happened to you?"

I kissed her pretty mouth. "Demons, they've been coming closer to the keep. We don't know why."

She gripped my shoulders, her eyes growing round. "I do."

Iris told me about Penny and Charity and that she'd threatened Iris's family and our pack. That she was behind the demons coming here, that they were behind everything.

"Charity and the crones are using Penny to get what they want," Iris said.

"Which is?"

"To be brought back from the dead. Charity just needs one more thing, and they'll get what they want."

"What? What does she need?"

Her throat worked. "Me."

Fear sliced me through the middle. "They want you dead?"

"They need my soul. That's why the crones called for me to take Charity's bones to Shadow Falls. And when that failed and you saved me..."

"They came to you in your sleep. That's why they were leading you into the woods?"

"Yes, to the cottage. It's in limbo and it's enchanted. That's where Charity and the crones are. But Charity can't reanimate without me there. Death won't just let her leave. She thinks with our similar powers and Thornheart blood in my veins, she can fool Death into thinking I'm her, so he won't come after her. Without me, she can't free herself."

"Fuck." I shoved my fingers through my hair.

She grabbed my arm. "She said, if I'm not there by dawn, they'll send more demons here, Draven. I...I need some time to figure out how to beat her. I can't ask my family. If I do, all this will have been for nothing. We'll lose the gifts the mother gave us, and it won't just be me who suffers. I can't take on Penny without some kind of plan or a power boost, not with Charity and the crones giving her their power as well. I just...I need time to figure this all out."

"I'll kill her," I snarled.

"She'll sense you coming and she'll send a forest full of demons into the keep." She gripped me tighter and shook her head. "And no matter what Penny said, Charity and the crones aren't going to just sit around and wait for me to come to them, I'm too important to their plan. They'll come for me sooner." She hugged herself. "The pack is in danger again because of me. I brought this here."

"No, that was Charity. Her and Penny did this, not you. I promise you, the pack is safe. Demons aren't getting in here, petal. I won't let them." I cupped her face. "I've got you. Just tell me what you need from me?"

"Don't let me fall asleep."

Chapter Thirty-Eight

Draven

I ris looked exhausted.

I had the windows open, the frigid air filling the room. She'd been scribbling in a notebook, muttering to herself, trying to come up with a spell or incantation to boost her power, some kind of a plan.

Christ, I felt fucking helpless. The first few hours had been fine, but she was starting to tire. We'd walked around the keep. I didn't want her outside, not with demons every-fucking-where. But the adrenaline she'd been running on was leaving her, and my mate was struggling.

"I think another coffee," she said, looking up from her book.

"I'll get the coffee. I won't be long."

She gave me a weak smile, and I strode out. Ebony was at the bottom of the stairs with Nia. "Ebs, I need you to go to my room and make sure Iris stays awake, okay? I'll be right back."

"Sure thing." She and Nia ran upstairs, and I headed for the kitchen. No one was getting much sleep tonight.

"We're under attack!" Asher yelled.

Fuck. "Kenric! Keep everyone locked inside!" I ran out.

The door locked behind me, and I shifted and tore into the demons running at the keep.

Charity could keep sending them, and we would keep tearing them to shreds. They weren't getting near my mate.

The ground around the keep was soaked with demon blood and ash by the time we finished. Hours had passed. Thank fuck, we hadn't lost anyone in the fighting, but we had injuries. The demons had just kept coming, wave after wave of the fuckers. It was like they had a death wish. Well, we'd given them what they wanted.

I hosed the blood from my skin in the yard, quickly dried off, yanked on some shorts, and rushed back inside. I ran up the stairs and was a couple yards away when I heard Ebony's distressed cries and Nia barking.

I sprinted the rest of the way and flung the door open.

Fuck. Iris's eyes were rolled back in her head, and Ebony was on the floor, arms wrapped around my mate's legs. Tears ran down her face. "I'm sorry, alpha. I-I only fell asleep for a minute. I don't know what's happened to her...I didn't know what to do."

I rushed over and scooped Iris up in my arms. "It's okay, Ebs. I've got her now. She can't go anywhere."

"T-there were demons outside, and she was trying to leave and she wouldn't wake up...and her *eyes*..." She sobbed. "What happened to her eyes?"

"Go to your mom, Ebs. This isn't your fault." I just had to keep Iris here, right? If I kept her here and woke her the hell up, she'd be safe? She had to be.

Iris lifted her head suddenly and turned to me. She stared at me blindly with milky white irises, then smiled. "Say goodbye to your mate, wolf." That wasn't Iris's voice, but it was one I'd never forgotten.

Charity.

Iris's eyes cleared for a split second. For a moment, they were back to their beautiful deep brown. But fear filled them. "Draven. Oh goddess, help me."

"I've got you. I won't let them take you. Fight it. Fight it, baby."

But her eyes rolled back, once again white—then she went limp in my arms. "Iris?" I shook her. "Petal? Fuck...Iris!"

She didn't move.

Her breathing grew shallow.

Then I felt it.

I felt her soul leave her body. She was just...gone. Still breathing, slow and shallow, but there was nothing there. *Iris* wasn't there. Even her face looked different. And somehow, I just knew that when Iris's soul reached Charity and the evil witch did whatever twisted thing she had planned, my mate would stop breathing.

And I'd lose her forever.

I roared, standing there with my female limp in my arms, not sure what the fuck to do.

Asher rushed through the door. "What the hell's going on?"

I shook my head, my mind buzzing, my heart racing. Iris's soul was on its way to that cottage, and I wanted her body to be as close to it as possible, it was the only thing that made sense. I held Iris close and ran for the door.

Asher immediately followed, and I forced myself to stop as more of my warriors rushed up the stairs as well. "Where I'm going, there will be witches." My gaze touched each of theirs. "Charity's evil spirit will be there."

Growls filled the small space.

"I won't ask you to come with me. I don't know what will happen. This could be a trap. I might get stuck again."

"Where you go, we go," Ash said, expression fierce.

There were grunts and growls of agreement. I didn't second-guess them, they knew more than anyone what was at stake.

"Two of you can come with me. The rest need to stay and protect the pack in case of another attack."

Asher and Dirk instantly broke from the group, and we rushed down the stairs and out to the demon blood-soaked earth surrounding the keep.

The moon was behind the clouds, and I allowed myself to partially shift, my eyes, ears, and muzzle transforming my face to enhance my senses. Ash and Dirk shifted into their wolves and flanked me as I ran full speed toward the cottage ruins.

I didn't know what I'd find when I got there.

But I'd do whatever it took to get Iris back.

～

Iris

It felt as though I were floating in the sea, caught in a riptide that pulled me farther and farther from dry land.

Nothing I did would stop my forward momentum, dragging me deeper and deeper into the forest. I knew where I was, and I knew where I was going. The crones' laughter was ringing in my ears. Their magic that had touched me before at Shadow Falls surrounded me now, cold and grasping, painful, as they gripped my soul and pulled me toward them.

This time I wasn't alone. This time I saw them—lost souls. They moved around me, wandering aimlessly, lost forever in limbo.

The cloaked figure appeared in the distance, in the shadows of the trees, tall and broad.

Death.

I was in his realm, and he knew I didn't belong here.

But the trees ahead parted again before he could come closer, and I was pulled into the clearing, the trees closing behind me like last time. Light glowed ahead, warm and inviting when I knew that cottage was anything but. I tried again to fight it, but I was drawn forward until I stood a few yards from it.

The trees surrounding it swayed and moaned, low and mournful. The only light coming from the cottage's small windows.

Something moved near me. I spun around. Penny rushed by.

"Penny!" I called.

She didn't hear me, didn't even look my way. She looked distorted, muted.

That's when I realized she was here, but not *here*. She was in the mortal realm, and I was in limbo, locked in Ortus Cottage's magic that Charity had created. Penny stood near the ruins where this cottage had once been.

She moved to where the stones we'd found lay, and I watched as she muttered a spell and waved her hand over the ground. A hatch door appeared, hidden by her magic. The cottage basement was still there from when it once stood. Penny opened it and disappeared down a ladder, shutting the door behind her.

I turned in a circle. It was impossibly dark all around me. I had no clue what time it was, but it couldn't be long until dawn.

I faced the cottage again, and anger filled me. They were trying to take me from my life, a life that I loved—from Draven. They wouldn't take me without a fight. "You called me here, so show yourself."

I didn't know if I was completely helpless or not. My powers had worked during my visions at the falls, and I prayed to the mother they worked here as well. Someone moved behind the door, a shadow through the window.

The handle turned, the old iron latch rattling.

Then the door swung open.

A woman, backlit by firelight, stood in the doorway. Her hair was black and wavy like Magnolia's, and her eyes were blue. She was stunning. Her full, red lips curved into a smile that was meant to be inviting, alluring, but instead lifted the hair on the back of my neck.

Charity.

"Iris, my dear, we finally meet," she said and held out a hand. "Come to me."

Her magic dragged me toward her. I tried to fight, but my magic was bound tight as I tried to call it forward. I was helpless. She stepped back, and I was pulled into the cottage.

The door slammed behind me; the bolt sliding in place.

"Why are you doing this?" I struggled against her hold on me.

She walked to a large pot hanging over an open fire and stirred it before she looked up. "Because I want to live again, of course. I want what I'd been destined for before my sister and her tedious husband murdered me." She was suddenly in front of me again, and her hand was cold as it cupped the side of my face. "The resemblance is remarkable. Even this..." She dragged her nails over my cold cheek. "Penny warned me, and I thought I was prepared to see this face again, but I find looking at you makes me...angry." She gripped my jaw tight, her pointed nails digging in. "Very angry."

"I'm not her. I didn't hurt you, Charity."

Her grip didn't loosen. "You're certainly as cunning. But she was also sweet, like you. She loved my mother and me and trying to protect us was all she cared about. She'd do anything for us. It was pathetic."

"Like trap Draven and his warriors, tying him to a rock with your hidden dagger for over three hundred years?"

"The wolf?" She laughed. "Yes, and she let me do it, but only because she'd planned to free him as soon as my back was turned. She saw I'd grown stronger, had worked out that I'd turned to dark magic. But my sister was a terrible liar, and I knew what she had planned. She was going to use *voltafaccia* on me—she was going to plunge the ancient dagger into my heart, and *change* me, try to *save* me." She laughed again as a low, deep sound echoed in the distance. Her form wavered, becoming less corporal for a moment. "So I locked it away, guarded by your wolf and his warriors, then used hemlock on her and a very special spell that made sure she forgot he and the dagger ever existed."

She'd wiped Draven from Selene's memories. Selene hadn't betrayed him, she'd been betrayed by her sister. "She did love him."

Her grip on me grew tighter, her eyes filling with fury. "Of course not. She never planned to stay with him, we needed his strength to destroy our enemy, that's all. She was Keeper," she said with a sneer. "She had things to do and staying with a wolf who wasn't even her mate wasn't one of them. My sister had a conscience, that's all."

"You thought you should be Keeper?"

"I was a far better witch in every way."

"But she bested you. She found out what you were doing and she stopped you. In the end, she won."

The sound came again from somewhere outside, louder, a *boom* echoing through the room, making the ground shake. I grabbed for the table.

Charity's form flickered again, but she ignored it. Her face twisted, her mouth opening wide, and she screamed. "She lied! She tricked me. She didn't win. I'm going to win."

Howling echoed in the distance and my heart soared.

"Iris!" Draven's voice roared from beyond the cottage.

"Draven saved me last time. He got me out of that cave before you could take my soul, and he found me here as well."

"I trapped him once and I'll do it again," she said.

I pulled from Charity's grip, yanked the door open, and ran outside. Draven stood there with my body held limp in his arms, Asher and Dirk in wolf form beside him. He called my name again.

"Draven!" I ran to him as he called for me.

But he looked right through me.

Oh goddess. He couldn't see me or hear me. I screamed his name again.

Charity laughed behind me, held out her hands, and used her magic to drag me back into the cottage.

Draven continued to call for me, the panic growing in his voice.

I spun around as the basement door opened, and three women climbed out, beautiful and powerful. The elder crones. Not old or ugly anymore but beautiful—and pure evil.

Penny came up behind them, no longer outside the cottage's magic. Her soul was here in limbo, like mine, while her mortal body was still on the other side.

Penny grabbed my arm. "You need to come down to the basement with the others."

Amy, Marina, and Kristi had to be down there, or at least their souls were.

The *boom* came again, closer this time, knocking several cups from the table and causing dust to rain down.

The crones ignored it and me and rushed to Charity. "It's nearly dawn, he comes," one of them said, and there was genuine fear in her eyes.

"We need the wolves gone to perform the ritual," another said.

"Then we must rise, if we're to use our magic beyond this realm," Charity said.

One of the crones shook her head. "But they're not ready."

"No, but enough for what we need them to do." The loud, *booming* sound came again. Charity looked up. "We can't wait."

I didn't understand what they were saying, what was happening. "Don't hurt him. You can have me, but let them go," I said. If anything happened to Draven, I wouldn't survive it.

Charity turned to me. "We already have you, you little fool."

Penny grabbed my arm again. "Come on."

"Let her watch us destroy him," Charity said. "Let her see what happens to those who dare to get in our way."

"No! Don't hurt him." I ran for the door as they walked out. One of the crones lifted her hand and a ward rose in front of it. I collided with it hard and was knocked to the floor. I scrambled back up and ran to the window, watching as Charity and the crones walked toward Draven.

He turned and froze. He could see them.

Somehow, he could see them.

Chapter Thirty-Nine

Draven

Four corpses lurched toward me.

Mainly bone held together by exposed sinew and ligaments, the flesh and skin still forming.

They were reanimating before my eyes.

The crones.

And Charity.

All four were focused on me.

Asher and Dirk growled beside me, moving forward.

"Give her to us," a disembodied voice said from one of the corpses. "And we'll let you live."

Skin, pink and raw, crept over their skulls and faces. Their hair sprouted, growing in seconds, until it reached halfway down their backs.

Then there she was.

Charity.

Her body was still catching up, but her head and face were

almost back to the way she'd once been. She lifted her bony arms. "Give her to me, wolf."

"Never, you evil bitch," I snarled.

"You are pitiful," she said, her eyes filled with hatred. "You are using my weak little niece as a replacement for my do-gooder sister. Males truly are the weaker sex. The organ between your legs has you ready to risk being trapped for another three hundred years." She laughed, and the crones laughed with her.

"Iris is my mate. Selene was nothing." I didn't know what the hell to do. We couldn't fight against magic. But this was where I needed to be. I felt Iris here, in this place. She was close, and she needed me.

I wanted to fucking roar.

She chuckled. "You sound angry. Are your feelings still bruised by my sister's rejection? You repulsed her, you know? When you put your hands on her, she shuddered. We both laughed at how gullible you were when I trapped you. Neither of us gave you a second thought. Now here you are, begging for me to do it all over again."

Ash snarled and snapped her teeth.

One of the crones slashed her arm to the side, and Asher was thrown through the air, crashing into a tree. She yelped and hit the ground and didn't get up. The crone on the other side did the same, and Dirk was thrown back. He hit the ground with a sickening crunch.

Then the four of them started toward me, their arms outstretched.

Iris

378

They were going to kill him. "No!"

That deafening sound came again, a massive *boom*, so close now, and Charity's form flickered again like it had before, but this time she flickered from beautiful to hideous. Hanging flesh and skin, bones exposed. Her soul was here with me in limbo, but her bones, her body, were trying to regenerate on the mortal plane.

Her hands were shaking.

Was she struggling? Was the barrier between realms somehow thinning?

She was using her powers here in limbo but channeling her magic through her corporeal form in the mortal realm.

Could I do that as well?

I couldn't leave the cottage, not with the ward there now, but I focused on my limp body clutched against Draven's chest. "Goddess, surround us with your protection, protect the wolves, ward us against evil," I called, reciting a protection spell.

"What are you doing?" Penny said, rushing forward.

I shoved her back. "Goddess, surround us with your protection, protect the wolves, ward us against evil," I repeated.

Charity screamed as she and the crones aimed their magic at Draven. He stood his ground, bracing for their attack—

But nothing happened. The magic didn't touch him.

It was working.

He looked down at my body in his arms. I don't know what he saw, but he knew it was me, that I was doing it. He pressed his mouth to my ear. "That's it, petal. I'm not letting you go. Don't you let me go either."

I heard him, his voice echoing around me, around us. Yes, the barrier was growing thinner.

Penny shrieked, and Charity spun to me, her face a mask of fury. The cottage door slammed, and the bolt slid into place.

Penny grabbed at me, digging her nails into my shoulder. "You're not ruining this for me."

I jerked out of her hold, spun, and punched her in the face. She dropped to the ground like a brick, unconscious. Thankfully, Willow had taught me how to throw a decent punch.

I didn't know if I could bleed here, but I had to try. Snatching a knife from the kitchen table, I sliced my arm. Blood bubbled to the surface. *Yes.* I quickly dripped a trail of it in front of the door. "Ward from evil, no witches four, no dark magic shall pass this door," I called, coming up with a spell that I hoped would be strong enough to hold them, and I ran back to the window.

Draven had his hand over my arm, blood oozing between his fingers. The cut I'd made here had affected me out there. That had to mean the barrier was still thinning, still weakening.

The cottage's magic is what made them strong, but outside the cottage, their magic was weakening.

Charity and the three crones screamed, their hands held toward the door, aiming every bit of power they had left at it.

It rattled, the heavy iron lock shaking and jumping.

They were still so strong. It was only a matter of time before they got through my hastily made ward.

There was only one thing I could do. Closing my eyes, I lifted my hands to the sky. "Come to me, animals of the forest, come to me. There is evil here. Come to me. Defend your home..."

Penny grabbed on to me, wrapping herself around my legs. I stumbled and fell, hitting the floor hard, and she attacked me like a wild animal. The bolt across the door rattled louder as we wrestled on the floor.

"You're disposable, Penny!" I yelled. "They won't keep you around once they have what they want."

"I only want Elmer. They can bring him back to me. They promised to bring him back."

"They lied!"

"I just need Isaac's body, then I'll have my Elmer back."

Jesus. "Can you hear yourself? You're willing to kill Isaac to get what you want? Everything you've done, Penny, it's wrong. You can't do this."

"You don't know me! I'm done being the one everyone forgets. Amy and her friends treated me like garbage, they deserve what's coming to them. But not Elmer, he loved me."

There was no reasoning with her. Penny had traveled down this path and there was no going back now.

Wood splintered behind us, and the door crashed open.

Charity walked in, her face distorted, twisted, as she screamed in rage. I could see the sun rising behind her. It was time. She was going to take my soul, my powers. My body was about to die in Draven's arms.

Her form flickered as that incredible *boom* sound hit again, the ground shaking so hard she had to grab for the doorframe. Righting herself, she used her magic to lift shards of splintered wood from the door and screamed, firing them at me. I rolled and they smashed through the floor and into the basement below. I threw up my hands, our magic colliding with an earsplitting crash.

My magic was working here, the barrier had to be incredibly thin now. Charity screamed louder.

Growls and snarls came from outside.

The crones were shrieking.

I scrambled to my feet. Draven had placed my body on the ground behind him, and he'd partially shifted, attacking their still reanimating bodies, tearing them to shreds.

"You won't win!" Charity cried as crows, so many they were a wall of black feathers, burst through the door, through the windows, the glass exploding all over us.

I didn't know if I'd called them from here in limbo or the mortal realm, but they went straight for Charity. She screamed as they attacked. Pecking and clawing at her, plucking the eyes right from her head.

Penny scrambled back, but the crows were only focused on Charity.

I twisted to where Draven had been. He stepped back from a pile of bones on the ground that had been Charity's reanimating body and lifted me again, looking down at me. I could hear him calling me back, begging me to come back to him.

That awful, deafening *boom* came again, the sound louder and closer together, and the barrier flickered faster.

Charity and the crones were severely weakened, but it was only a matter of time before they regained their magic and strengthened the ward again.

"I'm not going back," Penny cried.

"It's over, Pen."

Someone screamed from the basement.

I shoved Penny aside, hurried down the ladder. And there they were. Amy, Marina, and Kristi's souls were locked in cages, and through the wavering barrier, I could see their bodies laid out on the floor like I could see Draven on the other side. I needed to get back to the mortal realm, to their bodies. I had to reunite them with their souls before it was too late.

That's when I saw Penny's body. It was near the others, and the thick wooden shards from the door Charity had fired at me had pierced the thinning barrier completely and were embedded in Penny's chest. There was no surviving that. Her soul was here, still talking to me, but there would be no bringing her back now.

"You ruined everything!" Penny yelled.

I needed to get out of here. Now. I ran for the ladder, scrambling up—

Penny grabbed my ankle. I kicked back with my other foot, then fired a burst of power at her. It knocked her back, and she screamed, coming after me again.

The barrier flicked faster, the *booming* sound so loud now it hurt. The crones' ward in front of the door shattered, and I sprinted from the cottage, running at full speed for Draven.

His head snapped up, looking right at me. "Iris!" he roared.

The barrier was thin enough he could see me.

Death stood nearby, just beyond the cottage, and fury rolled off him in cold blasts.

Oh god.

He held his staff aloft, then slammed it down on the ground. *Boom.* That sound, it was like the end of the world was coming. Everything around me trembled, and the barrier collapsed for a split second. I jumped, throwing myself at Draven, at my body held in his arms.

He was knocked back a step, and I was smothered in darkness.

My eyes snapped open.

Draven was looking down at me. I was back.

He dropped to the ground, big body trembling, and pressed his lips to mine. "Thank fuck." He looked into my eyes. "I thought I'd lost you, petal. I thought I'd never get you back. Fuck, I love you."

"I love you too," I said, my heart soaring. "But it's not over, quick, the others are trapped."

He stood, lifting me to my feet, grabbed my hand, and we ran to the only part of the cottage still standing in the mortal realm, the basement. I grabbed the hatch door and flung it open, then spun back to Ash and Dirk. "Keep them in bits," I said, motioning to Charity and the crones. Their bones were scattered but still writhed, trying to reanimate even now.

Dawn light spilled down through the open hatch door. Amy, Marina, and Kristi were where I'd seen them, their white eyes blinking up at the ceiling, their bodies unmoving, their souls still in limbo.

Penny's body lay beside them. Her lifeless eyes staring into nothing, her skin pale, blood covering her chest from the wounds. I checked her pulse, though I knew there was no point. She was gone.

There was nothing I could do for her now.

I rushed back to Amy, pulled my blade from my pocket, and pricked her finger. I swiped up some of the blood as it bubbled to the surface, then smeared it over her lower lip. "Blood and bone, return home."

Her body jolted then her eyes rolled down. She blinked up at me rapidly. "Iris, oh, thank the goddess. I thought you'd left us there."

I squeezed her hand and rushed to Marina, then Kristi, repeating the spell to bring them back. I helped them to their feet, led them to the ladder, and they scrambled up to the surface on shaky legs.

Draven stood behind me, waiting for me to head up, but I stopped when my thigh tingled and turned to Draven. I opened my mouth—but pain sliced down my spine, and I dropped to the floor.

My mouth opened, a silent scream exploding from me. Power washed through my body, then again, the next surging even higher. The gifts the mother had given us when Willow passed her task were solidifying and strengthening.

Because I'd passed my task as well.

For now, our gifts would remain ours as long as I passed my combat trial.

Draven bent down beside me, eyes wild. "Iris? Talk to me."

I couldn't. My back arched when another great surge throbbed through my body. I stared up at Draven as the pain grew higher. No more. I couldn't take another second—

It smashed into a thousand pieces, like shattering glass, taking the pain away with it.

It took a minute before I was finally able to speak. I blinked up at Draven. "I passed my task."

An hour later, Amy, Marina, and Kristi's families arrived to take them home. They thanked me repeatedly, but I didn't know how worthy I was of their praise. I'd stumbled my way through this mess, and alternate outcomes of this night would haunt my dreams for the rest of my life.

My family was here as well. I had passed my task. And I was thankful for that, for a lot of reasons, but right then, I was most thankful that they could help me with this next bit. I wasn't strong enough to do it on my own.

"What will happen with Penny?" Else asked.

"The cottage needs a guardian, that's how the enchantment works. She's tied to it now and will forever remain in limbo."

We were about to send Charity and the crones to their rightful place. We didn't know where that was. A power higher than us decided that, but I had a feeling I knew where Charity and her crones would be going.

I turned to Mom. "Ready."

Death wouldn't thank us for interfering in his realm, but this had to be done. It was too dangerous for Charity and the crones to remain in limbo with that cottage and the power it held.

Unlike Charity and the crones, Penny wasn't as smart or powerful. We wouldn't be hearing from her in the future.

Mom nodded, and Else, Mags, and Willow joined me. As we stripped off our clothes, Draven and his warriors turned around, giving us their backs and some privacy. We surrounded the bones of Charity and all three crones. They jumped and wriggled on the ground, trying to reorder themselves, to reanimate again. Their souls were there, we could feel them, but they were trapped between realms.

Else began the chant, and one by one, Mom, Willow, Magnolia, and I joined in, creating a wall of sound and magic.

The ground glowed.

No one was surprised they were being called to Hell.

Something moved up beside me, dark and menacing, cold. Death. I knew it. He was here. I felt that familiar coldness slither down my spine. He wasn't happy we were taking souls from him.

I did my best to ignore his cold fingers lingering on my neck and chanted harder.

"You will pay for this. I'm coming for her. She will be mine," Death whispered in my ear.

He was talking about Rose; I knew it without doubt. Well, he wasn't getting her. Whatever it took, he would never have her.

The ground swirled and pulsed, and the forest floor disappeared beneath. The bones, along with their souls, were sucked down. Their screams echoed from the depths before being abruptly cut off when the ground closed behind them.

Chapter Forty

Draven

I ris lay over me, naked and warm. We were both sated, but she still held on tight. We'd almost lost each other a few days ago, and there would be no getting over that, not for a long fucking time—probably not ever.

And the danger wasn't over yet. Iris still had her combat trial coming up. Willow had been training with her all week, working on her magic, and I'd been helping with her fighting, in case it came down to that.

Nia growled in her sleep by the fire, and my beautiful mate lifted up and smiled at her familiar, then looked down at me. "There's something I haven't had a chance to tell you."

I ran my hand over her silky hair, and my wolf chuffed with pleasure. I looked into her eyes and saw concern there. "What is it?"

"Charity told me something when I was trapped in that cottage, something you should know."

I hugged her tighter. "What is it?"

"Selene did plan to release you. Charity knew her sister couldn't leave you there to suffer like that, and that she'd want to go back for the dagger. Charity suspected Selene knew about her use of dark magic and that she planned to use the dagger on her, to change her heart. So Charity gave Selene a potion and cast a spell so she forgot you and the dagger existed."

I drew in a sharp breath. "How do you know she wasn't lying?"

"Why would she? She had no reason to. She could have let us carry on believing Selene was this evil person, but Charity's ego was too big for that. She was jealous of her sister, that she was Keeper. She wanted me to know how strong she was now and what she was capable of even then. I believed her. Using a love elixir was seriously fucked up. There's no excuse for that, but she was always going to come back to release you. At the heart of her, I believe she was good, Draven."

I stared up at the ceiling. All this time, all the hatred I'd carried around for her. I'd made Selene the biggest villain in my story when it was Charity who had caused my pack all that pain. Yes, Selene had fooled me, but she'd believed she was doing what she had to for her family. And if I was honest, I knew that there wasn't anything I wouldn't do to protect the people I loved either.

She'd planned to set me free.

"I'm glad I know the truth." I pressed a kiss to my mate's lips. "And that Charity finally got what she deserved."

"Are you okay?"

"Yeah, I've got you."

Iris leaned in, pressing her lips to mine again. "I love you, Draven."

My hands flexed against her waist. It wasn't the first time she'd said it, but it hit me just as hard. "I'll never get enough of hearing you say that," I rasped. "I love you, too, my beautiful mate."

~

Iris

"Zinny! Jaz!" Magnolia ran to our cousins, and they embraced in a group hug, then Jasmine and Mags squealed and jumped up and down.

We didn't know Jasmine was coming, but it was a welcome surprise, and I laughed as I watched them together. Jasmine was seventeen, shy, loved pink, and was the complete polar opposite of Mags in every way. Zinnia was our free spirit and hardly ever made it to coven events. We didn't see her as much as we'd like, but she was here now, and we'd make the most of it.

They ran to us and we all took our turn dishing out the hugs.

"I've missed you," I said when Zinnia was squeezing the life out of me.

Zinnia's magic gifts had made her a powerful medium and highly sought after. Her profession, communicating with the dead and a few other things, took her all over the country.

"Missed you too." She tucked some of her wild red hair behind her ear and grinned. "So you got yourself a mate."

"I did."

"He's hot."

I laughed. "I know."

Her grin turned wicked. "He got any single friends?"

"He does."

"Nice." She chuckled. "Between the wolves and the hell-hounds, I'm not sure what to do with myself."

"You make the most of it," Else said with a cackle.

"Oh, I will, Aunty Else, you know I will."

"Seriously?" Jaz gave her sister a disapproving look.

"Loosen up, Jazzy, it's way more fun." Zinny gave her baby sister a playful shove.

Jasmine rolled her eyes then she strode over to Mags.

Else grabbed Zinny's hand. "I know Jazzy has to go home for school, but why don't you stick around? Willow and Iris's rooms are free now. Come home for a while. I worry about you when you're gone."

Zinnia slid her arm around Else's narrow shoulders and glanced at her sister, worry in her eyes. "I would love that...but Jaz needs me right now."

"What's going on?" Mom asked, following Zinny's gaze.

"She has the gift." Zinny slid her hands into the pockets of her faded leather jacket. "The spirit world came knocking. Jasmine woke up to a room full of souls, and she didn't take it all that well." She seemed to shake herself. "But we'll get to that a little later."

Poor Jasmine. Zinnia's gift had always terrified her.

We headed down the path to the cemetery, no mates or familiars, just Else, Mom, Mags, Willow, Zinnia, Jasmine, and me. Zinny was here to cleanse the grounds. We needed her expertise to remove any remaining dark magic that Charity's bones leached into the soil. The cemetery had started to come back to life, but there were still dead spots, and our main herb garden was struggling.

"So how do we do this?" Else asked.

Zinnia took off her jacket. "We get naked."

Mags huffed out a breath. "Of course, we do."

"And blood," Zinny added.

"Could have guessed that one as well," Mags grumbled as she pulled her sweater over her head.

Zinny laughed her throaty laugh. "Aw, you sound like younger me."

Mags smirked. "I'll take that as a compliment."

"Oh, you should."

We were all chuckling by the time we were standing naked in the middle of the cemetery.

Zinny started undoing her braid. "Hair down."

We all studiously let our hair out.

"What does our hair have to do with it?" Willow asked.

"I'm not sure, that's just how I was taught to do this, but you have to admit we look even more awesome," Zinny said and winked. "Man, if we had like, a coven newsletter or something, a pic of us right now would be front page material."

Mom groaned and Else snorted.

"I'm freezing my nips off," I said. "Are we ready to do this?"

"We're ready." Then all humor fled from Zinnia as she held a blade over her palm. We did the same.

Tilting her head back, she started whispering every name in this cemetery, over and over again, faster and faster. Until wind whipped around us, icy and cold, whistling through the trees.

Zinny finally lifted her head and blinked several times. "Good...everyone's here." She turned to the vacant space beside her and smiled. "Hey, Gran." She nodded. "I know. They're kicking ass."

Zinny turned to me. "Gran wants me to tell you how proud of you she is. She's been with you. She's been with all of you." Zinnia looked at Willow, then Magnolia. "She's proud of all of you, and she wants to make sure you tell Rose as well." Zinnia listened again, grinning, then turned to Else. "Gran says a man is coming your way, Else, and he's going to make you very happy."

Else's eyes went wide, then she shook her head. "She's cracked. You're cracked," she yelled where she thought her sister stood. "No man, no thank you."

Zinnia grinned. "She said, tough, it's happening, get ready."

"Hi, Mom," my mother said. "I miss you."

"She misses you, too, Aunt Daisy." Zinny listened again. "She loves Art. She says his heart is pure and overflowing with love for you."

Mom nodded, and her eyes filled with tears.

Zinny smiled at mom, then turned back to the rest of us. "Okay, ladies, alive and in spirit." She turned to someone behind her and rolled her eyes. "And Uncle Herbert and Uncle Jacob."

"They never did like to be left out," Else muttered.

Mom giggled. It was one of my most favorite sounds and something I hadn't heard much lately.

Zinnia clapped her hands. "Right, let's get this poison out of here and finish what Selene started. Coven Thornheart has no place in it for dark magic."

"Is she here?" I asked. "Selene, I mean."

Zinnia turned to me, and her smile gentled. "Yeah, she is."

"Is she listening?"

She nodded. "Say whatever you want to say, cousin."

My heart was filled with love and understanding. That's just how it was when Zinna was around, she had that effect on people. I took a steadying breath. "I'm so sorry, Selene, for doubting you..." I looked around, not sure where she was.

Zinnia pointed to a spot opposite me.

I looked straight ahead to where I thought she was. "Draven's free, he knows you didn't mean to hurt him."

Sun broke through the clouds and shone down through the massive oak tree branches, throwing dappled light over us—and I saw her. Her soul, translucent and ethereal. Tears shimmered on her cheeks, and she smiled a gentle smile.

"She's glad he has you," Zinnia said. "And she wants you to tell him she's sorry."

"He knows," I said, tears running down my own face.

"And she's thankful for what you did, for sending Charity away, when she hadn't been strong enough to finish it herself."

"It was a joint effort," I said.

Clouds slid in front of the sun again, and I couldn't see her anymore.

I turned back to Zinnia and nodded. I'd said what I wanted to.

Zinny winked and then cut her hand and dripped her blood onto the grass. We all did the same and then followed her lead and started chanting.

It took almost two hours to remove every last drop of darkness that Charity had left behind in the soil. Our voices were hoarse, our feet were numb from the cold, and I was well and truly ready for a nap.

I finished dressing, pulled my shirt over my head, and shoved my feet into my boots. "Okay, let's head back..." Something moved on the other side of the cemetery.

Zinnia turned and waved at the large red fox who had moved out of the shadows.

"Ren?" Willow's voice was husky with emotion.

She made a move toward him, but Zinnia stopped her, sympathy in her gaze. "He's here because I asked him to come."

Willow stared at our cousin in shock. "What? Why? How?"

"I got his number from Else. I wasn't sure he'd come." Zinnia rubbed Jasmine's back. "Jazzy has a message for him." She gave her sister a nod, and Jasmine's throat worked before she broke away from us and walked over to Ren.

We turned to watch, unable to look away as Jasmine crouched down and ran a trembling hand across his neck. Ren didn't move, his amber eyes fixed on Jaz.

She smiled gently. "Hey, Ren."

He blinked at her.

Her throat worked. "They want me to tell you, they don't blame you."

He jerked back, but Jasmine took his face in her hands, not letting him retreat. "Your guilt is keeping them here, Ren. They can't move on, they can't be at peace until you try to find it as well."

Ren shifted suddenly into his human form and stumbled back several steps. He looked shocked, like he hadn't meant to shift, and there were tears on his cheeks.

"Ren!" Willow called.

He backed up, then spun and ran into the woods.

Willow cursed, her pain visceral.

Jasmine walked back to us, eyes wide, haunted, and Zinnia strode to her and pulled her against her.

There was no missing what that message meant, and I hoped like hell it made a difference. I threw my arm around Will's shoulders, and we started back to the house. "Do you think Jazzy's message will help him?"

"I hope so. A year without him has been too damn long."

Chapter Forty-One

Draven

Two weeks later

The last week had been hell.

We'd finally received the summons for Iris's combat trial. The final test, then she was done with the mother and her bullshit. She'd finally be safe.

We'd continued with her training all week, and Willow had been putting her through her magical paces.

Iris was ready.

Still, as I watched her, my female, my whole heart. As she walked out into that clearing, my gut twisted in fucking knots.

Her family had been right. The male she was up against was from one of the losing covens that had competed in last year's official trials. He'd been given a chance to redeem himself—a second chance to reclaim the mother's gifts that had been taken from his coven. For one night only, the mother had given him back the power he'd lost to fight my mate. Something that never happened, apparently, but of course, these were special circumstances.

I curled my fingers into tight fists and growled as her opponent jerked his head from side to side and jumped on the spot, like a fighter about to engage in a heavyweight boxing match.

My nerves shot higher.

He may have lost his last battle, but the male they'd pitted against my mate was fucking huge. No, fuck this. I started forward but hit the fucking ward surrounding them, locking them in—and me out.

I cursed. I couldn't get to her.

"She's got this," Warrick said beside me.

How the fuck could he be so calm? "The guy's a fucking giant, and he's hungry to win. He's got nothing to lose, that makes him even more dangerous."

The clearing at Blood Hill Grove was surrounded by witches. Iris's family watched on, her mom gripping Else's hand. Some of the other members of the coven were here as well, and seeing their worry only made mine worse.

"Come on!" The big male taunted Iris. "I thought coven Thornheart was a big deal. You think you can take me, little girl?"

Iris had her eyes on the male, but she was focused inward on her magic, calling it forward. I had no idea what she was going to do. She'd worked on different options with Willow, depending on who her opponent turned out to be.

"She's got this," Willow said as well. "This guy is your typical bully. He uses his size to intimidate because his magic is lacking, and deep down, he's scared shitless." A small smile curled her lips. "And how do you fight a bully?"

You stood up to them.

"You think you have what it takes to best me?" he yelled at Iris, and held out his hands, fingers outstretched. "I'm going to crush you. I will fucking annihilate you." Rocks the size of his head exploded out of the ground.

"Fuck," I bit out, my wolf clawing to get to Iris.

The other witch fired a rock through the air, and Iris dove to the side before rolling back to her feet. I growled, desperate to get in there. Another rock flew straight for her. Again, Iris leaped out of the way.

He kept firing them, and Iris kept dodging, and each time she got closer and closer to him.

Willow snorted. "Fucking one-trick pony."

Iris's opponent was puffing and sweaty, and yelled as he threw another rock at my mate.

She dove once more, and as she rolled to her feet—she went animal.

Iris had called on one that she'd struggled with but had obviously been working on with her sister because her magic was strong, so strong I felt the power of it through the ward.

The male trapped in with her cried out, high-pitched and full of terror, and stumbled back.

Iris roared, loud and fierce, and started toward him, the lioness she'd become not backing down to the bully. He tripped and fell on the ground, and she stalked him. Weapons weren't allowed here —no knives, swords, guns—but smaller things that could be used for spelling were okay. I could barely see her now, the lioness growing more solid, but I knew she'd be taking the pin from wherever she had it in her clothes, like Willow had taught her, so she could prick her finger and draw blood. Her opponent tried to scramble back.

Iris closed the space between them. Her lioness had startled him long enough for her to make her final move. She slapped her hand to his forehead and muttered the spell to freeze him in place. The male stared up at her in horror.

The barrier dropped instantly, the mother's way of letting Iris know she'd won.

Iris released her animal form and spun to me, a huge smile on her face.

I ran to her and scooped her into my arms.

She laughed. "I did it!"

"Fuck, yeah, you did. You kicked his ass, petal."

"I love you," she said, then she grabbed my face and kissed me.

I loved her too. She was finally safe, and no one was ever going to hurt her again.

If they tried, I'd kill them.

Epilogue

Iris

Three months later

I ran from the five pups in hot pursuit. At this age, they had trouble staying in one form. And I had three tiny wolves and two naked toddlers swarming me, giggling and yapping.

I pretended to fall over so they could catch me, and they squealed and barked in delight.

"Cake!" Sally called out from the keep and they jumped up and ran away as fast as they came.

I chuckled and stood, dusting off my hands and went back to admiring my flourishing herb garden. My vervain right in the center and covered in gorgeous purple flowers. My phone beeped and I pulled it out of my pocket.

Willow: *You told him yet?*

I quickly typed out a reply: *Last night.*

Willow: *How did he take it?*

Being told you were immortal, and any children you had would be as well, was a lot. It was what Willow had tried to tell me on mine and Draven's mating day, and why she'd been so obsessed with finding me someone. She'd finally shared the news with me a few days ago. I still couldn't quite grasp the magnitude of it. Thanks to Warrick, and some favor Lucifer had owed him, Willow and I, and our mates would live *forever*. The same went for Mags if she found a mate, that was Lucifer's condition. Rose, she was a different story. Apparently, her future had already been set in stone, and Lucifer was reluctant to upset the fates. In other words, there was no guarantee where Roe was concerned.

That was the only part I hated about this whole immortal thing. If Lucifer was right, I'd have to live an eternity without her. I shoved that thought from my mind; it was too painful to even contemplate.

I typed my reply to Wills: *Pretty good? We're both still processing.*

"Have you finished for the day, petal?"

I turned and smiled as Draven pulled me into his arms. "I hadn't realized it'd gotten so late."

"It looks good," he said, taking in my handiwork.

"For only a few months, it's freaking awesome."

Draven's lips curled up on one side. "I need you to come with me, and you can't ask any questions."

I tried, but I couldn't read his expression. "What are you up to?"

"No questions, remember?" He took my hand and led me around the side of the keep then kept going, heading into the woods.

"Do I get any hints?"

He looked down at me and grinned. "Nope."

A larger area around the keep was now demon free. Which meant, Draven's warriors needed to patrol a far wider area. They'd been training up more members of his pack. He also had a group of adolescents, all in their mid to late teens, who Ash was training for the future.

Birds fluttered around us, squirrels scampered along tree branches to keep up and several rabbits were hopping along behind me. My powers had only increased, and Draven loved to tease me about it. I couldn't go anywhere anymore without several little friends following me. "It's so beautiful out here...you know, without the threat of a demon ambush. You want to go for a run later?" Draven loved it when we ran together.

He kissed my hand. "We'll be a bit too busy for a run, but I guarantee you'll still get a workout."

I barked out a laugh. "I can't believe you said that? I swear you've been corrupted by all those movies you and Ash watch." Seeing as they'd been locked away for over three hundred years, then were a little busy claiming territory, movies were still pretty new to them. Ash liked action and some comedy as well, and the corny lines my mate was coming out with were a constant delight.

He chuckled. "You love it."

"I do." He could read me so damn easily.

Draven led me to the edge of a large clearing, and I looked around. "What is this place?"

My mate walked over to a massive ancient tree. His eyes were bright with excitement as he turned to me and pressed his hand to the rough bark. The clearing shimmered, a rainbow of colors, that shot up as far as the eye could see.

"What...what is this?"

Draven strode to me. "Our oasis. We're on our honeymoon, petal. And before you ask, Nia's with Ebs."

I gaped up at him. "But I haven't packed anything?"

"You won't need clothes," he growled.

Excitement filled me, and I grinned up at him. "I can't believe you did this."

"If we have an eternity together, petal, I think we need to start it out right. You game?"

I grinned so wide my cheeks hurt. "Always."

He flashed his teeth, gripped my hand tighter, and we walked through the shimmering wall into paradise.

~

Rose

Music drifted into my window from outside.

It was Mom's birthday, and my sisters had thrown her a party. I'd been downstairs for a while, but when I'd started falling asleep, Art had carried me up to bed.

Else was sitting in the chair beside me, missing out on all the fun because, for some reason, I was still alive.

I was more than ready to die.

It'd be better for my family and for me if this would just...end. They'd miss me, but they'd been forced to take care of me my whole life. It hurt them to look at me, to watch me suffer, and I didn't want them to hurt anymore. I wasn't even strong enough to use my magic to help them. It was still inside me, I felt it there, but it was as weak as I was.

"You can go down, Else. I-I'm fine here on my own," I said and hated how weak my voice sounded.

"I'm not going anywhere, kiddo..."

"I can stay if you'd like," a deep yet quiet voice said from the doorway.

Ronan.

I didn't know why he hung out with me, but I was glad he did. He didn't treat me like I was made of glass. He wasn't bogged down with emotions, so he didn't feel the need to tiptoe around me or feel sorry for me. He told me the truth, always.

"You okay if I leave you with Ronan?" Else asked and winked.

My whole family thought I had a crush on him. They were wrong—I was completely and utterly in love with him.

I nodded.

Else stood, kissed my forehead and walked out, patting Ronan on the shoulder as she passed.

He walked in, and I ate up the sight of him. He was wearing trousers and a deep blue button-down shirt; the sleeves rolled up his muscled forearms. He'd let his hair grow a little longer, and tonight he'd combed it back. He looked sexy and dangerous, and I really wanted to see him naked.

Too bad I wouldn't be able to do anything with him if he was naked. I couldn't stand, let alone have sex. I was going to die a virgin, which sucked. Not that Ronan would ever want me that way—I didn't know if he wanted anyone that way, honestly, but a dying girl could dream, right?

"How are you this evening, Rose?" Ronan asked and placed a small plate of cheese and crackers beside me since his life mission seemed to be trying to feed me.

"Okay," I said and smiled up at him. The male had that effect on me. He didn't smile back. He never did. I didn't think he knew how. "Wouldn't you rather be down having fun at the party than up here with me?"

He moved to the bookshelf and scanned my collection. "No."

Which meant it was the truth. "Why?"

He turned to me. "I don't know."

Again, the truth. Ronan always told the truth.

The song changed to a slow song, and I heard Mags yell at someone, probably Iris and Draven, to get a room. I wanted to see my family enjoy themselves. I was used to missing out, but I loved to watch them when they were happy.

"What would you like to read?" Ronan asked.

We'd finished the fantasy he'd been reading me the day before. "I'm not sure I feel like reading tonight."

"No? What would you prefer?"

"Put on a pretty dress, go downstairs, and dance with my sisters," I said, and an ache started in my chest from wanting that so badly.

"You can't stand, Rose, so you can't dance."

"I know that, Ronan. I was just dreaming, you know? Wishing I could."

He nodded. "I see." He glanced at the window, then back at me. "Would you like to watch? Or are you too tired?"

I was always tired, but there'd be plenty of time to rest when I was dead. "I'd love to watch."

He strode over. "Would you like a cracker first? Some cheese?"

"No, thank you."

He frowned but pulled back the covers and scooped me out of bed. I forced down my humiliation as he covered me with a blanket and carried me to the window. The slow song drifted up, "Yellow Ledbetter," an old Pearl Jam song that Mom loved, and I watched as she and Art slow danced. Draven and Iris were there as well, and so were Willow and Warrick. Mags and Bram were standing a little apart, then he tugged her close, and she wrapped her arms around him. They swayed slowly, and the pain on Bram's face stole my breath.

"Poor Bram," I muttered.

"Is he injured?"

I turned to Ronan. "He's in love with Mags, but she doesn't feel the same way."

Ronan focused on them dancing. "Then why doesn't he find someone else to love?"

The way his mind worked fascinated me, it also shocked me at times. "That's not how love works."

He didn't say anything for a minute, then turned to me. "How does it work?"

"You can't control it, it's a feeling. Something you just know. You just want to be with that person. You want to protect them and care for them. You'd do anything to make them happy."

He nodded like he understood when I knew he didn't. "My sister loves her mate."

"She does." Luna and Gunner were most definitely in love.

Draven cupped Iris's cheek and kissed her. I glanced at Ronan, and there was a strange look on his face. "They make it look like it's something enjoyable," he said.

"It is." At least, I imagined it was. "Have you ever kissed anyone before?"

His lashes fluttered. "Yes."

Jealousy pounded through me. "You didn't enjoy it?"

"No."

I wanted to ask more, but when Ronan got a certain look on his face, I knew we were veering into territory he didn't like to discuss. He didn't get upset, that wasn't something he was capable of, but he did get quiet.

"I've never been kissed," I said. "I've been sick since I was little. I've never had the chance."

He glanced at me and back down to Draven and Iris. Warrick and Willow were making out as well now. "And you want to?"

I was still in his arms. He could hold me for an eternity and never tire. I was light, but he was also incredibly strong. "There are a lot of things I want that I'll never get to experience before I die. Like dating, like close dancing with someone. Like having a guy fall in love with me. Kissing...sex."

His lashes fluttered again, and his expression seemed to grow even more blank. "You might not die."

"I'm dying, Ronan. I can barely eat. I'm skin and bone. I'm in constant pain. I want to die. I want to free my family from the burden of looking after me."

He turned to me. "They don't see you as a burden, Rose. They want you to live."

"We can't always have what we want."

"No." He looked back down and his eyes narrowed on Bram and Mags.

Then he started to...sway, slowly.

I stared up at him, my heart beating faster as he held me closer, then took my arm and brought it up around his neck. "Is this right?"

Tears sprang to my eyes.

We were dancing.

He looked down at me and frowned. "Am I doing it wrong? I thought it might make you happy?"

"It does. You're doing it perfectly." I rested my head against his chest. I'd never been so happy. "Don't stop."

He didn't, and I silently prayed to the mother, asking her to take me now, because I couldn't think of a better way to go than in Ronan's arms.

And if she didn't?

Well, I just hoped Ronan agreed to do what I'd been building up the courage to ask him.

To help me end my life.

Because Death beckoned and he was getting impatient.

About the Author

Sherilee Gray is a kiwi girl and lives in beautiful New Zealand with her husband and their two children. When she isn't writing sexy contemporary or paranormal romance, searching for her next alpha hero on Pinterest, or fueling her voracious book addiction, she can be found dreaming of far off places with a mug of tea in one hand and a bar of chocolate in the other. Visit her at: www.sherileegray.com

Also by Sherilee Gray

Lawless Kings:

Shattered King

Broken Rebel

Beautiful Killer

Ruthless Protector

Glorious Sinner

Merciless King

Boosted Hearts:

Swerve

Spin

Slide

Spark

Axle Alley Vipers:

Crashed

Revved

Wrecked

Black Hills Pack:

Lone Wolf's Captive

A Wolf's Deception

Stand Alone Novels:

Breaking Him

Made in the USA
Las Vegas, NV
18 October 2024

10065191R00246